DESSA

Ann O'Connell Rust

Author of the Award Winning Series
"The Floridians"

Amaro Books
Fiction

Published by
Amaro Books
9765-C South West 92 Ct.
Ocala, Florida 34481

First printing 1996
ISBN NO. 1-883203-02-3 (softcover)
ISBN NO. 1-883203-03-1 (hardcover)
Library of Congress Catalog Card No. 96-97174

Printed in U.S.A.

Cover Artist: Karen Fulford

Books by Ann O'Connell Rust
The Floridians — a five-volume series
Vol. I Punta Rassa
Vol. II Palatka
Vol. III Kissimmee
Vol. IV Monticello
Vol. V Pahokee
Dessa

ACKNOWLEDGMENTS

The author wishes to thank A.F. Rust, Editor/Copy Editor, for his tireless efforts and enthusiasm, and Karen Fulford, whose dedication made the project a pleasure.

AUTHOR'S NOTE

This book in autobiographical and biographical. Many liberties were taken with the actual facts. Dessa, the real Dessa, was instrumental in helping me adjust to the trials and thrills of growing up in rural Florida. This book is a fictionalized account of that period.

Dedicated to our children, who grew up hearing *Dessa* stories: Peter Allen, Melissa Ann, David Hummel, Timothy Fennell and Amy Knight.

CHAPTER ONE

The morning Dessa showed up at Marsh's quarters, Sammy had just turned eight years old—the year was 1932. Catherine, Sammy's mama, never said when Dessa arrived. It was always "when she showed up." Sammy guessed that her mama didn't like Dessa much, or perhaps it was that she didn't understand her. Sammy always preferred the latter explanation. When she looked back on it, seems like she was having to explain Dessa to most everybody because they didn't understand her either.

Sammy remembered that she was hanging over the sink, looking out the kitchen window and hurriedly gulping down the glass of orange juice. Her mama was fussing at her to hurry 'cause Miss Howard was honking the school bus horn, and her brat brother Jamie, who was only a first grader, was yelling that she was gonna miss the bus if she didn't get a move on. But her mama knew that if she gulped her orange juice she'd throw up in her kitchen—goodness knows she'd done it before.

But there she sat, Dessa, that is, on an up—turned bean crate in front of the colored quarters behind Sander's place across the dirt road from Sammy's house. She was wearing a great big braided palmetto hat and clothes that covered almost all of her all the way to the ground. Her black shiny hands were sticking out of her shirt sleeves and planted squarely on her hips.

Sammy asked, "Who's that?"

"Who's who? Sammy, hurry up! Ida Howard's not gonna be late on account of you, young lady."

She took the last gulp, wiped her hand across her mouth to catch the final drop under the pursed lips and *don't-you-dare-young-lady* stare of her mama. She wasn't gonna wipe her hand on her skirt like her mama suspected, at least not with her standing there glaring at her.

"Who's that old colored woman sitting in front of Marsh's? And why didn't General bark at her?" Sammy continued.

Catherine grabbed her arm and yelled to Miss Howard, "She's coming, Ida. Hold up!" just like Miss Howard could hear her over the din those unruly kids were making.

Jamie was laughing at his mama's practically dragging Sammy to the hard road that ran in front of their house, but when he saw Sammy give him the "evil eye" his mouth quickly went from upturned to downturned. He knew that she'd get even with him for enjoying her discomfort in front of just about the whole town—well, almost the whole town.

It was that night at supper before Sammy found out who Dessa was. As was her habit when she got off the school bus at about three o'clock, she

1

rushed into the house and headed for her mama's kitchen. No one ever said "the kitchen"—it was always Mama's kitchen. Even Daddy called it Mama's kitchen or Catherine's kitchen or if he was funning with her, Kitten's kitchen. Anyway, Sammy checked the oven and sure enough, her mama and daddy had had ribs and rice for dinner, cooked together as they all liked it with sliced green onions and lots of black pepper. Sammy didn't even wait to lift that heavy iron pot out, just yanked the top off and dug in with the big wooden spoon that her mama'd used to stir it with. All the while she was savoring their goodness she was remembering that her mama didn't like for them to eat out of the pot and especially with the stirring spoon.

There he was staring at her—that Jamie. "If you tell, I'll tie your tail in a knot, James Patrick Carroll. You hear!"

He ran out the screen door, down the steps, onto the wooden walk that led to the bathhouse, pushed General out from in front of him and disappeared behind the bathhouse, heading toward the bean field. She stood watching, and when he and General didn't reappear, she knew that he had hidden in the stand of bamboo and would be covered with its sticky hairs, and about now he'd be itching to beat the band.

Sammy was debating whether she should cover the pot and put it back inside the oven or succumb to her temptation and catch that sneaky brat to make sure that he believed her, when she saw Dessa shaking out something at the quarters door that faced their house. Being curious by nature, Sammy forgot all about tattle-tale Jamie. Her daddy always said "Sammy, that curiosity will get you in trouble one of these days." Well, she'd admit that it had in the past done just that, but she simply couldn't contain herself. She dashed out the back door, but not before grabbing a biscuit from the oven—it was still warm. She ran—at least she did at first—towards where Dessa was standing. Then she slowed down so she could eat the biscuit and so Dessa couldn't see how curious she was.

"Who're you?" Sammy asked.

"And who wants to be a knowin'?" she responded in that sing-song talk that the island Negroes spoke.

Now Sammy knew that was no way for a Colored to talk to a White even if she was only eight years old, but she wasn't upset with the woman's defiance. That old curiosity had already set in and taken over.

"I asked first," Sammy said, expecting no nonsense from her.

The woman smiled then, and her face, which had been...well, you couldn't say that Dessa was ugly, but pretty she wasn't either. Well, that smile kinda started from her insides and leaped out of her face in an unexpected rush, making her head bounce up and down. At that very moment Sammy knew that she'd found an exciting friend.

Dessa waited for Sammy to identify herself, and Sammy knew by the way she was grinning down at her that she'd be forced to give in first. So she said, "I'm Sammy, that's who!"

"And I'm Dessa," and she didn't volunteer another word.

Now Sammy wasn't about to give her any more satisfaction and pushed her "curious" down as deep as she could and wheeled around, but before returning to the house she turned back just to see where Dessa was, and sure enough she was standing in the doorway watching her. So Sammy did the most perfect cartwheel you'd ever see, not caring if her skirt fell to her face and showed her underdrawers. When she turned to see if Dessa was still looking, she was, so she did two more cartwheels and would've done another, but she was already up to the clump of palmettos that grew beside the cabbage palm at the corner of the bathhouse. When she sneaked another look back at Dessa, she was still standing there grinning, so Sammy knew that her performance had impressed her.

About that time her mama and Aunt Clara showed up in Uncle Walter's new Hudson. They'd been to town grocery shopping 'cause her mama yelled for someone to help her. That's all Sammy needed to hear, and she ran as hard as she could to beat Jamie there.

"Where's Mary Catherine?" her mama asked.

Aunt Clara said, "Isn't this the day that she helps Miss Page at school, Catherine?"

"That's right," her mama said. "That child never seems to be around when I need her." Mary Catherine was twelve and got by with all sorts of things, at least to Sammy's way of thinking.

"I'm here!" Sammy piped up, out of breath.

"And so you are. Here, take this bag, and don't you dare drop it."

Why'd she say that? Sammy thought, I have never dropped a bag of groceries in my whole entire life. Here came Jamie struggling for breath and trying not to trip over General, who seemed to be always underfoot. He brushed by her with his arms extended for the other bag. Catherine reached down and kissed his sweaty cheek and said lovingly, "How's Mama's favorite son?" Well, how indeed, since he was the only son she had. Sammy never could figure out how he could be her mama's favorite, but that was how her mama talked, so they all just put up with it.

Clara said, "You suppose that Miss Page will drive Mary Catherine home? After all, she's the one who's asking for help."

Catherine spoke up. "She'd better, Clara. I surely don't want Patrick to have to drive all the way back into town for her. What with the season on him he's just too tired when he finally gets home to have to make that trip."

Well, "that trip" Catherine referred to was only one mile to Canal Point, but one mile to Catherine was near 'bout a hundred, Sammy thought, and the season was the third planting of green beans.

Clara put that big grey Hudson in reverse and wiggled all the way to the hard road. Catherine, who was skittish about any vehicle, yelled, "Clara, you be careful on that road." Clara didn't have to be careful but for about a block, 'cause Sammy could near 'bout throw her baseball to Clara's house, it was so close. But her mama wouldn't drive, so she was extra cautious about anything moving, and that included tractors and even Sammy's wagon when she pulled it with her bike. Catherine's concern wasn't that the Hudson cost a whole year's wages either; it was just that it ran on that hard road.

"See you later," Clara yelled over the motor noise. She always saw Catherine later, every night for as long as Sammy could remember. Aunt Clara would drive her mama to choir practice every Tuesday night even though she couldn't carry a tune in a bucket, as her husband said. But her mama needed to be there, 'cause she played the piano and had a strong alto. Then on Wednesday night she'd drive her to prayer meeting. Aunt Clara did know her Bible, and the folks at the First Baptist Church in Canal Point could attest to that.

They were only a year apart in age, and some folks thought they were twins. They did look alike, and Sammy favored them. At least that's what folks said.

That's how Sammy got her name. Grandpa Samuel, their daddy, whose house is the big one next to the Carrolls', is as bald as a billiard, and since Sammy didn't even have any fuzz on her head when she was born, someone said, "My gracious, she's as bald as Samuel". So, from that moment on she was called Sammy. Her given name was Helen Louise. Her daddy's middle name was Louis, and they were afraid that they'd never have a boy, so they'd planned to call her Louise after him. A good thing they didn't, Sammy thought. That was one ugly name to her. She liked Sammy.

"Sammy, you wash those sandy hands real good, you hear." Of course she could hear. Heck, her mama was just in the kitchen, and Sammy was just outside the door at the pump, but her mama always said that. "And don't you dawdle. You know your daddy wants to hear the fight."

Since her daddy never missed a fight on the radio, she hurried. Her Aunt Clara and Uncle Walter would be over with their brat youngun, Clarissa, soon's their supper was over, 'cause her Uncle Walter and Daddy had dibs on the living room with no noise allowed from a one of them. Her mama and Aunt Clara would be holed up in the kitchen doing something like shelling peas or snapping beans or just talking to beat the band, just like they hadn't seen each other near 'bout forever. Sammy knew for a fact that they had talked all the way to town, then had their coca colas with half the ladies in Canal Point at Doc Fletcher's drugstore, then gone to Hickerson's for groceries. Their mouths never closed for a second every Monday and Thursday just like always.

But hurry she did because she wanted to get to the supper table to ask her daddy who that old colored woman was and what she was doing in Marsh's quarters.

Catherine had served the ribs and rice and biscuits from the warm gas oven. She and Patrick just had biscuits and pickled beets and some sliced cucumbers and tomatoes, 'cause they'd already had their main meal at noon, same as always. They sat around the square table in the kitchen, because they didn't have a dining room like Grandpa Samuel did. Sammy dug into those ribs and rice just like she hadn't already sampled how good they were.

"Jamie, you eat those greens, honey. Mama mixed the mustard with the turnips just like you like them. Sammy, pass him the butter beans. I know he'll eat those." She sure loved to fuss over him, Sammy thought.

"Sammy, don't gobble your food. Some day, I declare, you're gonna choke." Her mama was always declaring something or other. Sammy was about to ask her daddy about that colored woman when Mary Catherine opened her busybody mouth.

"You'll never guess what Miss Page had me do today. I'll declare."

Guess she had already got a bad case of "I'll declares" from Mama, Sammy thought. So she said, "No, and we don't want to hear about it either!"

Sammy could feel her daddy's glare, so dived into those butter beans with a vengeance, her eyes lowered. Mary Catherine ignored her, as usual, and continued in that actress-sounding way she had when she had everyone's attention, except Sammy's. She just let her ramble on about how the young, new teacher had selected her to choose the spelling words for the monthly spelling bee that the whole entire town would turn out for. Sammy just stared at her and thought, grief! just like it was important or something.

Well, Catherine got so excited—and so did Patrick—that you'd have thought she'd beat Tunney with a knockout or something just as important. Heck, they didn't even get that excited when Janie Lowell won the chance to get hypnotized and got to sit in the window at Badcock's furniture store in downtown Pahokee only to wet her britches for the whole town to laugh at, Sammy thought. Now that was exciting! Spelling bee...grief!

Before Mary Catherine could expound on how important she was, Sammy said loudly enough to shut her up, "Who's that old colored woman at Marsh's, Daddy? She showed up and General didn't even bark."

He sort of smiled. Now Patrick Carroll was a big man with a big smile. Everything about him was big, especially his hands, that had found a need to contact Sammy's bottom on a number of occasions. So when her daddy smiled a little smile, she knew that she'd not be getting a full answer.

"I believe she's his wife, who he brought from Pahokee. Walter mentioned that Marsh was planning on going to Pahokee to get him one."

He winked at her mama, so Sammy was for certain sure that was not the whole truth. Her mama smiled too. That sealed it. So if she wasn't his wife, then who was she? She was too old to be his daughter—heck she was older than her mama, who was near 'bout thirty-five.

"I found out her name!" Sammy said excitedly.

"Of course, you had to, Miss Curious!" Mary Catherine stuck in.

Now Sammy didn't mind one iota if her daddy called her Miss Curious, but she sure as heck didn't hafta take it from that stuck-up sister of hers.

Patrick could see her bristle, so said, "That's enough, Mary Catherine." Boy howdy, that sat her down in a hurry.

"Her name is Dessa, 'cause she told me so." Since Sammy was getting all the attention she knew from past experience that Jamie was gonna hafta say something about her eating out of the pot, so she blatantly turned to him and gave him her "evil eye." He suddenly had a change of heart and resumed fiddling with his food.

Sammy's plate was already empty, so she asked her mama if she could have her dessert, and Catherine smiled and said, "It's your favorite, Sammy, banana pudding." Boy howdy! Not many things got her more excited than diving into her mama's banana pudding. Sometimes she'd let Sammy beat the egg whites for the meringue. She always said that Sammy had the knack just like her Aunt Clara. Catherine would separate the egg yokes from the whites, gently sliding the whites onto the shallow blue platter, and then Sammy would tip it just ever so slightly and take the wire whisk and froth up those whites. Catherine would add the sugar slowly and, at the very end, a pinch of cream of tartar to make that meringue stand up proud. There was no doubt that Sammy indeed had the knack. Heck, that was a lot more important than getting to select dumb ol' spelling bee words, Sammy summarized as she downed the pudding and asked to be excused to the sound of her mama reminding her that she'd eaten like a field hand and shouldn't run and play so hard. But Sammy was already out the back door and down the steps and over to the quarters to see if that woman was around. If she wasn't his wife, then who was she? I'll find out this very night, she declared.

She saw Floy, Jr. out in his front yard. He lived on the other side of Sander's houses. He was her boyfriend, sort of. Pretty soon Junie came out of the quarters, and before that woman came out, they already had a game of catch-me-if-you-can going. It was kind of like hide-and-seek but was harder, more grown-up. So Sammy forgot all about her intended mission of finding out about Dessa.

It was dusk, and Junie, being so dark, sort of blended into the shadows, but Floy, Jr. had golden curls. As much as Sammy liked him, she

6

that is. But tonight her daddy was listening to his fight, and Catherine didn't have time to supervise the younger children's bath in the bath house.

Clarissa was in the living room sitting on her daddy's lap sucking that foul smelling thumb—and her seven years old! Boy, did that thing stink! Sammy once told her that she was gonna get leprosy and that it would rot off and fall just in time for the buzzards to get it, so Clarissa stuck her tongue out at her. Big baby is all Sammy could think to call her.

She would have thought that her parents would have been mad at her when she missed being the bride in the Tom Thumb wedding that the Woman's Club put on when she was four. Jamie got to be the groom, and Catherine made him a little white suit and a tall top hat, but the ladies asked Abigail Faulk's little girl Marylee to be the bride. She wasn't half as pretty as Clarissa, everyone said, but at least she didn't suck her thumb. As soon as she fell asleep, Walter would put her down on Patrick's and Catherine's bed in the front bed room.

Jamie was already in bed when Sammy passed inspection and kissed her mama goodnight. He slept at one end of the front porch that Patrick had partitioned off for him. Mary Catherine was in the girls' room reading out loud just like she was a big movie star or something. Sammy hopped in bed on her side next to the wall, pulled the sheet over her head knowing that it'd do no good to complain to Greta Garbo about her elocution, and ended up putting the pillow over her head, too.

Before she fell asleep she thought of Dessa. That sweet smelling, pungent aroma filled her head as she eased into a deep sleep. She still couldn't figure out why General hadn't barked at her.

They awakened to rain. Not just *a rain*, but a Florida downpour. The gutters that surrounded the tin roof weren't deep enough to handle the rushing surge of water. Sammy looked out the window and wished that she didn't have to go to school, because there were few things that she enjoyed more than playing in the rain. The rain barrels below the valleys where the front porch and living room roofs met and near the kitchen door at the back of the house were overflowing, making deep trenches in the fine sand.

Catherine stood looking out the kitchen window, a troubled look on her face. "The rain tank above the bath house is already overflowing. Imagine that!" She handed Sammy the hot buttered biscuit, not even looking at her, but continuing to stare out the window.

"Where's Daddy?" Sammy asked, knowing the answer, but the silence was bothering her.

"He's already gone to the fields, honey. Go see what's keeping Jamie. That child has gotten so slow. He'll be late for school. Mary Catherine!" she called. She didn't have to call loudly, because the girls' room was right off the kitchen.

Catherine resumed talking, almost to herself. "Your Daddy and Uncle Walter rushed off soon after daybreak. Heavens, I didn't even get the biscuits out of the oven before he left. He'll for sure get one of those sick headaches if he doesn't stop by the store for something. I declare he will."

Mary Catherine was in one of her early morning stupors, as Patrick called it. She just sort of looked out into space and slowly ate the biscuit, letting the butter and honey drool onto her plate. Now she was as fussy as anyone in the whole world, so for her to let anything drip took Sammy's full attention. She started counting to herself and sure enough by the time she got to a hundred, Mary Catherine was awake enough to realize what she was doing and quickly got a paper napkin to wipe up her mess. Don't know why she doesn't wipe it up with her biscuit. That's what I'd have done, Sammy thought, but that was not her way. Everything had to be *just so.*

There'd be no work in the fields today, so her daddy would probably be home early. Hey, maybe he'll get to teach me some new power throws so I can show 'em to Snookey and Renner, Sammy thought, excited. Her daddy was an expert baseball player. But he probably won't feel like it what with all the rain. There'd be long faces at the supper table tonight she also realized.

Patrick and Walter farmed together. They both had ten acres behind their houses and also farmed for the biggest farmer in the Glades, at least in Canal Point and Pahokee, Mr. Eben Hunter. He was the talk of the entire Glades. Everyone called him the "mystery man." Came to the area back in '29 with a bundle of money, and before you knew it had brought all three of his brothers down from Georgia to help with his operation. Since Patrick and Walter were considered experts in farming the black muck, Eben hired them to oversee his farm.

The bush beans were ready for picking, and what with all this rain they'd probably end up sitting in the fields to rot. The irrigation ditches that had been dug along side the fields were already filled with the early spring rains, so there'd be no run off. That was why Catherine was so worried.

Catherine held two umbrellas over the three children as they splashed over the front yard, the only area where the grass grew thick, toward the bus. Miss Howard had the bus lights on, windshield wipers struggling to push aside the rain so she could see. There were three big trucks waiting behind her filled with bean pickers. They were huddled together trying to stay dry beneath the tarpaulin stretched over the back but not long enough to shield them from the rain blowing in the sides.

By the time they got to the bus their shoes were soaked, and Mary Catherine was having one of her dramatic fits about it. Sammy just took hers off like she did most every day, wet or not. She didn't like to wear shoes, and her mama declared that she didn't have a single school picture of Sammy wearing her shoes and that she didn't know why she went to the trouble to even buy her any. Sammy didn't either.

The bean pickers were being returned to their various quarters that the White people had built for them alongside the lake ridge out in the muck. The ones who lived in Turnerville worked for Patrick and Walter and for Hunters' Farms as did the ones who lived in Sander's quarters, like Marsh and Junie's mama DeeCee. There were lots of small quarters up and down Conner's Highway, the hard road that ran in front of the ridge homes following the shore of the big lake, Okeechobee. The road was finished in '24 and went from West Palm Beach on the Atlantic Ocean to Canal Point, then to Okeechobee City. The quarters folks lived in the area year 'round and weren't migrants.

As the bus passed Turnerville they could hear the music bellowing from the radio in the stucco building. Boy howdy! Sammy thought. I bet Mama would be giving those men a tongue lashing about now as she went about her dailies. She sure hated for them to waste their money on those slots instead of taking care of their wives and children.

Sometimes things would get so bad that her daddy would drive her mama and Aunt Clara to the packing houses to get crates of vegetables, corn or beans or whatever they were picking, to take to them. Her daddy sure didn't have any respect for folks who neglected their families. I bet we'll be getting an ear full of Mama's frustrations when we get home from school about those no good men, Sammy thought. Her mama was near 'bout as dramatic as Mary Catherine when she got going. Sammy loved school but was getting excited about getting home and hearing her mama's tirade—that and the fact that she was cooking Aunt Jenny's potato surprise, one of her favorites, out of her Aunt Jenny cookbook. Yummmm...

Sammy always made sure that she knew what her mama had planned for supper so she'd know whether or not to trade off one of her sandwiches. But not today, 'cause she'd made Vienna sausage sandwiches. Now she knew that she could get most anything for one of her mama's Vienna sausage sandwiches. She chopped up her bread and butter pickles and grated a little onion and then added her homemade mayonnaise to the mashed up sausages. Heck, Sammy could get liverwurst, with that rim of white fat surrounding it. She saved the fat for General and would fool Jamie into thinking that she was feeding General a worm. He never caught on, and when General sat up for her she'd sneak the fat out of its waxed paper and drop it into his mouth. Jamie hollered every time she'd do it. She could get baloney or most anything for her Vienna sausage, but she already had her eating planned for the day, and no matter how much Frankie Ogle begged her, she'd not trade that sausage, even if he offered her a nickel as a bonus like he sometimes did.

As Sammy expected, there was no school recess, and they had to eat their lunch inside the class room. Sammy counted! Twelve whole offers were made to trade for her sandwich. That was a record. She almost succumbed when Richard Anderson offered to trade his pork and bean sandwich. But when she checked it, his mama hadn't even added any sweet pickle or onion. That did it! Just plain old pork and beans. Not worth a genuine Vienna sausage sandwich, Sammy whispered to him inside the cloak room—that's where they handled their rainy day transactions. Miss Zander, her third grade teacher, never seemed to catch on to the number of times they visited the cloak room on a stay-in day. At least she never acted like she suspected anything.

The bell rang, and since they were already in their seats, Miss Zander began the geography lesson. Sammy loved geography and dearly loved Miss Zander.

"Class," she said in that funny way she talked—she was from way up north in Rhode Island—"get your geography book out and turn to page ninety-seven." She waited for all seventeen students to find their places. She continued, "Rupert Mock, would you begin, please?"

Rupert began. Sammy heard what he was reading, but her mind was doing flip-flops. In his halting voice he read "Zanzibar and Tanganyika." Quickly she forgot all about playing after school and tuned in to what Miss Zander was saying.

She said that they transported cloves from Zanzibar and that they were their main crop. Sammy wondered if that was what that sweet spice was that she smelled coming out of Dessa's room. She bet that those spices came all the way from Africa, across that big ocean to Canal Point, Florida, and right into Dessa's big black pot. How about that!

Then Miss Zander said that a long time ago thousands of African natives who had been captured by Arab traders passed through Zanzibar and were shipped into slavery in Arabia. Sammy began to wonder if Dessa's kin were among them. Miss Zander was a good teacher and made every-thing interesting, even dumb old spelling.

Sammy got so caught up in the lessons that she forgot about the rain, and before she knew it the school bell was ringing and the shuffling of anxious feet sped past her. She grabbed her canvas bag out from under the seat, shoved the waxed paper from her lunch sandwich back inside the front pocket and buckled it. Waxed paper was good for all sorts of things, like rubbing the slides in the playground. Boy howdy! You could really fly down that slide, it'd be so slippery.

Sometimes Junie and she'd play like there was poison on the paper and would rub it on the spears they made from palmetto fronds. She sure could come up with some dandy ideas, that Junie could.

Hey! Sammy thought, as she made sure that she splashed in the deepest puddle she could find, I wonder if maybe Junie's kin came from

Zanzibar. I'll ask her this very afternoon. Hey! Maybe Dessa's did too, and that's where she learned all about cloves and the like and....

She looked up at the sun trying to find its way through the dark clouds and was disappointed that the rain had stopped.

CHAPTER TWO

Catherine and Clara were sitting on the front porch glider having a glass of lemonade. It was Friday and their day to stay home. Every other weekday afternoon they'd go into town for the mail and to the drugstore for a coke with the other ladies after their afternoon naps—Monday and Thursday were set aside for groceries. Catherine called it their pleasure time. If anyone in the area was sick or had some kind of problem, then they'd pay a visit, usually taking something such as a tin of cookies or a cake; or if there'd been a death in the family, then, my oh my, they'd turn loose, as Ruby would say, and take dishes of most everything they could come up with.

The rains had ceased. Big puddles were alongside the hard road in front of the house. There was no sign of Patrick's truck when Sammy got off the bus, so she figured that he was still in the fields or down at B. Elliott's garage with the other farmers. Sometimes he'd let her go with him. The men sat around and talked about the early days. It sure must've been something to see.

Her daddy said that the year she was born, 1924, that things were really hopping in the Glades. Mr. Howard Sharp came out from West Palm Beach and started his very own newspaper, *The Everglades News*, and he wrote about her. He wrote all about her birth and said that her mama bought at least a dozen copies of it and mailed them all the way to Georgia to their kin.

He said that Canal Point was called Nemaha and that the real estate sharks in West Palm Beach were selling that custard apple and elderberry land fast as they advertised it. That's the year that Mr. Fingey Conner opened up his toll road from West Palm Beach to Okeechobee, and Canal Point was smack dab in the middle of it. And he hired her daddy and Uncle Walter to be the toll gate keepers. Out of all those men he hired her daddy. She knew that the year she was born was just about the most important year a body could be born in.

<hr />

Sammy was sure hoping that no one had died or had taken sick so that her mama had found it necessary to give them Aunt Jenny's potato surprise. But when she opened the oven door, there it was with only part of it gone. It was golden brown, and she could see the little squares of shiny onions and green peppers chopped up fine throughout. Her mama diced the potatoes as fine as the onions and mixed everything with beaten eggs and fine bread crumbs that she rolled out between two pieces of waxed paper and formed it in the shape of her blue, oval platter. Then she'd brown it in butter in the great big cast iron skillet, being careful when she turned it or it'd fall all to pieces. When it was golden brown on both sides she'd put it in the oven to finish cooking. Boy howdy! That Aunt Jenny sure knew how to surprise a person with that recipe. It was real crunchy on the outside and melt-in-your-mouth soft on the inside.

After checking out the oven and removing a hunk of corn bread Sammy headed for the back yard. When she looked toward the quarters she could see *that woman* sitting on an upturned bean hamper in the back, fanning herself with something. She for sure had to find out what it was. Maybe it was something from her kin from Zanzibar, Sammy thought.

Sammy somehow knew that Dessa knew that she was approaching even though she didn't acknowledge it. Just sat there fanning herself in the afternoon sun and looking out over the rows of beans as far as the eye could see. She's a slick one, Sammy could tell. That just made her more interesting. Sammy was almost on her when she whirled around. And when she did, she just sorta wheeled her entire body around on that hamper with her feet up off the dirt and with a studied look on her shiny face.

"Thought you'd sneak up on me, huh, Sammy?" she said. Sammy could tell by her voice that she'd never be *Miss Sammy* to her, but it didn't bother her. Now Mary Catherine would have had a glorious fit about it and would have extracted an apology from her or gone running to her mama and daddy to tell them on her. But Sammy thought the entire business of Miss this and Miss that ridiculous, simply ridi... whatever the word was.

"Just wanted to see what you were doing and if you had kin from Zanzibar." Sammy rushed as she said it. Heck, I bet she hasn't even heard of Zanzibar, Sammy thought, allowing herself to get disappointed.

"Zanzibah," she said, and when she said it, it took on a foreign sound, and Sammy could hardly contain herself, wondering what she was gonna say next.

"You know, where maybe your kin came from and sent cloves to you across the ocean for your cookin'. You know!"

"Zanzibah...hmmm," she said slow like she was in some kind of trance or in one of Mary Catherine's early morning stupors.

"Oh," she said after letting Sammy stew a little. "You mean dat island off da coast of Tanganyika Territory in Africa..."

"Yeah! That's the one. Miss Zander said that their chief export was cloves. Is that what that sweet smell was coming out of your room last night?"

Sammy realized when she said it that Dessa knew that she'd been snooping around, so she gulped and tried to cover her tracks.

"Me'n Junie were playing outside the quarters last night and I said, "My, my, Junie, ain't that a sweet smelling something or other coming out of Marsh's room? And she said..."

But Sammy could tell that she wasn't buying that pig in a poke, as Grandpa Samuel would've said. But she didn't let on, just kept that secretive grin on her face, and it was aimed right at Sammy.

Well, I can't figure that one, Sammy thought. But because I can't, it just makes her that much more interesting. So she said with confidence, "Dessa, are your kin from Zanzibar or ain't they?"

"Sammy, it don't make a bit of difference if dey wuh o' if dey wuhn't, now does it? You want ta know who Ah am and what Ah'm doin' heah, now, isn't dat so?"

She caught her by surprise, so she just shook her head up and down like Aunt Maude chewing her cud in the broad sunlight. She sure 'nuff was a slick one.

"Well, Ah'll ease youah curious nature and tell you who Ah am." And she proceeded to tell Sammy, at least a little, who she was. But wouldn't you know that brat Jamie came a runnin' over to get in on it, and then Junie came roundin' the corner of the quarters to get in on the act, and before you could shake a stick at a...whatever...here came Thelma and Wilbur. Well, I never! Sammy thought, disgusted with the turn of events.

They were sitting on the damp, brushed-clean sand, and Dessa was leaning up against the rough wood of the quarters. She had them just where she would have them for the entire time that she lived there. There was never such a story teller as Dessa—Sammy's Dessa, as she became. She told them about how she and her friend Alpha, who became Mr. Eben Hunter's maid, survived the '28 hurricane by hanging onto a dead cow and how their clothes had been stripped clean off them by the high winds. She told them that when she and Alpha were found, Alpha had been bleached almost white, and how the little, scrawny Miller boy had been scared to death when he reported that he'd found a ghost and a black woman. She knew everything that there was worth knowing, and when Sammy told her daddy this that very night, well, all hell broke loose in the Carroll household.

Patrick was glum, and being glum was just like being happy. Whatever Patrick was was BIG—glum or happy. Catherine had no smile on her usually happy face. The minute Sammy ran home from Dessa's she knew that something was amiss. She could feel it as she washed her hands at the pump. Even Jamie knew that something wasn't right.

Patrick said grace in a trance. Sammy couldn't stand the tension any longer, so she said, "Dessa's not from Zanzibar, but she ran rum from the Grand Bahamas! And she knows just about everything that's worth knowing, too. Now I think that she's done the most exciting things in the..."

Sammy could tell immediately that she'd said the wrong thing. What, she didn't know, but she was about to find out in a hurry.

"That'll be enough from you, Sammy," Patrick said real low like.

Catherine could tell that Sammy wasn't aware of why Patrick was so upset, so she proceeded to talk, just very slowly at first, then in a normal voice.

"Your Daddy and I, as well as your Uncle Walter and Aunt Clara, are very worried about getting the beans picked before they rot. If we can't, then the rest of the season will be lost and we'll have to plow them under. Your Daddy..."

"Catherine, I can speak for myself..."

"But, you weren't saying anything, and I felt that..." Catherine got up, stumbled into their room, sniffling all the while, and shut the door hard. It was not at all the way that she usually acted. Sammy looked at Mary Catherine, and sure 'nuff she started with those fat tears streaming down her round, pink cheeks, and then Jamie started hollering so loud that they both got Sammy mad as a...as a...About then Patrick shoved his chair back, scraping the linoleum, something Catherine would've had a fit about, and said real loud, "Hush up, the two of you! There's no need for all this commotion!"

Sammy replied, "I'm not making any commotion, Daddy!"

"And so you aren't. You're the only level-headed one at this table tonight, Sammy."

He added, upset, "I'm going to calm your mother, and I highly suggest that the rest of you calm yourselves, too. Sammy, you see to them, please."

"Yessir!" she almost shouted. Sammy did like being given the go ahead to take charge. Her daddy often said that she was a take-charge kinda person. He couldn't have said anything more important than that. Heck, that was a lot better than being told that she was pretty or sweet like folks were always saying to Mary Catherine. A lot better.

"All right, you heard what Daddy said, Jamie. Go out to the pump and wash your face, and Mary Catherine..."

"Don't you Mary Catherine me, Miss Smartie Pants!" she shouted and ran to her room hollering her head off. Sammy decided that it'd do no good to follow her 'cause she was in such a snit, so she grabbed Jamie's arm and pulled him down the steps and started pumping that handle to beat the band. Jamie took one look at her and knew that if he didn't put his hands under the stream of water and splash his face that she'd gladly assist him. She dried his face off with her shirttail knowing that he'd not squeal on her. Confidence was her companion.

Sammy could hear her mama and daddy talking and then their door opening, so up those steps she hurried with Jamie right behind her. She had hardly touched her potatoes, so when she started to dive in Catherine said,

"Here, honey, I'll warm those up in the skillet in no time." Sammy was going to protest but changed her mind when she remembered how much better they tasted warm.

"I'm sorry that I ruined everyone's dinner and promise..."

"Catherine," Patrick interjected, "You have every right to be upset. Don't berate yourself. We'll just have to hope for the best and..."

"I bet Dessa knows a secret chant to help you save the beans, Daddy. I bet she can..."

"Sammy, what on earth are you talking about?" Catherine asked.

"She's gonna give me a secret remedy to take off these ugly old warts and.."

"That's enough about *that woman*, young lady!" Patrick put in. Sammy could tell that he was mad at Dessa. "I'm gonna have a talk with Marsh this very night!"

Sammy figured that she'd better come up with a fool proof defense for her and said, "Well, you know how those island folks talk, Daddy. Talk, talk! I'll let her give me the remedy, but bet these old warts will be here clean 'til next year."

Patrick acted like he wasn't listening to her and continued, "She's already causing trouble with the Coloreds. One of them said that she made the remark that she wasn't about to pick any beans for anyone, White folks or not."

Sammy hurriedly responded. "Oh, that was probably that old lyin' nigger Ropia. Why that nigger can't tell the truth to save her soul. Junie said that is one lyin' nigger!"

"Helen Louise Carroll, I do not ever want to hear you say that word again! Do you hear?"

"But Junie is the one who called her that, Mama. I was just repeatin'..."

That got nosy old Mary Catherine off the bed and out the door in a hurry. There was nothing in this entire world that gave her more pleasure than seeing Sammy get in trouble, Sammy thought. Boy, she was big eyed and smiling.

Patrick could see her enjoyment and came to Sammy's defense, "Sammy, it doesn't sound nice to refer to a Colored as a nigger. How would you like to be called an unkind word?"

"Heck, that Jacob Scarborough calls me worse than that all the time. I just turn two deaf ears. Why just today he called me a rotten skunk with a baboon face, and just because I wouldn't let him take two turns on the monkey bars. It was Dolly's turn, and he was hoggin' it. I just yanked him off, but not before I asked him real nice to get down."

Mary Catherine just had to say something. "And guess what everyone in the entire school calls her, too. Miss Boss, that's what. Miss Boss! Miss Boss!"

"That'll do," Patrick said. "Sometimes it's necessary to step in and help a friend when there's a bully around."

"And he sure is a bully, that Jacob is. Why just the other day he..."

"I believe it's time to change the subject. I still intend to have a talk with Marsh, and I think that now is the right time."

Sammy didn't know if she could stand not knowing what he was going to say, so she said, "I'll help you. Daddy. Dessa is my friend, and I know she'll listen to me."

He reached down and kissed the top of her straight brown hair and said, "I believe that I can handle this by myself, honey. I just want her to know that she's living in the quarters, and as long as she lives there she'll be expected to pick beans or do anything else we ask of her. I'm afraid that your friend is just too high and mighty for her own good."

"She's not high and mighty, Daddy. She's just different. You know, like I'm different from Mary Catherine and Jamie, but that doesn't make me high and mighty, does it?"

"Sammy!" he said sternly, so she knew that there wasn't a thing she could do, so she asked her mama for dessert. Fresh coconut custard! Wow! She soon forgot all about Dessa's plight 'til she heard Junie calling her to come out to play. Sammy decided that they'd play real close to Marsh's room in case Dessa needed them.

Junie didn't want to have any part of Sammy's plan to eavesdrop on Patrick's and Marsh's conversation—she was scared to death of Mistah Pat, as the Coloreds called Patrick. And it didn't matter how many times Sammy told her that his bark was worse than his bite, she still was scared. So Sammy told her to go find someone else to play with 'cause it was her duty to listen so's she could protect her new friend if need be. Sammy's *curious* had latched on tight as a tick, and she wasn't about to let her friend go undefended.

Sammy could hear muffled sounds coming out of Marsh's. When she crawled around the corner of the quarters, first thing she saw was a chair leaning up against the wall and a long figured skirt going almost to the ground with shoes sticking out but not quite reaching the ground. Sammy hadn't figured on Dessa not being allowed in on the doings. It took her aback at first, but when she looked up, she saw Dessa sitting with her ear against the wall, grinning. Dessa shook her head from side to side. Sammy sat down beside her in the dirt and put her ear against the wall, too, but couldn't hear a thing.

They were both startled when they heard Patrick loudly say, "Now, Marsh, I'm not going to have to say anymore about this, am I?"

"Nosuh, Mistuh Pat, yo sho ain't. Not anothuh word. Nosuh."

Dessa quickly got her chair over to the stand of bamboo in the corner of the yard and sat there working some palmetto into a braid, just like she'd

19

been there all along. Sammy hightailed it over to Junie's front door and hung close in the shadows.

She heard Dessa say, "Good evenin', Mistah Carroll."

"Good evenin' to you, Cat Island."

"Now, Mistah Carroll, you know full well that Ah'm from the Grand Bahama Island."

"And so you say, Cat Island." And with that Patrick and General headed for the house. Soon's he was inside Sammy ran to where Dessa was.

"Why'd he call you Cat Island, Dessa? Why?"

"Ah would imagine dat he wanted to put me in mah place, Sammy."

"I don't understand. He knows that you're from the Grand Bahama Island, 'cause you said so. I don't understand."

Dessa sat there and grinned. "It'll take moah dan ya daddy ta find a place ta put me in, Sammy, 'cause Ah've got propahty. Ah'm a propahty ownah, Sammy. Da man Ah ran rum foh bought valuable land and deeded it ovah to me. An' ain't nobody gonna get out of me who he is, eiddah. Nobody! Yes ma'am, Ah'm a land owner and Ah knows mah place."

"Dessa, your place is right here livin' next to me. That's your place," and Sammy hugged her around her waist. She seemed ten feet tall to her, but truth was Dessa barely hit the five foot mark.

They were startled when Marsh's low, booming voice called out the back door. Sammy looked up at Dessa, and her expression didn't change one whit. But Sammy was frightened for her.

"Is he gonna beat you, Dessa? I won't let him if you say so. I'll take a big old stick and hit him. Dessa, don't you feel scared?"

"What Ah got to be scared 'bout, Sammy? Dat's de dumbest niggah Ah ever laid eyes on. He's gotta be de dumbest niggah..." She was talking real loud, and Sammy was sure that Marsh heard her. Now she was really scared.

But Dessa strutted up to that back door with that faded flowered skirt swishing around her slight figure and in she went. Sammy could hear them talking but couldn't understand what they were saying. So she sneaked around to the front and stuck her head up underneath the window shutter. She could see Dessa. Her back was to her, her hands planted on her hips, and she was looking up at Marsh, who was taller than Sammy's daddy, making him at least six foot three, and boy she was giving him a piece of her mind! He didn't say a word. Just stood there looking up at the ceiling, that wasn't very high to begin with, just like he couldn't hear a word she was saying.

When she was through, she yanked the washtub off the nail beside the table and proceeded to go outside just like nothing had happened, and Marsh sat down on the chair next to the table and was staring off into space when Sammy ducked down and ran after Dessa.

"What'd he say, Dessa? What?"

"Now, what's a dumb niggah say, Sammy? He din' say nuttin', just lak Ah 'spected."

"But isn't he mad at you for talking to him like that?"

"Is Marsh a land ownah, Sammy? Is he? Course not. He's too dumb to be one, and he knows it. Ya'll learn how ta treat people one o' dese days. When dey knows dat youah smartah dan dey is, dey'll back down every time. Every time."

"Boy howdy, Dessa! You sure are smart!"

<hr>

Sammy didn't hear any more about Dessa causing trouble with the quarters people, but she also didn't see her going into the fields with the others. Next thing she knew, Dessa had made herself her Grandpa Samuel's chief cook and cleaning woman. Since her Grandma Belle died, her Grandpa didn't spend much time in the big house. He had leased his grocery store out front and would go to Hot Springs, Arkansas, for the baths or back to Georgia where he came from, and usually when he came home to the big house he'd eat with the Carrolls or with Clara and her family. But somehow Dessa finagled her way into his good graces and got herself a job. At least, that's what Catherine and Clara said.

When Samuel and Belle Graham moved to the Glades back in '16 there wasn't any house for them to move to. Samuel had left Georgia to work with his brother in the hotel business in West Palm Beach. But when the Palm Beach Canal was dug all the way to Canal Point and people started moving in, that black muck beckoned to him. Samuel was an adventurer, everyone said.

Catherine often told her children about how exciting it was to move to a new place as wild as the Glades and that she and Aunt Clara and Uncle Wash and Uncle Watson had a new adventure every day. She said that the alligators were all over the place, as well as snakes and rabbits, and that the lake shore was hard the full mile to Canal Point and that they could ride their bikes on it all the way there and never get stuck either.

There was always lots to do at the church and school, and the hotels would have a dance every Saturday night without fail. That's where she met their daddy. She said he was the handsomest young man around but that Grandpa Samuel wouldn't let her be courted by him, 'cause he was Catholic and she was Baptist. But after a while he gave in. He did make them wait four long years before they were wed though. Aunt Clara and Uncle Walter didn't have to wait any time at all because Uncle Walter said he was Baptist to please their Grandpa. Truth was that he was Methodist. But Grandpa said that wasn't nearly as bad as being a Catholic.

Sammy didn't understand any of it. When Miss Mae, her daddy's mama, came down to Florida for the winter, they became Catholic in a hurry. But when she wasn't there they would go with their mama to her church sometimes, or their daddy would take them to Mass—that's Catholic for church at someone's house, 'cause they didn't have a church anywhere around.

It was interesting to her though, because they spoke in Latin and seemed to know what they were saying. Her daddy taught them to make the sign of the cross, and when Sammy showed it to Junie she got down on the ground and started yelling her head off. She said that Sammy was putting a spell on her.

Sammy had to prove that she wasn't by taking a stick and drawing a cross in the sand. "Now, Junie, have you ever heard of the man named Jesus?"

"Course Ah have. Everybody heard 'bout Jesus. He's de one who gonna save mah people."

"All right then. Now where did those bad people take him so's they could kill him, huh?"

"What you mean, where'd dey take him?'

"Did they take him and hang him on a cross or not?"

"Course dey did. Sammy, everybody in de whole world know dat."

"Well, when we Catholics draw the cross on our bodies, we are just reminding ourselves that is where Jesus died so we won't forget. Now, that's what my Daddy told me, and my Daddy doesn't even begin to know how to tell a lie."

"You sure, Sammy? Dat don' look lak no cross to me."

"Sure it does. Look here, it's got four points." Sammy drew the four points in the sand and had Junie trace them with the stick.

"See, Junie? Here's where they hung his arms on some old rusty nails and here's where they hammered in his feet."

"You best not be funnin' me, Sammy Carroll, or Ah'll tell on you and get Dessa to teach me one a her spells lak she used on Mistah Samuel an' Ah'll get back at ya, too."

"Take it back, Junie! Take it back, ya hear? Dessa wouldn't use her spells on Grandpa Samuel. Now you rightly know that. Take it back!"

Neither of them heard Dessa until she had grabbed Sammy's shirt collar and was pulling her off Junie.

"What you two fightin' 'bout? You supposed ta be best friends, aren't ya?"

"She said that you put a spell on Grandpa Samuel, and that's why he hired you for his cook and cleaning lady. She said it, Dessa!"

Dessa looked down at Junie. "Wheah'd ya evah heah of such a ting, Junie. Wheah?"

"My mama told me dat dat's what dey all sayin' 'bout ya."

Dessa began to laugh all over the place, just a shaking hard as can be. Sammy joined her.

"I told her that you didn't cast one of your spells on Grandpa Samuel, Dessa. I told her."

"Now what makes ya t'ink dat Ah din't, Sammy?"

"Cause you're my friend, and I know that you wouldn't do anything to hurt my kin, that's why."

"Well, young lady, ya be de smartest one around dis place, dat's what." And she gave Sammy a big hug, and that's how Patrick found them, hugging and laughing. He had a strange look on his face.

"Sammy, you're needed at home," is all he said, but Sammy knew from the way he was looking that something awful had happened. It couldn't be that the beans had rotted, 'cause they hadn't.

"Can Dessa come with me, Daddy?"

"No, she certainly can't!" he said emphatically. And not another word did he say all the way to the house.

CHAPTER THREE

When Samuel and Belle Graham moved to Canal Point from West Palm Beach, Belle's folks thought that they'd lost their minds. Belle wasn't sure that they weren't right, but she knew Sam, and when his mind was made up there was no need for her to argue with him. She'd felt the same way when he decided, out of the blue, to leave Glennville, Georgia, and head for Florida to work for his brother in his hotel business.

The farthest Belle had been from her birthplace, Glennville, was to Savannah, and there just twice. Sam was the adventurer of the family. She knew right from the start that the hotel business wasn't for him, but she did have to admit he tried very hard to adapt. But when he opened the small grocery store on Clematis Street, he seemed to have found his life's work.

Belle went into business with Sam's cousin making dresses and hats for the elite of Palm Beach. Their combined income was enough for them to consider buying a lovely home on Datura Street, and since the children were happy in their schools, their life seemed to have found some order. When the newspapers began printing articles extolling the possibilities in the Everglades, especially the rich muck land surrounding the southeastern area on Lake Okeechobee, the wandering bug bit Sam again. When the Palm Beach Canal was completed to the lake, that was all Sam needed to make up his mind. The canal became the waterway into the Glades, and Sam instinctively knew that the area would prosper. He was right. It was bustling. There were two hotels, and stores were opening up as fast as the saw mills could cut and ship the lumber from Indian Town or Moore Haven.

Patrick Carroll arrived from West Palm Beach in '17 and knew as soon as he did that his decision was a good one, also. He'd left a small Georgia town when he was but sixteen. After working for his uncle in West Palm Beach he, too, succumbed to the lure of the Glades just as Samuel had.

It was rumored that all a farmer had to do was drop a seed in the rich soil and in no time become wealthy. Some had done just that, but others had become discouraged and left for more civilized towns in Florida, for the Glades were wild, and it took a special type of person to last even a year.

There was something exciting about being in on the beginning of a town, a community, and Patrick took advantage of every opportunity. First, he got a job with Fingey Conner, the wealthy entrepreneur from up north, on his farm. He knew little about farming but was smart and observant and wasn't shy about asking questions of the successful farmers in the area. He also was a natural at repairing anything mechanical, and Conner found the tall, affable man an asset to his operation.

But Patrick wanted his own land, and when the lake ridge began opening up he went to Conner and secured his first business loan. Fingey Conner co-signed for him at his bank in West Palm Beach. That impressed everyone in town. The only discouraging event in young Patrick's life was the insistence from Samuel that Patrick and Samuel's daughter Catherine were to wait to be married. He knew that he had to be patient, and he was, but it was difficult for the vital young man.

Patrick continued working for W.J. Conner's Farms, but when Conner saw the need to build a hard road into the Glades from West Palm Beach in order for the pioneers to have access to the lake area, he hired Patrick as foreman of the work crew he brought in. Canal Point was the halfway point for this large undertaking with Okeechobee City at the northern point on the lake as the final destination.

Samuel had built the big house for his family in '17. While awaiting the completion of their home they had lived in a large tent with wooden floors and sides three feet high. Samuel had the workmen secure mosquito netting above the sides up to the canvas roof, where they attached canvas flaps to be closed when the heavy rains blew, and they did often.

Belle had her open front porch with large square columns overlooking the magnificent lake just as she had wanted. She had insisted on a Georgia dogtrot house, three rooms off both sides of a center hall with a long porch across the back of the house. The deep windows were plentiful, and the house was built three feet off the ground to allow any breeze in the vicinity to pay a visit, as Belle explained to Samuel.

There were a front parlor, dining room and kitchen on the north side and three bedrooms on the south side. Plans were made to add a bathroom on one side of the back porch at a later date. The family bathed in the lake when it was warm, and during the cold months used a number-two, galvanized tub. Sometimes Samuel would go to town to take a bath at the barbershop but usually joined the family in the lake.

Their lives were full. Samuel began building his grocery store north on their property and by 1918 had an active business going. Belle handled the fabrics, notions and ladies' garments, and Samuel managed the rest of it with the children delivering groceries by bicycle or wagon. They farmed the ten acres of muckland behind their house, which was built on the sandy lake ridge underneath towering cypress and rubber trees.

Samuel's fascination with the Glades knew no boundaries. If he heard of a new type of green bean or corn or strain of anything that grew, he'd investigate and usually experiment by planting a small portion of his acreage in whatever it was. Belle was almost as bad as he with her flowers. Getting a new seed catalog was like Christmas at the Graham household.

Catherine, the oldest, and Clara, Wash and Watson were involved in almost every activity in the small community. Catherine was the musical one of the family, and like her father could play a number of musical instruments. She was especially proficient on the piano. Samuel's preference was the organ, accordion and jews'-harp, but he also played piano. They were in great demand at the many social functions in the small communities surrounding the lake.

When Catherine and Patrick were finally allowed to marry in 1920, Samuel built them a small house north of the big house just behind the grocery store. Until their house was completed, they lived in the town of Pahokee south of Canal Point. And when Clara and Walter were wed, he built them a smaller house next to the Carrolls'. Sam liked having his family around him, especially since Belle had begun to fail.

The doctors in West Palm Beach said that she had a weak heart, and Dr. Spooner in Pahokee, in whom he had more faith, agreed with them. When Samuel was told that it was just a matter of time he was devastated. The girls were glad that they were living close by.

Belle lived to see the birth of Mary Catherine and Sammy, but the year Jamie was born in '26 the Lord chose to take Samuel's beloved one. He never forgave Him. He became a wanderer, going from state to state on the pretense that he was investigating better farming methods. But everyone who knew Samuel knew better. The year before Belle died they took a train trip to California, and Watson and Wash, who were still single, accompanied them. He had granted his Belle her last wish, to go from the Atlantic Ocean to the Pacific, and since then was biding his time until he could join her.

He had leased the store to the Lowell brothers, and his farms were doing well even with the floods in 1922 and 1924. The hurricane in 1926, which almost wiped Moore Haven, Miami and the Keys area off the face of the earth, came soon after Belle died, but Samuel didn't seem to notice. Not even when Jamie was born did he allow happiness to interfere with his grieving. Catherine and Clara were at their wits' end with worry over him.

So much had happened in the last few years! Exciting things! His children had thought that with the land boom and accelerated growth of the community he would have come alive again—the old Samuel would have.

<hr/>

The Everglades News, the weekly newspaper begun by Howard Sharp, a newspaper man from Palm Beach, was filled with the evolution of the Glades, the dormant area of the country touted as the last frontier. Sugar cane fields surrounded the lake. Thousands of train cars of vegetables were rolling. Tomatos, corn, beans and potatoes were rushed to the hungry markets up north. Five hundred crates of vegetables were shipped from East Beach each day for two months, and two thousand hampers a day for long periods. The government experiment station in Canal Point had 157 varieties to send to various areas around the lake to plant, the *News* reported.

The week before Sammy was born in March of '24 Belle had taken to her bed. Samuel had gone into town for a prescription, and when he got there he saw and certainly heard the throng of people surrounding the dock. The entire town was buzzing. It seems that 1,300 hampers of green beans had spilled into the lake on their way to Moore Haven when the barge that had been carrying them sank seven miles east of Observation Shoals.

The barge was towed by the towboats Lucille and Rosa Lee and belonged to J.P. Heimer's fleet. They had hired a colored man to pump out the water, but the motion of the water lulled him to sleep. About 5:00 in the morning Mr. Fultz came on the deck of the Lucille and heard the man call for help, but the front end of the barge was already under water, and the crates of beans were sliding off. All 1,300 of the hampers plummeted into the yellow, fresh water.

Petrie Jones, the colored man, said that his lantern had been put out by the rising water, and the barge and wind were so noisy that Mr. Arrington had not heard his cries for help.

They were towed back the next day to Bacom Point, south of Pahokee, and later to Canal Point, where the throng awaited them at the docks. When Samuel got there, the farmers were shouting their concerns about whether they would be compensated for their loss, as werethe buyers and shippers. Mr. Heimer assured them that the Canal Point docks would be paid $5000.00 for their loss of produce, which would have brought $8,500.00 in the northern markets, and all claims would be satisfied.

Samuel left town with a smile. He would have some exciting news to share with his Belle. That should get a smile out of her, he thought. When Samuel told Belle the tale of the spilled beans with considerable theatrics and that the folks in town had dubbed the negligent colored man who had caused all the commotion, Sleepy, he still did not evoke a smile. All she said was, "Poor old Sleepy." Being a loving man by nature, he understood her compassion.

He tried to keep her informed and alert by giving her the news of the day. He'd read the *News* weekly and would try to make it as entertaining as possible, but Belle seldom responded. "Listen to this, Belle!" he'd exclaim. "J.H. Snyder, up on the north ridge, is growing potatoes that weigh a pound each. How about that!" He'd chuckle then continue. "You know how he did it? Well, you know old Johnny. He had to add 200 pounds of fertilizer to that little old plot of 30 by 170 feet. Imagine that!

12% potash and 12% acid phosphate." Samuel laughed. "He exhibited them at the *Everglades News*, and five potatoes weighed in at five and a half pounds."

No response. "Well, my sweet," he said, patting her dry, withered hand, "I'll take those red bliss potatoes that you cream and that melt in your mouth any day. You know, the ones that they're growing at Torry Island. Bet their flavor is a heck of a lot better than that New Jersey Snyder can grow." Had Belle been alert she would have detected Samuel's competitiveness, but she was asleep.

He had wanted to share with her the excitement of their sons' selection for their high school cantata. She would have been so proud, for Belle, who was not musical herself, dearly appreciated anyone else's talent. He also wanted to tell about Patrick's new job as toll taker on the newly completed Conner's Highway. He and the others had insisted on Belle's attending the opening celebration at Okeechobee City on the 4th of July along with the rest of the family, but she responded very little, and Wash and Watson had to take turns staying in the car with her.

There were two railroads in Canal Point and Pahokee in 1924, and the new ice factory in Belle Glade meant delivery by boat at least twice a week. It was rumored that there would be daily mail deliveries from West Palm Beach now that the highway was opened. There was so much that he wanted to share with her. He was so desperate that he even had Clara accompany them to Safety Harbor, hoping that the famous baths would help her in some way. But they didn't. There seemed to be no magical cure for his Belle.

So much had changed since they moved to the Glades, not just in the tiny towns around the lake but in the crops as well. A number of the farmers had begun growing avocados commercially as well as peanuts, which were touted to have more rich oil for commercial use than their competitors' in the other southern states. Fishing was still a big business with 6,500,000 lbs. being shipped from the lake per season from Okeechobee to the terminal in Jacksonville, and that was just from the eastern side of the lake.

Even the movies had arrived in Pahokee, and Samuel thought that laughter should be a part of Belle's life as it had been ever since he had fallen in love with the beautiful, tall, grey-eyed girl of just fourteen. So Samuel asked Clara and Catherine to help her get dressed for the trek into town to attend the movie. Into Sam's new Ford they went to the opening of Mack Sennet's comedy, "The Winning Punch," but Belle's chin rested on her chest for most of the movie, while Clara and Catherine laughed and laughed and could hardly wait to get home to share their adventure with their families.

Sam insisted on stopping by Maggie's for an ice cream cone on their way home, for it appeared that Belle had rallied and seemed more alert. She sat with them and visited the other customers just like she always had, even joining in the conversation. But when she began talking about the opening of Conner's Highway, as if it had just happened, instead of happening the year before, Sam became embarrassed.

Catherine encouraged her to continue, but Sam went to the car and waited for them to finish. Belle was laughing with the others about Gov. Hardee's speech and the fifty decorated cars that participated in the parade, a lot of them from Canal Point. Clara reminded her that she and Catherine along with Sam had attended the masquerade street dance and that Mr. Hawk had told them that the fireworks committee had spent over $3,000 and that Mr. Conner had also donated four lots in Okeechobee City worth $1,500.00 to be sold with the proceeds going to the finance committee.

When Clara and Catherine took Belle to the car, Sam had his head down on the steering wheel—it was obvious that he had been crying. Catherine told him in her animated voice that Belle had everyone laughing when she told about the parade and celebration. Sam nodded and said barely above a whisper, "I didn't know that she was aware of anything that night. She hardly remembered anything about our trip to California the following year." He had such a grin on his face, but when he turned around to smile at Belle, she was as she had been at the movies, asleep.

"Daddy Samuel," Catherine said, "Maybe she understands a lot more than we think. Why, just the other day she told me that Sammy was going to have a little brother, and I hadn't even visited Dr. Spooner to confirm that I was with child. How about that?" Sam didn't answer. He was afraid to allow himself any hope. She died the August before the hurricane of '26 and Jamie's birth in October and left a grieving, devastated husband.

The big house was closed more than it was open. Samuel had hoped that Patrick would agree to move his family into it because their small house was no longer adequate for the five of them and was bulging at the seams when Miss Mae, Patrick's mother, came down from Georgia for her winter visits. But Patrick was a proud man as well as a practical one. He offered to purchase the big house from Samuel and sell him their small one, but Samuel couldn't part with Belle's dream home.

After the birth of Clarissa, Clara and Walt sold their little house to Silas Maxon up on the ridge, and his sons moved it for him to his small piece of land. The Halls moved about a block south to a larger house located on the ridge with ten acres of good muck land for Walt to farm.

Samuel's inability to cope with his loss kept his girls upset. He would sit night after night on the front porch ignoring the buzzing, biting insects. Rocking on the rush-seated rocker, he'd stare out over the reeds that grew thick along the shore of the lake as the lazy waves splashed against them, reflecting the evening sun that was taking its time to set. When the rose, gold and deep blue clouds converged with the night blue of the lake, his family would hear him hum *Amazing Grace*. There was not a dry eye among the adults, and to get their minds off Samuel's grief Catherine would usually begin playing something light and airy on the piano. In no time the group would surround her requesting particular songs. Her music was her solace, she said.

<hr />

Sammy could feel her daddy's big, hard hand clasp and unclasp hers. She knew that he was nervous, and she just hoped that it was not something that Dessa had said or done. The way that Junie had been carrying on about Dessa putting a spell on Grandpa Samuel made Sammy afraid to let her mind dwell on what was wrong, especially since Dessa seemed to have a special power so strong that even General had never barked at her. He had to be the best watch dog in all creation, her mother had often said.

"Well, there you two are," her mama said, rushing around the kitchen grabbing this and that and straightening it up just like Miss Mae was about to open the door and come for her winter visit from Georgia. But why is Daddy so nervous? she questioned. It can't be Miss Mae, or he'd not be acting this way.

Mary Catherine was all gussied up in her Sunday best. Her taffy-colored curls were set just so, and even Jamie's hair was slicked back, the unresponsive curls springing out around his ears like always when someone tried to tame them.

"Get yourself dressed, Sammy. I've been whistling for you for almost forever. Mister Eben Hunter is coming calling, and you look a mess. Here! Put this on," Catherine said, handing Sammy her navy blue serge dress with the middy collar. Oh, how she hated that dress, but she decided that it would probably do no good to make a fuss. Catherine Carroll was jittery, and Sammy was relieved that the reason for the nervousness was not some devil spell that Dessa had put on Grandpa Samuel, as she had feared.

Sammy gave in to her "curious". She couldn't hold back any longer. "What's so important about Mister Eben coming to visit, anyway? Is he mad at you, Daddy, 'cause the beans almost rotted and you couldn't pick as many as he wanted? Heck, he's not some kinda king or even president of the United States, so why's his visit so important?" she added, trying to think of some reason to not have to wear that dress,

"Enough!" is all Patrick Carroll said, drumming his fingers on the wide arm of the maroon mohair armchair, his chair.

"He's not a king, is right, young lady, but he is your daddy's boss, and when he sent James up to tell us that he'd be calling, there must be something important for him to tell your daddy. And, Sammy, I want you to be quiet as a mouse, do you hear?"

Sammy could feel Mary Catherine and Jamie stifle their laughter but decided to go into her room and get dressed as requested. Besides, she wanted to ask Mr. Eben a few questions about Alpha, his maid, who was the only friend Dessa really had and who had come from the Grand Bahamas either with her or, at least, about the same time. Sammy had never got a straight answer from Dessa on it. There was something that Dessa was hiding, and Sammy sensed it. Sammy liked things in order, and that included when and why Dessa moved to the Glades. Was she practicing that voodoo she'd heard about? Or maybe the law had shipped her out to sea to drown. She'd heard that they did that sometimes to witches. Or just what...

Catherine continued to comb Sammy's bobbed hair just like she hadn't just finished it. Sammy let her—she loved having her hair combed. Jamie was on the front screened-in porch sitting beside the fern planter on the lettuce-green straight chair that Catherine had painted for the summer. Everything on the porch had been painted lettuce green. Catherine had read that it was the fashionable color for out door furniture. Patrick had teased her, saying that she sure had a partiality to lettuce, but she thought that it freshened up the tiny porch. She was an enthusiastic homemaker, and he was proud of the interest she took in their home.

"He's here!" Jamie called to them loudly. General began barking like he usually did.

"For heaven's sake, son," Patrick said and put his finger to his mouth. "Mr. Hunter will think that you have no manners." He turned to Catherine, and she could tell that he was concerned. I just hope that it's not bad news. It's not his and Walter's fault that the rains came when they did was all she could think, biting her lower lip as she often did when she was worried.

The big, black Packard was polished to as high a sheen as James could get it. Sammy could see the reflection of the bright coral vine growing up on the side of the house in the side of it. James was Dessa's friend from the islands and Alpha's husband. James sat proudly in the driver's seat, and beside him sat Alpha, who opened the car door and began walking toward Dessa's quarters with General right behind her, barking his head almost off until Patrick yelled, "General Lee!" Not another sound did General make. He turned around and went to his master.

Sammy called to her, "Alpha, Dessa's at Grandpa Samuel's." When her daddy looked down at her, she mumbled, "I saw her go over there, Daddy." She thought, why's he looking at me like that? I didn't say anything wrong.

Eben Hunter was in the back seat and sprang out of the door next to the house. He was smiling, and when Sammy saw him she thought that he had to be the handsomest man she had ever seen—except for her daddy, of course. He was wearing an open collared, long-sleeved, tan shirt tucked into darker tan riding britches and high, dark reddish-brown boots. His curly hair was the color of the boots and his eyes a pale, cool gray.

He was the first to speak. "Patrick, I'm glad that James found you home. I was afraid I'd miss you."

He bowed slightly to Catherine, who had come down the front steps and was standing beside Patrick.

"Catherine," he said taking her hand. "Thanks for receiving me." He could see that they had all dressed for the occasion. It pleased him. He liked the respect they showed. He reached down and petted General, who immediately went back to Patrick.

Sammy was taking all of this in and wondered when she'd be able to ask him about Alpha. She ran down to stand beside her mama, just in case the opportunity presented itself. Then she'd be ready for him. She liked his manners. He talked just like they did in the movies, but with a soft bass voice. Next thing she knew, that Mary Catherine was pushing her aside, trying to get next to her mama. Sammy gave her arm a hard pinch, then shoved her to the side.

Eben saw her maneuver and, looking down, grinned at her. "You must be Sammy."

"How'd you know? I never saw you before. But before you and my daddy start to talking about your business, I got a question I want to ask."

"Sammy, that will be quite enough, young lady," Patrick interjected, afraid of what she might ask.

Eben put his hand on Patrick's shoulder and winked at him saying, "I'm sure that she won't ask anything that I've not been asked before, Patrick. Now would you, Sammy?"

"I don't have any way of knowing that, now do I?"

Eben Hunter had a glint in his eyes. "Alpha told me that you were an interesting child, Sammy, and that you were a good friend of Dessa's. She also said that you were a very curious child..."

Patrick decided that he'd not chastise Sammy but wasn't sure that Catherine would be able to hold her tongue much longer. He could feel her nails digging into the palm of his hand.

"And that's just what I wanted to talk to you about, Mister Eben. I can't get a straight answer out of Dessa, and that Alpha is as close-mouthed as she is. No point in asking James, 'cause he's as dumb as Marsh. Now, I'd like to know when they came to Pahokee and why? Me'n Junie got a bet on it."

For whatever reason, Patrick felt that Eben Hunter seemed relieved by Sammy's question but was perplexed by their interchange.

Eben began walking toward the house before answering. He virtually wheeled around and said defensively in a strange voice, "Well, young lady, I have no way of knowing the answer to your question. When I hired James and Alpha back in '29, soon after I moved to the Glades, they said that they'd been here during the hurricane and didn't venture any other information. And, frankly Sammy, I didn't care enough to inquire further."

He added, "Does that satisfy your curiosity, Sammy?" Sammy got the full brunt of his cool gray eyes and felt a little shiver. What had she said wrong, she wondered. Heck, she'd just asked a simple question about when they all came to the Glades. Now what could be wrong with that?

But when Sammy looked up at him the shiver returned, so she added politely, "Mr. Eben, all it told me was what I already knew." She could feel Eben Hunter close the door soundly on any future conversation. So could Patrick. And Catherine was so embarrassed by her direct young daughter that she hastened to say, "Sammy, Mr. Hunter has business with your daddy, and I think that you owe him an apology for your impudence, young lady."

Eben put his hand on Catherine's arm to restrain her and said, "Now Catherine, it's almost refreshing to hear a young lady be as direct as Sammy. But, of course, everyone does not have my respect for directness. It will probably do your young Sammy good to practice the art of observation and certainly of restraint, but then," he laughed a hearty, hollow laugh, "without the unexpected utterings of the young perhaps our lives would take on a dullness..."

What in the world is he talking about, Sammy wondered. Bored with his obvious dismissal, she shrugged and asked her mother if she could go to the big house to visit with Dessa and Alpha. Maybe I can extract some truth out of those two, 'cause I sure can't from that high and mighty man.

Catherine looked at Patrick for help. "Why don't you go on to Clara's for that visit we were talking about? Sammy can visit with Dessa another time." Sammy knew not to protest. Her daddy's tone of voice left no room for argument. When Eben heard their plans he insisted that James drive them to Clara's. He and Eben went to the kitchen, where Patrick kept a bottle of good Irish whiskey. He turned to tell General to go to the bath house, and he did without any further commands. Eben was impressed. He wanted that dog, coveted him, but knew Patrick well enough to not pressure him about him.

Getting to ride in the big Packard was the only thing that kept Sammy from pinching a big old hole in Mary Catherine's arm. It was obvious how delighted she was at Sammy's being put in her place by that mysterious Mr. Hunter. She could hardly wait to tell her best friend Dorothy about the encounter. Everyone in the entire Glades wondered just who he really was and where he came from.

Clara was surprised when she saw Catherine and the children drive up in Eben's Packard. She was also surprised that Walter had not been let in on the meeting, that is, if it indeed was a business meeting, as Catherine had said. Why, Walter Hall was as much in Eben Hunter's employ as Patrick Carroll, for heaven's sake. She knew that she would soon be finding out the answer. She could tell by how Catherine was leaning forward, hurrying to get up the porch steps, telling the children to go to the back yard to play, and they in their Sunday best, and sure enough, even before she opened the screened door, she was sputtering...

"You'll never believe that Sammy, Clara, not in a million years—I don't know what I'll ever do with that child—and how nice and gentlemanly he handled her behavior."

"Sit down and get your breath, Catherine. Now, what are you talking about?"

"That Sammy! That's what! Why, she asked him all about his servants and when they moved to the Glades and..."

"Well, what's wrong with that? Catherine, what could possibly be wrong with that? It's not like she asked him why he didn't have a wife, and him in his mid thirties for sure, or why he felt like he had to go all the way to West Palm Beach to get a whore? Well, you know what Walter said. Said that the Glades girls weren't good enough for him and..."

"You'd just have had to have been there to understand, Clara."

"Well, I wasn't invited and neither was Walter, Catherine," she said with a huff.

"Are you upset with me? Are you? Well, I had nothing to do with this entire matter, and you know it. And neither did Patrick. I don't know what he wants, but I'm about to die to find out. If it had anything to do with the farming operation, then of course Walter would have been included. Now, you know that! Or do you?"

"You don't have to get huffy about it! I don't know anything of the sort, and neither do you. I've never trusted that man, and neither does anyone else I know. Why, to come down here with a trunk full of money, and next thing any of us know, to buy most of the best farmland around the lake and hire those fancy servants and ...."

CHAPTER FOUR

Dunbar Anderson was not a big man in stature, but he was a BIG man in the town of Pahokee, Florida. He was one of the earliest settlers and had been a fisherman by trade and desire when he first arrived in the Glades in 1916. He was an easy going man with a sixth-grade education from the town of Lakin, Kansas, a small farming community on the banks of the Arkansas River. The nearest town of any size was Garden City, but when Dunbar mentioned that he was from near Garden City, no one had ever heard of it, so he started saying that he was from outside of Dodge City. They seemed to have heard of that.

Why he had set out to become a fisherman no one in his hometown of Lakin would have understood. Maybe it was because he hated the endless fields that stretched from butte to butte, horizon to horizon with no finality—never ending. Maybe it was because he never felt clean. There seemed to always be a skim of dust clinging to his body hair. Maybe his need to feel the easy coolness of rain running over his pudgy face down to his feet and to watch it puddle...maybe that's why he left Lakin at the age of thirteen, wandering down to Alabama and eventually to Florida.

But it all began much earlier and for a very different reason. Dunbar's mother Viola Stutzman had come to Lakin as a young bride of fifteen. She had been a pleasant woman, who was used to small towns and hard work. When her first born, Clark Lovin, had died before his first birthday, some of the happiness went out of Viola, and when her second child had been stillborn, she lost a little more of her glow, Dunbar's father, Edward, said. Dunbar was the third child and was born to a dour faced woman, who had aged greatly since her marriage and the loss of her children.

When Dunbar was five his brother Gordon was born. Dunbar loved him from his first lusty cry. He was a healthy child, a happy child and favored Viola. She began to smile more often. When the family went to town on Saturday afternoon, Dunbar took care of Gordon so Viola could socialize with the other ladies. In their small prairie home she'd spend hours telling the two wide-eyed boys about her grandfather's struggle to homestead his land, about his fights with the Pawnee and the Kiowa and about the land that her parents' home was on being the scene of one of the bloodiest battles that he'd ever had to fight.

Viola never worried about Gordon when he was with his brother. They became inseparable. If Dunbar went fishing, he took Gordon along. If he went to the adjacent farm to play, Gordon tagged along. If Dunbar had chores to do, Gordon wanted to help. Viola was a happy woman once more.

But happiness was not to be hers for long. When Dunbar was twelve and Gordon seven, tragedy struck the Anderson family again. As was their custom during the summer months Dunbar and Gordon would get their fishing poles and head for the river after their chores had been completed. They walked the train tracks that ran beside the river, ducked into the willows and before long were at Scratch Bottom, their favorite fishing hole.

On this particular day Dunbar had gone on ahead of Gordon, returning by the train tracks as usual, because he had promised their dad that he'd help him with some tractor repairs. He hadn't a worry in the world. He'd caught a few bream, and it was a beautiful, clear day. He heard the train's whistle but was not alarmed. He heard it twice every day. When he got to the path to their farm he heard the train's brakes screech, and when he turned to see what the problem was, he knew instantly. How he knew, he was later to say, was a mystery to him.

Returning to the tracks, he picked Gordon's broken body up and carried him all the way home. When Viola saw him walking toward her, she also knew. Dunbar was devastated. So were his parents. He left home the next year, and after working his way on farms from Kansas to Alabama, where he lived for three years, felt the lure of the Glades. He was only twenty years old but was already an old man.

His fishing business on the big lake had been quickly extinguished when he found out, quite by accident, what a tiny seed dropped in the black muck could do for a fellow and his pocket book back in 1917. He made his mark and his fortune, because fate took a hand in Dunbar's financial state. His small acreage that he'd bought the previous year, using the money from the sale of catfish, he'd planted in green beans. It had been the only acreage spared from the devastating norther that winter. A hamper of beans brought $24.00 in the northern markets that year. He was grateful, and his farm grew with the town, as well as his self esteem.

He shopped in the Glades and was upset with his fellow citizens when they went to town, as they called West Palm Beach, which was forty-five miles east toward the Atlantic, to shop. He bought his Majestic radio from Olaf Boe, his Ford from B. Elliott, his gas from the Pahokee Texaco station, his suits from Joe Kahn and his seeds and hampers from the Kilgore Company. He said that all his money was in the Bank of Pahokee and that when he died, J.C. Berry was going to handle his body at the Everglades Funeral Home in Pahokee and that his body would go to Port Mayaca Cemetery.

Practically the only time that Dunbar Anderson left the town of Pahokee was to attend the Palm Beach County Fair in West Palm Beach, and then he attended only the Glades' exhibits: the women's cookery, fine arts, needle work, the agricultural exhibit. He wasn't interested in hearing Gov. Doyle Carlton speak or see the vaudeville acts. He did attend the presentation of the blue ribbons, because Mrs. Coburn of Canal Point had won the blue ribbon for her hooked rug.

Dunbar always said that if people really wanted to see a good fair they should attend the annual Glades Bean Festival sponsored by the American Legion and held halfway between Canal Point and Pahokee. Now that was a fair worth visiting. They brought in the old steamer *Lily* for boat rides on his beautiful Lake Okeechobee. A silver loving cup was awarded the prettiest baby, boy or girl, in the six-month to fifteen-month age group, and a ten dollar gold piece was awarded for the prettiest baby girl and the handsomest boy baby of fifteen months to three years by the Woman's Club. His best friend Jessup's little Orin had won it the previous year. The prettiest child, three to five, won a shiny red tricycle. Now that was a fair to be reckoned with, he said to anyone who'd listen.

They could keep their high-faluttin' vaudeville acts. Dunbar had rather be entertained by the Negro performers competing in the dance contests: buck and wing, Charleston and black bottom and dances that the White people had never seen and had no names for. Twice every night Frederick Dobell did his high wire act, and it was held on the beautiful lake front and not in some fancy park.

The biggest Bean Festival the Glades ever had was held the year after Eben Hunter moved to Pahokee. Palm Beach County had sent airplanes to perform their stunts, and a drum and bugle corps. performed down Main Street. There were the Boy Scout jamboree, the fiddler competition and political speeches with Gov. Carlton right up on the stage with the locals. There were the baby show, the school children's programs, a singing convention and the big dance later with the Shawano orchestra playing. And there was one Eben Hunter, acting like the cock of the walk, dancing with every available lady there. Some who should not be thought of as available found their way into his waiting arms. Since Dunbar didn't dance, that really irritated him. Look at him! I'll guarantee that his suit wasn't bought at Kahn's. Probably went to town to Burdine's, he thought.

In 1929 when Eben Hunter arrived in Pahokee, Dunbar was a town councilman, a trustee in the Bank of Pahokee, the Sunday school president of the Methodist church, a founder of the newly formed Rotary Club, a fact that he was especially proud of, and served on the county school board. He was also a bachelor.

Dunbar was not a suspicious man by nature, so when he began getting strange feelings about the newcomer, he was distraught with himself. He liked being known as a fair man, a decent man, a God-fearing man. Dunbar liked himself, or at least he had in the past.

The newly completed city hall was a large, two-story building on Lake Avenue off of Main Street near the lake. The formal grounds were the pride of Pahokee. Stately royal palms surrounded it, and Jessup Spearman,

Dunbar's closest friend, worked as city clerk on the first floor. As was Dunbar's custom, he had visited Jessup at the hall, and they had walked to the coffee shop for their mid-morning cup of coffee to catch up on the local gossip, town happenings, etc.

They were just finishing their coffee when Eben walked in. Newspapers were lowered as every head in the small cafe turned, almost in unison. There was something magnetic about the handsome stranger, who appeared to be around thirty, April Mosley, the counter girl noticed. She said later that she knew immediately he was someone to be reckoned with and laughingly added that she was just the girl to assist the young man in getting acquainted with Pahokee. She was not, as it turned out, nor were any of the other young ladies who tried to capture the elusive Eben, or Ben as some called him.

He gave an ingratiating smile to all and sat on the vacant wooden stool next to Dunbar. His manner was casual and self-assured. Dunbar, who had been about to leave, took his hat off the counter and spoke to Eben.

"If you're new in town, I'd like to welcome you. I'm Dunbar Anderson." He laughed when he said it, because everyone in the room knew that the man was new in town, as they would have in most small towns.

"Well, I thank you. Yes, I am new. Was just in the city hall, and a Miss June Mosely, I believe her name was, said that I might find the clerk, Mr. Jessup Spearman, here."

April quickly said, "She's my sister—June, that is. I'm April and," she laughed again, a tittering high laugh, "we've got another sister named May."

"All lovely names and lovely months, as well." When Eben added that, Jessup would say later that he thought April was gonna wet her drawers, she was so excited.

Jessup rose and extended his slight hand toward Eben. "I'm Jessup Spearman. Was just finishing up here and heading back to the hall."

"Don't rush on account of me, Mr. Spearman. I could use a good cup of coffee and then..."

"Then you'd better go to Betty Ann's for a good one. April's tastes like lye water," someone at the table next to the large window overlooking Main Street said.

They all laughed at how red April's face got. But Eben smoothed everything by adding, "I'm sure it's delicious and that they're just having sport with you, April."

She gave the man who had made the uncalled-for remark one of her child-like faces. Her full mouth, wearing bright red lipstick, dissolved into a satisfied smirk. She could feel Eben's eyes take in every ample curve of her rounded body. She could also smell the subtle scent of his shaving lotion. She liked it...manly.

Dunbar, curious about the business of the stranger, said, "I'll have a second cup with you, and we'll walk over to the hall together. That is, if you don't mind, Mister...uh Mister..."

They had the attention of everyone in the small shop. Eben knew that the man was about to burst with curiosity and, not wanting to offend but needing to needle him a little longer, he said, smiling, "Oh, that won't be necessary. I don't want to take you from more important business. But thank you anyway." The onlookers had to stifle their laughter. They were enjoying the exchange between the stranger and Dunbar. No one left his table but just sat, waiting for Dunbar's reaction.

They were not enjoying it more than Eben. He loved a contest of wits. Unfortunately, he could read him. He knew that the man was not his match, but he waited for Dunbar's next move anyway.

Dunbar Anderson was not a man to be put off easily. His tenacious nature had been his ally ever since he left Kansas. He cleared his throat before resuming. He wasn't sure whether to put his hat on and leave graciously with a, "I hope that you enjoy your stay in our fair city," or to insist on being the stranger's guide. He decided to give it one more try.

"Now, I'm not the official guide for the town," he laughed a nervous laugh, "but I am a town councilman and a trustee at our bank," he said importantly. "So, if there is anything that I might assist you with this morning, I'll be only too happy to help."

Eben stood, extended his firm, tan hand. "You are being most hospitable, Mr. Anderson, and I do indeed appreciate it. But I've had a long journey and just want to relax and finish my coffee. I'm sure that I'll see you around if I decide to remain in Pahokee, and I do thank you."

That did it. The smiling patrons turned toward each other. It wasn't that they didn't like Dunbar. It was just that he'd become quite full of himself in the past few years, and they enjoyed seeing the stranger put him in his place. They enjoyed seeing Dunbar's expression of defeat, and that the stranger had not even given him his name.

J.E. Barnes turned toward Tommy Dickson and said, "I ain't ever seen Dunbar Anderson so frustrated. I'll be willing to make bet that he hangs around the hall 'til he finds out who the man is and what his business is." He chuckled and added, "Hey, Tommy, I'll lay a fiver on it that Dunbar don't find out unless that Jessup spills it. What ya say?"

"I'd lose the bet, that's what I'd say. That man ain't gonna give old Dunbar one ounce of information that he don't hafta." He, too, chuckled.

Eben had overheard them but continued sitting, enjoying April's deep breathing, as she knowingly accentuated her full breasts that tugged the tight, blue print dress. She often wore it. Found that her tips were much larger when she did.

After finishing his inquiries at the town hall, Eben went to the Dixie Hotel, recommended by Jessup. He registered, listing his former address as Savannah, Georgia. Harry Elliot, who was a co-owner of the hotel, showed him to his room on the second floor overlooking Main Street. Eben tipped Harry handsomely and as soon as he left threw himself on the double bed. He was smiling. I've done it! I've made the break! Tomorrow I'll visit the bank here, then take a little ride to Canal Point, and then I'll drive on over to Belle Glade and Clewiston to look them over for future investments. Maybe I'll take some of my money out of the banks in West Palm Beach and deposit it right here in Pahokee. All this money in the middle of a depression. My, my! Ebenezer Rahn Hunter. He loved the excitement he was causing.

❧

Eben decided to purchase an acre on the lake ridge in Canal Point for his house rather than build in Pahokee or Clewiston. But he did purchase farm land in Pahokee as well as Canal Point and north in the small hamlet of Sand Cut. The fact that he knew absolutely nothing about farming in the muck did not concern him or lessen his fervor for this new venture. He was and always had been a reckless man, though shrewd.

His daily visits to the Lakeside Coffee Shoppe were appreciated by April Mosely, and she made sure every one of her regulars knew it. He complimented her on her appearance and especially her pie-making talents, for Eben dearly loved fruit pies. April had Joseph Abel, the owner, order canned cherries and apples from West Palm Beach every week. The regulars also began ordering April's pies. She had become an accomplished pie maker since Eben's arrival.

Eben was the talk of the Glades. Who was he? Where did he get all that money? What was he doing in the Glades? Many questions but no answers, and the more people inquired, although discretely, the more they were confused, and the more Eben was delighted by it.

April Mosely said that it was obvious that he was a southern gentleman and had inherited his fortune, and she always added that it was also obvious that he had been brought up on fine food, especially pies. Dunbar Anderson said he knew that it was un-Christian of him to make such an observation, but he smelled something unscrupulous about Mr. Hunter, and they all should be cautious in dealing with him. Everyone laughed when he said it, for they knew that it rankled Dunbar no end to have been bested by the mystery man, as he was called.

Eben began bringing his brothers down from Georgia, one a year until all three of them had arrived and moved into the large house on Lakeshore Dr. in Canal Point, and that really got the tongues wagging. The first to arrive was the youngest of the Hunter brothers, Ralph, who came at the end of 1929. He was not as handsome as Eben but was taller, standing well over six feet, and had the same ingratiating smile and smooth way of speaking, an easy, Savannah, Georgia, genteel way of talking, or so said the ladies of the area. Those who had fallen under Eben's spell soon found another brother to cast their hooks for when it was obvious that Eben was not interested.

By 1930 Eben had brought Emerson, the middle brother, and again the ladies were agog with excitement. The poor bachelors were inundated with invitations to every picnic, cantata and church supper in the area, for there were seemingly a great many eligible young ladies in the Glades, because most of the men who moved into the area had already married and brought their wives with them.

The next brother to arrive was Thornton, and he brought his wife and two young daughters with him. He was well received but without the same enthusiasm. Thornton was to become the bookkeeper of the Hunter Brothers' Farms. He was the one who hired Patrick and Walter with the approval of the other brothers. Thornton was slight in build and bookish. The other brothers were outdoors men or, as someone had referred to them after they had all arrived, the three rascals. They enjoyed a drink of good whiskey, the sight of a good-looking woman, an off-color joke, a day on Lake Okeechobee fishing and a deer, quail or wild hog hunt in the Big Cypress. They were men's men, and that only made them more attractive to the local belles and the more suspect to Dunbar.

Eben had hired Alpha and James soon after building his house, and as the brothers came down he brought in a wash woman to spell Alpha. The Hunter Farms prospered under Patrick's and Walter's supervision. Soon Emerson found a local young beauty to share his life, and not two months later Ralph began courting the Raulerson girl in Okeechobee City. They were wed in the spring. Each built a nice house in the town site in Canal Point among the sugar mill houses, as they were called locally, and melded into the community.

The excitement of the Hunter brothers' arrival had died down somewhat, and rarely did anyone wonder, "Where'd they get all that money?" except for Dunbar Anderson. He was determined to find out and set about doing just that. He knew that he would have to be discreet because the Hunters had fit into the area in every facet. They were socially sought after and had all joined one of the churches. They had also joined some of the local men's clubs with Eben being accepted as a Rotarian. That really bothered Dunbar. They had become active in area sports. Ralph was an excellent pitcher for the newly formed East Beach team. Dunbar wanted to expose them for who they were, for in his heart he knew that they were not the exemplary specimens that they purported to be. The Glades were his to protect, just like he'd protected Gordon, or so he felt.

He could not do this alone. Who could he get as his accomplice? Jessup's wife Elsie was so demanding of his time that he'd be of no use. Besides, she was an avid gossip, and if he failed he'd certainly not want anyone to know of his attempt. Eben had endeared himself with their fellow Rotarians, and when he joined the Pahokee Methodist Church instead of the one in Canal Point, Dunbar felt that Eben was deliberately attempting to erase the progress that he, Dunbar Anderson, had made in the community. It was as if Eben were making a concerted effort to undermine everything that Dunbar had built in the years he'd been there.

Many sleepless nights were spent by Dunbar as he plotted his course. He was not an imaginative man and found even the slightest straying from the accepted bothersome, but he was tenacious, relentless in his obsession. Even so, he could not truly enjoy the pursuit. The solution of how to expose Eben came to him in an unexpected but thoroughly obvious source. Had he been a devious man he would have been aware of it immediately. APRIL!

Who but April Mosely was head over heels in love with the interloper? Who would do anything in the world short of murder for one Eben Hunter? April, that's who. He'd seen how Eben had looked at her. Lust! That's what it was. Lust! And if April could entrap Eben by gaining his confidence and could find out about his sordid past, then Dunbar could expose the trash. A Rotarian indeed! And a member of his church...HIS CHURCH...TRASH!

When Dunbar realized that he had the answer to who was to be his accomplice in exposing that Hunter tribe, he relaxed his ardor. Instead of pursuing the villain he became so satisfied by his discovery and hoped-for solution that he became smug to the point that Jessup said one day while they were consuming some of April's lye water, "Dunbar, do I miss my guess, or have you found yourself a lady friend?"

"What in the world are you talking about, Jessup Spearman? You ought to know better!"

"Well, everyone in town's talking about you looking like the cat that swallowed the canary, that's what! And you don't hafta get on your high horse with me! They say that you're hiding something, that's what!"

Dunbar had turned crimson, his pudgy face screwed up so that each fold of fat fought for its proper place, but he knew that he had to be calm. He'd found his accomplice but had not been brave enough to seek her help, plus he needed to come up with a plan.

"I'm sorry, Jessup. I've had a lot on my mind lately. Mind's been far away. Been thinking about returning to Kansas for a little visit, but just can't make up my mind. Still got an aunt and cousins there and haven't seen them since I left..."

Jessup looked at his friend of over fifteen years and knew that he was lying. He knew that Dunbar was an honest and truthful man, and this was totally out of character. Maybe he really did have a woman. Maybe she was already married. Maybe, like Elsie had said that very morning, "He has every sign of a love-sick cow, Jess, every sign. Wonder who she is?"

About then April came over, leaned down to pour them a second cup, and when Dunbar looked up he was staring directly at her deep cleavage. Shaken, he turned deep red and tried to redirect his gaze, but Jessup had seen the effect, and Dunbar had seen Jessup's reaction. Jessup mistakenly thought that what he had seen was his friend's yearning for April Mosely. He couldn't believe it! Of all the women in the Glades for Dunbar to want, he would have never suspected April. Not that there was anything wrong with April. She wasn't the smartest woman around, but then neither was his Elsie. She was as pretty as most, and he hadn't heard of her giving her favors to anyone in particular. So, why not?

When Jessup heard the familiar clearing of Dunbar's throat, he knew that was a sure sign he was unsettled. He couldn't help but smile and was about to bust to get home to tell Elsie that she was right. And wait 'til she heard who the girl was! She'd never believe it.

Jessup rose, put the coins on the counter and his hand on Dunbar's shoulder and said, "I understand, my friend. I understand."

Dunbar hopped up and sputtered, "You, you don't understand a blasted thing! Not a thing! Surely you don't think that I have a ...a..." and ran out of the coffee shop.

April called after him, "Dunbar...Well, I never! Ran out without even paying! Jessup, what's wrong with him, anyway? The last few times he's been in here, it's like he's not here. You know what I mean? Like he's a million miles away. He's just not himself." And she went about the business of being a counter girl, wiping the polished pine counter and straightening the napkin holder and smoothing her too tight dress. She was humming.

And Jessup was smiling. So my friend is a love sick cow...I mean bull! I can hardly wait to tell Elsie! Won't she be surprised! April Mosely...imagine!

***

Dunbar was beside himself with embarrassment. He tossed and turned, trying to get comfortable. He usually would have been at the church meeting to determine the annual budget but could not make himself attend, especially since he was sure that Jessup would be there. How in the world could he think that I could have any feelings for that April Mosely...How? And he was also sure that Eben Hunter would be there, acting like he had all the answers, and everyone hanging onto his every word—like they used to do his.

He had come home from the fields, fixed himself a can of soup and heated the leftover corn bread in the iron skillet. He wasn't hungry and couldn't make himself finish *The Everglades News*. He usually read every word in it. So he went to bed even before nightfall and before the Lum and Abner radio show, something he rarely missed, that and the news.

He lay still, his eyes fixed on a spider crawling across the wooden ceiling. Flopping over onto his side, he sighed loudly. To think that Jessup believed that he had a romantic interest in that woman. Heavens, she wasn't anywhere near his class. He'd needed her for just one thing, and that was to be bait for Eben.

It wasn't even light when Dunbar awoke. Gracie wouldn't come until 10:00 o'clock to start his main meal. There was no need to go to the fields. How was he going to kill all that time? He would have normally slept until 6:00 or 6:30, but then he'd gone to bed so early.

A man of habit. It suited him, and he saw no need to change. He usually had a piece of leftover corn bread or a biscuit for his breakfast along with a cup of coffee, which he fixed himself as soon as he got up. He was in his Ford and on his way to his fields by 7:30 at the latest. He spoke to his hired people, then visited the drugstore for his big breakfast, purchased the morning newspaper and took it with him to the city hall to see Jessup for their morning coffee at the Lakeside Coffee Shoppe. A man of habit. After his coffee with Jessup he would go back to his modest home on Bacom Point Rd. to check on Gracie and listen to the news on the radio while he finished the newspaper. His parlor was a small room off the screened front porch that fronted Bacom Point Road. There were two bedrooms and a kitchen and small back porch. A modest home for a modest man, he realized happily. There was nothing ostentatious about Dunbar.

He had built the house in '20 and bought the furnishings the same year. A large maroon, stuffed easy chair, an end table that now held the radio, and a floor lamp beside it. On the wall next to the front door was a matching settee with another table, and underneath the only window in the room was a fern stand with a magnificent fishtail fern hanging almost to the floor, his pride and joy. Gracie always said, "Mistah Dunbar, suh, ya sho got yose'f a green thumb...yessuh, ya sho 'nuff do." He watered it every Sunday just before he went to church, saying, "I now baptize thee..." It was a joke between Dunbar and his fern.

Gracie would come in five days a week to do the cleaning, cook his noontime meal, and once a week she gathered his laundry to take to her quarters to wash. If she was ill or couldn't come for any reason, she had Bark, her husband, or one of their six children tell Dunbar before he left in the morning for the rounds of his fields. That way he'd know that he should eat in town at one of the restaurants.

Gracie was given Thanksgiving and Christmas off and with Dunbar's blessing. He either ate leftovers or would be invited to Jessup's to share their festivities. But when Jessup's children began arriving, Dunbar felt out of place, so he usually stayed home and listened to the radio, or sometimes he'd go over to the lake to see what progress was being made on the new levee being constructed around the lake. They expected it to be completed in 1935, and since he'd been through the '28 hurricane, spending two frightening days and a night in the newly completed school, he and the other residents hoped that the completion would be earlier. They were eternally grateful to President Hoover for making the dike possible.

He turned on his side and began remembering how excited he used to be when he first awoke. He liked his life and his town. Now, with that scoundrel here, it seemed that everywhere he turned he felt his presence. Dunbar was losing his prestige, prestige that he had earned by hard work and community involvement. And this Eben waltzes into town with a ton of money and buys himself the respect that it had taken Dunbar almost sixteen years to acquire. It wasn't fair, he thought.

Maybe I will return to Kansas for a little visit. Serve them all right. With me gone, then maybe they'll realize how important I am, how much they need me. He dwelled on it and decided to visit Jessup like he did most every day, go to the coffee shop and pretend that nothing had happened. Then he'd tell Jessup that he had decided to take an extended holiday to the town of his youth. He wondered what his reaction would be?

But what if he's agreeable? What if he doesn't say, "And just who do you think will take your place on the budget committee? And who will they get to replace you as the Sunday school director?" What if he doesn't say that I'll be missed?

Dunbar knew that he couldn't take a chance on Jessup's reaction. He rolled over and faced the bare wall, staring at it and seeing nothing. That's how Gracie found him at 9:30.

CHAPTER FIVE

Eben took a long swallow of the whiskey that Patrick had poured into his best crystal glasses. "The Irish know their whiskey, don't they?" Eben said as he pulled up the kitchen chair. Patrick nodded yes and thought that Catherine would have a fit when he told her that they sat in the kitchen instead of the living room. But Eben was calling the shots.

"Well, Patrick, I know that you're wondering what I'm doing here on this mysterious mission and on a Saturday, too. Well, to tell you the truth, so am I." He laughed and reached for the bottle. "May I?" he questioned.

"Of course, help yourself. And yes, I am wondering. I know that it has nothing to do with the farm or you'd have had Walter join us..."

"Well, that's not actually accurate. It does in a way have to do with the farm. I'm almost embarrassed to tell you just what it is." Again he laughed. Patrick could tell that he was indeed uneasy.

Eben proceeded. "I'm leaving on an extended mission to search for a...wife."

"What?" is all Patrick could think to say. He wasn't certain that he had heard him correctly.

"I know that it probably sounds crazy to you, and to anyone else who I might choose to confide in, but I want you to promise me that you'll not share this information with even Catherine or Walter. Frankly, I was concerned that Walter wouldn't be able to keep the... uh...shall we say, secret from Clara. This is very important to me."

"Oh, you can count on my complete silence about this." Patrick didn't know whether to laugh or to believe Eben. He was well known as a prankster and practical joker.

Eben continued. "Since I'll be away for an extended period, I don't know how long you and Walter will have to make all the major decisions concerning the farm. Ralph, Emerson and Thornton have already been informed about that, so don't you worry about it."

They sat and savored their whiskey, and finally Patrick spoke, "I'm glad that you're feeling the need of a wife, Eben. As much as I like the Glades, I'd hate to live here without Catherine. Actually, I'd probably be a lot like Samuel, wandering all over the place."

Eben let out a long sigh. "That's what I've decided. Oh, I've sampled some of the local lovelies, but damn it, Pat, I want a WIFE. Someone who will give me a son. Someone who hasn't had another man, a virgin." He was feeling his third glass of whiskey, and so was Patrick.

"Of course you do. What respectable man would want a woman who's been tampered with, I ask you?"

"None that I know. Not a single one. When Emerson married that little piece from up in Sand Cut, I asked him how he could marry used goods? And, Pat, you know what he said?"

"No, what?"

"He said that at least he knew she'd learned a thing or two, and would keep his bed warm when he demanded it. Imagine!"

"No, I can't imagine that kind of thinking. Hell, Ben, what kind of wife and mother will she make?" He belched, wiped his mouth and poured them another round.

"I'm gonna find me the most beautiful young girl in the whole state of Georgia. You knew I was from Georgia, didn' ya?" He stared off in space, remembering.

"Seems ta me tha ya mentioned it a few times..." Patrick answered, slurring his words, too.

"Beautiful state. Born outside o' Savannah near the town of Springfield. Mother was a Salzburger. Ya know, from Salzburg, Austria. Fine ol' family she was from. Now, that was a beautiful woman, I can tell ya, and she was certainly not damaged goods when mah daddy whisked her away. Always said it was love at first sight. That's what I wan..."

"And ya should have it, too. Just like ya daddy. Ah remember when Ah first saw Cath..Catherine. She was wearin' the prettiest blue dress Ah evah saw..."

Eben seemed to be in another world. He wasn't listening to Patrick, but was remembering a young girl from his youth, a girl with whom he had fallen in love at first sight, too. But that was a long time ago, and he had to get on with his life.

"Now, as Ah was sayin', Ah had mah share of lovelies in town...Palm Beach. Yeh, some lovelies. Evah had a dark one, Pat?"

"No, an can't say Ah evah had a hankerin' for one eithah..."

"There's one in town that's part Spanish and Negro, an' she somethin' else. Nothin' that one won' do..."

"Mistah Eben," James called, knocking on the back door, "Is ya ready to go back home?" James had brought the car up front and had walked to the back door as was the custom for the Coloreds, and neither man nor General had heard him.

"Go on ovah ta Dessa's an' get Alpha, James. Mistah Pat and Ah jus' about ta finish up heah."

James laughed a good one. Those two is drunker den skunks. Ah do declare dey is. Wait'll Ah tell Alpha and Dessa.

47

James and Alpha had been informed about the upcoming trip to Georgia, and Eben had also told them why he was going. He wanted them to accompany him. They were both excited, because neither'd been anywhere but their birthplace, the Grand Bahama Island, and the east coast of Florida until they'd moved into the Glades. Eben assured James that he'd take over at the wheel of the Packard and would do the driving in the cities. That relieved James, and Alpha as well.

Alpha had not been told to keep their intended trip a secret from Dessa, so she'd spent the afternoon sharing her anxiousness with her. Dessa set her friend at ease, for Alpha was indeed a friend and had been since they were twelve years old.

Samuel was asleep on the day bed in the parlor. Dessa had made sure of that before she and Alpha sat down for their tea in the kitchen. It was their habit to have tea every Sunday afternoon either in Dessa's quarters or now in Mister Samuel's, but this being Saturday, it was a special event. James had permission from Mister Eben to drive Alpha to Dessa's on her day off, and that meant Sunday. Well, it wasn't actually her day off, because she always cooked a big dinner for the Hunters, wives and all, every Sunday without fail.

Eben insisted that they gather as a family on Sunday, as they had when they were youngsters, and that meant the entire morning in the kitchen for Alpha. That was the only time that she had help from that lazy wash woman Eben had hired. But Alpha made sure that she did her part. She had to do the wash-up after dinner, and that meant the best china, crystal and silver set on the long linen cloth from Ireland that Eben treasured so. Always said that it had been in his mama's hope chest. No one disputed it, because no one knew whether it was true.

That nigger called herself Russeen. Now what kind of name was that? She had been given the job of doing up that long table cloth, for which Alpha was grateful. She hadn't ruined it as yet, but Alpha, who had a great fondness for Eben, couldn't figure if he was crazy or drunk when he hired that woman.

Their big meal would consist of two kinds of meat, one having to be chicken fixed some way, and rice and gravy and biscuits and every vegetable that was growing in the garden, plus some of Mrs. Latham's pickled watermelon rinds and pears with lots of lemon slices spiced to a fare-thee-well, as Eben said, and at least two kinds of dessert. Well, by the time Alpha had her nap she was ready for a long visit with Dessa, and James was ready for her to have it. She was sure out of sorts if she missed that visit.

"Wheah you and James gonta sleep while Mistah Eben's stayin' in one of dose fancy hotels?" Dessa inquired.

"We ast him de very same question, an' he say dat he done took care of dat. We gonta stay in de big cities, an' he say dat dey all got real nice and clean boarding houses for us in colored town. He say dat in some o' de real fancy hotels dey got rooms set aside for colored servants. Ah'm not worried 'bout Mistah Eben takin' care o' us. He always has, an' ya knows dat fo' shuah."

Dessa rose from the straight-backed, wooden kitchen chair and reached for the teapot and the pitcher of Aunt Maude's rich cream. Marsh had commented just that morning about how much milk Aunt Maude was producing this year. She didn't ask Alpha if she wanted more tea because they'd been having tea together ever since they had arrived in the Glades, and Alpha was a two cupper, she knew. Dessa poured two spoons of sugar in the hot tea. She waited for Alpha to take a sip before she covered the sugar bowl. Alpha nodded that it was sweet enough. Dessa set the bowl back in the saucer of water to keep the ants from invading it. She reached into the cookie crock for another raisin cookie, Alpha's favorite.

"Is dat Mistah Samuel Ah heahs?"

"Shouldn't be. He always takes at least a two-houh nap, 'specially on Sunday. Dat man can shuah 'nuff put away a big meal on Sundays. Eats lak a sparrow all week long, and den on Sunday he jes shovels it in. Sammy told him dat he was gonta blow up lak a ol' blow fish, and he laughed lak he used ta, Miz Catherine say. He comin' long real good, Ah tink."

"He fo' shuah lookin' bettah. Seems ta have some roses in his cheeks. He talkin' bout goin' on one o' his trips?"

"Not say a word 'bout it, an' Miss Catherine is sho 'nuff happy 'bout dat. Say Ah work a miracle on her daddy. An dat Sammy roll her eyes ta da sky, an' start a hummin' lak she know Ah done put a spell on her grandaddy, but Ah shut huh up in jig time."

"How ya do dat?"

"Ah took huh han' and staht wit' da rubbin' on her wahts ta 'mind huh dat she still got 'em an dat all mah spells don't work. She got de idea. Dat Sammy is a smaht one."

"Ah tink dat he jes need someone ta talk ta. Ya know, someone dat din't evah know his missus."

"He can talk all de day an' into de night sometimes. Den udda times he quiet as a mouse. Dat's when Ah tell him de tales 'bout when Ah was little in de islands. He listens and don't say a word, but Ah know he 'joys it. He jes sit deah an smile an shake his bald head up and down. He a nice man, Alpha."

"Heah come James. Gotta go. Must be time fo' Mistah Eben ta go on back home. Bet Mistah Pat sure 'nuff surprise 'bout him goin' all de way ta Gawgia ta get him de prettiest wife a body can fin'. Bet he is."

"What day ya be leavin'?"

"Well," Alpha said scratching underneath her brightly flowered turban, "He say dis week fo' shuah. He anxious ta be on his mission. Not a word 'bout it, now, Dessa. Dis 'portant ta Mistah Eben dat nobody know."

"What ya take me foah, Alpha? He been mah friend jes long as he been yuahs and James', now ya knows dat. Afta all, he de one who buy mah land fo' me. And ain't anyone gonta get dat information outta me eidder. Not even mah Sammy."

"Ain't nobody's business if'n he got his money from de fields or if'n he got his money from runnin' rum. Nobody's, Dessa. Mind ya dey tryin' ta fin' out all 'bout him. Why jes las' week James say dat Mistah Hooks pry and pry, tryin' ta fin' out 'bout Mistah Eben an' wheah he got all his money. But he put him off by sayin' "'Ah don't know nuttin' bout nuttin', but dat Mistah Eben come from de state o' Gawgia'. But dat man kept on at him—hmmmuh! Finally, James say, 'Mistah Hooks, Ah gotta be runnin' along wid dese groceries, o' Alpha gonna tie a knot in mah tail'. Dat de only way he got away from dat curious man."

<hr />

When Gracie got to Dunbar's small house and found him in a fetal position and not saying a word, just staring at the wall, she immediately called Dr. Creel. As it turned out he was out and his maid took the call. Gracie was beside herself with worry. Not knowing what else to do, she called Jessup at the town hall. He was there inside of fifteen minutes.

He rushed in out of breath and sputtered, "What's this all about, Gracie? What's wrong with him?"

"Oh, Mistah Jessup, suh, he ain' movin'. He jes lay deah an look at ...at nuttin'. He jes lay deah."

"When did Salina say the doc was coming back? Did she even know where he was? Did you try to get Dr. Spooner?"

"Nosuh! Salina she say dat Dr. Creel he be ah...at a board meetin' 'bout de hospital dey plannin'. Ah'm scared dat sometin' dreadful wrong wid Mistah Dunbar, Mistah Jessup." And she began to sob.

Jessup sat on the edge of the double bed and shook Dunbar's shoulder gently and said softly, "Dunbar, it's me, Jessup. Can you speak?"

Not a sound did he make, nor did he even blink. Jessup got up and looked down at the distraught Gracie, "I think that he might have had a stroke, Gracie. He needs help now. I'm going over to the hotel and see if that's where they're meeting. I know that the Elliott brothers are on that board. Now, listen to me. Don't do a thing. Just sit here in case he comes to or says something. Gracie, are you listening to me?"

"Yessah, Ah heard ya, but, Mistah Jessup, what's Ah ta do if'n he start to yellin' or sometin'?"

"If he's had a stroke he'll not be yelling. Look, I'll have Elsie come over to sit with you. Would you like that?"

"Oh, yessuh, Ah sho 'nuff would. Ah sho 'nuff would."

When Eben got to church Sunday he was astonished by the news about Dunbar. Doctors Spooner and Creel had both attended him and neither had made a diagnosis. Not that he was particularly fond of the man, but he didn't wish him harm either. He was a pillar of the community, went to almost all of the baseball games on Sunday afternoon, and in the summer when the businesses closed Thursday afternoons, you'd usually see him at the games, never yelling or joining in, but there. It was said that Dunbar Anderson attended anything and everything that had to do with the Glades. He believed in supporting his town.

The minister announced the news about Dunbar, asked the congregation to pray for him and also asked them to visit him at his home. He said that the doctors thought that it might bring the poor man out of, well, whatever it was that he had.

Eben decided that he really should pay Dunbar a call before he went on his extended trip and decided to go to his home before returning to Canal Point and the feast that Alpha had prepared for him and his family.

There were already several cars parked out in front when he got to Dunbar's house. Eben was never hesitant, so he walked briskly up to the front door and knocked. Before it was answered he reached for the handle and opened it, walked in and smiled at the people gathered inside the small parlor. As he looked around he said to himself, this room is Dunbar Anderson all over: the overstuffed furniture, the pictureles walls, except the one of George Washington, the linoleum on the floor, a man of little taste.

"Jessup," he said, feigning considerable concern while extending his hand. "How is he?" Poor Jessup just shook his head, and Eben could tell that he had been crying. I wonder if anyone will feel this sad when I'm ill? he thought to himself. Probably not. He decided that very minute to leave for Georgia the next day.

On entering the room he saw a mound of covers surrounding Dunbar's small, round head. His eyes were open. Jessup was at the doorway watching, as he had been since the visitors began arriving. When Eben spoke, "Dunbar, I'm so sorry that you're not we..." Dunbar sat straight up and began to yell and speak in an unintelligible gibberish.

Jessup ran to him trying to restrain him. Eben backed up toward the doorway, not knowing what else to do, and the other visitors ran inside to see what on earth was going on.

"Someone get Doc Spooner," Jessup yelled.

Eben walked toward the phone that was on the lace doily on the living room table and dialed him. "Dr. Spooner, this is Eben Hunter, and I'm at Dunbar Anderson's home. It would appear that he's out of his ... He needs for you to come over as soon as you can, Dr. Spooner. This man's in bad shape."

<hr/>

The Packard had been loaded the night before. Eben had instructed James and Alpha the minute he arrived from Dunbar's that they'd leave the very next morning and that he wanted to get an early start. That meant first light. He was excited, Alpha could tell. She'd seen him like that before. When the lights would flash over their small boat as it made its way from the islands, and she and Dessa would have to crawl under the tarp shaking with fear while trying to conceal the rum, he'd get that wild look in his eyes. Why now? Why would setting out to find a wife give him that *look*? There's something more going on in his head. I'll not mention it to James.

There was only one thing that Alpha wanted to do before they departed, and that was to get word to Dessa that they were leaving. Because neither Patrick nor Samuel had a phone, that meant a trip to Dessa's by car.

When they pulled the car up beside the quarters, Dessa and Sammy were sitting beside the stand of bamboo in the side yard. Even before the car was stopped Sammy had run toward them.

"Alpha!" she shouted and reached for the door handle.

"Watch out, chile! You want dat James run ovah ya? Dessa, tell dis chile ta be careful!"

Dessa just laughed and motioned for her to sit on the other up-turned bean crate, which she did. James was busily wiping some smudges off the car door, and Sammy was assisting him by telling him where he'd missed. She ran back to Dessa and Alpha, but before she could join in their conversation, Dessa said, "Sammy, you go on an' play. Me an' Alpha got business to discuss."

Sammy looked perplexed and, not one to be put off, asked, "What kind of business would that be?"

"Now, if Ah wanted ya ta know den Ah'd ast ya ta join us, wouldn't Ah?"

"I suppose so, but for the life of me I can't think of any business that you might have that I shouldn't know about. Is it about your land?" she questioned excitedly. "I bet it is. I just bet you a hundred million dollars that it has to do with your land, doesn't it?"

"Sammy, ya lose de bet. It ain't got nuttin' ta do wid mah land. Now, go on an' fin' Junie and leave us be foah a little while. Go on!"

"She gonta drive ya crazy 'til ya tell huh, ain't she?"

"She shuah 'nuff gonta try. But Ah'll jes tell huh de trut' 'bout ya goin' on youah trip ta Gawgia tomorrow. Dat'll hafta satisfy huh."

Sammy ran toward the end of the quarters where Junie lived, but Dessa had her eye on her. She motioned to Alpha as she saw Sammy sneaking around the end of the quarters and ducking behind the row of sunflowers, which were used as wind breaks for the green beans.

"Deah she go. Ain't gonta let us tell huh what she can o' can't listen to. Dat's mah Sammy."

Sammy ran the length of their field, then cut in toward the big house. She ducked down behind the bee hives under the tall avocado trees and beside the grove of bananas, mangos and papaya trees. She looked to see if Dessa or Alpha was watching. They weren't. So, she ran to the cow pen and alongside of the barbed wire fence that kept Aunt Maude, formerly named Honey, inside. She was their milk cow, whose milk would be as sweet as honey, Mr. Kautz had assured her daddy when he sold her to him. She ducked down, scooted to the long, low chicken coop, then stopped to rest in the shade beneath the guava trees.

Out of breath she said aloud, "They aren't gonna pull that old dodge on me. Not on Sammy Carroll. Not today and not tomorrow." That was one of Dessa's favorite sayings, and naturally Sammy had adopted it.

She made it to the back porch of the big house, peered around its corner, then ran the short distance to the bath house. Almost home free, she thought. The stand of bamboo was only a short way from her position. She couldn't see Dessa, but Dessa knew that it was about time for Sammy to be squatting behind the bamboo so she could listen to her and Alpha's conversation.

When Sammy got to the bamboo stand she was gasping so that she had to put her hand over her mouth. Dessa began. "Now Alpha, Ah knows dat you an' James gotta go to Gawgia wid Mistah Eben tomorrow, but Ah do want dat ya be careful. Dey got dose men who weah dose long, white sheets an' hoods to covah deah heads so's no one will know who dey is an' dat hang an' burn Coloreds. Now ya rightly knows dat. Why jes de udder day Ah read in de *Palm Beach Post* dat a whole bunch o' Coloreds got rounded up jes lak cattle, and dey put dem ta de stake jes lak Joan of Arc in de story books dat de sistahs used to read ta us."

Sammy's eyes got big as saucers. By then she was sitting in the sand trying to brush the hungry ants off her bare, tanned legs. She cupped her ear hoping to hear more about the hangings.

"If'n Ah had mah way Ah shuah wouldn't be agoin' up deah, Dessa. Come on ovah heah an' hug me. Dis maght be de las time Ah evah see ya." And she pretended to cry loudly.

By then Sammy was beside herself. She jumped up shouting, "Alpha, I won't let Mister Eben take you and James. I won't!"

"So ya couldn't let us have ouah privcy, huh, Sammy?" Dessa said, laughing at her astonished expression.

"You were fooling me, Dessa! You were playing like! You were..."

"An' what if Ah was. Din't Ah tell ya dat me and Alpha had business ta discuss and dat ya wuhn't invited an'..."

"Yeh, but you didn't hafta fool a person. You didn't hafta..."

"Come heah, chile. Come on ovah heah ta youah Dessa. Dat ain't no reason fo' ya ta cry dose big ol' tears, now is it. Ya jes embarrassed, dat's all 'cause ya got caught. Heah, Sammy, now don't ya carry on so."

Dessa took the end of her apron and wiped Sammy's tears away, but before she could explain more, Sammy had recovered enough to say haltingly, "Alpha, do you really think that you and James will be burned at the stake by those Klanners? Do you?"

"No chile, Ah don't. Mistah Eben wouldn't let dem do dat ta us in de fust place. Mistah Eben always take care o' us. Dessa jes foolin' ya so's ya'd come outta youah hidin' place. She jes trying ta teach ya a lesson. Come on ovah heah, Sammy, an' give Alpha a hug. Ah 'preciate ya wantin' ta save me and James from de burnin' stake. Ah truly do."

Eben had mapped their trip out carefully, at least as far as Savannah. He expected to spend time there looking up a few old friends and relatives. They had been on the road for three days, and although they had experienced no difficulty, they were ready for a few days' rest.

The first thing Eben did when they arrived in Springfield, his hometown northwest of Savannah, was to call on his old friend, Judson Ridgeway. Judson was one of the few friends he had kept in touch with since he'd left twenty years before. For Eben to return a rich man, when he had left in shame, would be satisfying to them both. The shame that had befallen his family was difficult for Eben to handle. Judson understood that. He knew that Eben's heart was broken when Eleanor Easterling's father forbid her ever seeing Eben again. But he also knew that was but a part of the reason Eben had left Springfield and joined the army. Judson was one of the few who knew the truth.

The Effingham county court house's clock sounded twelve o'clock. Eben told James to drive up Pine and he'd show them where he used to have chinaberry fights with the prisoners at the old Effingham County jail. "Heck, they were even let out so they could umpire our softball games in that lot beside the jail."

James turned around at Early St., as he was directed, and headed south on Pine. Eben wanted them to drive past his school five blocks away. James slowed up, and he and Alpha both exclaimed about what a handsome building it indeed was. When Eben didn't respond she turned around to look at him hoping he would be smiling, but he was sullen, looking off into space. She patted James's arm and motioned toward the back seat.

"Mistah Eben, ya wants me ta keep on a goin'?" By then they were at Elbert St., and he and Alpha could see the cemetery as they approached the intersection.

"No, I need to get on over to Jud's. Turn here and we'll drive up Laurel commonly called Main Street. Slow down, James. I think I see Judson's building. Yep! There it is, the nicest looking one on the street." He also saw the building where his father had at one time had a business. It was one of many in downtown Springfield that Reddick Hunter had occupied only to fail time and time again.

Alpha could tell that he was happy to be back home, but she also felt his sadness. Now, why didn't he want to pay his respects to his mama and papa whom she knew were buried in the White cemetery? She decided that she would keep her eye peeled for that *look*.

It was a small town with seven major streets running north and south, all named for trees. It was also a town that had felt the recent depression with a number of businesses closed. There didn't seem to be the vitality here that one felt when in Pahokee. There were few cars parked along Laurel Street, so James had no trouble finding a place to park.

Eben had written Judson a few weeks before that he intended to drive to Springfield to pay him a visit but had purposely declined to tell him why. He wanted to feel out Judson first. After all, they hadn't seen each other in a long time, and although his letters sounded like the Judson of their youth, he no doubt had changed, as had Eben. So, cautiously he entered the brick building with the dark green awning over the door. The sign read Ridgeway Enterprises.

The main room was filled with beautifully upholstered, antique furniture. The deeply piled carpet felt like money underneath Eben's polished boots. He's done very well, he thought, as he looked around the room. A middle-aged woman came through the rich, mahogany door. Her hand rested on the heavy brass handle.

"May I help you, sir?" she asked, her expression approving the handsome man before her.

"You may. I'm an old friend of Judson Ridgeway's and wonder if he might be in."

"I'm so very sorry, but you just missed him. He always goes home for dinner on Thursdays. I'd ask you to wait, but he'll be gone for at least two hours. He lives just down on Oak Street, but he does like a short nap after dinner."

"That'll be no problem. I'm Eben Hunter or Ben, as Judson calls me. Actually my given name is Ebenezer, you know, like in New Ebenezer, the town over on the river. My mother was a Salzburger." He could tell that she was barely listening, so continued. "Judson and I were classmates at Effingham Academy a long time ago, I'm afraid. Played baseball and basketball there. I'll just find a restaurant in town, and by the time I've finished, he should have returned."

"I'm Ava Millward, Mr. Hunter. I've been with Mr. Ridgeway for eleven years now." She patted her pale blond hair and smiled. Eben noticed that she was not wearing a wedding band. She was a nice looking woman without being pretty—clear, fair skin and blue eyes edged with light lashes. Her figure was softly rounded, and she was stylishly dressed in a sensible, grey, shantung dress with black buttons. The medium white linen collar was opened modestly, slightly revealing the swell of her ample breasts.

"Would you care to join me for dinner, Miss Millward? I'd be honored if you would," he asked openly admiring her with his eyes fixed on her bodice.

She actually blushed. "That would be lovely, but I must remain in the office while Mr. Ridgeway is away. That was very thoughtful of you, sir."

"Call me Ben. I'll be around for a while, and if you are not otherwise engaged, perhaps we can take in a movie or take a ride in the country, so you can fill me in on the happenings of my home town. I've been away for a very long time."

She turned toward what Eben presumed was her desk, and when she turned around he noticed a distinct barrier had been erected. "I'm afraid that would not be possible, Mr. Hunter. Thank you for asking me. Now, if you'll ex..."

"I hope I didn't offend you, Ava. It was not my intention. Is there a restaurant that you might suggest? I..."

"There is only one in town that is still operating," she said curtly. "The Savoy just down the street. You can't miss it. It's only a few blocks from here, just past the bank and dress shop on your left." She sat down abruptly.

Eben put on his dark brown felt hat, but before turning said, "Judson always did have excellent taste, and I can tell by his furnishings and his choice in personnel that he still does. Good day, Ava." He tipped his hat then boldly winked at her. He opened the dark green door and began whistling a popular ditty, closing the door soundly behind him. Alpha looked at James and they both smiled. They loved seeing Mistah Eben in a happy mood. They didn't know that his smile was the result of one Miss Ava turning red with embarrassment while clutching her bodice. She was ripe, and she knew that he knew it.

⚜

The Savoy wasn't as plush as Eben would have liked for his first meal in his hometown. He sighed and thought maybe the meal would be acceptable, though. He could see that it had at one time been quite elegant. The brocade on the chairs was worn, and the dark tables could have used polishing, but the brass and crystal chandeliers were still handsome. There were about eight other diners in the large room. He was approached by a young waitress wearing a black uniform with a starched, white lace collar and apron, carrying a menu and her order blank.

"Here's the menu, sir, and I'm Jenny. I'll give you a few minutes to look it over. May I suggest the braised pork chops with onion gravy? They're awfully good."

"You may indeed, Miss Jenny. And I'll have rice with them." He glanced at the menu and asked, "And how's the squash? Is it fresh?"

"Oh, yessir, everything Mr. Green serves is fresh from the gardens right around here. He won't ever serve anything from a can unless he has to."

"Then, I'll have the yellow squash and the turnip greens. I hope they cook them with the roots like my mama used to. Actually, it was our aunt who fixed them like that. I used to live here."

"You did? Well, now isn't that nice," she said to be polite. Eben could tell that she didn't care one bit if he had or if he hadn't. She turned toward the table next to Eben's and said, "I'll be with you right away, Buford. Just be a minute."

Jenny left, taking the menu with her. Eben noticed the young man who was sitting next to the large window pat her bottom as she sashayed by. No wonder she's in a hurry, he thought. That must be her boyfriend. He noticed that he was having just a cup of coffee while he slowly smoked his Chesterfield. He's no doubt waiting for her to get off work so they can take a little ride in his car down a lonely lane and...I think I'm getting horny! That Ava putting me off must have affected me more than I care to admit.

57

When Jenny returned with his glass of water, he asked her where his colored chauffeur and maid could get a bite to eat. "There're a few places for Coloreds at Jack's Branch, but I don't know nothing about them. I'll ask Mr. Green, my boss."

"Thank you, Jenny." Eben saw that he'd impressed her when he said chauffeur. He also saw her glance out the large window that she purposely walked by to check out his car. When she returned with his meal, she was a little more receptive and certainly more friendly. Money definitely speaks, he thought. Now, why is that, I wonder. But I'll use it whenever I can if that's what it takes. Yessir! I'm going to buy me the prettiest little Georgia peach I can find. I'm getting the itch this very minute. Hope it doesn't take long.

Jenny had been right. The pork chops were delicious, tender and succulent, swimming in rich, brown gravy. She returned with a note written by Mr. Green, he supposed, with the name of two boarding houses serving food. Funny that there was only one restaurant in white town, but then maybe the depression hadn't effected the colored area as much, because it was in a constant state of depression.

He tipped a smiling Miss Jenny generously, and she suggested that he visit them often. There was an obvious invitation in her big, grey eyes, and when he lifted her hand and kissed it, every head in the room witnessed the scene, especially the young man seated beside the window. Eben could see him bristle. Bet she gets an ear full when she' finished here. When Jenny looked down at the large tip, she openly grinned at Eben and winked, licking her moist mouth, that she had opened suggestively. Now I know she's in for it, Eben thought, looking at the furious young man beside the window. But I bet that little trick can handle it. He enjoyed stirring up trouble. Always had.

⸙

James and Alpha went into the first house listed on the note. It was an unpainted, wooden, two-story building with a sign in the lower window beside the front door stating that meals were served and that there were rooms for rent. Eben remained in the car and read the *Savannah Chronicle*. He pulled out his pocket watch and noticed that they'd been gone from Judson's office for over two hours. He hoped that they wouldn't be long, because he did want to get settled for the night so he could spend some time with Judson after he finished work. He was getting anxious to get on with his business. And he was getting anxious to find out about Eleanor Easterling and her mother.

It was May, and all was right with Eben's world. Well, his world but not his family's world nor the world in Europe. But Ebenezer Rahn Hunter didn't care—not one whit! He was in love with the belle of Effingham County, Eleanor Anne Easterling. She was beautiful, she was bright, she was from the wealthiest family in four counties, including Savannah, and best of all, she loved him. She hadn't said it, but he knew...he just knew. So, BE GONE WORLD WAR—BE GONE FAMILY FAILURE—BE GONE OPPOSING FATHER! She's mine and I'll have her, even if I have to capture her and whisk her away to a foreign land. So help me God!

Eben had just turned twenty years old. He had been in Savannah for the past year working for his uncle Alex Rahn in his import-export business that had been severely affected by the war. Eben knew that he had taken him on simply out of love for Amarine, Eben's mother and Alex's youngest sister.

When Alex called him into his office in early February and told him that he had no choice but to dismiss him due to the lack of revenue, Eben understood. He had been an apt pupil and had learned the business quickly and well, his uncle had assured him. So Eben returned to Springfield and a concerned family.

Eben's income had kept the family from being paupers, his Aunt Tempie said, and didn't seem to care who heard her. Tempie was short for Temperance, but anyone who knew her agreed that she had indeed been misnamed. No one had approved of Amarine's marrying that Reddick Hunter. Heavens, no one knew a thing about his family, even though he claimed to be one of the Forbushers of South Carolina. No one had ever seen any proof of it, she reminded them at every opportunity. Why, Amarine had to have been out of her mind! And worse than that, dropping a child every time a year went by, just like a field hand, or worse, a Catholic!

But Amarine hummed and smiled and gave of her loving nature, not blaming her husband for his business failures nor for being forced to sell off the 803 acres of the best farm land in all of Effingham County, land that had been in the Rahn family since their ancestors came over from Austria. All would be well, she assured her love. For Amarine did love Reddick, and all the gossip and titters whenever she came to a gathering wearing fashions that were out of date and worn almost through did not affect her—she continued to smile.

"She's dense! That girl is empty headed. Now, mind you, she wasn't always that way. It was only when that Reddick Hunter looked her way.

She lost her mind on that day. And can you believe she talked poor, lonely old Papa into letting her marry that...that...TRASH!" Tempie said without provocation every chance she got. It never seemed to occur to Tempie that had she found herself a husband, she would probably not be in the position of having been awarded the family place for the years of service she had shown to their father. She never thought of herself as an old maid, but rather as the devoted first daughter of Papa Rahn. Tempie was just Tempie, and despite her feelings for Reddick, she loved the boys and they her.

When Eben returned home he wasn't sure just what he would do, and, being the oldest boy, he needed to do something to help out. The other three boys had odd jobs in town or on a local farm, but for whatever reason they all seemed to look toward Eben, including Reddick, for the major support. Eben had not told them, but he planned to join the army. It seemed the sensible thing to do. He just hated to face his mother when he made the announcement.

He remembered that he didn't want to attend the annual festival at the Jerusalem Lutheran Church on the Savannah River, where his ancestors had settled back in the 1730s. But his mother had looked so disappointed when he told her, that he gave in and helped the others get ready. It would be a day-long outing with a picnic on the green, and cousins, aunts and uncles would all gather, including Uncle Alex and his family from Savannah. He knew that it was his duty, so he went, as did over two hundred other Salzburgers.

Aunt Tempie had insisted that they go by wagon like they had in the old days, but everyone felt foolish until they arrived and saw that there were others who had done the same. Tempie had actually said to Amarine, "Why, Amarine, you look just like a school girl in that checked gingham dress. My, my, how all your old beaus will swoon at how you've kept your figure," hoping to make Reddick jealous. But Amarine just ignored her, hugged her husband to her and joined the others in unloading the baskets from the wagon.

Eleanor was the first one Eben saw as he hopped down from the wagon. She was not beautiful in the accepted sense. She was regal with strong, patrician features, a cameo face, a long beautiful neck, and a way of carrying herself that made him stare at her with his mouth open. Eben Hunter had been smitten that very day, he later told Judson when he got back to Springfield.

"God! I can't believe how beautiful she is. Judson, did you say that she was being courted by anyone? I'll die if she is! How well do you know her?"

"Hey, hold up, Ben. Grief! You do have it bad, don't you?"

"You can say that again. Well, does she have a beau or doesn't she?"

"She was seeing Baldwin Futrell before he went over. Don't know if it was serious or not, but since he is her father's partner's son, I'm thinking that old Martin would like to see them make it permanent."

"Do I have a chance, do you think?"

"Since when do you let anything like that get in your way, Ben Hunter? Huh, since when?'

Eben laughed a hearty laugh, hitting his friend soundly on the back. "Yeh! Since when?"

Eleanor had seen Eben jump down from the wagon and wondered who he was. She had been away at school in Atlanta for the past four years, coming home only for holidays, and didn't know many of the local boys. He has a presence about him, she thought. Not your usual country lad. She saw his expression, and when he smiled at her she openly returned it.

My, my, how brazen you have become, Miss Eleanor. I do hope Lillian didn't see the exchange. Lillian was not her chaperone, but Eleanor knew that her father had expressed his concern for her by sending Lillian. He and her mother weren't able to attend the homecoming, so he felt that she and her younger brother Roscoe needed to be accompanied. He was a very protective father—also a very shrewd father. His family needed to be present. Everyone in Effingham County knew that Martin Luther Easterling planned to run for governor.

Not looking right nor left, Eben headed straight for her. He's certainly sure of himself, she thought, but smiled when she thought it. I like that. Must be about twenty, I'd say. Got that self-assured swagger. I wonder if he's from Springfield or Rincon. Probably from Savannah or maybe even Charleston. Doesn't look local.

Amarine called to him to help take the picnic baskets. He continued to smile at Eleanor and yelled to her, "I'll see you after services." She ducked her head, but he could see that she was smiling. Oh, what a wonderfully rich voice, so polished, she thought. He returned to the wagon and helped his Aunt Tempie down with the assistance of Thornton, his brother. Tempie had become quite heavy in the last few years, and her knees were arthritic, so it took the two of them to assist her.

Always nosy, she asked Eben, "Who was that girl you were calling to, Ebenezer? I've not seen her around here before. Must have come up from Savannah. Did you know her there?"

Not knowing who she was and certainly not wanting Tempie to know it, he mumbled, "Just a friend of mine. Yeh, from Savannah."

Amarine heard him and, amused, shook her head at her oldest.

"Might as well tell Tempie the truth, son, or she'll bust with curiosity. Tempie, that's Martin Easterling's daughter. You know, the one who goes to school in Atlanta. A lovely looking girl she is, too." Eben's interest increased when he heard that, and he thought, my, my, she's not only beautiful but rich, too.

"Then why did you say you knew her in Savannah, Ebenezer? Are you trying to put your fat old aunt off the track?" She laughed and tweaked his ear, then hugged him to her. She loved that child and had often said that she'd be a happy woman if the Lord had given her Ebenezer, that he was so like her dear Papa. Then she'd cry. Tempie was always one to cry easily. She dearly loved a good cry.

Thornton helped Eben take their baskets down closer to the river and found a soft grassy spot beneath a giant elm. Reddick whispered to Amarine that he thought that he'd forego services and stay to guard their baskets. She knew that he wasn't comfortable in a Lutheran church and did not protest. After all, he had been guarding their food every homecoming for as long as she could remember.

The church, Jerusalem Lutheran Church, was the pride of the Salzburgers who had settled in that section of Georgia back in 1734. The church had been organized in 1733 in Augsburg, Germany, when their members had been exiled from their homes in Salzburg and were looking for a place to live and worship. The Society for Promoting Christian Knowledge in England came to their rescue by sponsoring their passage to the New World. And the first ship arrived in Savannah, where General Oglethorpe met the anxious settlers.

They founded the town of Ebenezer on Ebenezer Creek, but life was so hard and so many died that in 1736 they got permission from General Oglethorpe to move to the new site on the Savannah River. They named it New Ebenezer.

"I always get a lump in my throat when I look at this church, Tempie. When I think of how long it took them to build it and what hardships they had to endure, I'm ashamed at myself when I complain."

"Complain! When in the world do you ever complain, Amarine? You should, but you don't. I don't know how you put up with it..."

"Not today, Tempie! Not today. We will have peace this day and a wonderful reunion with our friends. Look! There's Mary and Sallie Smithfield. My," she said waving and smiling, "I haven't seen those two since last year. See, Tempie, what a glorious time we're going to have."

As they began walking up the path to the church, the bells, which had been brought from Europe, began ringing, and the congregation began smiling. Amarine squeezed Eben's shoulder, but when she looked up at him his gaze was directed toward the Easterling girl, who was only a few steps ahead of them.

Martin will never allow anything to come between them, she thought worriedly. I wish that I could warn him, but it would do no good. He has his father's persistence. I wish sometimes that my Reddy could pause long enough to plan his ventures, but if he weren't so delightfully full of surprises, he wouldn't be my Reddy. She felt warm when she thought of him sitting beside the river, relaxed, smoking his pipe and humming. He was the happiest man she knew. Goodness knows why, as Tempie often said.

Amarine took Tempie's arm, steadying her as they walked up the few church steps toward the impressive, white doors. Tempie held onto the brick wall that was made with the red clay of the area and was thought to be able to withstand any intruders, thanks to its twenty-one inch walls. But it hadn't withstood the British when they captured the small town and used their beautiful church as a hospital and Lord knows what else in 1779, Tempie thought, as she watched the sun stream through the tall windows.

It upset her every time she thought of those British stabling their horses in her church. It took General Anthony Wayne to drive them out in 1782. Remembering, Tempie began to sob loudly, as she did every year, and Eben and Amarine looked at each other, and, as they had often done in the past, hugged her to them trying to calm her. They knew that Tempie was reliving Sherman's march to the sea. They knew that she could see him give the order for his men to burn the hand-carved church pews and the fences. But, what was worse, they knew that she could see his soldiers savagely topple their ancestors' gravestones. Tempie always said aloud, when her fevered mind got to that point, "He didn't have to do that, Amarine! Not our people's gravestones! Sherman didn't have to do that!"

No one looked at Tempie except the children who didn't have their parents' control. They understood how upset she was, for they, too, were upset, and the clearing of the men's throats and the subtle wiping of the ladies' eyes revealed it. It took Tempie's outburst to force them back, back to that terrible time.

When the service was over, Eben began looking for Eleanor. "Aren't you going to help your aunt down the hill, son?" Amarine asked. She was very much aware of what was on his mind.

"Tell you what I'm going to do, Mama. I'm going to allow Emerson to have the honor. I've something extremely important to do." He reached down and kissed the top of her honey blond hair and, whirling around, ran to the top of the long, wooden walkway that led down to the river.

When he got to the top he had a clear view. There she was, not twenty feet from the family's spot. He bounded down the walkway, dodging happy picnickers and shouting, "The British are coming! The British are coming!" Orin Knight yelled back, "Then, by gum, they'd better watch out, 'cause the Salzburgers are armed and ready this time." Everyone laughed and Eben flopped down onto the blanket beside his father.

"What was that all about, Ebenezer? Why'd you make such a fuss anyway? The British, indeed!" Tempie said, out of breath. She was the only one who was allowed to call him Ebenezer. He had protested when he was younger, but to no avail.

Amarine knew, and Eben was aware that she knew, when he glanced at her. He just had to cause a fuss so the Easterling girl would know where he was and notice him, just like his father would've done. He's so like Reddy.

The commotion he had made did make Eleanor notice him, but then she had been following his whereabouts ever since they had got out of services. She returned his smile, and that's all he needed. He excused himself and headed straight for her blanket, leaping over everything and everyone in his way.

When he spoke, she told her best friend Nancy later, I thought I'd melt. I honestly did. Such resonance, you know, like Professor Trenton. So polished. I couldn't believe that he was from little old Springfield. I really couldn't. Perfect manners. Dressed beautifully. When he said that he'd recently come from Savannah, I knew that I'd be able to tell Father about him, and that perhaps we could have him for supper or something."

"Father, I met the most engaging young man at the homecoming, actually, one of the few young men that I have met who has any manners, except dear Baldwin, of course." Eleanor let that sink in while trying to eat slowly, pretending to concentrate on her food. But when she looked up, her father was not paying her any attention. That was unusual, for as she was his only daughter, Martin Easterling usually hung on to her every word.

Rachel Easterling noticed that her husband's mind was on something other than his daughter's chattering and intervened.

"What is his name, dear?"

"Eben Hunter, but he goes by Ben, and he..."

That information awakened Martin. "Who are you talking about and why! Are you speaking of Reddick Hunter's son?"

"I don't know who his father is, but he recently came back from Savannah and has the nicest..."

"He might have nice everything, but you, young lady, are to have nothing to do with that riffraff. Do you hear?"

Roscoe, who was six years younger than Eleanor, was enjoying his sister's discomfort. His napkin did not hide his joyful smirk, but Eleanor ignored him. His mother did not. She shook her head at him, and he quietly resumed eating.

Eleanor's expression was not of defiance but of disappointment. "I understand clearly, Father. You seem to have found it necessary to squelch every opportunity that I may have for some male companionship while I'm home. It would appear to me that only Baldwin is suitable for me to associate with while in Springfield, and, Father, we don't even know if or when he'll return from the war, do we?"

Rachel quickly intervened. "He is just trying to protect you, and of course Baldwin will return. What a terrible thing to say! Eleanor, that is not what your father had in mind at all."

"That is indeed what I have in mind, Rachel! That Hunter has gone through Amarine's entire fortune! All her land has been lost by that incompetent. He's gone into at least a dozen businesses that I know of and failed at every one. Why, she's living like a sharecropper in that tumble- down shack..."

"Martin, there's no need to get yourself upset about it. I know that you were at one time very fond of Amarine Rahn, as were half the young boys in Effingham County." Rachel didn't say it with bitterness nor jealousy. She made a statement of fact. She knew that her husband married her for love as well as for her position, and she also knew why he was so upset at Eleanor's even mentioning the Hunter name—he hated to lose. And when Reddick Hunter came to Springfield, Amarine Rahn dropped all the boys flat. Martin couldn't stand not being in the running. Rachel knew her husband very well.

"Father, I didn't say that I was interested in marrying Ben, I merely said that I thought it would be lovely to have a male companion while I'm home for such a short time. The fact that his father is a poor business man certainly..."

"Poor business man! Poor! The man is an absolute fool! And why the bank continues to lend him money, I do not know..."

"Eleanor, you have upset your father. Roscoe, you may be excused, and do not run and hop all over the yard. You'll get sick. Now Eleanor, it would indeed be nice to perhaps have a few friends in for an afternoon of croquet or lawn tennis, and perhaps if your father is home then he could meet this young man. Would that not be acceptable, dear?" she asked, trying to smooth everything over. Rachel disliked having her meal fraught with dissension, she had reminded them often.

Martin sighed and said, "If the occasion is well chaperoned and if there are a number of people invited...perhaps the Kicklighter twins. Their father's on the bank board with me, you know. They're fine boys. Then there are the Brewton girls. They're lovely." He looked at Rachel, and she was smiling knowingly. If he can have some of his business associates and the children of the influential families at the party is what he means, she thought.

"So, you see, Eleanor, all this fuss for nothing. Now, you may send invitations to the ones that your father has mentioned as well as the young man, and he'll not feel that he is being singled out for a suitor."

"Suitor! Rachel, that will do! Suitor indeed! He'll merely be a guest, and that's all. Is that clear?"

"Do not raise your voice to me, Martin," Rachel said calmly. "You know how I hate it. I'm right across the table from you, and my hearing is still very acute." She was emphatic. She placed her napkin on the table, rose from her chair and continued, "I'll be in the sun parlor when you decide to apologize."

Martin rose quickly and said to Eleanor, "She knows that I just get excited and don't mean to shout. She knows it!"

Eleanor rose, as well, and smiling to herself escaped upstairs to her room. I'm sure he'll come. I'm positive. She rolled onto her stomach. The pale gold bed coverlet felt cool underneath her. Staring through the heavy lace curtains, she saw her mother and father walking in the garden. They weren't speaking but were holding hands, so she knew that their encounter had been smoothed over by her father's apology. Roscoe had ignored his mother's admonitions and was rolling the large hoop up and down the side hill. He was not throwing up as predicted.

Rachel DeShields Easterling was a strong woman. She was also a clever woman, who admired her husband, understood him and, in her way, even loved him. She was a good mother, wife and an excellent hostess, and was admired by everyone. She was attractive, having kept her figure, and her dark hair showed not a sign of greying. She was also bored, and nothing gave her more pleasure than a problem to be solved, and dear daughter Eleanor had just provided her summer deliverance.

Eleanor restlessly flipped over onto her back and studied the carvings on the pale yellow ceiling. It seemed to her that her parents' outbursts were getting more frequent. She hated to hear them fuss. Ben and I'll never fuss like that, she thought. Never!

Restless, she got up, opened the heavily carved mahogany wardrobe and began going through her dresses. I must choose the perfect dress for the party. Perhaps white...yes, this white voile will be just demure enough. Perhaps he'll not be able to see my heart pounding through the embroidered blouse. And a wide black ribbon at my waist and in my hair. No baby blue or pink for Mister Ben Hunter. Eleanor Anne Hunter. Oh, I like that...I like that...

CHAPTER SIX

"But, Nancy, it won't take but a few hours by train. Please come. You've got to meet him. You've just got to!" Eleanor shouted into the phone.

Nancy Pinholster was Eleanor's best friend from the Margaret Primrose Academy, a finishing school in Atlanta. They'd been best friends from the first day and had spent most of their time together, even on holidays. Eleanor would go to the tiny town of Tusculum, northwest of Springfield and in the same county, to spend part of every holiday with the Pinholster family, and Nancy would do the same, visiting the Easterlings in Springfield.

They had often analyzed their attraction and had come to the conclusion that part of it was that they were both from small towns and from families with similar position, wealth and background. Some of the other girls were condescending in their attitude toward the young country girls the first year, but when Nancy and Eleanor proved to be exceptional students and began receiving the highest scholastic honors, the students formed a different attitude.

"If Father and Mother approve it, but Ellie, I don't think that they will." She sighed then continued, "I've not been quite honest with you. I've been confined to the house. Now, don't get excited. I've not done anything awful. Heavens! I wish that I had. You know Joseph Surrette..."

"Yes, of course I know him. What does he have to do with anything? Nancy, you didn't..."

"Of course, I didn't see him without Father's approval. What do you take me for, a dunce?"

"No, I do not take you for a dunce. It's just the way that you said it, that's all."

Nancy hesitated then said, "Well, I might as well tell you. You know that we've been corresponding when I'm at the Academy. Naturally, I hadn't told my parents about it—just a few little ol' letters. But when I received a letter from Joseph—and I had told him that he was NOT to write me at home—well all the bats in the belfry were loosed. I mean ALL!"

"Did they read it? I mean, it was your private letter and..."

"You don't know my parents as well as I thought you did. Of course they read it!"

"I'd die if my parents read any of my personal letters, not that I get that many. I mean really, Nancy. Why can't we have a little privacy? Now, the boys, well, Jacob was seen going into a *you-know-what* and in broad daylight! I'm sure Father knows about it, but to my knowledge he's not been chastised. I know he's twenty-two and at the university, but that doesn't make a particle of difference. Heavens, I'm eighteen, and I can't even look at a boy or have one over without a dozen chaperones. It isn't fair, not fair at all!"

"So you understand. Perhaps I can talk them into letting me come if I can prevail upon Cleon to take me. He'd dearly love to take a ride down to Rincon via Springfield. He's still sweet on that Helen Swift, you know. That twit! If I told him all that I know about her escapades at the Academy, then he'd be singing another tune, but then he'd also not be so willing to take me to Springfield, would he?"

<hr/>

When Eben received the invitation to the lawn party he wasn't surprised. He should have been, Judson said in that condescending manner he projected once in a while. Eben set him straight.

"I can tell when a girl likes me, and I can tell if I have to make the first move, dear friend Judson. I knew that Eleanor had to make the first move."

"And just how did you conclude that, dear friend Ben?"

"Well, dear friend Judson, by the fact that she is from a prominent family, and that's the way they do things."

"And how would you be knowing that, Ben? Tell me how?"

"I was not Reddick Hunter's son while in Savannah." Eben spoke softly when he said it. He looked seriously at Judson. "You know that I love my father...I really do, but it's not easy being his son here in Springfield. He always means well, and we all know it. That's why we put up with these ridiculous business ventures of his. That and the fact that we think that one of these days he's going to hit pay dirt. But it's not easy to be laughed at, I can assure you."

"I'm sure it's not, Ben, but that's not what we were talking about, if you remember."

"That's just what we were talking about. In Savannah I was Alex Rahn's nephew and had the pick of any girl from the best families in the entire city. I wasn't there a week when the invitations began coming in. Don't look at me like that! I'm serious! Those little rich darlings are hungry for dashing young men like the two of us, my dear friend, and surely we're smart enough to capitalize on it. Even my Uncle Alex suggested that I go that route."

Judson looked at his friend of twelve years. He was surprised by this conversation. Ben had always been his own person—that was one of his endearing qualities. Sure, he knew that Ben was ashamed of his father's being the laughing stock of the town, but in the past he had just shrugged it off. At least Judson had thought that he had. But this was a new side of his friend. He wasn't sure that he liked it. He wasn't sure at all.

Finally, Eben said, "Have I disappointed you, Jud? I'm sorry if I have, but I'm so goddamned tired of being poor and having to cover up. I think that if it's the only way I can get out of this mire, then, HELL YES! I'll marry for money and position if that's what it takes! I want to get all that I can get, Jud, old friend!"

Judson didn't answer right away. When he did, Eben knew that he had mulled their conversation over very carefully. That was Judson's way. "I understand what you're saying. I really do. But do you not think that, maybe in the future, you'll feel that you've cheated yourself? You have the intelligence, the cleverness, the charm, if you will, to accomplish everything and more. Ben, if you use all your gifts to achieve any ambitions that you might have, why would you settle for a wealthy woman you don't love and..."

"Hey, wait a minute, fellow! I didn't say I'd marry a woman I didn't love, at least a little, now did I? I'm too much of a romantic, Jud. You should know that."

"I'm not sure that I do anymore, Ben. I'm not sure..."

"You have certainly gotten serious this past year, Jud. Hell, when I left, you would have pissed in your drawers over what I just said about all the sweet little things in Savannah. Hell, you'd be hopping the next train down there to help me tame the little things. What's happened to you, anyway?"

Judson swallowed, then continued, "You know Abigail Walters. I told you that we've been seeing each other, but I didn't tell you that I'm really getting serious. I mean I've kissed her and everything..."

"Whoa! What's this *everything*?"

"Hell, Ben, not what you're thinking! I'm planning to marry the girl! I wouldn't do anything like that."

"Oh, you wouldn't, huh! That's not what I heard and saw about this time last year down at Wishing Hill Pond, now was it? And her name sure as hell wasn't Abigail, either. Seems to me her name was Hester."

"If you breathe a word of that to Abigail, I'll have your head on a platter, Ben Hunter!"

"I'm surprised. Really I am. You are finding my attitude toward the affluent young ladies of Georgia distasteful, but here you are playing footsie with Abigail Walters, whose father owns half of Effingham County and is a judge to boot. This entire conversation is hypocritical, Jud, old boy. It's all right for you to feign love for..."

"What do you mean feign? What the hell do you mean? I'm genuinely in love with Abigail, and I would be if her father didn't have a dime. Do you understand?

"What the hell are you laughing about, Ben? You're enough to drive a fellow...I hope that you do join the goddamned army! I do!"

<hr />

"Ebenezer, I hope that you realize what an honor it is to be invited to the Easterlings'. Amarine, tell him. And your manners. You've got to be brushed up on your manners. Even Reddick has good manners. I think that's what your mother saw in him..."

"Tempie, stop with all this fuss. Eben has always had excellent manners, for his father and I have seen to it," Amarine said with a smile. Pushing her dark blond hair back from her forehead, she resumed slicing the tomatos and onions for the pickling sauce she had boiled. They loved them that way.

The kitchen was large. A big, black, wood-burning range took up most of the side wall with a wooden work table on either side, scrubbed to a fare-thee-well, as Tempie always said. On the opposite wall was a cupboard with a flour sifter built into the upper part, and Amarine stored her baking supplies below the white enameled top. She was so proud of that piece of furniture. It had been in her family for as long as she could remember, and she had painted it a soft green.

The large, round, oak table with its center pedestal surrounded by eight ladder-backed chairs with rush seats dominated the room. They, also, had been in the Rahn family and had come to Tempie, the eldest daughter, when Papa Rahn died. It was a warm, bright, and loving room where Reddick was master—at least at meal times.

An excellent cook, Amarine enjoyed Southern cooking, which was her specialty, learned from her mama and the various cooks that the Rahn family had employed during her growing-up years. Living in poverty, at least according to Tempie, had not changed her cooking habits, and they dined every day at twelve o'clock sharp. Reddick Hunter habitually lavished praise upon his wife and her culinary expertise as they gathered around the oak table set with the Rahn crested china, silver and finest crystal. The linen napkins were washed and ironed by Tempie herself. "We may eat in the kitchen, but we shall dine in the style to which we have always been accustomed," she said almost every day.

Amarine felt queenly, and gazing at her Reddy, who masterfully carved the chicken, and once in a while a ham, with great elan, she was satisfied with her life, especially when she looked at her handsome sons.

How could anyone want more, she thought. It was only with Tempie's constant degrading of Reddy that she was uneasy, but never unhappy. Tempie had never received the love that she had. She understood and was compassionate. It was her nature.

When Papa Rahn passed away Tempie was bereft. She had tended to him the last six years of his life, never regretting nor resenting it. It was her duty as the oldest daughter. The other seven children had all married and had families, so naturally Papa Rahn was her concern. There was no one who argued with her, for they were relieved as well as grateful.

The Rahn homestead was situated on the only piece of land left of the original estate handed down by their ancestors, the Geigers, when they came to the area from Salzburg. Temperance had received it from her father, and no one resented it. She had earned it. Martin Easterling could have foreclosed on the parcel, but somehow couldn't bring himself to do it. His ancestors were Salzburgers, too. He didn't need it, and he didn't want Amarine to be without it, for when things got really bad for her and Reddick, Temperance took them in. Only Martin was aware of their financial situation. Reddick Hunter had no idea of the arrangement between Martin and the bank, and Martin intended to keep it that way. He had always had a soft spot in his heart for Amarine.

The boys adored their Aunt Tempie. Oh, how she fussed over them, always having a sweet smelling hankie in her waistband or apron pocket to wipe their sweaty brows or runny noses. She was a loving and caring aunt, but there was never any doubt about who her favorite was. It was Ebenezer this and Ebenezer that. Not that she didn't lavish love and praise on the other three, for she did, but Ebenezer was her special love.

At first Amarine cautioned her about the possibility of jealousy from the other boys, but to no avail. After all, it was Tempie's house, and they were guests in it. At first, that is. But in a short time it became the family place again with no regard for whom it legally belonged to. It was the Rahn Place to everyone in Effingham County.

The lack of paint, the lack of sprucing up, as Tempie called it, did bother Amarine and Tempie. The wide yard was always neat, brushed clean, hedges trimmed, but the metal roof was rusting through in spots, and the patches did little to hide the areas, and the front porch had begun to sag on the north end.

"And to think that our home used to be the envy of everyone in all of Effingham County, Amarine. To think of it! Look at it now. Would you just!"

"Don't fret so, dear. This is only temporary, and you know it. Reddy said just the other night that Sam Tillis had offered..."

"Don't you start that again, Amarine! Don't you dare! When that Reddick Hunter brings home a regular paycheck, then speak to me about it, but until then, please give your old fat sister some credit for brains. Really, Amarine!"

✦

When Eleanor Anne Easterling glided down the long staircase, just as she had been taught at the Primrose Academy, her mind was not on the party that her mother had taken great pains to bring about, but on Ben Hunter. *I wonder what he'll wear. Oh, dear Lord, please make it appropriate, so Father will let him call on me. But even if he is the most perfect looking and acting fellow in all of Springfield, Father'll probably have some objection.*

She heaved a tremendous sigh, and Angel, who was setting the long table for the buffet, laughed and said, "Miss Eleanor, ya gonna put a nail in youah coffin sighin' so big. Ah declare ya will."

"Oh, Angel, why do you say such as that? You know that's just an old wives' tale. Now you just wait and see. I'll live to be old and fat just like you, and there'll be no more nails in my coffin then in yours."

Eleanor began singing lightly as she patted Angel's shoulder and opened the French doors that led to the garden. Her mother was putting fresh flowers on the tables and straightening the bright green tablecloths.

"Oh, there you are. Would you look at these cloths? I'll declare I'm gonna hafta speak to Daphne about this. Look at all these wrinkles! I just bet that she didn't even dampen them. Honey, go to the summer kitchen and see if she's there. Now, hurry! I'll simply not stand for this!"

Rachel Easterling was an excellent hostess and had been since she first married Martin. If the guests arrived before Daphne had pressed the cloths, she would certainly lose her standing in the community. Not that the boys would even notice, but she knew full well that those Brewton girls would. They were as big gossips as their mother was, and that Lillian had a mouth that carried all the way to Atlanta.

Up the brick walk and around the stand of lavender crape myrtle Eleanor rushed. Her white leather slippers tapped enough for Daphne to know that someone was coming. She brushed the tears aside, straightened her long white apron but could not stop the sniffling.

"Daphne," Eleanor called, even before opening the glass door. "Mother is having a fit about...Daphne, what's wrong? Are you sick?"

"Noam, Ah ain't sick. Ah be fine inna liddle while. Jes gonna take some time, dat's all."

"Turn around here. Let me look at you."

"Ah gonna be fine, Miss Eleanor. He din' mean ta hurt me." She

72

laughed a little when she finally got up enough nerve to look up at Eleanor. Her right eye was almost shut and badly discolored.

"Just what I thought! Father's gonna have Wilam's head. That does it! Why do you let him treat you like that? Does he mistreat the children, too?"

"Oh, noam, he don' tech de chilren. Ah coul'n' stan' fer him ta tech mah chilren."

"Well, he best not. But why do you let him mistreat you? I don't understand why you put up with him. Why, if he were my husband I'd ...I'd ..."

"Eleanor! Now where has that girl got off to! Eleanor!" Rachel shouted.

"You stay put, Daphne. I'll talk to Mother."

"Yessum."

"In here, Mother. Daphne was very upset about the cloths, but she's not feeling well..."

"Has that Wilam got her with child again? Has he?"

"Oh, no. Well, I might as well tell you, because I think Father should do something about the situation."

"First things first! I want these cloths done over and I want them done now! Go get Angel, and she'll help her. Daphne, what's this all about anyway?"

"Miss Eleanor done got upset 'bout Wilam, Miss Rachel. He a good man when he sober. He jes move me 'round a liddle bit, but it don' hurt lak it done las' night."

"Well, that does it! I'll declare it does! I'm speaking to Martin this very minute. He needs a good talking to, and if he does not respond, then it's to jail for him to cool off. He has absolutely no right to beat up on you like that. Now, not another word. I've made up my mind!"

Daphne knew that when Miss Rachel made up her mind it would do no good to protest, but what if Mistah Martin put Wilam in jail? What would she do? When he got out he'd beat her for sure. She began sniffling so loudly that Rachel put her arms around her, patting her slight shoulder.

"Now, now, it'll be all right. I'll have Sheriff Carr talk to him and tell him that he'll be sent up for life if he ever touches you again. That oughta scare him into behaving like a responsible man. Now, come on Daphne, stop those tears. Angel will help you with the cloths. Not another sniffle, do you hear?"

<hr>

Judson Ridgeway received his invitation to the lawn party a day after Eben did. He was ecstatic! That could mean only one thing, that Abigail had asked Eleanor to include him, he figured. Then she is serious. In a way I hate to tell Ben. He'll make some kind of facetious remark, no doubt. I don't know what's happened to him. He's not the same Ben that I grew up with. He thinks he's so witty and clever. Well, he's not. I'm in love with Abigail, and it doesn't matter that she's rich or not. And I intend to marry her, too.

But Judson couldn't keep his news from Eben even an hour. He borrowed his Uncle Cal's Ford and drove out to the Rahn place just outside of town on the Clyo Road. God, look at how this place has run down, he thought as he drove up. Maybe I'm too hard on Ben. No wonder he's ashamed of his father and has become so belligerent. God, I can't even have a conversation with him anymore without his arguing.

Aunt Tempie was sitting on the front porch when Judson drove up the sandy lane. She waved and tried to get up but was struggling when he called to her.

"Don't you get up for me, Aunt Tempie. It's me, Judson Ridgeway. Hey, let me help you." He hopped out of the coupe and went through the opening in the hedge. At least they keep the place clean, he thought.

"Why, Judson, I've not seen you since before Ebenezer went to Savannah. You've grown, I'll declare you have. Bet you've grown two, three inches."

He reached down and kissed her upturned, soft cheek. "Not grown up, but I have added a few muscles, Aunt Tempie. You know working at Dad's feed store and lifting those heavy sacks will make a man outa you."

"How's Baker doing, anyway? Been a long time since I saw him and Verna. Saw her when Amarine and I went to Page's funeral. How long's that been? Two years? Or was it in '15?"

"Can't keep up with all that happens around here, Aunt Tempie. But seems to me that Aunt Page passed away spring of '14. Yep, Ben and I were in the eleventh grade. That's when it was. Folks are doing fine, and I'll tell them you asked for them. Oh, how are you, Miss Amarine?" he asked as she walked out on the porch. "Haven't seen you in a long time."

"Come here and give me a hug, Judson. It has indeed been a long time." She patted him on the back and held the screen door open for Reddick.

"How's it going, Jud? Well, well, what brings you all the way out here? If it's to see Eben, he's already gone to town to get himself outfitted for the big party at Easterlings'. Imagine that! Old Martin letting his daughter invite my son. Don't know what's got into the old skinflint. Heck, Eben can't even vote." He gave a hearty laugh and so did Judson.

"Well, I can't vote either, and I got an invitation. But then I've been seeing Abigail Walters, so I guess that's why. But then it could be 'cause so many of the fellows are over fighting the Krauts, and we're just about the only available ones left in town, huh?"

Reddick laughed again and said, "That could be. But I'm thinking that it just might be because you're two damned good-looking and smart young men. That's what I'm thinking."

Tempie just had to get in her barb. "Reddick, if you think for one minute that Martin'll let that daughter of his marry Ebenezer and make you a rich man, you'd better think again. I know Martin Easterling, and he'd rather put her in a convent than let a son of yours get near her. And he hates Catholics, too!"

"Now, Tempie, that's not a Christian way of talking, now is it?"

"And what would you be knowing about how a Christian talks, Mister Hunter?"

"You two stop it this instant! Gracious me, we have a guest and haven't even offered him any lemonade or tea or anything else. The very idea! Come on inside to the kitchen where it's cooler, Judson. Tempie, let Reddy help you up."

"I'd rather sit here until I die, Amarine! I'd rather."

"Here, Aunt Tempie, I'll help you," Judson said smiling down at her while extending his arm for her to grab. "These new muscles ought to be good for something."

"You're a sweet boy, Judson. Always have been. That Walters girl will be a lucky one if she latches on to you. She certainly will. Not like some people I know, like poor Amarine," she said glaring at Reddick's back and sticking out her tongue for good measure.

"I heard you, Tempie. Sticks and stones will break my bones, but words will never ..."

<hr />

"Never saw a more beautiful day, Miss Rachel," Martin said teasingly to his wife.

"Well, Mister Martin, you wouldn't be saying it if you had just been through what I've had to go through. I could gladly cane that Wilam Simpson, I could. You should see poor Daphne's eye, black and blue and swollen almost shut. You've got to speak to that no good..." she looked around and whispered, "nigger!"

"Why, Rachel Easterling, I've never heard you use that word before."

"Well, sir, that's what he is. Daphne is a fine young woman, and he had no reason to mistreat her. She did assure me that he never lays a hand on the children, though. Martin, you've got to take him in hand, now, I mean it. This very day!"

"You are upset. Have you forgotten that you're having a party that is supposed to start in a few minutes," he said, looking at his pocket watch.

"No, I haven't. But I want this matter resolved, and I want it done now." She looked longingly at him and added, "Please, Martin. Now."

"If that is what is needed, of course I'll speak to him. But I think that I'll drop down to the court house and talk to Hubert first. Will take only a minute, and he'll know how I should handle it, my sweet."

He certainly is happy this afternoon, Rachel thought. That merger must have gone through at the bank.

"My gracious, is that a car I hear coming up the drive? Who on earth would arrive half an hour early. The very idea!"

"Oh, Nancy and Cleon. I should have known. Martin, please have Angel put on her other apron and get to the front door. I'll round up the rest of the cloths and Eleanor can help. Now, Martin!"

Why can't he be of more help to me. Can handle international affairs and can't even...

"Eleanor," she shouted opening the door to the summer kitchen. "Daphne, is she in here?"

"Noam, she run to the driveway when she heard dat car a comin' up. Said dat it mus' be Miss Nancy and her brudder."

"Well, I never! Here she talks me into having a big fancy party for her and then deserts me..."

"Yessum, she sho done dat."

"Guess I'll have to take matters in to my own hands, as usual." She took the freshly pressed cloths from Daphne's outstretched arms and quickly rushed outside and down the brick path that led to the garden patio. There were six round tables circling the fountain. She could hear the laughing chatter coming from the house and then heard another car drive up.

I'll never make it, never! When she saw Eleanor and Nancy open the dining room doors she motioned to them. Eleanor could see how upset she was and called, "We're coming, Mother. Here, let us help."

"About time you showed. Hello Nancy. I'm sorry that I'm in such a dither, but we've had servant problems and ..."

"Mother, I said that we'd finish up here. Now, go on upstairs and get yourself together."

"Here, Mrs. Easterling, I'll take that one. Servants can truly be a bother. Mother has said that a million times, I'm sure."

"Gracious, Ellie, I thought she was going to have a stroke. What's so important about a few cloths, anyway?"

"You don't know Mother. She has a reputation to uphold, Nancy. Now, you and I would think the entire episode funny, but not Mother. Everything must be in place."

She stood back and said, "There! Now perhaps the catastrophe has been diverted and her face saved. They do look pretty, don't they?"

"Yes, they do, and unless my eyes deceive me I think that your new friend has just arrived."

Eleanor whirled around, but the smile she was wearing quickly dissipated when she saw one of the Kicklighter twins. She could never tell them apart.

She rushed toward them, turned back toward Nancy and shook her head no, and vivaciously said, "Welcome Elliott, or is it Elmore. I haven't been in your company long enough to tell you two apart. Oh, Nancy, come over and meet the twins."

Cleon Pinholster, Nancy's brother, bounded over the lawn and joined them. There were few people that Eleanor disliked, but she had never liked Cleon, and even Nancy knew it. Why can't he walk over like any normal fellow would, she questioned. And that fake grin, his eyes never reflecting his true feelings. Cold, calculating eyes like in a Shakespearean tragedy— probably like Brutus looked at Caesar. And what makes it worse, he knows that I don't like him. I don't care how handsome he thinks he is. Anyone who would be sweet on that Helen Swift must be addlebrained.

"Oh, boys, this is Nancy's brother Cleon. He was kind enough to drive her down from Tusculum. Wasn't that nice of him?"

Just who does he think he is putting his arm around my waist! Well, really! "Cleon, I must tend to my other guests. Would you be a dear and see to the twins?" she said while removing his arm forcefully. He's enjoying tormenting me.

"There you two are. Mary Ellen and Lily, I want you to meet my dear friend's brother. This is Cleon Pinholster from up Tusculum way. His sister Nancy is my suite mate at the Academy. Cleon, these are the Brewton girls, and they're not twins, even though most people think they are." She laughed, and the girls nervously stared at Cleon while giggling.

Good! Eleanor thought. That'll give him someone to talk to. Where on earth is Ben? It's a quarter after. And Judson and Abigail? Maybe they think it's fashionable to be late, but that is just not the case, and Mother is an expert on manners. I hear a car. Oh, dear Lord, let it be he...or is it him...oh, I don't care...

⁂

Rachel, refreshed and calm, checked the dining room table and sideboard and cautioned Angel about keeping the oysters and crab mousse cold. "I like the ham spirals surrounding the pickled cauliflower, Angel. Like this, dear. And the parsley sprinkled over the whole cauliflower. Put the pimento strips in a star shape. Now, doesn't that look better?" She stood back and admired the buffet.

"Oh, Angel, I hear a car. Would you be a dear and answer the door? I must go help Eleanor. Mister Martin is paying a visit to Sheriff Carr to ask for his assistance in warning Wilam about his terrible treatment of poor Daphne, or he'd be here to help."

"He jes a mean nigger, Miss Rachel. Dat's all he is. She oughta leave him and take dose chilren 'fore he give her 'nother one. Dat's de truth."

"I hate to see that happen, but I believe you're right. She said that he only does that when he's drunk."

"Yessum, an' he drunk mos' de time."

The Ford pulled up, and Judson, Abigail and Eben got out. Judson had borrowed his Uncle Cal's car because his father's was older. Still looked nice, but this occasion called for the best that he could come by.

So that's the young man Eleanor is smitten by, Rachel thought while peering out the side window. He is a handsome thing, I must admit. But then why wouldn't he be? Amarine was and is as pretty as a picture, and Reddick was the handsomest thing to come down the pike. He's aged well despite his financial set-backs and is probably the most cheerful man I've ever met.

Judson nervously opened the car door for Abigail. He was obviously unsure of himself. God, I'll probably use the wrong fork and say everything wrong. He looked down at Abigail, and she took his hand and squeezed it, reassuring him. I'm the luckiest fellow in the entire world, he thought. So what if I mess up. She won't care. She's so sensitive, and I never saw such eyes.

What on earth does he see in her, Eben wondered, looking at the two of them cow-eye each other. With those bulging frog eyes of hers, she'll look like a hooded lizard by the time she's thirty. But I can see that he's truly in love. Good for you, friend Judson. You'll be a millionaire when her old man croaks, and I for one hope that you are.

And here just might be my ticket out of misery headed right for me, and what a beautiful ticket she is, too. That must be her mother joining her. God, she's a beaut, too. Shrewd, though. Look at how self-assured she is and direct, not hiding her feelings as she assesses me. Good! I didn't want this to be too easy.

"Ben, I'm so delighted that you were able to join us. I want you to meet my mother. Mother, this is Ben Hunter. Or would you prefer that I call you Eben?"

"Just don't call me Ebenezer. That's my Aunt Tempie's prerogative. Mrs. Easterling," and he bowed slightly, raising her hand to his lips while looking her directly in the eye.

"Ben, I've known your mother and father and your Aunt Tempie for years. I hope that they're well." He's a cocky one and will definitely bear watching.

"They're very well, but Aunt Tempie wouldn't like to hear me say it. She dearly loves all her ailments." He laughed lightly, but Rachel could tell that he was evaluating her and his situation. A clever young man, who will do anything to get what he wants, and I do so hope that it's not Eleanor. I don't think that she's his match. I would have been at her age, but I'm afraid we've sheltered her too much. I told Martin that she needed to stay with Frieda in New York for a summer and experience another way of life. These southern girls are just too sheltered for their own good. But he wouldn't hear of it. Bohemian lifestyle, my eye. Frieda would help Eleanor get some starch in her spine. I hope I'm not too late. This will need some careful attention, I'm afraid. We're in for a long, eventful summer. Thank God!

"You willed a perfect day, Mrs. Easterling. I can tell that you have special powers."

"Why, Ben, you'll have Mother thinking that you're some kind of clairvoyant, yourself. Mother, I told you that he was very charming."

"He comes by it honestly, Eleanor. His father is as *charming* a man as we've ever had in Springfield." That'll put him in his place. Charming and the laughing stock of Effingham County. I wonder if he'll retaliate. She needn't have wondered.

"Charm is necessary when you're penniless, Mrs. Easterling." His head was bowed. He said no more. She was fascinated by his maneuver. Are you playing on my emotions, Ebenezer? Not today. I've been through a harrowing morning, and I'll not be enticed into feeling sorry for you, dear boy. If my prediction is correct, you'll be able to buy and sell all of us before you're through.

She smiled slightly, a Cheshire cat smile. You missed your chance to charm me. I'm not Lillian Brewton or any of your other girlfriends' mothers, all willing subjects no doubt. Dear boy, I'm Rachel DeShields Easterling! But I'll admit that you're a fascinating addition to an otherwise dull summer.

CHAPTER SEVEN

Eben was just finishing the newspaper when Alpha and James came out of the boarding house. "How was it? Was the food good?"

James looked at Alpha and replied, "Ain't no ways as good as Alpha fixes, but it was tol'able."

"I tought dat de biscuits coulda used a little moah shortenin' and dat slaw was weepin' a little bit, but udderwise it was all raght, Ah reckon."

James slid into the driver's side, and Alpha adjusted her hat, straightened her skirt and proceeded to tell Eben about their experience. "Mistah Eben, we ain't complainin', now Ah wants ya ta know dat. It was a real nice place and de folks dat works deah was real polite. We tol' dem who ya was, and de owner, he say he knew youah pa, and dat he was shuah sorry ta heah 'bout de typhoid takin' him an' youah ma."

She turned around to see his reaction and noticed that he pulled himself up and sighed like he did when he was bolstering his strength. He still miss dose two. Ah can tell.

"What was his name, Alpha?"

"He don't 'dentify hisself, but Ah heard de woman call him Philbert oah sometin' lak dat."

"I remember him. He used to work for my daddy when he had the furniture store. Unfortunately, it didn't last a year, like most of his other enterprises." Alpha noticed his fingers nervously drumming on the dark grey seat. Ah'm not shuah dat comin' back heah is good fer Mistah Eben. He shuah is nervous.

"Where ya wants me ta drive ta now, Mistah Eben?"

"Go back to Judson's building, James. He should be back from his dinner by now." He sighed again, but Alpha didn't turn around to check on him. She had known Eben for so long that she could read his every mood.

They passed by the now defunct bank, where Martin Easterling had been king. Eben should have been happy when Judson wrote that the bank had failed and that the Easterlings were almost penniless. Why wasn't he? It would have been sweet revenge. He had also written that Martin had had a stroke and that he and Rachel had moved up to New York state to live with Eleanor and her husband. Eben was still not satisfied. He had wanted to return, flaunting his wealth, but now there was no one left in Springfield whom he could impress or who would care.

He rested his head back, closed his eyes and remembered the last time he was on this street. It was just after the war, and he and about twenty-four other soldiers were marching down Laurel St. to shouts and cries from the celebrating townspeople. He saw Eleanor and Rachel on the sidewalk waving small flags, and Eleanor was shouting "WELCOME HOME!" He remembered that she was wearing a red dress. Rachel was in soft blue. Their eyes locked; then she averted her gaze for fear someone would see her.

Judson was the only one who knew the story. Oh, others speculated, even his mother, but only he, Rachel and Martin and, of course, Judson really knew the truth of why he hurriedly left Springfield to join the army. His mother thought that he was heart broken over not being allowed to court Eleanor. Dear, sweet Eleanor. That was the problem. She was too dear and too sweet for him to really love. He could have faked it if it had not been for Rachel. He would have faked it had she not seen through him. He tried to outsmart them but ended up outsmarting himself.

⁂

"I'm so happy that you accepted my invitation, Ben," Eleanor gushed. She took his arm and led him over to the assembled group beside the fountain. After introductions they walked down the lawn toward the green and white striped tent that had been set up beside the playing field. Martin's man Russell was serving cool drinks to the young ladies who preferred sitting in the shade to playing croquet.

Eleanor was admiring his dress and decided that he was undoubtedly the best dressed man there. His white gabardine slacks and V-necked sleeveless sweater over the navy and white striped shirt were so appropriate. The Kicklighter twins were not nearly as attractively dressed. He might be penniless, but he certainly had taste. She could see that her mother approved by the way she looked at him. I believe that he's won her heart, she thought. She almost drooled. Oh, I'm so happy! Now she will work on Father, I'm sure. I certainly need an ally.

Eleanor had put on a large leghorn hat that tied under her chin, and she and Ben took the field. She wasn't a bad player, but would not have been his match had he not let her win. She knew it and smiled her appreciation. Rachel had selected a chair in the shade of the tent and watched, never taking her eyes off them.

Why couldn't someone that exciting have come into my life when I was young, she thought. I'm afraid that he can read my mind, so I must be careful. Heavens, I'm actually having a difficult time breathing. I'm sure that I have no worry with Eleanor nor Martin, but Ben, my dear, you have an uncanny way of seeing through me, I'm afraid.

"Russell," Rachel called, "Please see to our guests who seem to enjoy being in the afternoon sun. They must be thirsty, and Russell, you might suggest to them that it's much more pleasant under the tent. Thank you." She motioned toward the fountain, where she saw Martin.

Now's the time to begin my little game. "Martin, aren't you going to change, dear?"

"And why must I? I have to get back to the bank in a short time. When can I eat?"

"The game is almost over. Did you succeed in your talk with Wilam? You're back sooner than I thought." She was staring at Eleanor and Eben as she said it.

"No, I didn't. Hubert was out on a call, so I decided to postpone our little talk until he returned." He followed her gaze. "Is that the Hunter boy with Eleanor?"

"Yes, it is. He seems harmless enough, dear. Has just a smattering of Reddick's charm and is nice enough looking, I suppose, if you like unrefined features and an indifferent smile. Frankly, I think that Cleon Pinholster is much more attractive and definitely more polished and suited for our Eleanor. I must remember to mention it to her."

"I see what you mean. Doesn't look a bit like Amarine, does he? You're right. Definitely not as attractive as Pinholster."

I hate having to put ideas in your head, dear Martin. I wonder how you have ever succeeded in banking, but I'm glad that you're clever at something. Certainly not about women and how we think. God! He's the most exciting thing I've ever seen. He moves with such grace and assurance. I can't understand why my husband can't see it, but I'm glad that he can't, or he'd spoil everything.

"Dear, have Angel fix you a plate so you can run off to the bank and make us lots of money," she said teasingly.

"You're a good wife, Rachel. You've always taken good care of me, and I think that I'll do just that. I really do need to get back. Will you join me?"

"I'll wait for Eleanor and her friends, dear. What I'd really like to do is take a long, hot tub and curl up with a book. These young people can be very tiring. Don't worry if you're late this evening. We'll probably still be clearing up from the party." She rose and kissed his cheek and putting her slender arm around his ample waist said, "Don't be concerned about Eleanor. I'll personally keep an eye on those two."

"Now that I've seen him, I'm not as concerned. And you're right. He certainly doesn't have much of Reddick's flair, does he?"

"No, he doesn't, not at all." If you were more observant you'd see that Reddick could take lessons from his handsome son, dear Martin.

"Isn't he charming, Mother? Isn't he?" Eleanor gushed.

"Don't gush so, Eleanor. He seems to be nice enough, but I'd not classify him as charming, dear. More like pleasant, I think. Now I think that Cleon Pinholster is definitely charm..."

"Cleon! Really, Mother, he is a bore with a capital B. He simply has no class, even though he thinks he does. How Nancy can have such a brother, I don't know. Cleon! Really!"

"Don't raise your voice or everyone will hear. Now, be a dear and have Angel replenish the nearly empty bowls. I had forgotten how young men eat. Would you look at the oysters, or what's left of them? Oh, and Eleanor, have Russell see to their drinks. I'm sure that the young men had rather have some *sweetening* in theirs, but your father had to return to the bank. Do you think it out of order if Russell asked them?"

"Why not? If Father were here, he certainly would. I'll tell him. Is it still in the chest in Father's study?"

"I'm sure it is. Anyway, Russell will certainly know its whereabouts. Your father usually has a nightcap before retiring."

Good, that'll keep her busy for a while. Rachel knew exactly where to find Ben. She smoothed her soft peach lawn dress and walked determinedly toward him. He sensed her nearness even before he turned around.

"I'm glad that I found you alone, Ben. Now don't interrupt, because it will do you no good if you choose to. Please, let's walk down to the tent. I can tell that you are a sensitive man and a very alert one as well, so what I'm about to say should come as no surprise to you."

He walked beside her and could feel her anxiousness. He said nothing.

"Martin is determined that Eleanor have nothing to do with you. The fact that he was sweet on your mother at one time and Reddick beat him out is really what dear Martin cannot stand. He hates to lose. It wasn't that he was in love with your mother, although he thought that he was at the time. It was simply that he was a poor loser. Do you understand?"

"Yes, completely. You see, I don't like to lose either." He took her arm and could feel her flinch.

"Does that offend you, Rachel? I may call you Rachel?"

"It doesn't bother me. Why should it? After all I've certainly had men, other than Martin, hold my arm in the past, and I dare say that they'll have the opportunity to do so in the future. Ben, you're a grown man. I would, however, prefer that you call me Mrs. Easterling in public. Others might feel that you're too forward..."

"But you don't, do you, Rachel?"

"Of course not! Why should I? Heavens, I'm not as old as Methusellah and so out of date as to ..."

"Indeed you're not! You're a vibrant, handsome woman in the prime of her life."

She stopped, looked at him and almost laughed at his presumption. "I like everything you just said but the handsome woman part. I've never thought of myself as handsome."

"Poor choice of words. I could have said that you're "pretty" like a little girl dressed in pink and white. What adjective should I use for you, Rachel? Beautiful? Or perhaps..."

"Do not toy with me, Ben. I'm not one of your little, empty-headed conquests who'll giggle nervously at your every phrase..."
"Thank God!" He laughed heartily. She joined in but with restraint.

She sighed loudly. He could tell that she was uneasy and not sure of her approach. *Should I help her? I think not. Let her proceed. I need to know just what she's up to, for I'm sure she's plotting something. This woman enjoys intrigue. Not one bit like her sweet, innocent daughter. Not one bit. Perhaps I'm after the wrong fish. She excites me, and it's obvious that I excite her, or why is she having such a difficult time formulating her thoughts and controlling her breathing.*

She could feel him gaze at her heaving breasts but could not seem to control herself. *What has come over me? I've never behaved like this. Never!* She allowed herself to look up at him. She felt so weak that she was glad that they had reached the tent. She sat down on the first chair, and when he knelt beside her she could not find her voice. He spoke, "May I get madam something cool to drink? You look flushed."

Damn you! "Flushed? Do I really? I had no idea."

"Not like my other empty-headed conquests, Rachel? Then don't behave like one."

She stared at him—it seemed like forever. Then finding her voice, she said, "I'm not used to being flirted with by one of my daughter's suitors, Ben. And I find it quite unnerving and would ask you..."

"Ask me what? Ask me to stop admiring you openly? Is that it? And just when I was beginning to think that I had finally met someone with whom I could have an intelligent conversation and be myself..."

"Yourself! Are you ever yourself? Or do you even recognize Ben Hunter? I rather think that you take great delight in pretending, while skirting the perimeter of the true Ben Hunter, so as to confuse your opponent."

"Oh, Rachel, you are a wise and astute adversary. I'll have to brush up on my parrying. And to think that I was so sure of myself when I left Savannah, relishing my...ah... accomplishments as well as my conquests. Then to meet you, my dear one. You have indeed put me in my place."

"You have no place, Ben," she said softly, then added haltingly, "but I could help you create one..."

"Mother, there you two are. I've been looking all over." Eleanor stopped. "Is something wrong? Have I done anything..."

"Of course not. What on earth could you have done?"

"What your mother means, Eleanor, is that we were deep in conversation about the...war. And you know how that affects..."

"I'm so glad. I was afraid that I had caused you some concern."

Stop grovelling, Eleanor. God! Was I ever that dense?

***

"But, Mother, why can't I see him openly? You said yourself that he seemed like a nice young man. Now didn't you?"

"I'll admit that I did, but, Eleanor, you know how your father feels about the young man. I'd be going behind his back if I gave my approval."

"But he could come calling, and we could sit in the parlor. I could even ask Nancy to stay for a while, and she could chaperone. Oh, please, Mother. Please!"

"It's against my better judgement but, well, I'll ask your father. And, Eleanor, his word is final. Do you understand?"

Rachel smiled. It was a secretive smile. It had been over a week since the lawn party, and she and Ben Hunter had had several "accidental" meetings. My Lord! I'm in love. For the first time in my life I'm in love. How did it happen? Why did it happen? We must be careful. Martin might be slow, but he is not stupid. If he found out he'd...he'd...what would he do? Could he chance being made a fool of in such a small town? No, his pride would not stand for it. But how can he not see that I'm changed? I feel like I'm on fire. Every nerve in my body is alive. Oh, Ben, where are you today? Are you down by the pond...our pond...

***

"Well, Ben, how nice to see you again. Eleanor is upstairs..." Don't you dare grin at me like that, my love, or I won't be able to carry this through. And don't stroke my arm or I'll die on the spot. "I'll tell her that you've come calling. How are your folks? Well, did you say?"

He whispered, "That's not what I said, and you know it, my love. I said that I love you, and that if you don't meet me tomorrow during your nap time, I'll come here to join you upstairs."

"You wouldn't!"

"Try me! Oh, there you are, Eleanor. Looking lovely as usual. And Nancy, how are things in Tusculum?"

"I guess they're fine, Ben, but I'm sure that you didn't come here to ask about Tusculum, did you?"

"You are very astute, Nancy. You bet that I didn't. Eleanor," he said, taking her arm, "you two go into the parlor, and I'll join you in a minute.

I want to have a conversation with your mother." Ben closed the double parlor doors, looked around and seeing no one reached for Rachel. He felt her hard against him, the jet buttons on her bodice dug into his chest, and when he kissed her she responded passionately without restraint.

When he released her she was panting—so was he. "My God, you're the most desirable woman I've ever known. Tomorrow, and don't be late. I'm not sure I'll be able to wait..."

"Neither am I, my sweet..."

Neither one saw Russell. Martin was not the fool his wife took him for. He had indeed noticed her heightened color, nervousness and evasiveness. Her mind was definitely not on running the house. Even Angel had asked him what was wrong with the Missus. No, Martin was no fool, and suspecting that something was amiss had engaged Russell to keep his eye on her, stating that he was concerned for her health.

"How's Ah gonna tell Mistah Martin 'bout dis? Deah Lord in de mohnin'! She sho got me in a fix! Hmmmm."

The pond was a five-minute stroll from the main house. Rachel was not concerned about anyone's discovering them, because Roscoe was the only one who actually used the pond, and she had sent him to their farm in the eastern part of the county for a few weeks. It was not unusual for him to stay two or three weeks each summer with the Dunkirks, who were the caretakers and whose sons, Luke and Randy, were close to Roscoe's age and attended the same grade school with him.

She couldn't believe how easy it was for her to slip outside her upstairs bedroom, down the stairway and out the side door of the dining room. Russell always worked the front flower gardens at that time of day when it was shady on that side of the house, and Angel and Daphne were cleaning up the kitchen after their main meal and enjoying their rest off the summer kitchen. Rachel always rested for one to two hours every day, either napping or reading and sometimes doing handwork. It was her quiet time, and unless there was an emergency she was not to be disturbed. All the servants knew it, and so did Martin.

She rushed, her pale lavender, voile dress clung to her damp back. He had said that he liked her in pastels, that their softness contrasted with her dark coloring. Her vivid, colorful dresses quickly found their way to the back of her tall wardrobe. She had softened her hair around her face, even cutting bangs and curling them. Martin had noticed and said that he liked her hair that way. Eleanor had said, "Why, Mother, you look like a school girl with your hair like that." She had responded, "I don't think that forty-two signifies old age, Eleanor. Actually, I feel as young as I did when your father and I were married."

"I didn't mean that you were old, for heaven's sake! Seems like I can't say anything right these days." She was out of sorts because Ben had not come calling any more, and she had no idea why. Their last meeting seemed to go very well. Even Nancy had said so.

Rachel could see him waiting beneath the weeping willow. Watching her approach, he removed his straw bowler. He threw her a kiss, causing her to quicken her pace until she was actually running, ending up in his anxious arms.

"I thought you'd never get here," he gasped. "God, I've dreamed of this all morning..."

"So have I. Oh, Ben, I'm sure Martin suspects something. No, he hasn't said anything, but I catch him looking at me in a strange, questioning way. Now, that's not Martin. He rarely notices anything. At least he hasn't in the past."

"Maybe we should stop seeing each other for a while if..."

"No, my love. I couldn't stand it. We'll just have to change our meeting place. But where?"

"We'll worry about that later. Now come here and let's live what I've been dreaming about..."

He couldn't finish. Her open mouth hungrily found his, and the only sounds were the hurried movements as he pushed up her skirt. Discovering that she was wearing no undergarments, he said, "You were anxious, my love...my Rachel." Her moaning was squelched as she bit her lower lip.

His hungry kisses enveloped her. "We mustn't rush so. I want to savor this, but...it's too late...Now, my sweet, now!"

"Yesssss.....

<hr/>

"Thank you Russell. You are not to breathe a word of this to anyone, do you hear?" Martin rose from his easy chair in his study.

"Oh, nossuh, Mistah Martin. Ah sho nuff won't."

So that's what's been going on. I can't believe it! Rachel! This will not get out. This is my town, and I'll not allow her to destroy what I've built and make me the laughing stock of the whole county. No, Rachel. He'll be horsewhipped and sent packing. I don't think she knows how much influence I have in this town, but she'll soon find out.

Martin had left the house after presumably resting in his study like he did every day. But this day he had poured himself a stiff bourbon and removed his revolver from the desk drawer before leaving. He drove the

Maxwell a few blocks, then took a dirt side road, pulled up into the heavy brush and left the car. He felt that it was necessary to catch them together, so he had to rush. Going through the woods was not as difficult as he had thought it would be. The underbrush had been cleaned out by the convicts just the year before.

He was panting, and his shirt was soaked with perspiration. He was glad that he'd left his jacket in the car. When he got to the wooden fence, his property line, he knew that the pond was not far beyond.

He stopped, catching his breath. Do I want to do this? Maybe I should just sit down with her and talk it out. No, Rachel has always been able to outdistance me with words. This will take action and threats. She'll not back down unless I threaten to kick her out and disown her, and my ace in the hole is that he is penniless. Rachel does love money and the power that it gives her. A romp in the hay cannot replace what I can give her, and she's clever enough to know it.

Well, it's now or never! He slowly approached the pond from the south side, where the willows that they had planted their first year of marriage were thick. That was twenty-two years ago. He heard nothing at first, then as he got closer he could hear muffled sounds. I don't want to see this. God! I hope I don't get sick. He could feel the bitterness crawl up into his throat, but he continued.

Parting the willows slowly before him, he was shocked when he actually saw them. They didn't hear him. Pulling the pistol out of his belt, he cocked it. They became still. Eben rolled over to find the muzzle pointed at his head.

Rachel, disheveled, looked up, hopped up and said, "This is no way to settle anything, Martin." Why was she so calm?

"You are wrong, my dear. This is indeed one way, and there is not a man alive who would not agree with me!"

Eben should have been frightened or at least surprised to be caught in such a predicament, but from his expression no one would have known it. "Your husband is right, dear Rachel. He has my permission to do whatever he feels is justified by the situation."

"That's ridiculous! He has no such right! I came here of my own accord—no one forced me. If you disagree, then I suggest that you take up the matter with the one who is at fault! And that, Martin, is your wife, and that is the last word I'll utter on the subject until you come to your senses!"

She brushed off her skirt, smoothed her hair, whirled around and proceeded to walk back to the main house.

The two men stared at her, not believing the scene they'd just witnessed. They turned and looked at each other. "That is one helluva woman you've got there, Martin." Eben shook his head, put on his bowler, brushed himself off and followed Rachel, thinking, he'll have to shoot me in the back if he has the nerve.

Martin did not have the nerve to shoot Eben, but he did have the nerve to yell after him, and that was even more devastating. "Ben Hunter, if you're not out of town by sundown, you and your family will feel my wrath. You think that Tempie owns that land...well, she doesn't and hasn't for years. I hold the note on it and will foreclose immediately. Do you hear that, Ben Hunter?"

Mistah Eben, we's heah suh. Ya had yose'f a nice little nap, din't he, Alpha?"

"I was just remembering the big parade down this street years ago, James. I'd seen some of the heaviest fighting at the end of the war, as had my army buddies, but wasn't 'til I came home that I was scared."

"How's dat, Mistah Eben?"

"I didn't know what the hell I was going to do with the rest of my life! I just knew that I couldn't stay in this one-horse town."

"What'd ya do?"

"Went to the coast and learned how to run rum, that's what I did." He looked up and down the street and grinned. "That's the best goddamned decision I ever made. Hell! I can buy the whole town with what I've got in the banks. Look at it! Half the stores are closed. It's a pathetic looking place."

They didn't see the tears slide down his cheeks as he approached the green doors of Ridgeway Enterprises.

CHAPTER EIGHT

Dr. Creel and Dr. Spooner had both attended Dunbar Anderson for almost two weeks. They declared the man to be well, but neither had been able to diagnose his illness. Dr. Creel thought that he had a nervous breakdown but, Dr. Spooner did not agree. He had known Dunbar since his arrival in the Glades and didn't think he had the temperament for a breakdown. No medication was prescribed, but with bed rest and the loving visits by his friends and neighbors he seemed to respond and return to normal.

"Jessup, I do believe that now is the time to return to Kansas for a little visit. I spoke to Dr. Spooner, and he felt that I was well enough to travel. Now don't look at me like that! I'll be fine."

"I think you're rushing it. Why don't you give yourself a few more weeks?"

"I can't! I mean that I feel like now is the time. My aunt is getting up there in age, and I haven't seen my cousins since I left."

Jessup sighed, knowing that arguing would do no good. "Well, I hope that you don't try to drive and will take the train."

"Haven't decided how I'm going to go yet. Would like to take my time, so might just drive and do a little sightseeing while I'm at it. Never have been to Savannah or Charleston or even St. Augustine, as far as that goes. Yep, think I'll do a little sightseeing."

"How long you gonna be gone? You've got a lot of responsibilities right here, you know."

"I'm not one to shirk my responsibilities, and you know it."

"What with Eben Hunter gone and now you, who're we gonna get to take the helm at Rotary and the church?"

"You got along very well without Mr. Hunter for a lot of years, so don't know why you're concerned now!"

"Well, Mr. Anderson, I didn't mean to get your balls in an uproar! You can't stand that man, can you?"

"I never said that, Jessup, and you know it!"

"You don't hafta say it. I can tell how you feel, and so can everyone in the entire city of Pahokee."

"That's ridiculous! I don't particularly like Hunter or trust him for that matter, but you can't say that I've ever been anything but pleasant to him. Frankly, I'd like to know how folks would feel about Mr. Hunter if they found out where he got all that money. And I'm not the only one who's suspicious, Just the other day Delmer Hooks was saying that he'd give his right arm to know where that Hunter crew got all that money. It's my bet that he came by it dishonestly!"

"You don't have any proof of that, Dunbar. I've never known anyone who has done more for the Glades then Eben Hunter and his brothers..."

"And how long have you known him, Jessup?'

"Just as long as you have, but I don't have your suspicious nature!"

Dunbar looked at him sternly. "I don't know why I feel like I do, but I'm certain he's a charlatan. And I don't like feeling this way, I can assure you. He's hoodwinking the entire Glades, and I, for one, resent it. I would think that you'd feel the same way..."

"Dunbar, I don't think I like what you're saying. It seems to me that you've taken it upon yourself to be the number one caretaker for the Glades. There's no one who loves this place more than I do, but I can't see what harm Eben Hunter and his brothers are doing. Just how do you think he made his money? And why do you think he came by it dishonestly? Do you think that he robbed a bank? Is that what you think? Now, if you had a shred of evidence, then I'd understand, but even you admit that it's just a gut feeling. I don't think that's fair."

Dunbar lowered his head, pursed his lips and mumbled, "This is the first argument we've ever had. Do you know that, Jessup? And he's the cause of it."

"He is not the cause of it. You're just overreacting, that's all. Now, let's go on over to Bolton's for a coke and stop this nonsense."

"I don't feel like it. I think I'll take a little rest and then write my Aunt Julia that I plan to pay her and my cousins a visit."

"Suit yourself! I declare you've gotten peculiar. I declare you have."

Well, maybe I have, friend Jessup, but when I come back from my trip and can show you proof about that Hunter crew, then you'll change your mind. I'll just take a little trip up to Savannah and do a little digging into the past of that wonderful man. At least, you and all these other fools think he's wonderful. I'll show all of you. Just might run into him up there and catch him red handed at whatever he's up to...

<hr>

I don't know why I've been feeling sick at my stomach lately. I'd better get down to Dr. Spooner's for a check up, thought Catherine Carroll. Gracious, I haven't had to visit the doctor since Jamie was almost two, and that was over four years ago. This isn't like me at all.

She walked down the back steps to the wooden sidewalk that Patrick had Marsh build between their little house and the big house and called Sammy. No answer. I bet she's at the quarters. That child is going to drive me insane before school's even out.

"Sammy Carroll, you come home this minute, do you hear!" Jamie came running from the groves and yelled, "She's warring with Wilbur, Mama. They're fighting with the hollow palm sticks the bumble bees live in. She's gonna get stung for sure..."

"She is what?"

He stopped, out of breath, and said, "You know! The sticks where the bumble bees bore into and make that loud humming sound when you put your ears to them. Then you war..."

"I don't have any idea what you're saying, Jamie, but I can assure you that I'm going to have to spank that child before this day's over!"

Oh, boy, she's gonna catch it now, he thought. I hope Mama lets me watch.

"Where is she?"

"Under the avocado trees, but they might have moved by now. Boy, they were really going at it, fencing like in the movies, but they hadn't broken the sticks yet," he said wiping his sweaty face on his shirt sleeve.

"Well, it's good for her that they haven't, or she'd be covered with bee stings. What possesses her, anyway? When I wanted her this morning she was up in the tallest coconut palm in the yard getting a coconut for Dessa. Said that she had promised to get her one for the pralines they were gonna make. No concern for what I want."

"You oughta spank her good, Mama. I mean a real hard one."

Catherine looked down at Jamie, his pug nose covered with those Irish freckles, and thought, you'd like that wouldn't you, son? Poor little Jamie. It isn't easy being the youngest and kept out of everything. Not easy at all. She stopped then. You don't suppose that I'm with child again. Dear Lord! What will Patrick say? No, I can't be. But, why not? I'll not think about it.

Catherine saw Dessa as she came out from the back porch closing the screen door. "Miz Carroll, I jes' saw Sammy playin' out back. You wants me ta go foah her?"

She thought, always covering for her, aren't you, Dessa? "No, thank you, Dessa. Jamie and I'll tend to her."

The way she said it made Dessa know that Sammy was in for trouble. Her first reaction was to intervene, but she decided to bide her time. Sammy's gonta hafta take care of huhse'f one of dese days, so she maght as well staht now. Ah hates ta see it. She lak mah own. Now wha can't Ah feel lak dat bout mah own flesh and blood? But Ah can't. He so stuck up wid his highfallutin' wife and younguns ovah in West Palm Beach jes waitin' fo' me ta die so he can get mah land... But Ah ain't a goin' ta tink on dat dis day. Bes tink 'bout mah Sammy and dat trouble she got huhse'f inta.

Dessa stayed on the screened back porch so she could see the commotion. Sure enough, Mrs. Carroll had Sammy by the ear and was giving her a tongue lashing, while Jamie was trying to smother his delight, his grubby hand hiding his mouth. Wilbur was saying that he was sorry, that he didn't know that Sammy wasn't allowed to war and that he meant no harm. But Sammy, for once in her life, had her mouth shut.

"If I ever catch you doing such a dumb thing again, young lady, then you'll really catch it! Just how do you think I'd get you to the doctor? Huh? How? You know I don't drive, and what would happen to you with all those bee stings? They could kill you! Do you want that?"

Sammy stopped up short. Oh, oh, thought Dessa. She's gonta explode.

"Mama," she said trying to hold her temper, "In the first place, I've been bumble bee warring since I was knee high, and to this day I've never been beat and I've never been stung, either. And the day that I'd let Wilbur best me in a bumble bee fight, then that'll be the day that I'm old as Methuselah!"

Catherine began to sniffle, then cry openly. Dessa was out the door, down the steps and over to her, saying, "Miz Carroll, heah, let me he'p ya. Ya jes distraught. Sammy din't mean no hahm. She jes rambunctious, dat's all."

She held onto Dessa's arm for support and said, "I don't know what' the matter with me lately. I've just not been myself."

Dessa looked back at Sammy and motioned for her to take her mother's other arm. "Mama, I didn't mean to make you sick, honest."

"She didn't mean anything, Mama," Jamie said, worried.

"I wish Patrick were here." She sighed, then began to sob.

"Sammy, ya go on ovah to de big house jes in case Mistah Samuel wakes up. Now, ya go lak Ah says. An, Wilbuh, ya go on home. She jes don't feel good."

"Ah'm gonna fix ya a nice cup o' tea wid some sweet honey in it jes lak youah daddy laks. Dat'll fix ya raght up."

Catherine sat with her head down on the kitchen table. When she raised her head, she was sure. Well, we always wanted four children. Guess we'll have to move into the big house now. Patrick won't like that, but it can't be helped. She smiled at Dessa. "Thanks Dessa. I'll be all right now. It's just that Sammy gets me so upset sometimes."

"She gets me upset, too, Mama," Jamie added.

"She jes got a lotta energy, dat's all. Now, ya wouldn't want huh ta be sickly, would ya?"

"Of course not! But I'm afraid that she's going to get hurt playing those dangerous games."

"Well, Miz Carroll, she say dat she ain't evah got stung, so maybe dey's not as dangerous as us grownups tink."

"Perhaps you're right. Thanks, Dessa. This tea hits the spot. Oh, have you heard anything from Alpha and James?"

"Not a single word, but den dey only been gone a little ovah a week."

"Mister Patrick said that Mr. Thornton had a phone call from Mr.

Eben and that they're having a wonderful time. Said that he's visiting his old school chums in Georgia."

Dessa thought but did not dare say, Ah wondah if he found hisse'f a wife? Ah miss Alpha and wish she'd come home soon. Ah'll need her when dat son o' mine comes out next week. Ah bes tell Miz Carroll 'bout his visit so Ah can get someone ta take care of Mistuh Samuel.

"Oh, Ah neah forgot ta tell ya, Miz Carroll. Mah son John comin' out ta see me next week an' Ah was wonderin' if ya could get someone ta stay wid Mistuh Samuel."

"Why, Dessa, I didn't know that you had a son!"

"Oh, yessum, Ah had mah John fo' goin' on tirty years now. His papa was drowned off de island a long time ago. He live in West Palm Beach wid his wife an' girls."

"Of course, I'll have someone stay with Daddy Samuel. You need time with your own. That will be lovely. I'm anxious to meet him and his family. Would you like me to prepare something special for them? Have lots of fat hens that I would be happy to cook up for you with some rice and..."

"Oh, no mahm. John, he'll want some fancy island food lak Ah used to fix foah..." She almost said Mistuh Eben, but caught herself in time... "Foah de man Ah used ta work foah. But dat was a long time ago back in de Bahamas."

<hr>

"Judson, old boy, you look great! Abigail must take good care of you."

"She always has, Ben," he replied getting up from his desk and shaking Ben's hand firmly. "God, it's good to see you." He stood back and said, "Damn you! You've not changed one bit, and look at me," he patted his stomach, "I've added a paunch and have only half my hair. Hell, I didn't think one did that until they hit forty."

Eben could see Ava through the door, pretending to be busy but not missing a word. I wonder if there's something going on between these two. No, I don't think Judson would be a part of a love affair. He's too solid.

Eben took his arm and moved him over by the window that faced the street. He whispered, "I want to talk to you without the keen ears of your secretary. Is there anywhere we can talk without her overhearing and spreading my business all over Springfield?"

"Of course, Ben. What's this all about?"

"Can you get away for a little while?"

"Well, yes, but I'm sure that Ava wouldn't be able to hear us if I closed the door."

"Wrong, old friend. This is too important to take a chance on. Wanta take a little ride? Let's go out to the old place and..."

"You don't want to go there, Ben, and you know it."

"I have nothing but happy memories of the place. I was upset that Aunt Tempie had such a lingering illness, but I saw to it that she had the best care money could buy. And in retrospect, I'm glad that Mama and Daddy went within days of each other. That's the way they would've wanted it."

Eben looked at Judson and continued, "You didn't know that I bought the place from the Aherns, did you?"

"No, I certainly didn't. When did that happen?"

They walked to Eben's car and Eben reached for the back door handle and continued, "About four years ago. Old Easterling had gone under by then and was not on top of things. You know he vowed that I'd never get my hands on anything that belonged to him."

"Yes, I was aware of that, but I didn't know you'd managed to outfox him. I should have known better," he said with a muffled laugh.

"James and Alpha, this is my dear friend Judson Ridgeway."

"It is sho nuff a pleasure ta meet one ah Mistah Eben's friends, ain't it, James?" Alpha said with her bright smile.

"James, you keep heading down this street, and we'll tell you when to turn."

They passed by the Easterling place, and Eben was surprised at how small it appeared. He had remembered it as tremendous. The grounds were well kept, and he turned to find Judson studying him.

"Who owns it now, Jud?"

"Someone from Atlanta bought it a few years back. His name is Champlain. A Yankee, I'm told. Hasn't gotten involved with a church or club or anything. Is into developing land or something like that. Met him briefly."

"Things have surely changed, haven't they? In the old days we'd have known him, his family and most of their secrets, huh?"

"You're right on the changes, Ben. The crash swept down even to little Rincon, and money's been tight ever since."

"But you're doing all right, aren't you?"

"I'm doing the best I can. Could be a lot better, though. We'll make it. Abigail is my strength. She always has been, and I make sure that she knows it, too." He laughed contentedly.

Now's the time to tell him about my mission, Eben thought. "James, when you get to that fork in the road, turn right. Now, friend Judson, I'll confess why I'm here. You're the only one to know about this besides a few people, and I know that you'll understand the necessity of keeping mum."

Eben unfolded the story of his quest, and while he was talking, Judson thought who but Ben would come up with such a harebrained way of selecting a wife? No normal courtship, no normal anything. He just wants the most beautiful girl, not a woman, but a girl, to father his perfect child, not children. He's in for a great deal of trouble, but I'd better not let on to him what I think, for it'll do no good. He seems to think that he can buy anything.

"Well, what do you think? Do I have a chance in hell of pulling it off?"

Judson gestured with his long arms and said, "Well, why not? Some men marry for love and take a chance on their children's health and good looks, and then there are others who marry for money, and then there are people like Ben Hunter who marry for...what did I hear you say? The most perfect woman...whoa...girl, not woman, and the most beautiful one to boot, who'll give him the handsomest son and..."

"You've missed the point, Jud!"

"Have I? You could have fooled me, Ben. Not one word about intelligence or a loving nature or..."

"I want it all, Jud! I want her to be everything any man could ever desire."

"All I heard you say was beautiful and young..."

"Well, hell, let me finish, will you? Oh, James, turn here."

Judson hadn't been out to the Rahn place in years. Had no reason to. When they drove up he noticed that the hedge was clipped just like he remembered and the front lawn was short, but the most obvious change was that the house had been painted white. He looked at Ben, and he was grinning.

"This is the Rahn place, James and Alpha. This is where I grew up."

"It be a handsome lookin' place, Mistah Eben. Look lak a nice place, sho 'nuff."

"They've done a nice job of keeping things up, haven't they?" He thought, they ought to; I pay them enough.

"And, Jud, I bought the two hundred acres that adjoin the place, too. Thinking about putting in field corn. What do you think?"

"I think that you should discuss it with Johnny Ahern, and you can start right now 'cause here he comes."

It was obvious that Johnny Ahern knew who the visitor was by the way he rushed out to greet him, smiling broadly as he came.

"Well, now, and is it my landlord that I'm having the pleasure of meeting?" he asked gleefully.

"Indeed it is, Johnny, and this is my friend Judson Ridgeway, and my friends from Florida, Alpha and James."

They shook hands, but Alpha and James got behind Eben, holding back, embarrassed. As the three men walked up the brushed path Eben noticed that every window in the house had several faces peering out at them. Johnny laughed again and whispered, "My missus is very excited about your visit, and the children are beside themselves with the wonder of it all. Maureen said that she had never had the pleasure of meeting a real landlord in the flesh before. She's my oldest."

"Well, she'll discover that he doesn't have a forked tail like Simon Legree, nor does he have a ..."

He didn't finish his sentence, because out of the front door walked the most beautiful creature he had ever seen, and Judson could attest to it. They both stood dumb struck.

Eben whispered, "My Lenore, Jud. My God, it's my Lenore."

Johnny didn't see their reaction, for he was motioning to the parlor window for his missus to come out. She was quite shy, so she'd sent Maureen.

Her eyes were sea green and almond shaped, fringed in long, black lashes and set in milk-white skin. Her hair was the color of a raven and just as shiny.

Eben gulped and looked at Jud, who was looking at him. The girl must have been about seventeen or eighteen, Eben thought, assessing the situation. Have I found her? My God! Is this really my Lenore? She was as tall as her father, almost five foot eight, and slender, but it was obvious that she was all female, curved where she should have curves.

Mrs. Ahern finally managed to come outside, and Eben could see where Maureen got her looks. She was not as tall, but having her eight children had not destroyed her shape. Good breeder, he thought.

"Mr. Hunter, sir, this is my eldest. Maureen say a greeting to Mr. Hunter. Maureen's completed the twelve years and made the highest marks in all of..."

She grimaced and quickly said, "Da, that'll be enough. He doesn't want to hear..."

"Oh, but I do. I want to hear all about...your school and..."

Judson intervened. "Ben, I bet Mrs. Ahern's got the tea on, and we can all relax and have a nice visit. Right, Mrs. Ahern?" God! He's salivating. He'd better calm it or he'll spoil everything. Slow down, friend of mine, he indicated, pinching his arm.

At the idea of fixing tea for the guests, Nora Ahern relaxed and invited them inside. She shooshed the other children outside, who seemed to be pouring out of every door, and told each one what his chore was. Eben could tell that she had gone to special pains to fix the parlor for his visit, but he would have preferred to sit in the kitchen as he had as a boy.

But he'd sit anywhere where he could look at Maureen and listen to her. Had Poe seen her he would have used her as his inspiration instead of his wife Lenore, he thought. She spoke with a slight Irish lilt but had added the soft southern way of expressing herself. He loved it but knew that when he took her to Pahokee the Irish part would have to go. A good finishing school in Atlanta or maybe Savannah would definitely be necessary.

"Ben, where are your manners? Mrs. Ahern has asked you twice if you want cream?"

"Oh," he sighed, "I'm just remembering when I lived here as a young man." He turned to Maureen. "Maureen, it is Maureen, isn't it?"

Nora continued to pour his tea. "Yes, that is my name." Nora might be shy, but she was not blind. It was obvious that Mr. Hunter was taken with her eldest.

"Did you say cream, Mr. Hunter?" she asked, breaking the spell.

"Call me Ben, Mrs. Ahern. There's no need to be formal, now is there?"

Johnny slapped his knee and said, "I told that very thing to Nora last night. I told her that I could tell a man's nature by how he wrote, and that your letter was a very friendly one, and that we had not a worry in the world."

"You're correct, Johnny. I'm not a formal fellow. Never have been. I like things very casual and relaxed. Isn't that so, Judson?"

"It was when you lived in Springfield, Ben, but people change, you know."

Now why did he say that? Just when I'm trying to get her to relax and be herself—my beautiful Lenore.

They drank their tea, and Johnny tried to keep the conversation going. Ben added little to it, he was so nervous, something unusual in him. Finally, when he knew that his control was slipping, he excused himself with the excuse of checking on Alpha and James.

"My missus will get them some tea or lemonade, Mr. Hunter. And there's a nice bench underneath the oak in the side yard for them to enjoy the shade. No need for you to go out in the heat of the day. Sit! Sit!"

"Thank you, Johnny." He turned to Maureen and asked, "Would you be so kind as to get them some cool lemonade, Maureen? I'd like to go over some business with your folks."

Maureen stood, smoothed her pale print dress that hugged her rounded hips, straightened the bow in the back and looking at him directly, answered, "No trouble at all, Mr. Hunter. It's really much too hot for them to be out in the sun."

She's compassionate. I like that.

"Could you use some assistance?"

When he said that, Judson, Johnny and Mrs. Ahern all looked at him. He knew immediately that he had tipped his hand, so added, "They're very shy. From the Islands, you know, the Bahamas, and aren't used to being served by a White."

Whew! Think I got out of that one, but when he looked at Jud, Jud shook his head as if to say, you messed up, old friend. Now Johnny and his missus are suspicious, not to mention your Lenore.

Judson jumped up and said that he would accompany Maureen. Eben knew that he was aware of his nervousness, and that would give him a chance to calm down. You're a good friend, old buddy, he thought. Put in a good word for me.

Eben stood and walked to the window so he could watch them. "I've decided that I need to work more closely with you on the farm's future, Johnny. We need to visit the farmer's bureau here and see what they think of the field corn suggestion, and there are a number of other things I need to discuss with you. I'll be around for a while yet." He was talking to the Aherns, but his eyes never left the window and Lenore.

He was smiling when he said it, so Johnny relaxed. He and Nora were unsure why their landlord had decided on a visit. After all, Johnny and his family were being well paid, but then the farm had made money, not much, but it had done much better than most in the county.

Nora watched him as he watched Lenore.

<hr>

When Dunbar Anderson arrived in Savannah, the first thing he did was ask the proprietor at the small hotel, where he had found an inexpensive room, the locations of the largest banks. If Mr. Eben Hunter was who he said he was, then surely they would have heard of him and known his business.

He had eaten a large breakfast in the hotel dining room. He usually didn't have more than a leftover piece of corn bread or biscuit and his coffee while in Pahokee, but he felt like celebrating. What, he did not know. His energy seemed renewed.

First Bank on Oglethorpe St. was his first stop. It was one of the oldest banks in the city, and he was sure that he would be able to gather the information he sought. It was an imposing building, about ten times the size of the Bank of Pahokee, but he gathered his resolve and entered with confidence. The elderly man at the teller's cage seemed the appropriate one to question. The other employees were probably too young to have known Hunter.

"Excuse me, sir, but I have a number of questions to ask and need to know if you're the one with the information."

The teller said, "We'll both know after you've asked, won't we?"

Dunbar didn't care for his impudent manner but was committed, so proceeded. "I am Edward Anderson from Kansas and need some information on a Mr. Eben Hunter, formerly of Savannah, I was told."

"And what kind of information do you seek, sir?"

"I need to know if he has ever done business with your bank, and what his financial standing is and..."

"Then you'll need to speak with our vice president, Mr. Appleby. I'll see if he is busy."

The teller left Dunbar standing, looking as uncomfortable as he felt, with the other tellers all staring at him—at least he felt that they were. He turned and pretended to be studying the large paintings on the walls.

He heard his name called, and when he turned, the teller with whom he had been speaking motioned to him to follow. They entered a large room, and behind the long, highly polished oak desk sat a very small, bald-headed man wearing spectacles, peering over them at Dunbar. He, at that moment, would have gladly said that he had made a mistake and left, but he couldn't. He had come this far, and these city slickers were not going to deter him.

He extended his hand to the minute man when he rose, and again introduced himself, using the name of his father.

"Mr. Anderson, be seated. Now what is this all about?" His voice was as small as its owner, and Dunbar had difficulty hearing him.

"As I explained to the other gentleman, I am from Kansas and have need of information about a Mr. Eben Hunter, who, I was told, was from Savannah. This concerns a business transaction between him and my family, whom I represent."

"It is not customary for the bank to give out confidential information, but I will at least search our files to see if we have ever done business with the man. If you'll be patient, I'll have Shirley go into our back files. When was the man in Savannah?"

"I'm not sure, but he's about thirty-four or five now, and it was my understanding that he and his family lived in this part of the state. He has brothers with the names of Ralph, Emerson and Thornton."

"This might take a while, but if you're in no hurry I'll get Shirley on it immediately. In the meantime I would suggest that you take a stroll around our beautiful city and return about," he pulled his pocket watch out and resumed, "shall we say, ten o'clock."

Dunbar stood, shook his hand and said, "That will be fine, Mr. Appleby. My family and I shall appreciate any information you can give us. There are so many charlatans around these days that one cannot be too careful."

"You are certainly correct, Mr. Anderson. Correct indeed."

Dunbar did as Mr. Appleby suggested and walked around the city. It was indeed beautiful. He spent the last hour sitting on a bench in Columbia Square watching the people, but he wished that he were back in Pahokee. He had already made up his mind that as soon as he got his information he was going to return. He truly had no desire to proceed to Kansas. He never had. That was just a ruse to satisfy Jessup.

His watch said nine fifty-five. He began his walk back to the bank, deciding that if First Bank didn't have the information, then he'd go to every bank in the entire city that had been in operation for the last twenty years. He'd get what he needed, and if none of them had information on that Hunter trash, then his suspicions would be correct. They were imposters and had got their money by devious means. He was sure of it.

Mr. Appleby received him with the news that First Bank had no record for the past fifty years of anyone named Eben Hunter nor of his brothers. Dunbar thanked him profusely and said that he would do as he suggested and visit the other banks in the city.

It was after three o'clock when Dunbar returned to his hotel. He had visited three other banks, and none had ever heard of the Hunters. He was elated at first, but when the man at the last bank said that there were a lot of small towns around Savannah and that perhaps the Hunters had done business with them, he felt dejected. He hadn't thought of that.

He asked the man about how many towns he thought there would be. He scratched his head and answered, "There must be at least two dozen or so. There are a lot of very wealthy people who prefer to do business in their own hometowns, you know."

Dunbar realized that he was right. After all, he preferred to keep his money in Pahokee instead of West Palm Beach. He hated to return to Pahokee empty handed. He was right back where he started. What should he do? He missed his home, his town, his friends, but an answer to Eben Hunter was necessary. He wanted his town back.

<hr />

Catherine Carroll was now sure that she was expecting. The early morning nausea had returned. Dashing out the back door and heaving until she felt her toes would be the next thing she'd toss was an every-morning occurrence. It was the bacon! That had done it every time with the other three children. She'd have to tell Patrick, because he wanted his bacon or ham every morning without fail.

Waving to Marsh, who was on his way to milk Aunt Maude, she returned to the kitchen, turned off the fire underneath the frying pan, took a cold cloth to her face and decided that this would be the day, whether she wanted to tell him or not. And wouldn't you know that summer was just approaching, and it would be hot as Hades, and the children would drive her crazy with their fighting, and Patrick would be bored with little to do during the summer months, and...

General was at the back door waiting for his master to awaken. Catherine looked at him wagging his tail and said, "General Lee, you're going to have to share him with a wee one in about seven or so months, sir. Don't know how you'll take to that as jealous as you are. But, old boy, you'll have to. Your master dearly loves his babies."

She heard Patrick stir, then their bedroom door close, and decided that after he had paid his call to the bathhouse she would tell him. She wanted to get it over with before the children awakened, so that should give her a half hour.

"Good morning, my love," she said giving him a hug. "Have your eggs going in a minute."

They saw Dessa go into the big house, and she waved a greeting.

Dessa thought as she went into the kitchen to get Mistah Samuel's coffee going, Ah wondah if she tol' him, yet? Frankly, Ah wondah if she even know dat she carryin'? Dat Sammy gonta have a quiet summer wid all dat goin' on. Ah best tink o' somet'in' foah dose chilren ta do. Maybe Sammy can staht dat milk delivery business she been talkin' 'bout. Aunt Maude got moah an' moah every day, Marsh say.

General found a place underneath the kitchen table as close to his master as he could, but Catherine pushed him with her shoe and told him to go into the living room, that the kitchen was her domain. Patrick laughed at the two of them, shook his head, and Catherine sat down across from him.

"I have something to tell you. No, go ahead and eat." She hesitated, then gushed it all out before she gave in to tears.

"Are you sure?"

"I'm sure. This is the fifth or sixth time that I've had to dash for the door. You know how I can't stand the smell of bacon or ham in the morning..."

"You're a wonder, Mrs. Carroll. You truly are. And here I wasn't even looking forward to the summer. Come here to me."

She rose slowly, he put his arm around her waist and pulled her down to him. He kissed her lightly, patted her bottom and stated, "It'll be another boy."

"How on earth do you know that?"

"I just do, that's all. Oh, I know that there's a lot of years in between, but he'll be a special child, I can tell."

"I wish I were as sure. I hate the long dog days of summer even when I'm not with child. But I do so hate the swollen legs and feet and the insufferable heat. Should I tell the children?"

"Why don't you hold off 'til you've seen Dr. Spooner?"

"You're right, but I'm sure. Think I'll not tell Clara. She'll have a fit! I promised her that this was definitely the summer that I'd go with her to the coast to the baths, and again something has come up."

"Why can't you go? You'll be in your early months. Will do you good."

"I wouldn't feel right about it for some reason, but maybe you're right. With Dessa here to take care of Daddy Samuel and to watch the children, it might be the only time. I'll think on it."

"Thornton said yesterday that Eben had called and that he'd decided to stay for a while longer. Guess he's having himself a high old time of it." He wanted to share the news about the possibility of an upcoming wedding, but he had promised Eben. This whole town will be set on its ear when they find out, he thought, chuckling. Catherine laughed with him, thinking that he was just showing his happiness about the new baby.

Patrick got up and so did General. He turned toward him and said, "Come on, old boy. You're going to have to share me before long." He began whistling even before he got out the back door.

Why was I worried about his reaction? There never was a man who loved his babies more than Patrick Carroll. I'm a lucky woman. She began humming, and when Mary Catherine came into the kitchen mumbling something about how she had to practice *Andalusia* for the school program, Catherine was all smiles. Normally she would have given her what for for waiting til the last minute to practice.

CHAPTER NINE

The Ridgeway house was the same one that Judson and Abigail had moved into when they were first married. It was spacious and charming and suited the two of them. He could walk to work and she to most of the club and church functions she attended. Their two children, Gale and Jacob, were thirteen and ten years old, respectively. The ideal family, Eben thought, as he sat with them on the warm veranda. He and Judson sipped a tall, cool scotch and water, and Abigail had iced tea. Their conversation was about the olden days and the children they'd grown up with.

Abigail was the first to bring up the Ahern family. Eben looked at Judson and realized that he had told her at least part of what was happening. How much he didn't know.

"Thornton contacted me down in Florida, oh, in '28, and said that there was a family that was interested in renting the place from Martin Easterling. How he found out I don't know. So I said to contact the family and tell them that I'd front them with the money and that perhaps they could buy it, that is, if old Martin would sell it. So, that's what happened. Martin was desperate, and everyone knew it. He had over-extended himself at the bank, and any money was better than no money at all."

"I was wondering how you'd pulled that off, 'cause I knew that he'd never sell it to you directly," stated Judson.

"It was easy as pie. Johnny Ahern bought it, then deeded it back to me with the understanding that he and his family would be paid a sum to run the farm and that, if they did a good job, the place was theirs for as long as they wanted it. I knew that I'd never return here to live, and the boys wanted to get out as badly as I did."

"It's not a bad place to live, Ben," Abigail said.

"I know that, Abigail, but it's a dead-end place. When I walked downtown this afternoon, I could feel and smell the decay. I'm not sure it'll ever come back like it was when we were growing up..."

"Maybe not the same, but I can see signs of better things to come, Ben," Judson interjected.

"Is that the scotch talking, Jud?" he questioned with his full, rich laughter.

Abigail looked at the two of them and smiled. "I love seeing you two together again. It's like old times. Ben, we're just going to have a cold supper, if that's all right with you." She rose and called to the children, who were playing in the side yard with some neighborhood friends, and went into the house to see to their light supper.

Ben called after her, "I need my strength, Abby, but guess a light supper will have to do." He looked at Judson and asked, "Did you tell her, Jud?"

"I only hinted, Ben. I'd promised that I wouldn't actually tell her until you gave me permission."

"Well, now's the time."

"Now! When did you pull it off? Have you actually spoken for her hand, and Johnny's given his approval?"

"Might as well say that I have."

"Have you or not?"

"Well, yes and no," he said pouring himself another drink. He looked at Judson and said, "I've got to have her. You know that."

"I knew that the minute you saw her. But, Ben, you don't know a thing about the girl except that she's beautiful and apparently bright. I did tell Abigail that we'd met the most beautiful girl either of us had ever seen. She said that she'd heard what a beautiful girl she was and also how smart. Falkner Bennett at the bank has already asked her to work there. Said that he'd train her and give her a good salary, Janet Albritton told Abigail. Said that she was the best student she'd ever taught."

"She'll not be working at any bank, I can assure you."

"Do you really think that she'll be happy moving all the way down to Florida away from her folks? That is what you have in mind, isn't it?"

"Hell yes, that's what I have in mind. What do you take me for? Any wife of mine goes where I say she'll go!"

"This one might not take to your high handed ways, sir. This one seems to have some get-up-and-go about her!"

"That's another thing I like about her. She has some starch in her spine. She'll make a good mother for my son."

"I never in all my life met anyone who was as sure of himself as you are, Ben Hunter. She might not like you. Did you ever think of that?"

"Yes," he answered softly, "I've thought of that. I even mentioned it to Johnny. But he said that it would just take her some time."

"When did all this take place? When did you talk to Johnny?"

"This afternoon, early. We discussed it over a pint."

"I thought that you seemed to be all mellowed out when you arrived. Well, what was the outcome?"

"He gave his permission. What did you think he'd do? Hell, the man's got ten mouths to feed."

"So, you bought her. That's what you did, just like a prize cow!" Judson was feeling his scotch too.

"You best not be slamming that door, Maureen. I've made up my mind." He belched and Nora slammed down his dinner plate not caring if the gravy splashed all over creation.

"I want more for our daughter, Johnny Ahern, and you best be a knowin' that, sir. I don't want her droppin' a babe every year. She's smart, and her school teacher said that she should be goin' to the teachers college in Savannah. You know that is what she wants..."

"Stop your busy mouth, Nora Elizabeth. 'Tis my decision to make, and I didn't come by it lightly, either. Ben Hunter assured me that he'd take good care of her, set her up in a big mansion, and treat her like a queen. Now what's a father to do when a man comes a courtin' and promises him that for his first born? Tell me, what is a man to do?"

Maureen came out of the room that she shared with her four other sisters and said, "I'll be tellin' you what a man is to do, Da! First, he should ask his daughter if she's a wanting to wed the man. That's the first thing he's to do. Then he's to ask her if she's not interested in marrying the man, what's she to do with the rest of her life. Then his daughter will answer, 'well, da of mine, I'll be taking the job at the bank that Mr. Bennett has offered, save my money and then go to the teachers college in Savannah', like she's been dreamin' about. Da, that's what you should do!"

What Johnny did not tell either one was that Eben had promised him the farm for the hand of Maureen. How could he refuse? His own land...his own land...

<hr>

When Eben left Judson's, he drove himself out to the farm, telling Alpha and James that they could have themselves a nice evening at the boarding house in colored town. They did not look forward to that but decided they'd explore the area, what there was of it, then go back to the boarding house for the evening. They were very uncomfortable without "Mistah Eben" around.

Eben was apprehensive. He and Johnny had decided that he could start his formal courtship this evening. He wondered how Lenore had taken the news of their impending betrothal. She seemed to have a spark and a self-assurance that he found enchanting, but if she was stubborn then she might reject her father's commitment. He'd know soon.

He could see the children playing in the field next to the house, just like he and his brothers had done. Dusk was a great time to play kick the can or tackle football. He pulled the Packard up alongside the hedge and got out. Special pains had been taken with his dress. He didn't want to be formal and wear a suit, so he dressed like he did in Florida, wearing his riding britches, open necked shirt and boots.

Maureen saw him drive up and stomped her foot. Who do they think they are, planning my life without even asking me? I think I'll run away, that's what! But then, what would Mum do without me? She has to work so hard, and the boys are always in the fields, and Clare is only eleven, so what help is she, and...there are too many ands, that's what!

She saw her da practically run out to greet that Eben Hunter, and he was grinning his head off as they talked about her, no doubt. She threw herself onto the closest double bed and beat it with her fist. Her mum called. She didn't answer. She heard the door open quietly and felt her mum's hand on her shoulder.

"Mum, I hate this, I really do."

"I know, my precious one, I know. You haven't known any of the local boys 'cause you've been so busy with your lessons. I know."

"You don't understand, Mum. You don't. I've had my life planned for a long time now. Miss Albritton and I've been talking about the teachers college ever since I was in tenth grade. Da doesn't understand that I don't even want a husband. Does he know why I wouldn't go with Donal Sullivan to the school dance? Why? 'Cause I don't want to get involved with a fellow, that's why. I want to teach, Mum. I want to teach!"

<hr />

"It's understandable that she's upset, Johnny. I understand completely. But when I explain about my town of Pahokee and all the advantages she'll have there, I think she'll come around. It'll take some time, but I hope not long. I'm warning you that I'm not a patient man."

"She's got a stubborn streak like my sister Mary Ellen, she does. Never a man would she have a thing to do with 'til she was nigh on thirty year old. Just up and married a fine man from Boston. Gave him five healthy lads, she did, and seems as happy as God intended."

"There's no reason that Maureen and I won't have the same luck, Johnny. No reason at all. Let me handle this. I've been told that I have a way with women." He winked and they both laughed.

Here they come to examine their prize sow, no doubt, Maureen thought. Think I'll just put Mr. Hunter in his place, I will.

She came out of her room and went to the parlor where Eben, her da and mum were in conversation. Eben looked up when he heard her. He couldn't seem to get his breath. He could see that she had changed into another dress, and that pleased him. Guess she knows that it is inevitable.

"Mr. Hunter, I've been informed that you've asked for my hand in marriage. Is that correct?"

"Yes, it is, Maureen," he answered, taken aback by her directness. "But I did not know that we would start our..." he winked again at Johnny, "courtship without you and me discussing the matter. If it pleases you, I think that we should spend a great deal of time together to see if we are suited. If that suits you, that is."

She was a little surprised by his explanation, and so were her mum and da. Johnny started to protest, but Eben held his arm and continued, "Johnny, I know that you and I have had a serious conversation about this, but I know that modern girls don't like to be treated like, shall we say, cattle." He laughed and turned toward Johnny and gave him a wink to indicate that he was playing Maureen along. Maureen wasn't sure whether it was a genuine laugh or not, so let no expression show on her beautiful face.

Have I scored, Eben wondered. She shows no emotion. He proceeded. "I was wondering if we could take a little walk down to the pond and get to know each other before we continue the proposed arrangement. Would that suit you, Maureen?"

She shrugged and said, "Then I'll change my slippers. These are my good ones."

He wanted to say, I'll buy you hundreds of slippers before I'm through, my Lenore, hundreds.

They went through the kitchen, and Eben was disappointed. None of his mother's things were there, but why should they be? The boys had taken everything of value out before the Aherns moved in. But he was still shocked.

He decided to let Maureen begin the conversation, but when she said nothing the silence bothered him. So, he began. "That willow tree is the one where we almost hung Thornton, my brother. Lucky for him that Mama saw what we were about and came to his rescue. He was our nuisance brother." He laughed when he remembered.

Maureen looked at him and saw that he was enjoying remembering. She said, "My brother Liam is our devilish one. He's always getting one of us in trouble."

"I guess every family has one," he added.

They had arrived at the pond by then. Eben said, "It'll be dark soon, Lenore."

"Why do you call me that? That's the second time you've called me that. I like my name and prefer that you call me by it."

"It's just that the first time I saw you I thought of the poem by Edger Allen Poe—you know *The Raven* and the line where he referred to his long lost Lenore."

"Yes, I remember it. We had to memorize it in English class, but I still wish to be called by my real name."

"Wouldn't it be all right, if we do wed, that I have a special name for you? Is there anything wrong with that?"

She thought a while and said, "*If* we wed, then I guess it will be all right. But only *if* we wed."

"Thank you for your permission, my dear," Eben said with a mischievous grin as he raised her hand and kissed it.

She smiled, enjoying his humor. Good, he thought, she has a sense of humor. I'm beginning to think that I've found the most perfect woman in the world for me.

"It's getting dark, Maureen, and we need to go back to the house. I was wondering if you would do me the honor of dining with me tomorrow evening? Savannah is not that far away, and we could leave early and have a leisurely ride. There are so many lovely restaurants that I'd like to show you."

She lowered her head and said softly, "I don't have the proper dress for a fine restaurant, Mr. Hunter."

"Stop calling me that. Please! My name is Eben or Ben, whichever you prefer, but my dear Lenore...oops! I did it again..."

"That's all right, Eben. It doesn't sound so funny when you call me that now, like it did at first."

"I'll have my man bring out a special dress for you to wear, if you'd like that. Would that suit you? I desperately want you to accompany me, and if the only way that can be accomplished is for you to have a new dress, then a new dress it is."

"Oh, it isn't that I want a new dress, it's just that I don't have an appropriate one."

"The matter has been resolved, Lenore. Do you have a preference as to style or color?"

"Oh, no. But I am partial to soft colors like lavender or peach or..."

"Lavender it is then. It'll bring out the green in your eyes." He took her arm, turned her around to him and said, "You are the most beautiful woman I've ever seen, dear Lenore. I've known a great many women and have seen none to compare."

She blushed and could not, for once in her life, find her tongue.

⁂

"Abigail, stop stewing!" Judson admonished her. "She is not the queen of England. She's just a poor girl who happens to be blessed with an incredible beauty, that's all. The rack of lamb with mint sauce is appropriate. The Irish enjoy their lamb. And roasted potatoes with Brussels sprouts are another good choice. You've had prominent women and men to our home numerous times, and I've never seen you like this."

She sighed loudly. "You are absolutely correct, dear husband, and on those occasions I knew exactly what the conversation would be, how they would dress and just what to expect. On this occasion I haven't the foggiest idea what will happen. It's unnerving, to say the least. Why can't Ben take us out to dine instead of coming here?"

"And just where do you think he could take us in this town? He wants to get her used to his friends, honey. This is all so new to her, and he does want to break her in to her new life easily."

"That's commendable of him, seeing as how he bought her like a...a rack of lamb!"

"Stop it, Abigail. I should have never told you that. Not a word of this to anyone, and I mean it!"

"We've never had a fight in fourteen years of marriage until Mr. Ben Hunter came on the scene. Never!" She ran from the room with Judson right behind her. "Honey, I didn't mean to be cross...Abigail, honey..."

When she didn't respond, he went to his study and poured himself a stiff scotch. Sitting in his hunter green easy chair, he put his feet on the ottoman and looked through the French windows that overlooked the back yard. You know, she's right. What is it about Ben that brings the beast out in me? He smiled and remembered some of their escapades, rose and poured himself another stiff drink and began laughing out loud. Abigail opened the door softly, and when she saw his outline and heard him laugh, she closed the door and realized that he was re-living his boyhood with his friend.

Jud's laughter swelled the room. I can't believe that Ben's naming his new house Elsinore. God! I wonder if anyone remembers that's the name he and Aunt Tempie named their pig pen when they thought that they'd get rich raising those hogs. What did they name them? Oh, yes. Hamlet and Ophelia, and the others were Romeo and Juliet and Cleopatra, and what was the other sow...had to have them butchered when Reddick went in the hole in that get-rich-quick scheme he and John Harrington got themselves into.

Abigail leaned against the closed door. I shouldn't disturb him. He has become so serious these past years that it's good to hear him laugh once more. She retired to their bedroom. In a way Ben is good for him...he's good for me, too. We've been in such a rut.

Unbeknownst to the other brothers, Thornton Hunter had been given the go-ahead to purchase a piece of land on Bacom Point Rd. in Pahokee for Eben. Eben wanted to begin his dream home for his bride. He had not told it to Thornton, but he'd hired an architect in West Palm Beach the year before, when he decided to seek a wife.

While in Savannah he had visited several firms for information on the finest artisans he could hire for the interior. He knew what he wanted and was willing to pay for it. He was told that the best cabinet makers and interior finishers were in Thomasville, Georgia. He intended to visit there on his way back to Florida, but first he needed to find a finishing school in the area for his Lenore.

He didn't expect it to take long, for she was an apt pupil and needed just the rough edges smoothed. He hoped that she would be as apt in their other pursuits, for he was having a difficult time restraining his ardor. Their Savannah trip had been a huge success. There was not a head in the dining room that had not turned toward them when they entered. She was glowing in the soft lavender silk dress. She had the presence to follow his lead as to which utensil to use, and even before they were into their entree she had relaxed and had kept him charmed with her animated conversation. The wine had helped, for she was not used to it.

He had been away from Pahokee for three weeks and was anxious to return. He spoke with Johnny and Nora about the finishing school in Atlanta, and they suggested that he also speak with Maureen. Things had been going so well that he was hesitant, but he saw the wisdom in their suggestion.

He was expecting an outburst of rebellion, but there was none. She said that if she was indeed to become his wife there were things that she needed to know. He was relieved. He asked her if she wanted to wed before she went away to school or afterward and where she would like the ceremony.

"I think that it would be better if we wait 'til after I've finished. Maybe I'll not pass, and you'll not want me." When she said that, he grabbed her and kissed her hungrily. He was as much surprised as she was.

"I'm sorry, I hadn't planned on doing that 'til later, much later."

She was flushed. When she recovered her composure she said, "If I'm to be your wife, Eben, then kissing me should be part of the arrangement, don't you think?"

"You bet it should!" He kissed her again, this time a long, smoldering kiss. She returned his kiss, and it was Eben who pushed her away.

"Whoa, young lady, this'll have to wait until after we're married."

"Maybe we'd better marry before my schooling then." She was serious when she said it.

"Father Rooney, sir, 'tis about my eldest, Maureen, and her intended, sir," Johnny said, embarrassed to even be in the presence of the priest.

"Sit, John, and unburden yourself." The priest could tell how nervous the man was by the way he was folding and unfolding his felt hat brim. *She's probably with child, and he wants to hurry up the bans.*

Father Rooney was absorbing the news when Johnny quickly added, "Ah, Father, the problem is that he is not Catholic. Now he is a God-fearing man, but he is not Catholic. Now the man is a wealthy man and can give her everything money can buy, and he's even offered me the title to the farm." He was short of breath but continued, "That is not to be repeated, Father, for I've not even told my missus. He wants to send her to a fancy school in Atlanta to teach her how to be a lady, so she can run his big mansion in Florida, where he lives."

"Aye, and is there a nice church for her to attend when she gets to that wild state?"

"There's one in progress, I'm told. Mr. Hunter says that the area where he lives is growing by leaps and bounds, and that their future looks bright."

"And I would say that your future looks bright too, aye, John?"

"Aye, that you can."

"I find no problem with such a marriage, provided that the man signs the papers, stipulating that their children be raised in the faith, but then I'm sure we'd have no reason for concern regarding that, or should we?"

"My Maureen would see to it, Father. Of that you can be sure."

"Send the man to me, and we'll get acquainted, then. And when does this marriage need to be?"

"Mr. Hunter wants it to be performed during the Christmas season. He said that'll give him time to complete the big house he is having built and time for Maureen to finish her schooling and to get her wedding finery ordered. He'll be up here to oversee everything—with her assistance, of course."

"I see," Father Rooney uttered, and thought, *I'm anxious to meet the man. Perhaps he will be as generous to the poor in Springfield and even assist us in building a church here. This business of having to drive out from Savannah every Sunday and holy day does take its toll. A feather for Johnny and all his kin. A real feather.*

Dunbar had decided to travel to two or three towns outside of Savannah to see what he could find out about Eben. He went to the small town of Midway, simply because it was on his way back to Florida. If that failed, then there were others that he could visit close by.

As he feared, no one had heard of the Hunters. It wasn't in his nature to abandon a mission as important as this one, but he was so homesick he gladly aborted it. When he got to the Florida-Georgia border, he heaved a huge sigh of relief. Only two more days and I'll be home. This should satisfy Jessup. Not a single person had heard of that trash in an entire area. That should stand for something.

<hr/>

Clara told Walter the news about Catherine's pregnancy as soon as she knew it. He became very quiet. They had both wondered why they had not been able to have more than one child, and it did bother him. They were grateful for Clarissa, but having a son would have been their wish fulfilled. She had prayed on it for five years, but the good Lord hadn't heard her, she told Catherine.

"I'm still going to Safety Harbor with you, so don't you get upset about it. Patrick has insisted. Dessa has been spoken to and has agreed to take care of the children, and since Daddy Samuel will be with us, that'll relieve her somewhat. Even Marsh has said that he would help. You can send Clarissa over here for the time we're away."

<hr/>

"She's what!" shouted Sammy when they were told at the supper table about Clarissa's coming to stay. "Does Dessa know? She might not stay with us if that brat is here."

"That's enough, Sammy. Quite enough! She's not that bad. I know that she's a baby about a lot of things, but you have to understand that she's an only child."

"I wish I was an only child! Bet I wouldn't suck an old stinking thumb! That thing's gonna fall off, it's so rotten."

"Maybe you and Dessa can put a spell on her, Miss Smarty," Mary Catherine interjected between bites.

"Yeh, just maybe we can, toad face!"

"That's enough, you two," Patrick said firmly.

They both concentrated on their supper while Jamie got quiet and poked at his food.

"Jamie, son, are you all right?" Catherine asked.

"I'm fine. How long you gonna be gone?"

"We'll be back even before you can miss us." She looked at him and realized that he was truly upset. She looked at Patrick for help, and he said, "Hey, son, you know what we can do while your mama's gone? We can take the boat over to Salerno and go fishing for blues. They should be running about then."

"I don't wanta."

"I do!" shouted Sammy. "I'll go with you, Daddy. Boy howdy, I bet we'll catch a whole boat full."

"You'll have to stay here to help Dessa, honey. She'll have her hands full with this tribe."

"Well, son, if you don't want to go fishing, then why don't we go to Lake Worth to the big pool they've just built? The paper said that the Lido pool is the finest one in the country."

"I can't swim good. I might drown. Then what would Mama do without me?"

Catherine got up and took him by the hand, pulled him to her and said, "Jamie, I don't know what I'd do without you. You're my little boy..."

"But you might get you another one," Sammy said.

"But it wouldn't be my Jamie. It would just be a little baby, and Jamie'd have to help me with it and teach it all sorts of things. You'd be the BIG BROTHER. How about that?"

He sighed and said, "Do you mean that I'll have to teach him how to fish and swim, 'cause I can't do those real good."

"You can't now, but by the time he's big enough to learn, you'll know how real well."

"You mean good like Sammy does?"

"Yes," she nodded with a smile, "just like Sammy does." She hesitated then added, "Maybe even better than Sammy."

He hopped up on his chair and began eating his greens, forgetting that he didn't like them.

Patrick found Catherine's hand beneath the table and squeezed it. He was smiling. So was she.

CHAPTER TEN

"Mama, Mama, Dessa got a letter from Alpha, and they're coming home for the Fourth of July picnic! Boy Howdy!" Sammy shouted as she ran up the back steps. "And Mama, that son of Dessa's is coming out to see her and bringing his wife and his brats, Dessa said!"

"Sammy, I was resting. What about Dessa's son?"

"He's coming out Sunday, so you can meet him before you and Aunt Clara go on your trip."

"That's nice, dear." I don't ever remember being this tired with the other children. I do hope everything is all right. Dr. Spooner said that I seemed in good health but that I must remember that I'm older and should take things easy. Maybe I shouldn't go to Safety Harbor after all.

"Sammy, did I hear you correctly? Did you say that Eben is returning for the 4th?"

"Yep. Can I have some cookies? I'll take one for Dessa, too."

"Why don't you play with the children and leave Dessa alone. I'll declare, you're going to drive her crazy."

"She likes for me to drive her crazy. She told me so. She also said that she likes me more than her own flesh and blood, and that means that son of hers, who is trying to get her land."

"Don't repeat things like that, dear. She's just talking and..."

"Mama, Dessa doesn't ever say anything that's not the gospel truth. That son of hers is just being nice to her so he and that wife of his can get her land. Now Dessa told me that."

"All right, dear. Think I'll lie down again. Would you keep an eye on Jamie for me? That's a good girl."

Sammy added another cookie for Jamie. Boy, her mama sure took a lot of naps lately. Her daddy said that sometimes when a woman is carrying a baby she gets extra tired and sleepy, and that when her mama was carrying her she slept 'most all the time. So Sammy understood.

"Jamie, here's a cookie. Mama said that I had to look after you, so you better mind, do you hear?"

"I bet she didn't say any such, Sammy. I'm going home to ask her."

"Oh, no you're not, mister! Mama's taking a nap, 'cause that baby makes her tired."

"No he doesn't! You're just sayin' that! I'm going home to ask Mama!"

"You two stop dat dis minute. Come on ovah heah to Dessa, Jamie. Now ya mama needs extra rest when she carryin', and she ast me ta see ta ya, and she even let Sammy hep me."

"See, mister! I told you, so maybe now you'll listen!"

"Sammy, Ah wants ya and Jamie ta hep me grate dis coconut fo' de pralines. Mah son dearly love pralines made wid coconut. When he little he used ta eat neah 'bout a whole pan of 'em."

"I can eat a whole pan of them, Dessa," Jamie shouted. "I can eat two pans of them!"

"Yes, and you'll get sick and throw up all over creation, and Mama'll be mad at me, too," Sammy said fussing at him with her face not three inches from his.

"If ya two don't stop dis fussin', youah not gonta hep me do a blessed ting, do ya heah?"

Sammy and Jamie both knew that Dessa had her fill of them, so shut up and sat down on the bench in her room. There was only one room. The double bed that she shared with Marsh took up most of the space. The big, black wood stove and the long, narrow table and benches took up the other area. They loved being in that room, even when it was summertime.

It was the middle of June, and the afternoon rains had not started yet. By the time Catherine, Clara and Daddy Samuel got back from their trip the rains should have arrived. This was the time of year that roof repairs would be made on the houses, and that meant excitement for the area children. Dessa had already planned how she was going to keep the children occupied during the summer. Miz Carroll needn't worry 'bout those chil'ren fo' t'ree whole months. Then it would be time for school to start. She'd tend to them. And she did.

Every summer since Sammy had learned to swim well—that was when she was five—the neighborhood children scoured the area looking for people who were replacing their tin roofs. They'd take the old sheets, bend them in two, hammer the edges so as not to get cut on them and pound the ends together to form their boats. They'd beg melted tar from the workmen to fill the old nail holes and to paint the boats' numbers on the side. Sometimes they'd have twenty or more boats for their races in Lake Okeechobee.

The paddles all had to be uniform, and that meant pulling the largest fronds off the cabbage palms, cutting the thatch off so they'd have just the heavy rib, and nailing a flat piece of wood to that for the paddle. The entire operation usually took two or more weeks to build their fleet. They'd stage races throughout the summer months. Since they had to contend with the afternoon thunder showers, they usually had their races about two o'clock or right after the folks got up from their afternoon naps, as was the custom in the area.

"Sammy, did ya know dat Mistuh Watson gonta put on a new roof next week?" She watched her out of the corner of her eye.

"How do you know that? Floy, Jr. didn't say a word to me about it. That horny toad! He oughta know that I have to know these things. I'll have to *get him* for sure!"

"Now, don't ya go an' get yase'f in a uproar! It ain't 'portant foah ya ta know everytin'."

"It is about an old roof coming off! How does he expect me to make arrangements with the workmen if I don't know?"

"You not de only one who wants dat old tin now, Sammy. Maybe dey's some poh folks who needs it, too."

"Yeh, Sammy, you can't take the poor folks' tin. They might need it."

"Shut up your mouth, Jamie! Now you ought to know that I'd never take the tin away from the poor folks, but that I'd share it just like I always do. How're we gonna build our boats for our fleet if I'm not told what's going on? Huh...how?"

Dessa began humming while stirring the dark cane sugar water for the pralines. She'd got Sammy all charged up about that tin so she could count on at least three, maybe four weeks of keeping all the kids in the neighborhood busy.

"Dessa, do you mind if I go over to Floy, Jr.'s to see about that new roof?"

"Course not, chile. Ah watch Jamie fo youah mama, an' he hep me wit de stirrin', huh, mah little man?"

She pulled the bench up to the stove, and Jamie jumped up on it, took the wooden spoon from her and began the important job of watching the boiling syrup turn color. When it got just the right color, he knew to let Dessa know. Then as soon as it cooled enough, he got to lick the pot and spoon. Jamie dearly loved his sweets, and Dessa knew it.

When Sammy got to the Watsons', no one was home. She saw old Hambone out back in their garden, so ran over the sand ridge to the muck and called him. "Hambone, where are the Watsons?"

"Dey downtown Pahokee seein' 'bout dat roof."

"I got dibs on some of the best sheets, so you better spread the word, you hear? I don't mean all the best sheets, 'cause I know you might need some," she said as an afterthought to cover herself.

"Yessum, Miss Sammy. Ah heah." Ah knew de minute Ah seed her comin' wid dat back straight up dat she done heard 'bout dat tin. She gonna sho 'nuff git on Floy, Jr. 'bout tryin' ta keep it secret. Hmmmm. He gonna catch it from Sammy. He continued humming and hoeing.

I can't believe that Floy, Jr. didn't tell me about it. Don't suppose that he made a deal with the Ogle boys, do you? I'll never speak to him again if he did. Not ever!

Dessa had the rest of June planned and had started on July. She had mentioned to Sammy that her tree house in the big rubber tree south of the big house sure could stand some work. Maybe with some tin from one of the houses she and her friends could put on a roof. It might also be convenient to have an elevator. So Dessa and Sammy went about drawing up the new plans for the old tree house. That should take care of July.

August was usually beastly hot, so morning swims in the lake and fishing, even if they weren't biting, would take care of the morning hours. And while their folks napped Dessa planned to spin her yarns about the island and her near escapes from the Feds when she was running rum from the Bahamas to the Florida coast. They would sit beneath the catalpas and bamboo that surrounded the quarters, hanging onto her every word.

Last summer during August Sammy and Junie had set up a stand by the hard road and sold lemonade, making a nice little profit so they could buy comic books for their tree house. That plus the money she made delivering milk to the Harringtons kept them in the money, she said.

Sammy had told Dessa that this year they were going to add on a room to their stand. That meant another orange crate or two, so they could sell coconut milk to the truck drivers who passed by. Dessa reminded her that she'd better check with her folks. She had got in trouble when she and Junie had taken all the shoe boxes, that Sammy's mother stored their shoes in, and covered them with wallpaper from the wallpaper books that they got free from the Sears and Roebuck catalog. Along with flour paste and tape they had built doll houses and sold them to the colored folks who walked beside the hard road.

Catherine made them return the money and retrieve the shoe boxes so she'd have a place to store their shoes for the winter, even though she had to cover up the holes where the girls had cut out the windows and doors.

That wasn't nearly as bad as the year that Sammy, Wilbur and Floy, Jr. decided to operate their own toll gate on the only road back to the quarters out behind Daddy Samuel's fields. It was bordered on one side by a wide, deep drainage ditch and on the other side by the fields. Sammy figured out that if she climbed up several stalks of bamboo, that grew in a clump beside the road next to Aunt Hannah's shack, and went high enough, they would bend over the road, and if Wilbur or Floy, Jr. held the bamboo down then it was a perfect barricade. She collected the toll from the cars which needed to pass, and it became quite a lucrative operation until some snitch told Mister Patrick about it. Another money making scheme aborted, and a tongue lashing that Sammy still remembered a year later.

Sammy saw her daddy's Diamond T truck pull up in the sand road in front of their little house. She ran as hard as she could, but there was no way that she ever beat General to her daddy. "Daddy, Daddy, Mama's resting so you'd better be quiet. Jamie's at Dessa's. When are you and Uncle Walter going to Salerno? Can I go with you? Can I, huh?"

"Not this trip, young lady. Maybe while your Mama's away."

"But, that'll be a whole week away!"

"That's enough, Sammy. Not another word. Did you say that your Mama was resting?"

"That's what she told me she was going to do, and that I had to take care of Jamie."

"That's a good girl." He held the letter away from General and petted him. "Down, boy. Down."

Sammy ran back to Dessa's with the news about the tin. Dessa could tell she was excited even before she came through the open door. Patrick was anxious to share the news about Eben with Catherine. He decided to let her rest a little longer. He sat on the hard chair on the end of the screened porch and read the letter once more.

June 10, 1932

Dear Patrick,

Everything that I had ever hoped for has come to pass. I found her! Right in my own hometown and living with her family in the Rahn house, that has been in my family since the early 1700s. Imagine! She's the most beautiful girl in the world, and intelligent with a keen sense of humor. We plan to be married in December before the Christmas season. You'll be delighted to know that she is Catholic and that we'll be married with the Church's blessing.

I plan to be back in the Glades for the July 4th celebration and to oversee the building of my new home. I'm sure that by now everyone in the Glades knows that I bought that piece of land a mile south of downtown Pahokee, and Thornton has informed me that the land is being cleared.

I plan to go to Thomasville, Georgia, to talk to some workmen about the interior work before I return home.

I do hope that this finds you and Catherine well and everyone else is fine.

> *Sincerely,*
> *Eben*

P. S. She's Irish...Given name is Maureen, but I call her Lenore, my beautiful Lenore.

"Patrick, is that you? I'll be up in a minute, honey. Was just resting."

"Don't you dare get up. You need your rest just like Dr. Spooner said."

He went inside and told General to sit and stay in the living room. He obeyed, crawling beside his master's easy chair. "That's a good boy."

"I feel fine, honey, really I do. It's just that I'm so tired. Guess this little fellow is going to take a lot out of me. What's that? A letter from Miss Mae? We've got to write her and suggest that maybe this year she can spend the winter with Joe and family. I really don't think I can handle her visit this year."

"We'll do what needs to be done, and, no, this is not a letter from Mother. It's from Eben. And he has a surprise for us, or I should say for you."

"For me? What on earth?"

He watched her expression as she read it and began laughing as her mouth dropped open, getting wider and wider. "Well, I never! When did you know about this? Patrick Carroll! I can't believe that you could keep such as this from me. Why you bugger! Getting married in December. Patrick, I'll be as big as a house and won't be able to have any kind of welcoming party for them or anything else..." She began to sob.

"Hey, honey, you are excited about this baby, aren't you? Why the tears?"

"I don't know. It's just like starting over again. I'm too old to be having another baby. I'm too old."

❧

The entourage of John Whitson, his wife Andrea and daughters Adassia, named for her grandmother Dessa, and Penny arrived Sunday afternoon from West Palm Beach. Sammy was ready for them and so was Dessa. They'd worked all week sprucing up Dessa's room and yard and planning and preparing the big meal.

The last time they had visited in the Glades, almost two years before when Dessa was living in Pahokee, Alpha and James had been present. John was their god-son, and Dessa had begged them to visit. Neither looked forward to it, thinking that he was visiting just to pester Dessa about her land. He was determined to find out who had purchased it for her. John Whitson was trouble, and they knew it.

When Alpha and James had driven up in Eben's Packard, they had but one purpose in mind. That was to make sure that Dessa was all right. "Ah nevah trusted dat John no' Andrea. Nevah!" Alpha said to James. "He a snake an' Dessa know it. A snake! Ah don't care if he ouah god-child."

"What he comin' out here in de Glades foah, Ah wondah," James had said. "If he out heah ta make trouble fo' Mistah Eben, den we bettah be on ouah toes. Mistah Eben got 'nuff folks wonderin' wheah he got all dat money."

Alpha had chimed in, "Yeh, an' Dessa know he runnin' numbahs. She know but won't say. He lookin' fo moah money ta play on dat Bolita, an' Ah knows it."

"He bettah not be lookin' down Mistah Eben's way. He tie dat little niggah's tail in a knot. He have dat sheriff aftah him an' t'row him in de penitentiary fo' shuah."

The Whitsons arrived about two p.m. in a fancy car and dressed to kill, as Sammy's mother often said. Addy—that was her nickname—had on a pink ruffled dress with lace and ribbons all over it, and just about as many in her hair, and Penny was almost as bad, but was dressed in white. Sammy wondered how long that dress would stay white with all that black muck around but decided that was her problem.

Sammy figured that she had done her best for Dessa, and now the rest was up to her. Marsh had on his Sunday suit when Sammy saw him come out of the quarters to greet them. He shook hands with John, and Sammy was having a fit because she couldn't hear what they were saying. She was scrunched down behind Jamie's bed on the front porch so they couldn't see her, but that meant that she couldn't hear them either.

"This is ridiculous!" she said out loud. She had promised her mother, who was taking her nap, that she wouldn't interfere, but she hadn't promised her that she wouldn't go over to see what was going on. Seemed to her that was the neighborly thing to do, just to greet them, sort of.

So she tucked her shirt in her play pants and down the front steps she went. She was glad that her daddy had taken Jamie into town with him so they could deliver the cake that her mama had baked for Mrs. Luther, whose husband had died. That Jamie would have spoiled everything. All the way there she went over how she was going to greet them and what excuse she was going to use for her surprise visit.

Dessa saw her coming. Ah knew dat she couldn't stay 'way. Not Sammy. Oh well, let huh come. She pretended that she hadn't seen her.

"Dessa," she called. Dessa turned to her, and so did everyone else. Sammy could see the expression on that daughter-in-law. She sure doesn't like me. Already doesn't like me and she doesn't even know me. Just 'cause I don't have on my Sunday clothes makes her think that I'm white trash. She's stuck-up, just like Dessa said.

"Why heah comes Sammy. She de daughter o' Mistah Carroll, jus 'bout de richest man in dese Glades, ain't he, Marsh?"

Marsh knew what she was up to, so he agreed. "He gotta be. Own lots o' land."

Sammy could see their expression change quickly, and the girls showed every white tooth in their heads, they were grinning so.

"Dessa, after you finish with your meal, you think that the girls would like to go to the lake for a swim? Mama said that I could go when she gets up from her nap. It's so blasted hot that it ought to feel good to them. And that would give you a chance to visit with your son and his wife."

"We can't swim," they said in unison.

"I could teach you in jig time, couldn't I, Dessa?"

"Now Sammy, ya know dat it ain't good to swim aftah a big meal, and Ah got a big one fixed. Leave de girls 'lone foh a little while."

Sammy pursed her mouth, not liking to be put off. After all, she had been nice as pie. She replied, "Well, you can't swim, but I sure hope that you're hungry 'cause me and Dessa worked near 'bout a whole week fixing that big meal for you."

She walked away in a huff but needed to say one more thing, so she turned around and yelled, "And furthermore, you'd sure as heck better appreciate it, 'cause your grandmother is my best friend in all the world, that's what!"

She wanted to say, but knew that she shouldn't, that they weren't gonna get her land, either.

Dessa couldn't help but smile. Dat Sammy shuahly latches on to evah'one she love. She 'fraid dat Ah gonta get hurt. Dessa was happy that she loved her, 'cause Sammy was her special child.

<hr>

John and Andrea glanced at each other curiously when Sammy came over to invite their daughters for a swim. John got up and went behind Andrea, leaned down and whispered, "I wonder if she is any kin to that Hunter fellow?" They were both suspicious about their Mama's association with Eben. John remembered seeing him at their house in the islands when he was just a little tyke. He was always with Juan Picone, and it was well known among the natives that he was big in the rum trade. When Dessa and Alpha and James all came out to the Glades and began working for Eben, then John knew something was going on, but just what he had been unable to find out. Dessa refused to give him any satisfaction.

After they'd eaten, John decided that he and Andrea needed to have a little talk alone, so he said, "Mama, me and Andrea gonna take a little walk to work off some of that delicious meal. Come on, honey."

"We wanna go, Daddy," both girls called.

"Not this time. Hand me my hat, honey. This sun too hot," he said wiping his black brow of sweat. His gold tooth with the star was shining in the sunlight. He had taken off his tan sharkskin suit jacket and thrown it over the back of the straight chair. Dessa noticed that there was a bulge in the inside pocket. She nudged Marsh, and when he looked down at her she whispered "gun." He shook his head affirmatively.

"What he want wid a gun?"

"Don't say a word ta nobody, but Ah'm hoppin' mad. Ah'm gonta warn Mistah Eben when he come back. Dat Ah am. We in fo' trouble, Marsh. Ah tink dis time Ah'm not gonta be able ta put him off. He gonta fin' out Mistah Eben bought dat land fo' me. He gonta. He runnin' dose numbers an' mus need money real bad."

"Sammy, is that you yelling?" Catherine called from her room.

Oops! Sammy thought. I'm in for it now. She rushed inside and got to her mama's door just as she was coming out. "I just went over to Dessa's to invite her granddaughters out for a cool swim, Mama."

"That was very thoughtful of you, honey. Are they going with you?"

"Heck no! They don't even know how to."

"That's too bad, dear. Are your daddy and Jamie back from Mrs. Luther's yet? They're supposed to pick up Mary Catherine from Dorothy's."

Sammy knew that her mama was in one of Mary Catherine's stupors and hadn't heard a word she had said. She shrugged and replied, "No, Mama, they aren't. Can I go over to Wilbur and Thelma's?"

"That would be nice, honey."

Sammy thought, I sure hope that I don't hafta put up with this for seven more months. Whew! That baby sure as heck better be worth all this!

Jessup Spearman was having his mid-morning cup of coffee at the Lakeside Coffee Shoppe, and April was chattering about the new house that

Eben Hunter was building down on Bacom Point Rd. "It's going to be a mansion, I mean a real big mansion, Gene Pickering told me. What on earth is he going to do with such a big house, anyway? Just ramble around in it all by hisself, that's what. No wife or younguns to help fill it up."

"Would you like to help him fill it up, April?" John T. Pickett asked with a smirk on his face.

"Wouldn't mind a bit, John T., and neither would any woman with any brains that I know of. He's the handsomest and the richest man to ever hit the Glades, and *HE* knows how to treat a woman, too."

"Yeh, it's rumored that there are a lot of them in West Palm Beach who have been treated real good by Mr. Eben Hunter."

"And so what if they have? I'm sure they got paid real good for their pleasure. Isn't that right, Jessup?"

"How the hell should I know, April? Don't you go and get a rumor started about me, young lady. What would Elsie say to that, huh?"

"She'd probably say 'good riddance', Jessup."

"I've had just about enough of this conversation. Think I'll be taking my future business over to Betty Ann's."

"For heaven's sake, can't you take a ribbin'? We all know that you're straight as an arrow. What do you hear from Dunbar? He get to Kansas yet?"

"You know as much about him as I do. He's got so peculiar of late, I don't know what he's up to. Probably didn't even go. Said something about going sight-seeing the last I heard."

Elmer Crews overheard them and said, "Hell, he's already home. Saw his car out in front of his house this morning on my way to the store."

"You what? Well, I never!" exclaimed Jessup. "See what I mean! You just can't read Dunbar anymore. He used to be one person that we could count on, but not anymore." He rose, paid April and put on his snap-brimmed hat and left.

April laughed. "He'll be on his way over to Dunbar's. You can count on that. Old man curious done got hold of him."

<hr/>

Jessup went into the town hall and told Betty Jo that he would be gone about another thirty minutes and to cover for him. Then he got in his Buick and headed for Dunbar's. Can't believe him. Maybe he had a seizure, like before. Maybe that's what happened. But why didn't he call me? Maybe he got in late and didn't want to disturb me. Maybe that's what happened.

Sure enough, there was his Ford parked in his spot, just like it had never left. Jessup wondered if Gracie knew that he was home and had fixed his breakfast. He'd soon know.

He knocked again, this time harder. He could hear stirring, and soon Dunbar came to the door. It was obvious that he had just awakened. Grief! It was nine thirty in the morning.

"Dunbar, you all right? Elmer Crews said that he saw your car, and I wondered why you hadn't called me."

"Got home after dark and was just too tired, Jessup." He unlatched the front screen door, smoothed his thin hair back and yawned.

"I can come back later if you're tired. I was just worried about you, that's all."

"No, come on in. I am still tired. It was a long trip..."

"There ain't no way that you could have gone all the way to Kansas and back, now Dunbar, so don't say that you did."

"Of course I didn't. Got up to Savannah and was having such a good time decided to stay for a while. That's all."

"Yeh, and spent the whole time checking on y*ou know who!*"

Dunbar's face turned red with anger. "And what if I did? Someone in this stupid town had better!"

"Well, Mr. Know-it-all, while you were out on your wild goose chase, Mr. Eben Hunter had land cleared not a quarter of a mile south of you right on Bacom Point Rd. and has started building a mansion...did you hear, a mansion!"

"Not on my street, he'd better not! Who told you that?"

"Hey, take it easy, Dunbar, I didn't want to get you upset. Hey, sit down before you drop. You're just tired, that's all. I'll get you some water."

"I'll not have it, do you hear? Not on my street!"

"It's all right, really it is. Hey, take it easy. You've let this get out of hand. So what if he builds on the same street? That doesn't mean a thing, not a thing. You want me to go get Gracie?"

Dunbar hadn't heard a word Jessup said but just sat there on the edge of his over stuffed chair, rocked back and forth and kept muttering that trash had better not build on his street.

"I'm going to go get Gracie, and then I'm going for the Doc. You just rest right here. Dunbar—are you even hearing me? My God, he's daft. Gone right out of his mind!"

Eben had not been to New Ebenezer since before he enlisted in the Army. He had forgotten how peaceful it was. It was good to just lie back, rest his head on the soft grass and gaze at the muddy Savannah River meander by. He was glad that Lenore had decided to come with him. He wanted to share everything with her.

Am I in love, he wondered? Or am I just overwhelmed by her beauty? I know it's not what I felt for Rachel. God, that was pure lust, passion, and yet, I want her. I want to bed her. When she's near, I have to restrain myself from grabbing her and having my way.

"Oh, there you are. I was wondering if you'd decided to steal the Packard and leave me stranded."

"Now, why would I do such as that? I had to visit Miss Jones, as my grandmother used to say. Do you want me to bring the picnic from the car?"

"Wait up and I'll help you," Eben replied.

"Mum fixed the blueberry tarts, like you like, and I deviled the eggs and added some of Da's horseradish."

"Are you trying to spoil me, Lenore? Are you?" He grabbed her around her small waist. She didn't pull back as she had in the past. They were getting used to each other's ways.

"I'm practicing how to be a good wife, Eben, and it's becoming easier for me than it was at first."

"Everything worth-while takes time, my sweet. Someone wiser than I once said that, and I, for the life of me, don't remember who it was."

"He had to have been a very wise man."

They walked up the long, wooden steps to the grassy hilltop, he holding her hand and she clasping her skirt to avoid the rough timbers of the rails. After all, she didn't want to ruin her new dress. He was the most generous man she'd ever known. Her da said, and why not? He has the money. But she knew some who were very wealthy who never shared. At least that's what Fr. Rooney had said.

Eben was surprised that they were the only ones around. He had thought that there would be some visiting the church and graveyard, but it was a week day and uncomfortably warm for June. He was glad that they were alone, and so was Maureen. They had so little time without others around.

"I already miss you, you know," he said, almost in a whisper.

"We have the rest of the day...and the night."

"Don't say that, Lenore, please. I'm having a difficult time as it is. Every time I look at you, I want you. It's a good thing that I am leaving tomorrow. There is no way in hell that I'd be able to last until December, my sweet."

She wanted to say that she didn't think it necessary to wait, but she knew better. She couldn't believe that she could feel this way about a man. She never had before. All she had ever wanted was to go to college and be a teacher. That was all. Now, she could hardly wait for the next day and one of Eben's surprises.

It wasn't that she wanted all the new clothes or jewelry that he showered her with—they didn't matter. She just liked the excitement of it. Everything was so new—everything was unexpected. Her life had been predictable, every blasted moment of it, and now every day was an unopened present anxiously awaiting her gasp of delight.

I wonder what *it* will be like, this being with a man. She had tried to find out from her mum, but got nowhere. She would avoid the subject or make some excuse to leave the room. Maureen wanted to be prepared. She wanted to behave right, but she had no one to ask. Her best friend, Agnes Goodson, had been with a man, got pregnant, and moved away. She had written her several times, but Agnes never responded.

What if I don't do it right? Will he still love me? I'm so confused...

"What is this long face you're wearing, my Lenore?"

She blurted out without even thinking. "I don't even know what to do, Eben. I mean I don't know the first thing about being with a man, and I..." She began to sniffle, then to sob.

Eben was amused, but also concerned. He couldn't believe that her mother hadn't talked to her about her role as a wife. Perhaps she was too shy. I don't like being in this position, but guess that I have been thrust in it, so here goes.

He held her close and said, "Lenore, let's go down to the river and have our picnic, and then we'll talk." He figured that would give him time to think about what he should tell her.

She had calmed down by the time they got to the bottom of the wooden steps. He took the blanket from her, spread it on the thick grass and sat down beside her. She slowly took the food out of the basket, and he helped her with the plates.

She looked up at him and said, "I'm ready when you are."

"Let's eat first." He thought it over and said, "No, I think that I can see some symbolism in this repast. You see this spread of food?"

"Of course."

"Which one of these dishes will you put on your plate first and why?"

"My favorite, the deviled eggs."

"All right. You chose the eggs because you like them best. I have chosen you because I like you the best. I like your looks, I like your wit, your humor, your figure, and I prefer you, just like you prefer the eggs over everything else here."

"Eben, what are you getting at?"

"I'm getting at why certain men fall in love with certain women and vice versa. Some call it chemistry, but whatever they call it, the outcome is the same. We are drawn to each other, and no explanation is necessary. So, when this happens, there are certain actions that we perform that satisfy us, our desire, our hunger. You know how you feel when we kiss and I open my mouth and you respond?"

"Yes, but what..."

"Now, be patient. That is satisfying that particular part of our love making." He sighed. "Lenore, this is more difficult than I thought. Why don't we do this? On our wedding night, I will show you and explain to you everything you need to do...and I don't want you to be embarrassed, because it is a natural way for a man and woman to act. Do you understand?"

"Oh, Eben, I've been so worried. I didn't know who to turn to, honest."

"You can always turn to me, my sweet. Don't you ever forget that."

If she only knew how much I want her this very minute. God, I don't know if I can make it until tomorrow. Maybe I should leave tonight. Hell, I don't know if I can even walk. He took the napkin and draped it discretely over his lap.

She saw his maneuver and was amused, then excited. I'm not sure that I can get through this night either, my sweet.

CHAPTER ELEVEN

Elsie and Jessup Spearman were listening to Dr. Spooner explain what he thought had happened to Dunbar. It was his opinion that he had indeed had a breakdown, and he felt that he should be taken to the hospital in West Palm Beach for another opinion. "He needs the kind of help that I'm not prepared to give him. He needs psychiatric care, Jessup. When did all this start, anyway?"

Jessup decided that he would not be going behind Dunbar's back by confiding in the doctor. After all, Doc had taken an oath and was not a blabbermouth like some he could think of. So he began, "Well, I know that you probably know Dunbar as well as most in the Glades, but I, being his best friend, have had his confidence. It all began when Eben Hunter arrived. Somehow Dunbar has got this idea, because of Eben's obvious wealth, that he came by his money dishonestly and that it was his job to expose him."

Elsie spoke up. "Jess tried to talk some sense into him, but he wouldn't listen. You know how he feels about the Glades, like he's the grand protector, as Jess says..."

"But that's not the half of it, hon. He just couldn't stand to see Eben and his brothers being accepted into Rotary and the churches around here. They were taking advantage of us, hood-winking us, or so he thought. In other words, Dunbar felt that because of Eben he was loosing some of his standing in the community, and to tell you the truth, he was right on that count."

"How's that, Jessup?" Doc asked.

"Well, while he was off traipsing all over creation trying to find out about Eben, the vestry did vote Eben in as head warden. You know that Dunbar has held that position for ten or more years. I was wondering how I was going to break the news to him. Now, I won't have to."

"Doc, Jessup's been making himself almost sick worrying over how he was going to tell Dunbar. I've been scared silly that something was going to snap when he finally had to tell him—he snapped even before Jess got around to it! Heavens, all he said was that Eben was building a house down the road from him, and Dunbar just went crazy. Started yelling and carrying on and saying not on his street he wasn't building his house. Went crazy just like I feared..."

"But that's no reason for the man to go off the deep end. Heavens, he's still the Sunday school president, isn't he? And what's wrong with Eben living on Bacom Point Road? There're dozens of houses on this road."

"Doesn't matter. Dunbar thinks that Eben is out to destroy everything that he's been able to build since he got here. And from the looks of it, he's right. Not that the man purposely tried to, mind you. It just happens that he's succeeded, and with tainted money, according to Dunbar's suspicions," Jessup explained.

"Well, if that's what he thinks, then he'd better point a finger at half the people in the Glades. Heck, I could name many who got their money from illegal shine and slots, and so can you. And as we all know, most of them are the pillars of these communities. There must be more to this than meets the eye. The doctor in West Palm will be able to uncover the real problem, I'm sure."

"I'll be only too glad to drive him over, Doc," Jessup volunteered.

"I was hoping that you'd do just that, Jessup, but I want you to have someone go with you, just in case he has to be restrained, you know."

He was speaking to one worried man, he could see. Elsie went outside with him and whispered, "Doc, I'm real concerned about Jess. Dunbar's been his best friend all these years, and he's taking this real hard."

"I know, I know. Be watchful, and if he gets really down I'll pay him a little visit. Don't want two of our best men to be out of it, do we?"

She couldn't hold back her tears. "Sometimes praying isn't enough. Sometimes I just have to do something," she said aloud as Doc drove off in his beat-up Ford. "Don't know what, but I'm gonna have to do something. Maybe I'll just have to take up where Dunbar left off. If those Hunters did come by their money dishonestly, then perhaps I can find out how," she said aloud. But she wasn't serious, just worried.

"Jamie, you hold still! Daddy's not gonna let you go to the movies if you don't hurry. You'll hafta stay with Dessa," Sammy warned. It was Saturday afternoon, and they were getting ready for the matinee, just like they'd been doing ever since the new theater opened in Pahokee the year before. It was a beauty with three hundred seats on the main floor and one hundred in the balcony.

"I don't even care if I go. You make me sit on the first row and my neck just about breaks in two trying to see."

"Stop your complaining, you hear! You know how I hafta fight to get those seats! Heck, just about get bruised to a fare-thee-well fighting for those spots."

"Well, I'd rather sit farther back with Mary Catherine."

"Good! That suits me just fine, mister. Heck, you go to sleep every blasted time, anyway! I don't know how anyone can go to sleep during a Hoot Gibson movie, I surely don't. And I'm not going to miss a one of the episodes of *Sheena, Queen of the Jungle*, do you hear? Hold still or I'll never get those blasted curls to stay down! Sheena's gotta be the prettiest woman I ever saw and the bravest, too."

"Is that who you think you are when you try to swing from one rubber tree to the other over at Floy, Jr.'s? Wait'll I tell Mama when she gets back."

"Well, mister, I for one don't care if you tell the whole entire world! 'Cause I can now swing on those rubber tree vines from tree to tree all around the Watson yard and not touch the ground a single time. Not even once! And that's from every rubber tree on the whole place, smartie. Did you see me do that? Did you? Now, that you can tell everyone, 'cause I'd sure like for them to know about it!"

"What're you two yelling about, Sammy?" Patrick called. He was searching for a fresh shirt from his bureau drawer. "Sammy, do you know if Dessa got those shirts done?"

"She sure did, 'cause I had to help her. She's afraid of that washing machine. Said she was gonna wash the next load in the tub and on the board like she used to."

"No, she's not. Your mother wants her to learn to use that machine. Says it's not as hard on the clothes."

"Well, she's gonna hafta be the one to tell her, 'cause she said she wasn't gonna have her arm wrung off in any *Easy* wringer washing machine. She said that she needs both her arms, and I, for one, agree."

"What did you say, young lady? It's your daddy you're speaking to."

"I didn't mean any disrespect, Daddy. I was just repeating what Dessa said, that's all."

"You'd better watch your mouth, Sammy. One of these days someone else, who doesn't understand your directness, will take offense and set you straight, young lady."

Sammy whirled around just in time to see Jamie try to cover his grin, but Patrick came out of his bedroom in time to save him.

"Daddy, I don't want to take care of Jamie at the movies this time. Can't Mary Catherine take him for once?" She almost said that she didn't feel too good but knew if she said it that he'd make her stay home with Dessa and Clarissa, and there wasn't any way in the whole, entire world that she'd miss a Hoot Gibson movie. So she gulped instead and tried to ignore the pain in her stomach.

"No, I can't!" Mary Catherine answered while trying to position the golden curls around her full face. "How would that look? Heavens! I'm sitting in the balcony with Dorothy and Martha. They'd never stand for it," Mary Catherine was speaking while biting her lips trying to get some color in them. She'd read that was what the movie stars did, and she'd almost bit her's to a bloody pulp, Sammy had once told her mama.

"The only reason that you're sitting up there with them is so you can flirt with those football players from Pahokee, miss!"

"That will be quite enough from the three of you. I don't wonder that your mother wanted to get away. You've got to stop this fighting, do you hear?" he said rushing to the car.

He had no sooner said it than Jamie and Sammy began fighting over who was going to sit in the front seat beside him. "She got to sit by you the last time, Daddy. I remember."

Patrick looked at Sammy and sighing loudly said, "Sammy, I tell you what I'm going to do. I'm going to let you sit beside me if you promise me you won't mistreat Jamie at the movies. Is that a promise?"

"I don't ever mistreat him at the movies, because he always falls asleep, and it takes me near 'bout half the night to wake him up when the lights go on. He's a pain!" Sammy looked over at her daddy, shrugged and said, "Oh, all right. But I think that Mary Catherine oughta take turns with me. It's not fair that he has to sit with me every time."

Patrick, smiling, said that he understood, but was surprised that she had given in so easily. "I'll speak to your mother about it when she returns. I think that you have a point. Are you feeling all right, honey?"

"I do think I have a point, and I feel just fine, Daddy," she lied. Sammy enjoyed having the last word. She decided that she would speak to her mother herself, just in case her father forgot.

⁂

Patrick met Walter in front of Bolton's Drug Store on the corner of Main like they did every Saturday afternoon. There seemed to be an unusual number of men hanging around, and he wondered why, even before he got out of the car. The children had been let out at the Prince Theater, and it would be after dark by the time the movies were over. First would be the news, then at least two cartoons, then the serial and then the main feature, usually a Western. That would give the grown-ups a good three hours to enjoy their cokes and gossip at the drugstore.

"What's going on, Walter? The Canal Point Bank fail again?"

"Nothing like that but just about as bad, to hear some of them talk. It seems that Dunbar Anderson went off his rocker again. Jones said that Jessup is taking it real hard."

"What set him off this time? Do they know?"

"Doc Spooner explained it to the men at Rotary that sometimes something that happened to you when you were just a little baby could surface and cause the damage, if you can believe that."

"That's too bad. He seemed like a real nice man and certainly was a pillar of the community."

Patrick walked over to Jones Maxon, and they began to talk about the new packing houses that the Hunter brothers were building in Canal Point, and someone called to him and asked if he knew when Eben was coming home.

"Heard from him a while back, and he said the Fourth of July in time for the fireworks and bar-b-que."

"That house of his is coming along real good. Almost got the foundation in, and when I stopped by the other day, must have been twenty curious people just watching the workers. Dalton Padgett said that if they were going to drive his men to distraction, they might as well take a hammer and help out or go on back to their farms and businesses. He's on a tight schedule, 'cause Eben said that he needs that place completed by no later then Thanksgiving."

"What's happening on Thanksgiving that's so all-fired important?"

"Dalton didn't say, but there sure as hell is something going on. He was sheepish and close mouthed and wouldn't give the men the time of day."

Patrick excused himself and went into the drugstore. He turned to Walter and called, "Walt, you want a coke?"

"Not unless you brought some sweetnin' to dress it up, Patrick."

"Look underneath the front seat of the car. Might just have a pint in there."

The exchange wasn't lost on Marthann Sewell and her sister Ruby, who were sitting in their car in front of the drugstore with the windows wide open, hoping for some cool air. There were several cars parked alongside them with ladies from Canal Point and Pahokee sitting and talking, having their drinks while their children were at the movies and their husbands visited.

"Bet their wives would be surprised about those two if they were here," Marthann said.

Ruby responded, "I'll not be the one to tell on them. Stuck up as they've gotten since their husbands began working for those Hunters, they'd not listen to me even if I did. I don't care if they get drunk as skunks. Serve those smarties right!"

***

Sammy was literally dragging Jamie's body along Main Street protesting as she went. "This is it! The last time you'll spoil my Hoot Gibson show.

133

And the best one he ever made or will ever make, too! "The Long, Long Trail" has gotta be the best movie ever made in the history of the..." She looked up in time to see her daddy and Uncle Walter animatedly laughing and carrying on with the other men on the street corner. She felt real funny, and her side was hurting to beat the band. Probably 'cause I hafta drag this brat brother all over town, she reasoned.

Wonder what's going on? When she got there and asked, her dad continued to laugh and said, "You know Mr. McGouirk up in Sand Cut, Sammy? He planted rhubarb and it grew so tall that he had to break the stalks in two so as to get 'em in the tomato crates."

Sammy looked up at all the men on the corner, and being Sammy, wondered what was so all fired funny about having to break that funny looking rhubarb in two so's to fit into a crate. Men do beat all! as Dessa would say. Now if they really wanted to see something funny they should have gone to the movie with her, and they'd have seen a movie short with a trained skunk doing tricks. Now that was funny. She'd be glad when her mama got home. Her daddy was acting peculiar.

Mary Catherine sauntered down the street with that Dorothy hanging all over her, and they were taking their own sweet time, too. "Daddy when are we going home? Jamie slept the last half of the movie. We're tired."

"Well, here come the other passengers, so guess it'll have to be in a few minutes."

"I want to go home now. I don't feel too good!" Sammy said weakly as she proceeded to throw up all over Patrick's boots.

All the women who were sitting in their cars along Main Street hopped out and started fussing over Sammy with Patrick almost yelling at them that he'd take care of her. Dr. Spooner was summoned, and before anyone knew it, Sammy was whisked off to the hospital.

She said later that she didn't even know she was sick when they attacked her. I mean just because my mama wasn't around and my daddy had been tippling didn't give them the right. Turned out that she had appendicitis and should have been grateful to them...but she wasn't. Heck, they'd probably spoil her chance to build her boat, and that Frankie Ogle will probably steal her number 7 for his very own. Just up and steal it! He always wanted it, she sniffled. Why, every one in the whole town knew that her number was SEVEN. Everyone!

They kept her in the hospital two days with her protesting loudly every chance she got. She knew full well what those traitors were going to do behind her back, and to think that Floy, Jr. was probably right in the thick of the conspiracy. She couldn't make the nurses nor Dr. Spooner understand how important it was for her to get home to protect her position.

When Catherine, Clara and Samuel returned from the west coast, Catherine was fit to be tied, Sammy told Dessa. "My mama told daddy that if he ever did a foolish thing like that again she'd...she'd, well she couldn't think of anything mean enough to do to him. But she was sure mad at him for not telegraphing her about my appendicitis. Whew!"

"He t'ought he was doin' right, Sammy. Yuah mama need to have a good rest and you in good hands wid Dr. Spooner. I fo' one tink he did right."

"How does this look? Look, I got the braids real little just like yours." Sammy held the palmetto hat out from her so Dessa could inspect it. They had gone into the hat making business, and Dessa told Samuel that she never saw anyone work as hard as Sammy at hat making. But she also said that even though she was as patient as Job, it was obvious that hat making was not Sammy's calling.

Dr. Spooner had confined Sammy to the house. She was to have no physical activity for two weeks. Sammy said that he might as well have sent her up to Alcatraz. Her ex-friends were busily building their boats and getting ready for the regatta on the lake. The only ones she'd speak to were Junie and Wilbur and Thelma. And she'd give them the time of day only because she needed allies to assist her in her grand plan for when she got well.

The day came for Sammy's release from jail, as she referred to her confinement. Dessa had kept her busy with the hat making, but her main activity had been orchestrating her grand plan.

"Boy howdy! They'll be so mad when they see what we're gong to do! Boy howdy!" she exclaimed to her three conspirators. They were in Sammy's room with her grandpa Samuel's map spread out on the floor. Besides those who were going to participate in the trip only Dessa and her daddy were in on the plan.

Sammy had the three of them round up all the orange crates they could confiscate and wagons, wheels and axles. They'd need all they could get for their big trip to CALIFORNIA. Yep! All the way to California they would go and leave that small minded bunch right in little old Canal Point. As Dessa had said, they just didn't have her imagination. They surely didn't.

Regatta! Shoot! What is that to compare with a caravan all the way to the Pacific Ocean. Heck! Maybe they'd even discover gold out there.

When she told Patrick about her plan he had a devil of a time concealing his amusement, but knowing how bored his daughter would be stuck in the house for two weeks, he decided that it would give her something to do besides moan loudly and beg them to let her at least go to town to visit friends with the promise that she would be quiet as a mouse. Knowing Sammy, he knew that would be impossible.

The regatta came and went with none of her gang participating. They didn't even go to the lake to watch. They had more important things to do. Frankie Ogle came in third in the race. That should have pleased Sammy, but she had her mind on bigger and better things, she said. They had a deadline and needed to be in the Carrolls' garage to assemble their cars. Each would have his own car constructed of an orange crate placed in the wagon bed. Her daddy had added a metal tongue on the back of each in order to pull their wagons that would hold their supplies. It was their plan to camp along the way, and he had spent hours with them going over the ways to live off the land.

Sammy was confident that she could get all the money that they'd need from the sale of the palmetto hats, and Patrick and Dessa had promised them that they'd match their funds. It was difficult for Patrick to keep the Grand Plan from Catherine, but he had promised Sammy. Actually, he was enjoying the excitement of the venture as much as Sammy and her friends.

The time came for their plan to be revealed. Mary Catherine was the only one who made fun of their efforts. "California! You've gotta be out of your mind, Sammy Carroll! Do you have any idea how far that is?"

"Course I do. I've got grandpa Samuel's map, miss smartie!"

Catherine looked at Patrick and, trying to show some enthusiasm, said, "Sammy, that sounds like a delightful trip. Why, the year before mama died they took that trip and sent us postcards of the giant redwoods. You know the ones where they can drive a car through that big hole in the middle of them. You remember that postcard, don't you?"

"Yep, I sure do, and we plan to drive our wagon train smack dab through that big old cut-out redwood, just like in that picture."

She jumped up and ran around the kitchen table to Catherine. Sammy hugged her around her shoulders and sighed. "It'll be some kinda grand, won't it, Mama? Imagine! Who cares if that old Frankie Ogle stole my number seven, anyway. Heck, he'll be stuck in old Canal Point, and I'll be headed for California!"

Mary Catherine could not contain herself any longer. "Are you gonna let her go, Mama? Why, you know she'll not get past Pt. Mayaca before she gets homesick or hungry or those ridiculous wagons will break down!"

Patrick spoke before Catherine could. "Mary Catherine, Sammy has a well thought out plan, and she and the others have been working on it for over two weeks now. If for some reason they don't get all the way to California on their first attempt, then they'll just regroup and try again, just like our other pioneers did. Why, this country was built with her kind of vision, and I, for one, am proud of her."

Sammy thought about sticking her tongue out at Mary Catherine, but when she looked at her she changed her mind. Holding herself up straight she proudly said, "Daddy, I'll not let the Carroll family down. Not now, not ever." Then she turned and ran out the back door, forgetting that she was not supposed to let the screen door bang, and headed for Dessa's.

"Boy howdy! Wait'll she hears what daddy told that busybody sister of mine. Whew! He sure put her in her place."

⬥⬥⬥

Because Mary Catherine and Jamie had told all their friends about the proposed trip, the news spread fast. Clara berated Catherine about even considering letting Sammy do such a dangerous thing, but Catherine informed her that she and Patrick had talked it over and figured that the children would indeed not get past Ammon's store, just a mile away, or certainly not far enough for them to worry about them.

"I can't believe you're even letting her attempt such as that! I truly can't! Why if Clarissa even mentioned such..."

"Clara, listen to me. I would never allow Sammy to do anything that would harm her. Now you know that."

"Well, then you don't know about her swinging from the trees all around Watson's place, do you? Why, Clarissa said that she thinks she's Sheena, Queen of the Jungle, just like in the movies. You didn't know about that, now did you?"

"No, I didn't, but it obviously hasn't hurt her, has it? Sammy will probably get her bumps and bruises or even broken bones. But I'd rather have her like that then sitting around sucking her rotten old thu..."

"Clara, I'm sorry. I didn't mean it. Clara, don't you dare leave here with that look on your face. Clara!" she cried after her....

⬥⬥⬥

"You had every right to say it, honey. Now stop those tears. You need to be happy, just like Dr. Spooner said. Kitten, dry those tears," Patrick said, smiling down at his distraught wife. "Besides, someone needs to say

137

something to Clara and Walter about Clarissa and that stinking thumb. Now, now..."

The onlookers were lined up all alongside the hard road in front of Turnerville and the Carrolls' place. Must have been thirty of them. Even Floy, Jr. and his family were outside waving their flags and shouting their good wishes to the enthusiastic youngsters, but Sammy ignored him. Even Howard Sharp, editor of the *Everglades News,* was there to interview Sammy and her friends. He was a good friend of Samuel and Patrick.

When Catherine saw Howard, she said with a wink at Patrick, "Patrick, you didn't. You're taking a chance, you know. What will she say?"

"Does it matter? She's having the time of her life, and so am I. You have given me a unique child, Mrs. Carroll." He hugged her to him.

Sammy had given Dessa the honor of christening the lead wagon—that was Sammy's—with a bottle of Dr. Pepper. Dessa had got dressed up in her Sunday best for the ceremony. She had added a lace collar to her flowered dress and a ribbon to her palmetto hat. Sammy whispered that she looked so pretty. That grin just jumped up from inside, just like Sammy had remembered it from the first time she had seen her. I'm gonna miss Dessa, she thought. My Dessa.

She choked back a frog in her throat and called, "Wagons Ho!" just like Hoot Gibson would have done. She slung her leg over the side of the crate and began pushing with her other sturdy leg. The others followed suit. No trouble all the way past Watsons', about a city block. They got to Ericksons', and that old red dog of theirs started chasing them, and Junie, who was scared to death of a dog, abandoned the wagon and ran all the way home, crying to beat the band.

That did it! Sammy told the others to pull off to the side of the road while she went to see Mr. Erickson about that blasted dog.

Patrick saw what was happening and told Catherine that Sammy could handle it. "But, honey, you don't want her to lose face, do you?"

"Sammy won't lose face. She's in control. Look, she's going up to see Floyd to get him to tie old Red. Then Junie will rejoin the group. Now, just be patient."

Everyone was laughing and saying what a short trip they'd made when Howard Sharp spoke out, "Now folks, let us not make fun of our Glade's youngsters. They've worked very hard on this project, and I intend to do my editorial on this very group. They remind me of the first pioneers who settled these Glades. Yessir, I'll do a grand editorial on this venture."

Not another titter did he hear as he went about getting everyone's name and occupation and thoughts on why they had ventured to this wilderness.

Old Red was tied, and Dessa had accompanied a frightened Junie back to rejoin the caravan. Again, Sammy called out, "Wagons Ho!" And they were off again.

Patrick, his arm circling Catherine's waist, said, "I hope they do get all the way to Pt. Mayaca."

"Patrick, that's almost ten miles. They'll be half dead if they go that far."

"Only physically, my sweet."

Howard Sharp approached Patrick. He was smiling. "I know that you didn't hear my interview with Sammy, Pat, but I'm here to tell you that you and Catherine have quite a daughter. I asked what inspired her to take such an arduous journey, and she answered, 'My imagination, Mr. Sharp. My friend Dessa said that I had more than my share, and Dessa always tells the truth, just like my daddy and mama.'" He chuckled and said, "Then she added that if I decided to print what she said in the *Everglades News*, she sure wanted me to put that a wagon train trip to California was a lot more important than an old boat regatta in the lake. What did she mean by that, Pat?"

"Howard, let's just say that our Sammy sure as hell doesn't like to be bested...not our Sammy."

⚬⚬⚬

Patrick put the Diamond T into reverse and called to Catherine, "They'll be at McGouirk's store in Sand Cut, hon. Harlan just sent word by Sweet and said that they were some kinda beat. I'll be back with them in no time. Now you get some rest, you hear!"

An hour had passed and Catherine and Dessa were on Daddy Samuel's front porch peering north hoping to see Patrick and the youngsters. "It's been longer than I thought, Dessa. Why's it taking him so long?"

About then they heard horns honking and the biggest commotion they'd ever heard. Seems that Harlan Sears had got a bunch of his buddies to form a parade to accompany Patrick and the kids back home. Dessa shouted as she ran toward the hard road. "Miz Catherine, heah she come. Heah come ouah Sammy back from huh big trip!"

There must have been fifty or more gathered in the yards around the

Carrolls'. Catherine brought out the pound cake that she had made for Sunday dinner, and Dessa got her coconut pralines and when Catherine looked up from the front porch, she saw Clara bringing a plate of something.

It was printed in the Everglades News that there had never been a bigger homecoming than the one witnessed at the recent arrival of the aborted wagon train venture to California. Unfortunately, the caravan had experienced technical problems. A later trip was planned.

When Patrick tucked Sammy in bed that night, he asked her, "Sammy, are you sorry that you didn't get to California?"

She replied sleepily, "Oh, I'll get there some day, Daddy. But I know one thing. That Frankie Ogle will never try to steal another thing from me...not ever. Number seven is mine, and now he knows it!"

When he later told Catherine what she said, she asked what on earth she meant. Patrick answered, "I think she means that she bested him and that he'd better think twice before he tries to outsmart one Sammy Carroll. At least I think that's what she means."

"Is Eben getting back tomorrow, hon? I seem to remember that Dessa said that is what Alpha told her.

"Tomorrow's the day, all right. I'm anxious to hear the news, aren't you?"

"I sure am!" she said as she dozed off. Patrick, his arms behind his head, began to speculate about Eben's return. He's gonna set this town on its ear, he thought with a chuckle. Gently removing Catherine's arm from across his chest, he rolled over and was soon asleep.

CHAPTER TWELVE

"They're here! Dessa. They're here!" Sammy and Jamie yelled. Their bare feet, hardened against the sandspurs, kicked up the sand as they ran in front of the Packard. James and Alpha had their heads outside the windows and were waving to Dessa where she stood in front of the quarters, her hands planted on her hips in the familiar position.

"Sammy," she called, "You and Jamie gonta become like little birds and fly away, so's me and Alpha can catch up, ya heah?"

"That's not fair, now you know that, Dessa. I've been waiting just as long as you have for them to come back!"

Sammy knew as she protested that Dessa had made up her mind, and it wouldn't do her one speck of good to carry on. So, pursing her mouth, she grabbed Jamie by the elbow and dragged him kicking and screaming back to the front porch.

She turned back around and yelled to James, "Where's Mr. Eben? You leave him in Georgia?"

James knew that she knew better but that he'd have no peace without answering her. "Noam, Miss Sammy, we sho 'nuff din't. He up at Mistah Thornton's goin' ovah deah finances. Dat big house gonta set him back a passel. Gonta hafta grow a heap o beans ta pay fo' it, he say."

"Sammy," Catherine called, "Is that Eben's Packard I see at Dessa's?"

Sammy and Jamie had come up the front porch steps and remembered to brush their feet off on the rush mat. Plopping down on the glider Sammy sighed loudly and answered. "It's his all right, but he ain't in it..."

"Isn't, dear. Please don't use that word. You know how it upsets me for you to talk like Junie and..."

"I meant isn't, Mama. James said that he was at Mr. Thornton's going over how much money he has left. Said that big house cost him a passel of money and that..."

"That's really none of our business, now is it?"

"Mama, I was just telling you what he said. Can I go over to Wilbur and Thelma's? Dessa doesn't want me to get under her feet. Said that I was to fly away just like a bird and..."

"Only if you take Jamie with you."

"Well, then I don't even wanta go. He's a pain! I'm going to the tree house."

Catherine watched her go slowly, dejected. She fingered Jamie's brown curls. It's going to be a long, hot summer, I'm afraid. I just wish I felt better. She looked down at Jamie, brushed the sand off his arm and asked, "Son, how about a nice glass of lemonade? Wouldn't that taste good? Go get your mama some lemons and also a lime or two to give it some bite."

<hr>

"He got jes what he went fo', Dessa. Evah blessed ting," Alpha said, reaffirming, her head bouncing up and down. "You know dat Mistah Eben don't take no fo a ansah. An' she sho is a beautiful young lady. Hair lak a shiny blackbird and eyes de colah o' de sea...dat clear green. An' she jes as nice as she beautiful, ain't she, James?"

"You say dat right. An' Mistah Eben look lak he could eat huh wid a spoon. Ain't nevah seed him look at a woman lak dat." Dessa could tell how pleased they were.

Dessa poured them another cup of tea. She was smiling. "He been lonely foah too long. He be needin' him a permanent woman. Hey, won't it be nice to have a baby in de house once moah? Heah we got Miz Carroll gonta give us one, and Ah be willin' to bet dat Mistah Eben an' his lady gonta give us anoddah one in no time at all."

"He be goin' back to fetch huh in December right aftah Thanksgivin'. He say dat de house bettah be mostly finished by den, 'cause all dose folks he brin' down from Georgia is artisans. Dat means dat dey knows deah business, and dey gonta put de finishin' touches on it." Alpha emphasized grandly.

"Oh my, Dessa! You oughta see what he got planned fo' de gran' party when Miss Lenore come ta Pahokee. He already got me an' James a workin' on dat menu. He gonta bring in folks from Palm Beach to hep us. Not Wes' Palm Beach, mind ya, but de real fancy Palm Beach itse'f. Hmmm. We gonta have us a real fancy shindig ta welcome Miss Lenore. Dis town gonta be set right on its eah, ain't it, James?"

"Well," Dessa interjected, "if you needs me den Ah'll be right deah beside ya. You can sho 'nuff count on dat. Aftah all, widout Mistah Eben where we be, huh? Back in de Bahamas jes 'bout starvin', dat's what. An' Ah wouln't be a land owner, either. Wouln't own a blessed ting." Dessa was getting into Alpha's and James's mood, but something told her to not get too excited. It was a long time from July to December, and she had a stirring in the pit of her stomach, a sure sign of trouble to come. She thought of John.

That blackbird had flown low over her that very morning and dropped at least five feathers, and they landed next to her feet. She scooped them up and tucked them inside her apron. Looking around quickly to see if anyone saw her, she dashed inside her and Marsh's room. Closing the heavy wooden door behind her, she rested against it. "Gotta t'row dese inta de wind dis night and scatter dem to de far co'nahs, oah Mistah Eben gonta have as bad a luck as old Lube had."

Everyone on her island knew the story of old Lube, and when those feathers fell at her feet she was definitely thinking of Eben—he was the target for sure. She hoped she was wrong, and she had been on occasion, but rarely. After she heard Marsh breathing deeply, she eased off her side of the bed and out the door she went, making sure that his breathing had not broken rhythm. To counter the spell she had to throw the feathers without anyone's seeing her, and it must be in the pitch black of the night.

She decided to not tell Alpha and James. No need to get them upset. And upset they'd be for sure, 'cause they were as protective of Mistah Eben as she was. None of them wanted to see him go into one of his dark spells like they'd seen before. Sometimes they'd last for days, but Alpha had confided to Dessa that since he'd moved to the Glades he'd had only one that she knew of. She never found out what brought it on, but it was a scary time for her and James.

***

The summer sped by. Dessa had done just what she said she would and had kept the neighborhood children occupied. Sammy and her friends had finished their tree house, and Catherine had begun to feel better. It didn't seem quite as hot as it had other summers, she said.

Lew Ayres and Spencer Tracy were the new stars in the movies, and locally Patrick Carroll and his East Beach baseball team were the talk of the Glades. Patrick had the highest batting average in the league, and Sammy was his number-one fan. Catherine said over and over again, "Thank goodness for baseball."

The Mayaca Co. in Port Mayaca, ten miles north of Canal Point, had begun growing citrus and avocados commercially, and the Pahokee football team had a new coach, Frank Hobson. Patrick and the local men predicted a perfect season. The street corners in downtown Pahokee were busy on Saturday nights with the area men discussing the levee being built on that side of the Lake. Everything was going smoothly, and a 1937 completion date was expected. That was good news for the area residents. Another disaster like the '28 hurricane would end a lot of dreams.

***

Thanksgiving was approaching, and Eben was unusually calm, at least to the unknowing eye. Alpha and James, along with Patrick, knew that he was a powder keg waiting to be ignited. He and Lenore had been writing several times a week. She had finished her school in Atlanta, and Eben even noticed a difference in her letters; there was more self-assurance. But the house was not going as he had hoped. One of the craftsmen had a disagreement with the cabinet maker from Rome, Georgia, and had left during the night. Eben threatened the man left behind, and he, too, had quit.

"You have to rely on the locals to finish up," Thornton warned him.

"We have carpenters, Thor, but no one with that deft hand that I need."

"Have you ever seen their work? Have you?"

"Well, no, I guess I haven't."

"Leonard Geiger, Coot as he's called locally, is a fine carpenter, Eben, and I'll have him come talk to you and look at the unfinished work. If he can't do the job, then I know him well enough that I'm sure he'll be the first to tell you. What's wrong with that?"

"It's just that I'm getting anxious, that's all!"

"I understand. He's done work on some of the finest houses around here and..."

"This is not just another Glades house, Thor. This is Elsinore, Lenore's house..."

"I had forgotten what a romantic you are, Eben. I wonder if anyone in this entire world has ever understood you except Mama and Aunt Tempie. You were always the favored son." He continued. "Oh, don't restrain me. I and the others have always known it, and," he actually laughed, " it never bothered us one whit, not a whit."

"Goodnight, Ebenezer." Thornton climbed into his beat-up Ford and headed back to his modest home in Canal Point. All the way back home he reflected on how they had come to the Glades. He knew that they should all be grateful to Eben, and they were, but he was getting a little worried. Eben had always been so positive. He didn't like this nervousness. He hoped that it would not bring on one of Eben's dark days, as his mama and Aunt Tempie called them.

Thornton was not given to curiosity, but he did wonder if perhaps Eben's past was catching up with him, and that was his concern—not the upcoming wedding. Neither he nor Ralph nor Emerson had ever had the nerve to question Eben about his newly acquired wealth. They all suspected though.

When Thanksgiving arrived, the finishing touches had finally been completed on Elsinore. The furniture had been purchased in Savannah and Charleston by an interior decorator and brought to Canal Point by train. Eben was at the depot to meet it, and Patrick and Walter supervised the transfer to the bean trucks. Their only problems had been the grand piano and large breakfront. Eben kept reminding them that all were antiques.

Catherine and Clara were having a fit about the furniture and must have asked their husbands nine hundred times what it looked like, according to Sammy. But it was all in crates, so they couldn't tell them. She was helping Dessa devil the eggs for the big dinner that was always held at Grandpa Samuel's. Jamie was allowed to help Sammy pull the big mahogany table apart in order to put in the three leaves, and Sammy was giving him what-for, 'cause he wasn't pulling hard enough to suit her.

"You two gonta cause Dessa ta mess up dese eggs if'n ya don't quit dat fussin'! Sammy, heah, ya'll do de rest o dese eggs an' Ah'll hep Jamie. Den Ah wancha ta stuff dat celery lak youah Granpa laks. Don't fo'git ta put a slice o' olive on top an' make shuah dat de pimento is in de middle. He lak it ta look nice. Come on, Jamie. You an' Dessa gonta git dat table pretty lak youah mama want. Next yeah we gonta hafta add a highchair foah ya little bruddah or sistah."

Dessa noticed that every time the expected baby was mentioned Jamie got sad. She had discussed it with both Catherine and Patrick. They had noticed it, too, but had tried to make light of the upcoming event. Guess Ah'm gonta hafta do some takin' charge mahse'f, Dessa thought. Gonta hafta come up wid sometin' special fo' de little fellow.

⚓

The main topic at the Thanksgiving table was Eben and Elsinore. Uncle Wash and Uncle Watson had both heard about the mansion all the way in West Palm Beach. Their wives were as curious as were Clara and Catherine. Why did Eben want such a grand house? They had no suspicions about a wife.

For the past two Thanksgivings the conversation centered around the new levee, or dike as most called it, that President Hoover and the Army Corps of Engineers were building around the southern part of the Lake. The president himself had visited the area after the devastating hurricane of '28. Every farmer in the Glades knew that if they were to stay in business, flood control had to be put into effect. They had a friend in the new president, since he had been an engineer.

Eben's secret had been kept well, and even Catherine had been able to

145

keep the news of Lenore from Clara. It had been difficult, and Patrick didn't know how much longer she'd be able to hold out. Only one more month to go, he thought. Eben planned to invite hundreds of the townspeople to a housewarming and surprise them with the introduction of his bride. At least that was the last word that Patrick had on it.

The table was filled with special dishes. Catherine had insisted on preparing her fresh corn pudding, and Patrick had been able to have Rupert bring oysters out from West Palm Beach for the stuffing. Walter had smoked a haunch of venison on his homemade cooker—used an old oil drum—and Mr. Ammons had got in the fat turkeys, like he did every year for Thanksgiving and Christmas. Dessa said that she didn't have to lard it much at all, "cause dat bird must've eaten real good." The rich gravy proved her to be right.

"Patrick, dear, don't give Jamie the giblets in the gravy. You know that he doesn't like them," Catherine said.

"I'll eat 'em, Mama!" Sammy offered.

"Sammy, don't talk with your mouth full, dear. It doesn't look ladylike."

Mary Catherine tried to ignore them and proceeded to dominate the conversation with her cousins hanging onto her every word. Sammy was disgusted with her airs. Shoot! I bet they think she's the Queen of Sheeba, the way she's talking. Look at that Bertha taking in all that bragging she's doing.

"Mary Catherine, I imagine that your cousins would like to add to the conversation," Grandpa Samuel said, noticing that Sammy was about to explode.

"Granddaddy Samuel, you know how I carry on when I'm stimulated, and this has to be the most exciting year of my entire life..."

"How does choosing a bunch of spelling words get to be exciting! If that's all you got to be excited about..."

"Sammy, that's quite enough. This is Thanksgiving, and we all have a lot to be grateful for, even Mary Catherine's being selected by Miss Page to help at the spelling bee," Patrick interjected.

"Well, Daddy, you didn't hear me carry on about my trip almost all the way to California nor..."

"Sammy Carroll!" Mary Catherine shouted. "You didn't get past Sand Cut in that old orange crate, and you know it!"

Patrick rose, went around the table, pulled Mary Catherine's chair out from the table with her hanging onto the sides, and proceeded toward Sammy. She pushed her chair back and headed for the safety of the kitchen and Dessa.

"Now, why ya wanta spoil youah Mama an' Daddy's big dinnah, huh Sammy? Now why did ya, huh?"

"It was all her fault. Every bit of it. Now I bet he won't let me have any of Aunt Clara's coconut pie or Mama's mincemeat tarts or...I just bet ya! I hate her! I do!"

"Now, now, Sammy. Come ta Dessa. Ya don't hate huh, ya jes don't lak huh much. Ya'll lak huh bettah when ya gits oldah..."

"No I won't! She's just a big old priss, that's what!"

"Maureen, I'm not sure that staying in Savannah with Eben is such a good idea. Oh, I know that you'll have separate rooms. That's not my concern. It's just not the proper thing to do, and your da..."

"Mum, shush now! Eben did say that he was going to invite Jud and Abigail to accompany us, but frankly I'd rather be alone with him. We've had so little time to ourselves."

They were sitting in the warm kitchen. There had been frost the previous night, and both were concerned that the trousseau that Eben and Maureen had selected would not be heavy enough for the cold Georgia nights. Eben had been the one to suggest another trip to Savannah to supplement it.

The final plans had been made for the wedding itself. Maureen had been adamant about keeping it small and simple, but Eben had insisted on a formal gown for her. He had won out on the design, but she on the heavy Irish lace. The short train was edged in a heavier scalloped lace as was the off-the-shoulder neckline.

"Your swanlike neck is one of your loveliest features, my Lenore. We don't want to hide it. It is a sign of royalty, I've been told."

Maureen could not help but laugh. "Yes, Eben, I'm the princess of the potato patch."

"Don't mock your heritage, my sweet. Some of the most beautiful ruins I've ever seen were in Ireland. It was once a..."

"You and Da should discuss this over a pint. He swears that we are of royal lineage. I don't know that, but Uncle Timothy swears that we go back to the Geraldines. At least they like to think that we do."

"And," he took her pale hand in his, nibbling her fingers, "Perhaps you do."

She giggled. She had always been such a serious girl that giggling was foreign to her. She found that he delighted her one minute and distressed her another. When she lay awake at night, trying to be quiet even in her breathing, so as to not awaken Helen, she had to keep her thoughts focussed on unimportant things or she might actually give in to her giggles. It became increasingly difficult the closer the time came for the wedding. She deduced that it was just nerves.

Abigail had arranged for her housekeeper to care for the children so that she and Judson could accompany Eben and Lenore to Savannah. Actually, she was excited about the trip. Judson had been so serious for so long that Eben's and Lenore's betrothal had become a source of new life, she had confided in Lenore after a few glasses of wine.

She liked the girl! She really did. It was almost like reading Cinderella and being allowed to participate in her metamorphosis. She was very bright, and as Abigail explained to Judson, "Every time I'm with Lenore it's like being in a candy store and being allowed to have all the candy I can eat. Or something like that. I feel childlike and free. And at other times I feel that she is the mother and I the child. She is very innocent, but wise beyond her years. Yes, Jud, I really like her, but I wonder if Eben is good enough for her."

"Were you this concerned about me before we were married, Abby?"

"No," she smiled conspiratorially, "I knew the minute you held my hand that we were right for each other."

"Perhaps Lenore feels the same about Eben. Did you ever think of that?"

"Oh, Jud, they're from two different worlds. Now you know that. You said yourself that he actually bought her and..."

"That was at first, my sweet. Now, I actually believe that he's in love with her. And it's not just her beauty that has attracted him. Oh, I know that at first that's what I thought, but, like you said, there is a lot more to her than we thought, and it is obvious that she's an apt pupil. Her manners are impeccable. The Atlanta school was a good idea, after all."

"A full day of shopping is not my idea of a day on the town, Ben!" Jud admonished. "What ever happened to the old days when we'd ...whoops! I'm not to divulge to our sweet companions what we used to do when you first came to Savannah, am I?"

"You certainly are not, Jud, old friend. But I think that perhaps they already know that it was not a day of shopping for finery for a beautiful lassie, especially not one who is about to be married."

Abigail reached for her jubilant husband, grabbed his arm, then turned back toward Lenore and Eben and said, "See what you two have wrought? My stodgy Springfield husband has indeed come to life in your presence."

⁕

The wedding was beautiful. Abigail and Judson and only a few of Eben's old friends had been present. Mostly the Aherns and their kin in the area witnessed the ceremony. Eben had insisted on an evening ceremony by candlelight, and the soft glow enveloped the beauty of Lenore. Abigail told Judson later that she felt she was watching the Virgin Mary. She got such a lump in her throat that she wasn't sure she'd be able to be a proper hostess.

Since there was no church in Springfield, Fr. Rooney had performed the ceremony at their home. The double parlors were filled with floral pieces from Savannah. She and Judson had insisted on having a small reception afterwards with Eben's and Lenore's approval. The big bash would be held at the farm later. Timothy said that there would be washtubs of the good stuff awaiting any fellow who'd be man enough to attempt it.

"Eben, I'd feel strange not to return to the farm for my proper send-off," Lenore whispered after they left the Ridgeways'.

"So would I, my sweet," he replied hoarsely.

Where all the people came from even Lenore couldn't answer. The fiddles awaited them and havoc ensued. Jud later told his friends, "Those Irish truly know how to properly throw a party. I thought that in the old days the wealthy knew what to do for a couple...you know, with the champagne and rice throwing and the horns honking and shoes tied to the cars and such...but you've not ever seen the likes of that night."

"I heard," Everett Jones said, "that Eben never made it to his wedding bed. Imagine that!"

"But, Mum, they didn't hafta give him Murphy's shine, now did they? They've spoiled my wedding night. Mum, why'd you let them?" Lenore lamented.

Eben tried to make up to his upset bride all the way back to Florida. They had driven to Savannah the morning after their wedding to the hotel he had engaged for their wedding night, and they would have stayed the night, but as Eben had informed Lenore, "We are having a party, the likes of which you've never seen, awaiting us in Pahokee. The invitations have already been sent out, and the hosts won't even be there. What should I do?"

She was disappointed by the turn of events, but not wanting to show her distress, she held his arm close around her and whispered, "We'll have time for us later, Eben." Looking up at his soft smile, she kissed him warmly. He responded, but before his ardor overwhelmed them she pulled away, gasping.

They proceeded to Jacksonville and found a delightfully homey hotel on the St. Johns River. Lenore was pleased that it was not one of the fancy, more formal ones like they had stayed in when they were shopping for her trousseau in Savannah.

She waited in the foyer while Eben made the arrangements and called the porter to take their bags upstairs. Everything seemed to be of a palm design, she observed. The carpet, wallpaper and the entire room was covered by palms. There's no doubt that we're in Florida, she thought. He joined her. He was grinning, and when she questioned him he said loudly enough for the clerk to hear, "I informed them that we were newlyweds, but that an early morning call was still necessary. His look of disbelief was worth the escalated price he charged me. Didn't you see him? First he looked at you and, shaking his head, began clucking. He couldn't believe that I'd want an early call...not after feasting his envious eyes on you, my beautiful one."

"I guess he doesn't understand that we'll have the rest of our lives for our lazy mornings." She said softly, blushing.

Eben firmly took her elbow and side by side they ascended the carpeted stairs.

He began apologizing even before they opened the door. "The bath is down the hall, Lenore. I'm so sorry, but..."

"Eben, if you remember, the bath at the farm was outside with only a pump beside the kitchen for our washing. Have you forgotten your beginnings, my sweet?"

He grabbed her to him roughly, closing the door soundly. Nestling his face into the nape of her neck he said, "There are four beautiful baths awaiting you at Elsinore, all the color of the sea, the color of your eyes."

150

He could no longer wait for her response. He fumbled with her bodice buttons, and she stilled his nervous hands and whispered that she would unbutton them herself. He turned away and pulled back the heavy drapes. The moonlight was bright, the river glistening, and he quickly removed his coat. He heard Lenore pull the coverlet back and the crinkle of the bed sheets heightened his desire.

❦

His heavy breathing interrupted the evening's quiet. *I hope that I wasn't too impetuous, and that she's not frightened. This is all so new to her. I'll be more gentle the next time.*

❦

He was supposed to tell me what to do. I don't even know if I did anything right. I hope he's not disappointed. She sniffled and buried her tear-stained face into her pillow. *Why didn't Mum tell me? Why...why... Am I now his wife? Am I?*

She felt him move closer. His arm reached for her and pulled her over on her back. "I...I'm sorry, my sweet. I was so hungry for you that I didn't properly prepare you..."

"Oh, Eben, I want to be a good wife and do all the right things and pray that you'll never be disappointed in me and..."

"Shush. You're the most desirable woman I've ever known. Stop the tears. Shush, my Lenore." She buried her head under his muscled arm and rested her damp face on his chest, sighing.

"Am I your wife? How do I know if I'm your wife? I don't feel like I've given myself to you. How will I know?"

"I promise you that you'll know before the sun comes up over the Atlantic, my sweet. I promise. Now get some sleep. We have a long night before us."

❦

He awakened and realized that Lenore was sleeping soundly. Looking at her he wondered how he could have been so fortunate. It was meant to

151

be. I don't know why, but I know that she was meant for me, just me. She smiled, then she stirred. Pulling her to him he stroked her beautiful face and lowered his hand, clasping her breast, caressing it. She murmured, "My sweet," and became more passionate. Her arms held him tightly to her. She felt a stirring deep in the recesses of her being and she gasped, "Eben, I want to become your wife now...this very minute...please..."

Slowly he stroked her hot, responding body and found joy in her ecstasy.

"You may be assured that you are now my wife. Never forget that, my princess."

"Is that a potato princess?" she laughingly asked. "You may attach any title to her you wish, my sweet. Just make sure that I am the king, the master, the ..."

"Oh, Eben, you can be assured of that. Always and always. But why do I feel...well, funny? I feel like I'm floating..."

"You feel like you're what?"

"Like I'm floating, like I'm me looking down at this other person—you know, separated from my body. Perhaps it's my spirit! Could that be?"

"Well, my sweet, I've made love to many women but have never had such a delightful explanation of my effect on them. My Lenore, you're, shall I say, refreshing."

"Now let's get some sleep."

She heard him chuckle when he turned over. I hope I didn't say anything to displease him, but that's just how I felt, like I was floating. You don't suppose that the Almighty placed a babe inside of me, and that's why I feel as I do? Oh, I do hope so. I want to give Eben lots of sons. And they'll all be just as handsome as he...

The sunlight streamed into the soft shadows of the room. Lenore awakened. He was in the shadow of the window peering down at her. She almost spoke. Why is he so troubled? Is he sorry that he married me? Perhaps he has the dark side like Uncle Sean. May the saints preserve us! I hope not. He was so peculiar. But I'll not give him up like Aunt Clare did Uncle Sean! Never! Never!

CHAPTER THIRTEEN

"April Mosely, you'd best watch your tongue!" Jessup warned. "Who'd you think he'd marry, anyway? You?"

"You know better than that, Mister! Of course I didn't!" April spewed with her face not six inches from his.

"It was just the way he snuck her here in the dark of night. Then to throw that big, fancy party, and I've been told that she was dressed fit to kill. All I'm saying is that it was sure a blow to everyone here, Jessup."

"It's no one's business but Eben's and his missus', April. And you're right about her being all dolled up. Elsie said that her dress was pure silk and came from Savannah. And how else you gonna dress for a fancy party, anyhow? Elsie had me drive her all the way to West Palm Beach for her dress. She must've tried on a hundred, 'cause I was even late picking Dunbar up from his session at the doc's."

Milton Salvatore interjected, "How's he doing, anyway? Haven't seen him at Rotary in a long time."

"He came in for morning coffee just the other day. When I asked him if he went to that party he mumbled that he didn't intend to set foot in that place. What's got into Dunbar, Jessup?" April questioned, a worried look on her face.

"Well, let's just say that he's not himself. The doc thinks it'll take a long time for him to come around, but that his friends shouldn't give up on him. I'm for sure not going to."

"Don't mean to change the subject, but Joy Moon said that she'd never seen such a beautiful house as that one of Eben's. When they opened up those folding parlor doors, she said, there was a big hallway that led into two parlors big enough for a skating rink. The dining room had a table in it that had to be fourteen feet long, and except for that ice sculpture there wasn't an inch that didn't have food on it. Eben and his wife really put on a spread. Said that the mousse was the creamiest she'd ever tasted. Now, April, that ain't a four-legged moose like you might think..."

"I might have been born in Pahokee, Florida, Cletas, but even I know the difference between a moose and mousse. Lois Morgan served the best crab mousse you'd ever eat at Betty Jean's coming-out party, Mister! And another thing, if you don't think I'm smart enough to know the difference, why've you been coming in here every blessed morning for nigh on ten years to pester me, huh? "And another thing you might be interested to know, Cletas, is that Eben ordered two dozen blackberry pies from right here in this Lakeside Coffee Shoppe, and yours truly baked them, that's what! Yep, lovingly made by these hands right here." She held her hands out from her for all to admire. She didn't care that her bright red polish was chipped.

"And another thing, Cletas, every mouthful of my pies was eaten, and I heard that they had a ton of those fancy desserts left over from that high-and-mighty outfit in Palm Beach and that they didn't taste one bit better 'cause they were served on silver trays by those fancy dudes dressed up in those monkey suits, either."

Cletas laughed at the other men on the bar stools and said, "Think I just got Miss April all riled up. The truth, April, as to why we all come in here don't have a thing to do with your pie making or your coffee making either. We just like to see you bend over to clean off the counter, especially when you're sporting that low necked, tight blue frock you wear a lot. Ain't that true boys?"

"You better get outa here while the gettin's good, Cletas," Milton said, laughing. Cletas made a dash for the door and waved back toward April, whose face was red as a beet, but before he closed the door he asked, "Hey, April, you gonna wear that blue dress tomorrow, 'cause if you are, you can bet I'll be here."

"Now, April, don't let him get to you. You know that he's just funning..."

"I know, but he makes me so blasted mad!"

Milton continued, "To get back to the party, when Patrick and Walter came to the packing house the other day, Dorothy Chastaine asked them all about the shindig, and they must've talked for nigh on an hour telling her all about it."

"What'd they say, Milton? Now, mind you, I've been told plenty..."

"April, Patrick gave it a real good description. Now, you know that Catherine is about to deliver, so he said that they didn't stay 'til the very end, but the way he described that mermaid ice sculpture...whew! That must have been something! Said that it was five feet high and sat up on a pedestal in the middle of this long table with orchids floating all around it..."

"That's not what Nelle Sears said. She said that it was only three feet high and that they were gardenias..."

"Now, April, I think that Patrick knows the difference between an orchid and a gardenia. Heck, Catherine grows gardenias all over the place and is past president of the Canal Point Garden Club."

"Well, Nelle's just as up on her flowers as Catherine Carroll any day, and she said that..."

"And they also said that there were about a dozen different kinds of fruit salads served in fresh pineapples and cantaloupes and watermelons, and so on. Said that they were sweetened with honey and orange wine and fresh mint and limes, and you name it, they had it all. They were all circled around that mermaid in a bed of ice, and he and Walter never knew that men liked fruit salad so much and kept eating that fruit 'til they almost burst. Truth was, they couldn't take their eyes off that naked mermaid." They all laughed, even April.

"Nelle said that they gave that house some fancy name out of a Shakespeare play. Now why couldn't they have named it for the Lake? Maybe Lake View or Lake..."

"April, bet you wanted him to name it for the Lakeside Coffee Shoppe"

"That's not what I meant, and you know it! Elsinore! What kind of a name is that, anyway?"

"Prof. Speare said that it's the name of a castle in Denmark or somewhere like that, and it's in one of those plays, just like you said."

"I don't care how fancy a name it is. They should have named it for some place around here, that's what! Heck, the next thing we know is they'll try to change the name of our Lake Okeechobee to Buckingham, that's what!"

"Now, April..."

<hr/>

"Eben, it's a palace—no, it's more like the White House. Oh, hon, it's so beautiful! I love the clean, classic lines. I don't like a lot of gingerbread on a house. Oh, I love you!"

They had driven in from Palm Beach, where Eben had checked with the caterers before driving on out to Pahokee. He was excited. How can she help but delight in it, he thought. I'm glad I decided on the black shutters instead of dark green. Ethan was right. More elegant. And the plaque done in white and black with ELSINORE in shiny brass was perfect. I chose Ethan well.

It was dusk, and Lenore and Eben walked side by side down the red brick walk that curved around the back garden overlooking the lake. "We'll get to enjoy the lake for a few more years, Lenore, so let's, while we can. The sunsets are unbelievable. We need that dike, though. I'd never have built here if there were no protection. I didn't go through the '28 hurricane, but I know those who did. It was devastating. Over two thousand people were killed—most drowned. We are still uncovering skeletons in the fields when we clear them for planting."

"Oh, Eben, how awful! You came out the next year didn't you?"

"In '29. Best move I've ever made." He squeezed her slender hand and smiled down at her upturned face, "The next best move I've ever made," he said, laughing forcefully.

He took his arm from around her shoulder and reached inside his pants pocket. "What are you grinning about?" Lenore asked, knowing that he had another surprise for her.

"I want you to have this for our party tomorrow. I bought it especially for your dress. Now don't say a word. I just had to have it."

"Ahhh, Eben! It's the most beautiful necklace I've ever seen. Is that a real emerald?"

"Of course! And the pearls and the diamonds that encircle it are real too. Here, let me."

She turned around for him to clasp it, and when he turned her back around, she was crying softly.

"I hope those are tears of joy, my Lenore, for you have made me the happiest man alive." He took her hands in his and kissed them gently. "I could not find the earrings that I wanted, so wear the diamond ones that I gave you for our wedding. They're not too ostentatious for our Pahokee friends.

"We have some lovely people in the area, and I'm sure you're going to enjoy them. Oh, I spoke to Margaret Bleech about giving you bridge lessons, and she said she'd be delighted. She'd better be. Her husband is into Hunter Farms for a bundle. Two bad years is enough to break a man out here. Let's hope that I don't have to retrieve that necklace to pay debts, my sweet. Now, don't look like that! I was only teasing you."

She had not noticed his dark side since Jacksonville. Perhaps she had been wrong.

⁘

"Sammy, run ovah ta ya Aunt Clara's, an hurry 'bout it. She gotta go ta Pahokee fo' Doctor Spooner. Ya Mama's time is come! Hurry now!" Dessa said.

Sammy took time out to ask a question. "How do you know it's her time?"

"Did Ah tell ya ta hurry? Git!"

General was on her heels the whole way, barking the news as he went. Sammy saw her Aunt Clara open the front door just like she knew what Sammy wanted.

"I've had my bag packed since two weeks ago, Sammy. How she's gone this long, I'll never know. That little fellow must weigh ten pounds if he weighs ..."

"How do you know it's a boy? Maybe it's a girl and they'll name her Sheena, like I want. Maybe."

"I don't know it's a boy, honey. I just hope it is so your mama will have two boys to go with you and Mary Catherine. That's all."

"Well, I don't think it makes any difference if we're all even. Daddy doesn't either..."

"Sammy, can't you see that I'm trying to hurry. Now go to the back yard and tell Clarissa that she's to stay here with you until I get back."

"I'm not going to stay here, Aunt Clara. Dessa didn't tell me that I had to. Besides, my mama might need me..."

"Sammy Carroll, you do just what I told you. I'm going for the doctor, and I'll stop by the packing house to tell your daddy. Soon's I'm through with that, then I'll send Dessa to stay over here with you all. Now don't argue with me. Clarissa is in her playhouse."

And with that she wiggled that Hudson all the way back to the hard road and headed for Pahokee to get the doctor.

Sammy didn't hear Dessa come up behind her, and as usual, General didn't bark.

"Sammy, Mama is sure yelling about that baby that's coming." Jamie said breathlessly.

"What do you mean she's yelling?"

Dessa intervened. "She's yelling 'cause she's got a bunch o' joy. Dat's all, Sammy."

"Junie said that her mama yelled her head 'bout off when little Jack was born 'cause it hurt something awful to birth a baby, Dessa. Was she telling the truth?"

"It sometime hurt, but it still a joyous yellin', 'cause ya mama is happy to bring a babe inta de world."

"Well, I for one hope that little Sheena doesn't up and die like little Jack did. They had him all the way to that colored cemetery even before I could see him. When can we see little Sheena, Dessa? Did Daddy say?"

"No, he din't say, but Ah'm shuah it'll not be too much longah. She been laborin' fo' neah 'bout six houahs now. Wouldn't be surprised if he come up in his truck any minute now to fetch ya."

Mary Catherine was sitting on the swing under the mango tree reading, unconcerned. When she heard Patrick's truck, she barely looked up, but Sammy and Jamie ran as fast as they could to get the news.

"Is little Sheena alive or dead, Daddy?" Sammy shouted.

"What on earth are you talking about, Sammy? Of course he's alive, and his name is Joseph Graham, named for my father and granddaddy Samuel. Your mother and I have decided to call him Gray, short for Graham. How do you like that handle?" he asked jubilantly.

Mary Catherine had joined the group and expressed her approval. "I think it's a handsome name. I especially like Graham. I'll call him by his real name. I think Gray is..."

"Why can't we just call him Buck or Buster or...?" Sammy inquired.

Jamie was the only one who didn't have an opinion. Even Clarissa joined in. "I like Johnny. That's a nice name."

Sammy couldn't help but pinch her. "Whose baby is it, anyway, Clarissa? He's ours to do with, isn't he Dessa?"

"Ya jes too excited, Sammy." Dessa said shaking her head at Sammy. "Clarissa jes saying a name she lak, ain't dat right, honey?"

"I like Johnny best, Dessa. I'll call him Johnny if I want to, Sammy Carroll."

"Hey, you three quit fighting. I'm a daddy to a beautiful nine-pound, healthy boy, and Kitten did just fine, as I knew she would. Are you ready to go see our new creation? Are you?" He lifted Jamie up high as he could but could not evoke a smile. He just twisted his mouth around and shifted his eyes like he didn't know how to act.

Poor little fellow, Dessa thought. He bes spen' de night wid me an Marsh. He gonta need a heap a lovin'.

Even Sammy saw how sad Jamie looked. "Here, Jamie, you can ride beside Daddy if you want. I can ride in the back."

"Well, I'm not going to ride in the back, Sammy." Mary Catherine shouted. "It'll blow me all over creation. My hair will be a mess..."

"It's only a block away, Mary Catherine. Besides, you can comb the blasted stuff, you ninny!"

"Stop it this minute!" Patrick yelled between clenched teeth, his nerves obviously frayed.

"I'm sorry, Daddy," Sammy said, and Mary Catherine said that she'd rather walk and that Dessa could ride in the cab with Jamie. After all, it was just a short distance, like Sammy said, and besides, that way her hair wouldn't get mussed.

When Patrick backed up and turned the truck around, he saw General out of his side mirror. He called, "General, old boy, come on and meet Master Gray."

Jamie spoke up, "I bet he won't like him, 'cause he made Mama hurt and yell. General doesn't like for Mama to be hurt."

Patrick glanced at Dessa, who was shaking her head from side to side. She looked at Patrick and her hands were patting Jamie's head. She decided that she had to say something, so she asked, "Mr. Carroll, da ya tink dat Jamie can spen' de night wid me an' Marsh? Marsh been wantin' him ta hep him wid peelin' some of dat sugar cane he cut up at Mistah Tucker's. I know how Jamie lak sugar cane."

"Yeh!" Jamie said excitedly, "Can I, Daddy? Can I, huh?"

"The only thing I can think of to keep you from it is your mama might miss you too much. But do you want me to ask her, anyway?"

"I wanta stay with Marsh to help him with the cane, Daddy. I wanta."

Patrick winked at Dessa and thought, when she first moved here I would have gladly booted that know-it-all islander off the place. But now, I don't know what we'd do without her. She has great insight. I've always wondered if Sammy is right and that she has those special island powers. She's also right about General never barking at her. Not once have I seen him even go up to her like he does Marsh and all the other Coloreds around here. Even when Sammy and Jamie are playing at Dessa's, he lies down beneath that catalpa tree and just watches. But when they are playing in our yard and Dessa's not around, he's right there with them, running and jumping. It's a puzzler all right.

"Patrick, are you sure? I know how much General means to you," Catherine said. They were on Samuel's front porch having a glass of limeade. They often sat there in the cool of the evening enjoying the lake breeze.

"You know how Eben has always wanted him, and the truth is I'm not sure that he won't harm Gray. Now, I mean it, Catherine. You saw him the first time I showed the baby to him. He actually growled and tried to paw him."

"But, honey, we could keep him outside the house and..."

"And keep the whole neighborhood awake with his howling and barking, like he did the few times I did put him out. No, I've made up my mind. I know that the children will miss him, but it just can't be helped. We have to think of the good of all. Besides, we're going to be so busy fixing up this place that I'll not have time to go hunting next season."

It was Samuel who suggested that Patrick and Catherine move into the big house and he into their smaller one. The only change he wanted was that a bathroom be added to the small house.

Sammy was ecstatic. She was to be allowed to stay with her grandpa in her own room without Mary Catherine. She could hardly wait. Her grandpa Samuel promised her that she could paint her room any color she wanted, and she said, "You can bet that it won't be that lettuce green, Grandpa Samuel. I want it sunshine yellow—that's what. And I want bunk beds, and I want..."

"Hey, I didn't say anything about new beds, Sammy." He laughed at Dessa, who was drying the dinner dishes with Sammy's help.

"Oh, I don't mean right away. But if sometime in the future you've a mind to buy new furniture, I sure could use bunk beds. That way Junie or Thelma could spend the night with me, and we could put on a show for you, or maybe even scratch your back while you listen to Lum and Abner, and then I could pop some popcorn for you...that would be fun wouldn't it, Grandpa Samuel?"

Samuel chuckled along with Dessa. "Dessa, I believe our Sammy would make a right good lawyer. What do you think?"

Dessa shook her head up and down and grinned. "Our Sammy gonta be anythin' she wanta be, Mistah Samuel, an' we gonta hep her."

When school began in September, the exchange of houses had been made and General was at Elsinore with Eben and Lenore. Eben had insisted on paying a healthy sum for him, and Patrick had appreciated it. The painting and papering of the big house had cost more than he expected, and with another mouth to feed he was struggling financially, but he never let on to Catherine or to Samuel that he was concerned. He had even considered letting Marsh go but knew they could not manage without Dessa, neither the Carrolls nor Samuel, and it would have killed Sammy.

Lenore had been accepted by the ladies of the area, and although she missed her family and Georgia, her life was full but for one thing—she had not conceived. It did bother her. She knew that Eben was concerned, although he had not voiced it. She had become sensitive to his moods, of which there were many, but the dark side had not surfaced again.

Alpha and James kept Dessa informed about the happenings at Elsinore, and Sammy was privy to some of their conversations. Alpha said, "Miz Lenore sho' 'nuff lak ta run an' play wid dat dog, an' Mistah Eben, why he t'ought dat dog was de best dog he evah seed. Miz Lenore taught dat General ta fetch de papah, an' she t'row sticks in de lake, an' dat General swim aftah it wid her laughin' lak a little girl."

"I bet she likes General near as much as we do, huh, Alpha?" Sammy asked.

"Ah, yeh, Sammy, she sho 'nuff do. But he miss ya. Ah can tell. Don't he miss 'em, James?" she said while winking so Sammy couldn't see her.

"Mistah Eben, he say dat dog won't evah really be his'n 'cause he miss Mistah Patrick an' y'all too much. Dat's de trut', Miz Sammy. I heared him say dat wid his own mout'."

"Well, I already got it figured out how we're gonna get General back." She looked at each to see their reaction, but none gave away his feelings. They just looked puzzled. Sammy continued. "When Miss Lenore decides to have a baby then General will get so jealous, just like he did when Gray was born, that they'll hafta sell him back to Daddy. That's what!"

"But what if Miz Lenore don't have a baby, Sammy?" Dessa asked.

"I heard Daddy say that Mister Eben wants a baby in the worst way. Now I heard him say that, Dessa. He's always asking Daddy about Gray and saying that he'd like to have a strapping boy just like him—that's what!"

"Well, lakin' ta have one an' havin' one ain't de same, Sammy. De Almighty have sometin' ta say 'bout dat, Ah'm believin'."

"I heard my Uncle Walter say that Mister Eben thinks he's God, so maybe he can do just about what he wants..."

⬥

Elsinore was lit up like a Christmas tree, Alpha told Dessa. "Now, mind ya, it jes' 'bout Christmas, but de fust anniversary for Mistah Eben an' his Lenore was de big occasion. She tol' him dat she din't want any fuss, but ya know Mistah Eben," she chuckled. "He gotta make a big show 'bout most everyt'in'."

"He look tired ta me de las' time he here, Alpha. Is he worried 'bout anyt'in'?" Dessa had been unable to warn Eben about John. She just couldn't...her own son...

Alpha didn't dare tell her about John showing up at the party with that other colored man from the catering outfit in West Palm Beach. She about dropped her teeth when he came to the kitchen door. There he stood grinning his head off just like the cat that swallowed the canary.

"Ya know, James say de same t'ing jes de othah day. De very same t'ing."

"Pass me dat othah pan o' beans. I gotta git on de stick 'fore Mistah Samuel start hollerin' fo' his dinner. Miz Carroll say dat she nevah see him eat so good, not even when his missus was alive."

Alpha changed the subject. "James," Alpha called, "Is Mistah Samuel an' Sammy come back yet?"

James got out of the front seat of the Packard, where he had been sitting, reading the paper, and went around to the side yard and looked in the garage. It was an open, four-stall, wooden building with a tin roof that Samuel had built that fall.

He called to Alpha, "Not deah. Nuttin' but Mistah Patrick's Diamond T truck. You an' Dessa got time ta visit some moah."

Alpha and Dessa left their shady spot underneath the Catalpa tree and went up the wooden steps into the kitchen. The aroma of smothered pork chops filled the small house. Dessa took the heavy pot lid off the cast iron frying pan and gently lifted the chops up through the onion gravy and added a little water from the kettle.

"Wait'll Sammy see what Ah'm fixin'. Hummm, she gonta have one o' huh Sammy fits, sho 'nuff. Alpha, han' me dat black peppah. Mistah Samuel lak his good an' hot an' even add moah ta his rice an' gravy."

Dessa sat down at the kitchen table, and she and Alpha resumed their visit. "Lak Ah was sayin', dat house look lak a Christmas tree. Mistah Eben had de dinin' room table so full o' flowers dat he could hardly see Miz Lenore. He sit at one end o' de table and she sit at de othah. He even hire him two servants from Wes' Palm Beach ta serve dat big dinner." She didn't dare mention that one of them was John.

Did you an' James hafta do all de cookin'?"

"My, my, no. Miz Lenore din't even know 'bout all de fuss he a goin' ta, oah she maght o' stop'd him. We din't hafta do a ting."

"Did he have fancy food lak at deah big pahty?"

"Lamb. Dat's what dey had. A great big leg o' lamb lak Miz Lenore lak, an' roast potatoes, an' Brussels sprouts an' a whole bunch of othah tings. Ah did make de mint sauce lak she lak, an' Mistah Eben ask me ta make de ambrosia wid fresh coconut lak in de island. She sho lak dat. He put some orange wine all ovah it, and my, my, it was good."

"Ah din't know James still makin' dat orange wine. Ah'd lak some fo' Mistah Samuel's fruit if he have extra."

"Oh, he got a plenty. Well, de pahty wasn't no pahty at all. It was jest de two o' dem. Mistah Eben had a violin player deah, an' he an' Miz Lenore dey dance all ovah dat big room, him in his ridin' britches an' boots an' she in a long, blue, silk dress, wearin' a new necklace he bought in Palm Beach at one o' dose fancy stoahs. It shuah was pretty wit' pearls an,' he say, diamonds. Dey laugh lak two little kids just a singin' an' a dancin.'"

<hr>

Eben had not recognized John. After all, he had not seen him in over fifteen years, when Dessa brought him to West Palm Beach to live with her cousin's family. He had noticed the unconventional interest the slight Negro man was taking in Lenore's necklace. I'm going to have to check the agency about this one, he thought. He's too surly to suit me. But Eben was so immersed in pleasing Lenore that he soon forgot his suspicions. He shouldn't have.

James, who was a mild mannered man, had John Whitson cornered in the kitchen with Alpha behind him agreeing with everything he told him. "Don't know wheah ya gits de idea dat Mistah Eben has anytin' to do wid youah mama's lan', John. Mistah Eben jest a good friend of Juan Pecone, an' he visit him in de islands. Ya bettah git ya head on straight befo' youah mama bust it—dat's what!"

"I'm beginnin' to think that there's more to this than I thought, James. What're you and Alpha hidin'? Would it be that this Mister Eben made a lotta money runnin' rum, and you two helped him like Mama did? Hmmmm? Is that what it's all about? I think I've just stumbled onto something that just might put some jingle in old John's pocket. Yessir, I think I might've."

"James, we gotta tell Mistah Eben 'bout John. Hate ta mess up his holiday, but we gotta."

Christmas of '33 came and went. Lenore and Eben began making their plans to return to Springfield for a spring visit. She hoped that she would have good news for her family by then. She had not told Eben, but she had visited Dr. Spooner to see if there was a problem. Married over a year and still not pregnant. It wasn't for lack of trying, for Eben was a very attentive husband and she a responsive partner. She had on occasion been the aggressor—he liked that.

Dr. Spooner had examined her and found nothing physically wrong. She was built small, and he could see a problem with carrying and delivery, but he had seen many similar cases with no problems. He informed Lenore of his findings and suggested that they exercise patience. He was well aware that Eben was short of it and wanted his way immediately.

"The good Lord will handle this in his own time, Lenore. You just tell Eben that. He won't like it, but there are times when we have to bow to God's will." He laughed and continued, "You can tell him that, too."

She told him nothing of the visit. He had been mentioning a well known doctor in West Palm Beach and had suggested that perhaps she should visit him before they went north. She shrugged and thought about what Dr. Spooner had said about leaving it to God, but she didn't mention it to him. "We'll talk about it after the Fair. You know how busy I'll be with that. Sue Maxville and I seem to have the entire program to put on. I don't know why I get myself in these messes."

"It's because you're such a good organizer and work well with everyone. I'm proud of you. Do you realize that you're the youngest coordinator they've ever had? You bet I'm proud!" To himself he said, I just hope that you'll always be proud of me. Think I'll just hire Tut to keep an eye on that John. James and Alpha seem to think that he bears watching.

<hr />

Clara and Catherine were sitting in front of the drugstore having their afternoon cokes when Lenore and Sue Maxville drove up in the new Buick Eben had bought Lenore for Christmas. Clara put her head out of the window and called to them. "Hey girls, Catherine needs an entry blank for the baby contest. I told her that you should just go ahead and award Gray the prize. He's gotta be the prettiest baby God ever made, aren't you, Gray?" she added clucking him underneath his chubby chin.

Lenore and Sue got out of the car and went over to them. "You know, I believe you're right, but we have to abide by the rules. Catherine, may I hold him?" questioned Lenore.

"He has gotten so big. Bet he weights almost thirty pounds, don't you, Gray? Look Sue. He likes me. Look at that smile!"

Sue had become close to Lenore since they had taken on the chairmanship of the Everglades Fair and knew of her longing to have a child. It's so sad to want one as badly as she does, and here every time Jack drops his trousers I'm pregnant. Doesn't seem quite fair. We have to struggle to make ends meet, and Eben owns practically all of Pahokee, according to some. But she's right about that adorable child. Think he favors Patrick with his reddish hair and those big blue eyes. He'll no doubt win his category hands down.

Catherine took Gray from Lenore and asked, "When are you and Eben going to Georgia, Lenore?"

"Right after the Fair. I had wanted to go up for St. Patrick's Day, but that's right in the middle of it. So, we'll leave the following week. I'm sure I'll need a good long rest by then. I don't know how Sue does it! With four little ones at home I'm sure I'd be too tired to take on such responsibility. But she's a trooper, aren't you, Sue?"

"Seems that the more I have to do the better organized I am. Mama said that I've always been that way."

"How is Grace, anyway?" Clara asked. "I haven't seen her in so long."

"Same old aches and pains, Miss Clara. Her knees do bother her, and with Daddy gone on that hunting trip with Arden Geiger, she has all the chores to do."

"Who all went in that biplane? And did they take the dogs with them? I don't know how they get all that equipment in that small a plane, even if it is a three seater."

"Well, they didn't. Dad had Cracker drive up ahead of them to set up camp, and he took the dogs. That's why Mama is so tired. Without Cracker to help with the milking and chickens she has it all to do, now that Bernice up and left him."

"Well, Walter had better get help before he and Arden fly up to Georgia, I can tell you that. Is Eben going on this trip, Lenore?"

"He was, but he'll wait 'til the fall now. Arden will scout the area for him, and I believe he said that Patrick wanted to go, if I'm not mistaken. They want to give General a good workout. Catherine, Patrick does plan to go, doesn't he?"

"He said that if everything is going well at the farm, then he planned to. His brother Jim is coming down from Georgia sometime about then to help work on the new Catholic Church. I know you'll be glad when it's finished, Lenore. Driving all the way to Clewiston is such a long way."

"Oh, Eben and I don't mind. We always stop at the Inn for a delightful dinner, and that gives Alpha and James the day off. Actually we'll miss the trip."

Sue called a greeting to Mrs. Bordeaux, then joined the conversation. "Jack said just last night at dinner that he never saw such growth as we're having, and he hopes that dike will be completed before we have another bad hurricane. The new Canal Point school will be finished by next year, and so will the Pahokee Methodist Church. And the Golds are adding on to the canning plant in Canal Point."

Catherine added, "Mary Catherine said last night at supper that they're going to build a big skating rink in Pahokee, and Patrick informed us that the Mayaca Corporation has donated land for a golf course north of Canal Point, and they've already named it the Big Lake Golf Club. Said it's one of those non-profit groups, just for the area people to join."

"Now when do they think these Glades people will find time to play golf?" Clara asked.

"If they can find time to fly all over creation to hunt deer, turkeys and wild hogs, then I'm sure they'll find time to play golf," Sue said.

"Eben wants me to take lessons. He's already said that we should join. I think it'll be fun," Lenore added, but to herself she said, I hope I'm so big with child that I won't be allowed to. Oh, I so hope. Eben's been so down lately, ever since the holidays. Even Alpha asked me if he was feeling poorly. My dear husband, I know it's because of me.

Little did she know...

CHAPTER FOURTEEN

When Lenore and Eben traveled to Savannah on their return trip to Florida, Savannah was wearing its bright spring foliage. The flowering trees, dogwood and redbud, and azaleas surrounding the hotel's gardens were the perfect setting for Lenore's announcement to Eben. She had been so busy with the fair that she had lost track of her overdue days. When she realized that she was almost a week late with her period, she was too fearful to even mention it to Eben. But now she was sure.

Actually, Nora was the first to mention it to her. "How did you know, Mum?"

"There's always a special glow when a woman is expecting and also when she's in love. Her color becomes heightened. I'm so glad that the church in Pahokee will be finished in time for the christening. Liam said he'd drive me down for the birthing, but I'll take the train, I'm thinking."

"Oh, Mum, I can hardly wait to tell Eben. It seems that we've waited for so long, even though it's only been one and a half years. So much has happened!

"I knew it! I was positive! Something told me, and when Johnny and I were sipping out by the barn the other night, he said that you were prettier than he'd ever seen you. And he also said that he'd be very surprised if you didn't bring a wee one back on our next trip. I did tell him that I'd begun to worry..."

"Oh, hon, I was almost beside myself with worry. Father Finnegan said that I needed more faith and should be ashamed of myself for pressuring the Almighty."

"I want to call Ethan and have him decorate the back bedroom as a nursery. It will be the most beautiful room any little boy ever had and..."

"Wait a minute, hon. I'm only just beginning this babe." They laughed and hugged, oblivious to the passersby. When Eben noticed the inquisitive onlookers, he laughed "It's spring, and anything can happen in beautiful Savannah in the spring."

Eben insisted on Lenore's going to West Palm Beach to the top obstetrician there. "I know that Doster Spooner is an excellent doctor, but I want the best."

"But what if we can't get to town in time. Those things do happen, you know," lamented Lenore.

"All right. I'll speak to Doc myself and explain. He's a sensible man and should know how much this baby means to both of us. You can visit him so he can keep abreast of your progress, and then if you go into labor and it looks like we won't have time to get to town, then..." Eben rambled on.

The dog days of summer came and went without a hurricane to test the new dike. Lenore said that she must have drunk a gallon of limeade every day that summer. Her friends came to visit often, for Eben insisted that she take it easy. "He watches her like a hawk!" Sue Maxville told their friends. "You'd think that this was the first and last baby ever born. I declare you would."

"He told Ralph that he wanted a son and then they'd call it quits."

"I bet Lenore doesn't know that!" Sue almost shouted. "She comes from a large Irish Catholic family, and they believe in big families. One son, indeed!"

"Well, you know Eben. He always gets his way."

"I hope that Lenore has enough backbone to put a stop to this kind of acting. I surely do! The audacity of the man! Just who does he think he is...God?"

"You might just say that, Sue. There are some around here who think just that. Poor old Dunbar for one. There are those who think that his jealousy of Eben pushed him over the edge. Now don't look like that! That's what I've heard more than once. I've also heard that there is a suspicion as to just where he got all his money. Now I'm not going to start any rumors, but that's just what I heard. Why just the other day at Hickerson's Grocery I overheard a perfect stranger say that it was well known that some of the rum runners had bought up most of the Glades. Don't look at me like that! They said it right in front of everyone there."

⁘

Lenore carried the baby well. She was into her last month but barely showed. Eben was concerned, but Dr. Spooner and the doctor in town both assured him that although the baby was small, all signs pointed to a healthy baby. She felt well and was as happy as she'd ever been. Eben's constant presence did annoy her at times. Patrick had tried to get him to go hunting earlier in the fall, but he would not budge. So Patrick and Walter took their swamp buggy to Big Cypress rather than Georgia, and Eben let him take General.

⁘

Tut Guthrie had reported just what Eben had suspected. John Whitson was knee deep in the numbers racket and owed money all over town. Tut had said that he was just about at the breaking point, and Eben gave him the go-ahead to contact the sheriff with the information. John and thirty others were picked up and convicted in September. They were sentenced to eight years.

Dessa was distraught, but as Alpha and James told Patrick and Catherine, "He brung it on hisself. He know he do wrong." Secretly, they were relieved. "Ah tol' ya dat little John too big foah his britches. Comin' out heah tryin' ta make trouble fo' de bes friend any o' us evah had. He jes no good, Alpha, no good, an' Dessa know it."

⁘

The grey, concrete jailhouse loomed in front of them as they rounded the corner. Marsh patted Dessa's hand and said, "Ah know he youah son an' dat you upset 'bout all dis. Well, he youah son, an' ya love him, no mattah what."

"Ah gonta be all right, Marsh. Ah gonta be fine. He gotta learn his lesson. Maybe dis help."

John scowled at the two of them. The jailor told them that they had ten minutes to visit, and they took their seats in front of the cage where John sat. Dessa was the first to speak. "Ya know dat ya done wrong an ya gotta pay fo' it..."

"And when I get out I can tell you who is gonna pay for his part in it. You can bet your black ass! That white son of a bitch best be looking over his shoulder, 'cause John Whitson's gonna make him pay for..."

Dessa was furious. "Now ya listen ta me fo' once in youah life. If ya talkin' 'bout Mistah Eben, den ya can quit raght now. Yes, he buy mah lan' fo' me. Dat what ya want to heah, ain't it? He bought mah lan' fo' me 'cause Juan Picone ast him ta. Dat's what. Juan couldn', 'cause he ain't a citizen. Mistah Eben did it as a favah ta Juan. What wrong wid dat? Huh?"

"Ain't nothing wrong with that, Mama. It's just that I know right here in my brain and my heart that one Eben Hunter was the Florida man who was receiving all that rum from Juan. And you know it, too. Don't you? And the law oughta be catching him, just like he had them catch me, and sticking him in the stinking jail right beside me! I'd like that. There ain't no way in hell that he'd get out alive! On that you can lay a wager!"

"Why ya gotta make trouble fo' youah Mama, John? Why?"

He lowered his head and mumbled between clenched teeth, "That white son of a bitch got everything, and I ain't got nothin'! But I aim to have some of what he's got! I hear that he's having him a little white bastard baby. That's right! And when I get out, that white baby gonna have a little visit from old John..." His voice trailed off. When he looked up he saw Dessa and Marsh drop their mouths open in amazement. Laughing loudly, he turned to the jailor and said, "I'm ready. Don't have any more to say to these dumb niggers!"

The jailor shook his head with disgust as he led him away.

Marsh helped Dessa up and squeezed her to him. "He jus' angry, honey. He din't mean it."

"He mean it. He mean it..." But she thought, no, Baby John. Not while youah mama's alive. Deh won't be no trouble by mah flesh an' blood for Mistah Eben. No, my Baby John, Ah'll tend to ya fust.

⁂

Alpha and James, like always, had planned a big Hunter dinner for Thanksgiving. Eben kept making remarks about not being there to enjoy it, because he and Lenore and Rahn Ahern Hunter would be in West Palm Beach at the hospital, enjoying turkey and dressing.

Lenore awakened Thanksgiving morning with a few twinges of pain but said nothing to Eben. She was sure that they would go away, as they had before, but by ten o'clock she knew that her time had come. She stayed upstairs, as was her custom of late, awaiting her tea. Alpha immediately saw that she was uncomfortable. "Ah'm gonna git Mistah Eben dis very minute, Missus. How come ya din't fetch me, huh?"

"I wasn't sure. It's not that I'm afraid, because I assisted Mum with the last three babes, but..."

When Alpha saw the puddle on the carpet, she shouted, "Ah'm goin' fo' Mistah Eben. Ya watah's broke. Ah'm goin' now!" She rushed down the winding stairway, holding on to the bannister for dear life. James saw her coming and knew what was going on. He was at the garage when Alpha got to Eben, who was on the back patio having his coffee. By the time Lenore was ready to go, James had the car engine running, and Eben was already telling him that he was going to drive because James drove too slowly.

"Hon, please let James drive. I'd like for you to sit here beside me."
She patted the seat, and Eben saw her concern. He told James, "I'll sit with
the Missus for a while, James. Then I'll take over when we get outside
town. I know you don't like traffic."

Lenore squeezed his hand and kissed his cheek. "There shouldn't be a
lot of traffic on a holiday, hon. What did Dr. Hebron say when you called?"

His face dropped. He sighed. "James, turn around. I forgot to call. I
can't believe that I'd do such a harebrained thing! James, what're you
laughing about? Lenore, you two had better stop it this instant!"

"Mistah Eben, Alpha done call de doctah, an' she call Doctah Spooner
jes in case." He continued to chuckle even though Eben was flushed with
embarrassment, and James, who had witnessed Eben's temper more than
once, should have known better.

About then Lenore had a hard labor pain. Eben felt her nails dig into his
hand. When he looked at her white face he told James to step on it and he
didn't care if he got every cop in West Palm Beach on their tails.

"Hold on, my sweet! Hold on!"

<hr>

Alpha called Thornton and he called the clan. "De dinnah already in
de oven, Mistah Thornton. Ya might as well come on ta eat. Mistah Eben
say he call soon as de little fellah show up. My, my, he some kinda excited."

"We're gonna have a very upset father if that baby isn't a boy baby,
Alpha. Poor Lenore will have to get busy to give him another one in a hurry
if it isn't a boy."

"She sho 'nuff gonta. Yessah, she sho gonta."

<hr>

Dinner had been over for two hours. Ralph had suggested that they all
go to the back patio to let it settle, and so the children could let off some
steam. Emerson had pulled out a bottle to sweeten the men's coffee. He
turned toward his wife and said, "It's time to celebrate, hon. Just a little
sweetnin' won't hurt." Damn, that woman is gonna drive me crazy. Ever
since that revival she's been watching me like a blooming hawk.

The phone rang in the foyer, and Ralph rushed to answer it. All the
grownups were right behind him. "Hello. Yes, Eben. IT'S A BOY! Six
pounds, eight ounces. Lenore and Rahn doing fine. Is that all? What time

was he born? Two forty-two. Well, old man, we all congratulate you and give our best to Lenore. How is she, by the way? What do you mean you don't know? They won't let you see her? Well, you should have had her delivered by Doster. He'd have let you help like I did with Junior."

Ralph turned to the smiling group and said, "He sounds exhausted. You'd have thought that he had the baby. Bet we won't be seeing much of brother Ebenezer for a while. That means more work for us all, but then he deserves it."

The wives looked at each other when he said that and thought, but did not dare to say, and who's been running the farms for the past three years? Ever since he married that teenager from Georgia, he's been throwing all the work at you three.

Eben was the doting father and Lenore the conscientious mother. Rahn was never without attention. His skin was as fair as Lenore's and his eyes darkly fringed and green as hers, too. But he was all Hunter in every other way. Alpha and James doted on him and called him Lil Eben when his parents weren't in attendance. A happier baby you'd never see with a smile for everyone.

The summer of '35 was approaching, and Patrick and Walter had a decision to make. Should they apply for a trucking job to haul fruit from Georgia and the Carolinas to the northern markets to tide them over the summer, or should they try fishing the Gulf again? It was a dilemma. Neither wanted to be on the road for six to eight long weeks, but neither did they want to borrow money from the banks to make it through the summer, when there was no farming.

Catherine and Clara both wished that they would stay in the Glades and hire on as carpenters like a lot of area men did. After all, there was the new Canal Point School being built to be ready for the school term, and Duke Tucker was building a large, two-story building in Canal Point. Plus Nola Dragon's new dress shop was going into a new building at the corner of Lake Avenue in Pahokee. The place was booming!

Patrick and Walter were to make their decision by Sunday dinner time, Sammy had told Dessa. Sunday seemed to take forever to arrive, and when it did, all were anxious to hear the decision. Grandaddy Samuel had finished the blessing, and Clara and Catherine turned toward their respective husbands for their answer. But before a word could be said a nervous Sammy just had to say something.

"You could work on the new sidewalks in Pahokee, or you could help them put in the street lights or even help build the dike, and then you wouldn't hafta go traipsing all over creation for work!" Having said her piece, she sat back in the dining room chair and swung her long, eleven-year-old legs nervously. She saw Dessa duck around behind the new refrigerator with her hand covering her mouth. She just hoped that she wouldn't be punished for her outburst 'cause she sure as heck wanted to go fishing while everyone else napped.

They all waited for someone to speak.

Finally, Patrick said, "Sammy has a point. But what they're paying those workers wouldn't put enough on our tables to carry us, and Walter and I know it. We've looked into the matter carefully. Heck, we don't like to be gone for so long, either."

"Oh, for heaven's sake! All this racket has awakened Gray," Catherine lamented. She got up, threw her napkin onto the table and went into the back bedroom. She was met by Dessa. "I'll tend him, Miz Carroll. You go on back ta ya family."

Catherine almost hugged her but restrained herself. She thought a lot of Dessa but was hesitant to show it. She used to hug Ruby all the time and really missed her when she and her boys, Snookey and Renner, up and moved to Miami without even a week's notice. She never wondered why she felt as she did about Dessa, rationalizing that she was just Marsh's wife and a hired servant, although a good one. But if she decided to move away, Catherine wouldn't have been overly concerned. She was totally wrapped up in her family and community and allowed no particular feeling for Dessa. She did recognize Sammy's adulation but passed it off as a child's need for approval. It didn't occur to her that she might be a little jealous of Sammy's affection, but Patrick had noticed it on occasion as had Samuel.

Sitting back down, Catherine replaced her napkin on her lap, smoothed it and asked, "Now, where were we? Dessa is tending to Gray, and I'd like for the conversation to be quieter, please."

"I'll be quiet, Mama," Jamie said.

She patted his head and Patrick resumed. "As I was saying before Master Gray perhaps saved our necks," he laughed, but no one else joined in except Walter and Sammy. "Walter and I have decided to go with the Latham Growers in South Carolina to truck their peaches to Baltimore for six weeks. Of course, they'll handle fruit from Georgia and North Carolina as well. The pay is good, and even if our own land doesn't do well this year, we'll be able to make it. The Hunter Farms do still pay us handsomely for our assistance."

Walter interjected. "We don't know how long that will go on, though. The boys have learned the ropes and might not need us much past this year."

Clara said sadly, "And what with his Missus and little Rahn, Eben'll not be traipsing all over the country either!" She quickly put her hand over her mouth, then brushed a tear away. She wanted another baby so badly. It just wasn't fair, she thought.

Daddy Samuel saw how ashamed she was of her jealousy, so added, "Eben would go, too, if he needed to, Clara. Just like every man in the Glades. We take care of our families..."

Sammy shouted, "Not those men over at Turnerville, Grandpa Samuel! Mama and Aunt Clara hafta..."

"That's enough, Sammy!" Catherine said. "I said no more shouting!"

"I didn't shout, Mama, and look, I finished all my dinner, too." A proud Jamie said hopping up and adding that he wanted to go fishing with Sammy. He knew when he said it that she'd be upset with him.

Patrick saw Sammy's recoil on hearing Jamie's request, and Mary Catherine threw her hands up in dramatic fashion, declaring that all of them and their trials were upsetting to her in her moment of despair.

Catherine and Patrick stood looking at each other, both wondering what they had wrought, when Samuel began to laugh. "What's so funny, Daddy Samuel?" Catherine asked in dismay, while taking his arm and leading him to the front porch.

"I was just thinking about how much Kate would love to be here listening to all this ruckus in our house. She dearly loved family, I told Dessa just the other day. You know, your mama would have appreciated Dessa. Those two would've talked a blue streak..." He looked out over the dike and thought how Kate would have hated to see that monstrosity. She loved to look at the lake and had great solace of an evening, just sitting out with him watching the waves splash onto the white, hard beach and enjoying a soft breeze.

But we're fortunate to have it, he thought. This place wouldn't be booming like this if Hoover hadn't pushed it through congress. Now, people will stay here instead of migrating to other areas. The packing houses are bustling, and those migrants have put down roots. Their children can now go to the same school all year round and become a part of the community. No, my dear Katie Belle, you'd moan about your beautiful lake shore but would revel in the activity that the dike is creating. But it is a monstrosity, even if some people do liken it to the Great Wall of China.

Patrick and Walter left for their job up north late in June. It was a sad day for the two families, but Samuel told them that he'd not go to Arkansas for the summer as he had in the past. They were grateful to have him stay.

Dessa had assured him that she'd help keep the children busy so they wouldn't bother him. And she did.

Junie Mae's ma, DeeCee, had taken on another "husband", as she referred to him, and Dessa was concerned about Sammy's spending any time over there. She told Catherine that she felt that maybe Sammy shouldn't be wandering in and out of the quarters like before, and Catherine agreed. After all, none of them knew this new man, and Marsh didn't take to him very well. There was just something sneaky about the fellow. If Patrick had been home, he wouldn't have allowed him to move in.

Spike was a slight man from up New Jersey way. He talked a lot and loudly and drank plenty. Spent a lot of time at the juke in Streamline and was said to be fast with a switchblade. And a good thing that he was, because he loved a confrontation and provoked one at any given opportunity.

"Marsh, ya gotta git dat man outa DeeCee's place oah Ah'm gonta do it mahself. Marsh, ya listenin' ta me?" Dessa questioned as she turned to leave for the little house to check on Samuel.

He could tell by her voice that she wasn't gonna take any excuse from him, so he reluctantly got up off the wooden chair in the shade of the catalpa tree and began moving toward DeeCee's quarters.

"Hey, Marsh, ya make shuah dat de chilren ain't deah, ya heah?" Dessa warned as she walked up the worn sand path between their quarters and the little house.

She hadn't needed to warn him, because Marsh was as responsible as she and just as concerned for their safety. He mumbled all the way there. "Now why dat woman gotta have a man lak Spike aroun'? She oughta know bettah what wid Junie Mae deah. No tellin' what dat niggah do wid dat liddle gal. Don' wan' Dessa ta know, but Ah saw him eyein' her jes de othah day, and her jes a buddin' inta a young lady, too. She ain' but twelve year old an him jes a yearnin' ta poke her jes lak he doin' her ma when he able. Drunk mos' da time. No, Ah ain' a gonna let on ta Dessa. She tear dat niggah up if'n she know."

When Marsh got to DeeCee's quarters, he could hear Spike snoring his head off. So he knocked loudly and DeeCee opened the heavy wooden door and sneaked out.

"Shhh, Marsh. Spike sleepin', an' Ah don' wan' him ta wake up. He come home drunk as a skunk, an' Ah sen' Junie ovah ta Aunt Hannah's. He don' lak her aroun' when he fust wake up."

"What fo' ya let a niggah lak him stay wid ya, DeeCee? He ain' nuttin' but trouble, an' ya knows it."

"He say he gonna take us away from all dis hard work, Marsh. He promise."

"An' how he gonna do dat? Huh, how?"

"He got a way o' makin' lots o' money, he say..."

"DeeCee, you de onliest one ovah heah a workin'. So how he gonna do dat?"

"Oh, Spike be real smart. He fin' a way. He promise."

"Me an' Dessa don' want ya to let Sammy in heah. We don' trust dat niggah. An' DeeCee, ya bes' watch Junie, too. Ah saw him slobberin' all ovah hisself while a eyein' huh when ya was out in de fields workin' ta pay fo' his groceries. He ain't nuttin' but trouble..."

"He ain't a goin' ta git to Junie, Marsh. Ain't none of mah men evah gonna touch her o' Ah kill em. None of em, do ya heah?"

⁕

"Sammy," Dessa repeated, "Ya mama an' Marsh and me don't want ya ovah at Junie's. Now don't ya fuss no moah. Dat's dat! No moah! It ain't gonta do ya one speck o' good ta carry on. Youah mama say dat she can spend de night wid ya, an' dat's dat."

Sammy was fuming. Wasn't a blessed thing to do but fish and swim. Wilbur and Thelma's mama had them working with their daddy at the new Canal Point School, that had to be finished by September for the school's opening. Floy, Jr. and his folks were up in the Carolinas working the peaches, and she swore that she'd never speak to the Ogle boys again, and frankly, she was bored.

Normally Dessa would have come up with something to keep her occupied, but the green pepper scheme she'd tried hadn't worked. She and Sammy decided to go into the green pepper business. Dessa knew that they'd probably burn up in the summer heat but thought that watering and weeding them for a few months would keep Sammy's active mind going. But even Sammy could see that the peppers weren't going to make it, and they'd not get rich enough for that trip to California that she and Dessa had spent days planning.

It was Grandpa Samuel who finally convinced them that they might as well give up on the peppers. He had suggested to Sammy that she catch as many fish as she could and sell them at the Canal Point fish house, but she reminded him that since no one had anything to do in the summer but fish, she'd not be able to sell them. The market was glutted. Even she could see that, she informed him.

So Sammy was bored. Her daddy and Uncle Walter weren't due back for another month. Her mama spent so much time taking care of Gray that Sammy was saddled with Jamie most of the time, especially since Mary Catherine had decided to become an actress and practiced every blasted day with her friends in downtown Canal Point. I mean, you'd think that going on fifteen was just the most important accomplishment in the entire world, she told Dessa. "She is such a priss that I can't even ask her a question anymore without her going into one of her tirades. Frankly, I wish she'd move to New York City like she and that Dorothy Simms plan, and that they'd move in a hurry—like tomorrow!"

⁘⁘⁘

Patrick had had Marsh build a small bridge across the canal that the Army Corps of Engineers had dug alongside the dike, in order for the family to have access to the dike and the lake. Sammy and her friends liked to fish off the bridge, even though they caught only perch and cats, but when Sammy wanted to go for bass, she needed to fish the lake. Catherine didn't like for her to go to the dike, because the workers who were finishing the dike and who drove the heavy equipment were a wild bunch, she'd heard. But Sammy prevailed, and she gave in.

"If your daddy were here, young lady, he'd not let you. Now you know that."

"I'll take Jamie, Mama. But he'll have to be good and mind me. We'll be at the orange pontoon. There's not a thing to do around here but fish, anyway. I'll be glad when Daddy gets back. He said he'd take me to Salerno when the blues are running."

"Why don't you ask Marsh if he'll go with you?"

"He can't. He's in Pahokee in Daddy's truck getting Dessa's kettle fixed at Mr. Denton's hardware store. Mr. Coburn didn't have the right size pot menders or something like that."

"Well, don't you stay long, and when you get back, you come over here. And don't you dare disturb your grandaddy, you hear?"

"Yes ma'am. Come on, Jamie. Now you heard mama say that you had to mind me. And don't you scream every time the worms wiggle. How do you expect the fish to see them if they don't wiggle? Just how?"

Sammy had hold of Jamie with one hand and their poles with the other. Jamie had the old tomato can filled with earth worms and was trying to keep his hat on while carrying it.

"If you dump those worms, I'm gonna tan your hide! Do you hear?"

They crossed the hard road looking both ways, just like they'd been told a million times, and headed for the pasture. Sammy separated the barbed wire fence for Jamie to climb through, then crawled through herself. Picking up their poles she told Jamie that she'd run across first to attract Mr. Marcus's bull, then he could run to the other side and be at the bridge, but that he was to wait for her there and not go to the dike until she got there.

Outrunning that red bull was almost as much fun as fishing, Sammy often said, but Jamie was scared to death of him. Patrick told Catherine over and over again that the bull wouldn't hurt them, that he just liked to have something to chase.

"How do you know, Patrick? How? Have you ever seen him catch anyone?"

"No, my sweet, but I can walk right up to him and stroke his head, and he almost purrs."

"Well, I don't trust him. I don't know why you don't ask Mr. Marcus to put him in the other pasture so we could all walk to the dike. I used to love to walk up there with Clara, and now we have to crawl through fences and, well, it's just too much trouble to even go anymore. Clara said just the other day that we'll have to ride all the way to town to use the dike from now on. You know how I like to take Gray for a walk. You can't even walk beside the hard road anymore what with those big old trucks just about running you off the side of the road. Why are you laughing?"

"You look like your mama when you get riled. Samuel said that the other day, and he also said that Sammy was looking more like you. She's almost a young lady, Catherine. Going on twelve. Seems just like yesterday when she was born. Have you ever heard such a lusty cry as she had?" He shook his head in disbelief as he remembered.

Catherine bit her lower lip. "You're right about growing up, but she doesn't seem a bit older than she used to. By the time Mary Catherine was her age she was paying attention to her dress and made sure her hair looked nice and even kept her side of the room nice and neat. But not that Sammy. She doesn't act one bit older than when she was eight. I think a lot of it has to do with how Dessa treats her. Seems to me that she encourages her to not grow up."

"Now, Catherine, I don't think you're being fair to Dessa. She keeps those children busy all summer long and..."

"Yes, she does, but look at what she has them do! Building tree houses and planning crazy trips to California..."

"And making palmetto hats so they can earn money for their tree house and gardening..."

"You always take up for Dessa, Patrick Carroll. And if the truth were known, I believe you're partial to Sammy. That's not fair to the other children, and you know it!"

"Well, if it appears that I am partial, then I'd better mend my ways. I'd not ever hurt any of them purposely, and you know it. And, young lady, I'm not partial to Sammy. It's just that I get a kick out of her antics. That's all. Mary Catherine is certainly more beautiful, and Jamie pulls my heart strings, and Gray is undoubtedly the prettiest and best baby we've had. No, I'm not partial. I just have more fun observing Sammy, hon."

When Sammy and Jamie arrived at the orange pontoon directly at the bottom of the Carroll path at the edge of the lake, Sammy yelled to Jamie to wait and she'd help him climb up on the straight bar that joined the two metal pontoons. The workers had left about six pontoons up on the lake shore from Canal Point to the Carroll place one mile north. They were great to fish off of but got beastly hot, so the people who used them had to take either a heavy blanket or towel to sit on. In her anxiousness, Sammy had forgotten theirs.

"Here, Jamie, I'll throw some water over the end here to cool it, and then you jump up high as you can, and I'll steady you."

"But I'll get my britches wet and..."

"Stop your whining. Right now, do you hear! Or I'm gonna take you right home!"

Sammy could see the bulldozers running up and down the dike putting more shell on it. She hoped that they wouldn't come all the way to where they were, because the noise might disturb the fish. Her Uncle Walter told her that if you weren't quiet the fish would know you were there trying to catch them. So Sammy wouldn't allow any of her fishing buddies to talk.

"Here, I'll bait your hook the first time, but you'll have to from now on out. Now watch me. You hafta slide the hook inside the worm starting at the head and make sure that some of the tail is left over to wiggle. That's how the fish knows it's there. See!"

"I don't like it when the gooey stuff comes out, Sammy. That's the part I don't like."

"Then just wash your hands off in the lake water, silly."

"That's not what I mean. I don't like to see it. I bet the worms don't like it either."

"Now how much thinking do you think a worm can do, Jamie? Huh? Do you see any brains in this worm? Do you?"

"Maybe that gooey stuff is their brains and..."

"How can that be their brains? If that is their brains, then they don't have anything but brains up and down their entire body. Now does that make sense? Does it? Of course not. That's just what they eat. That's just muck or earth. That's why they call them earthworms, 'cause that's all they eat."

She splashed water on the area where Jamie was to sit then jumped up beside him. She had worn her long pants so the hot steel didn't burn too much. She threw out her line and leaned back on the other pontoon to wait for her bobber to announce that a fish liked her bait. When she glanced up toward Canal Point, she saw that the dozers were working their way to where they were.

"Confound it! Here they come. Why can't they just stay in town... Whoa, I've got a bite. Jamie, now watch me if you want to see how to catch a fish." She stood up and started working the line slowly at first then would give the line a little jerk. She could feel the fish take hold. "Wow! It's a big one, Jamie! Look at him bend my pole. It's a bass! It's a bass! I told you we'd be in luck today. Must weigh over two pounds! Wait'll mama sees this. It'll be enough for a meal if Mary Catherine doesn't come home. Wow!"

Sammy took the long sharpened tree limb with the short hook at the opposite end that she kept beside the pontoon and ran it through the fish's gills, sliding it down to the hooked end. Tying the string securely on the straight end of the stick she lowered the fish back into the water at the lake's edge. "Don't want you to dry out, you beauty," she said. Jamie sat watching her and wondered if he'd ever be able to do what his sister had done. Not being able to stay quiet, he said, "Sammy, how do you know that doesn't hurt the fish when you run that stick into it that way?"

"I don't know, but I bet cutting it open to gut it would hurt more. What do you think?"

He wanted to say that he thought he was going to be sick, but knew that he couldn't. So he just sighed and hoped that his bobber wouldn't go beneath the water.

The loud noise of the dozers got closer. When Sammy looked up she saw one heading for them. "What in the deuce are they coming down here for?"

The dozer stopped about twenty feet from where they were. A burly, red-faced man got off the seat and headed right for them. He was built square and kept wiping his face, but the sweat didn't notice his persistence. Just kept pouring down his pudgy face. Sammy stood up and said, "All that noise is gonna scare the fish, mister."

He laughed. She didn't like his laugh. She didn't like him one bit. "What you two doing way out here away from home?"

"We're not far from home. We live right over the dike there," she answered pointing toward home.

"Ain't your mama scared to let you two go off by yourself? Ain't she afraid that a boogie man will catch you?" Sammy could feel Jamie grab her arm tightly.

"Our mama knows that there isn't any such as a boogie man, mister. Now, what can we do for you?" She didn't like his manner, and she didn't like his voice. Acted like he was making fun of her. Sammy didn't like for anyone to make fun of her. "I asked you what we could do for you?" Are you deaf?"

"Smart ass, ain't ya?"

"Don't think so, mister, just want to know what you want, that's all."

"I just wanted to know if you'd caught any fish. What're you getting all riled up about ?"

"Sammy's not riled up. You oughta see her when she really gets riled up!" Jamie shouted over the noise of the engine.

She could feel him stare, first at her face, then way down her body to her feet. She also saw the knife scabbard stuck inside his pants belt. If he thinks he's scaring me he'd better think again. I don't like the cut of him and aim to make sure he knows it. I got a knife, too. She was getting angrier by the minute.

"I just thought that you'd be able to sell Hawkins some fish. That's what I want, little miss."

"I don't sell my fish, mister, and I'm not a little miss either. That bass is the only one I've caught, and I'm gonna give it to my mama for our supper. If you want to buy some fish, why don't you get on your dozer and head for Canal Point to the fish house. They got a lot of fish there."

Sammy saw the other dozer, that had been working with the man, head down their way. Why she felt comforted, she didn't know, but she did. Jamie had begun to sniffle, and she told him to shush.

"Got you a crybaby for a brother, little miss?"

"No, he's not a crybaby. He wasn't feeling too good, so mama asked me to distract him. Said as how Marsh would be coming to fetch him soon to take him home. Jamie isn't a crybaby, are you, Jamie?"

"And who's Marsh? He your other little brother?" he asked while kicking the crushed shell into the water, never taking his eyes off Sammy, the smirk never leaving his scruffy face.

I've out stared Wilbur and Snookey and Jenner and every boy in the Glades, mister, and you ain't gonna best me. She pulled Jamie to her and reached down to the bucket she kept beside the pontoon. The other dozer stopped, and a nice looking man in clean blue overalls got off and headed their way.

"What you doing way over here, Hawkins? Boss is asking for you. Who're these kids, anyway?"

"We're Patrick Carroll's kids. That's who we are. And I don't like the cut of this man. He was trying to scare us, too. And another thing, when I get home I'm thinking that you and your boss just might be getting a visit from my pa, who just happens to be the sheriff in these parts. Are you hearing that, mister?" She was angry as all get out and couldn't help but think that Tim McCoy sure would be proud of her. Heck, he'd said almost the very same thing in "Riding Wild" at the Saturday movie.

"Scaring you, was I? You don't know the first thing about Hawkins scaring..."

Sammy'd taken her knife Marsh had made for her out of the bucket and started flipping it into the sand. She'd flip it then retrieve it, then flip it again. Every time she did, she'd stare at Hawkins.

She could see how nervous the other man was getting. He grabbed Hawkin's dirty shirt sleeve and said, "Come on, Hawkins. Leave these kids alone. I'm not foolin' 'bout the boss lookin' for you. Come on!"

Hawkins laughed at Sammy. "You think flipping that little knife is going to scare me...?"

"Come on! Now, I mean it. You'd better go on home, miss..."

"I came here to fish, and fish I'm gonna do, mister. You can tell your friend that my pa will be rounding up a posse when I get home. You can tell your boss, too. Your friend would be real smart to ride outa town, and he'd better be quick about it!"

Hawkins looked at the other man and asked, "What the hell's she talking about? Is she so crazy that she thinks we came to this one horse town on a horse?" He began to laugh so hard and was bent over trying to keep from choking. The other man was restraining him. "What's a little shit like you doing telling Hawkins that he's gotta get outa town! Huh!"

"That's enough Hawkins! You got no quarrel with these kids."

Sammy really got riled up then. "When I said that you'd better ride outa town I meant in your truck or car or on your jackass, whatever you came here in. That's what I meant. Now I've had all I'm gonna take from you. You'd best see to it that he's outa here by sundown, mister!" She grabbed Jamie by the arm and jumped back up on the pontoon to resume her fishing. Out of the corner of her eye she could hear the two men yelling at each other with Hawkins kicking the crushed shell hard with his boot.

"Stop your sniffling, Jamie. They're leaving and won't be back." She patted the top of his head, picked up his pole and baited his hook.

"I didn't like that mean one, did you, Sammy?"

"No, I certainly didn't. And I just bet he knows it."

"You were real brave, Sammy. Do you think I'll ever be brave like that?"

"Of course you will. You just have to get a little older and work on your muscles." She thought a while and added, "And you've gotta practice your staring. It helps to be able to stare mean people down. That's one of my secrets. Why, Wilbur and Jenner and me had a staring contest for a whole afternoon once. I practice in the mirror every chance I get. I'll show you how. Come on now, don't start that sniffling. They've gone."

"You what, Sammy Carroll? I'm going for Dessa this very minute. You've gone too far this time. Now, don't you worry your grandpa with this, do you hear?" Catherine was beside herself. Why that man might come after us. Why isn't Patrick here when I need him? Why is he off traipsing all over the country when we need him...she began to sob.

⁂

"Marsh, you'd better go to town to tell the police chief what that child did so he can take care of it. Do you want me to go with you?"

"Yessum." He shook his head that he did indeed want her to accompany him. Heck, that police chief might not believe him.

"Better yet, why don't you drive me to Eben's. He'll know what to do," Catherine added. This is one time I wish that we had a phone.

When they got to Elsinore, Eben happened to be home. He was so amused at what Catherine told him Sammy'd done that he could hardly wait to tell the chief. "But you did right in coming here, Catherine. That man shouldn't be around here trying to scare children. He might be dangerous. You can never tell about his kind. I am proud of how Sammy handled him."

When Eben and Chief Cross got to the equipment building in Canal Point and confronted the boss, they were told that the man they described had quit that very afternoon. He had drawn his pay and taken off in an old flivver.

Mac Quaid, the foreman, told Eben that they'd had trouble with Hawkins before. He seemed to have a penchant for young girls, and he had been closely watched.

"Not watched closely enough, Mr. Quaid. You should have reported him to the authorities."

"We did over in Kissimmee, but he seemed to straighten himself out. Best damn dozer I ever seen."

"I'd advise you to hire a better class of worker from now on," Chief Cross said. "These Glades men don't take too kindly to men who mistreat their younguns."

"You don't hafta worry no more, Chief. He was the only trouble maker we had around. No need to worry."

Eben drove to Catherine's and sat at the kitchen table to explain what the foreman had told them. "My gracious, Eben! The children could have been killed!"

"Catherine, it could have been worse. I think it's about time that you told Hopalong Cassidy about men like Hawkins. It could have been much worse." Catherine understood. She sat at the kitchen table for a long time after Eben left trying to figure out how she could tell Sammy about the relationship between men and women and about people like Hawkins. She knew that Sammy would ask a million questions, and Catherine knew that she'd have to go into great detail. When she told Mary Catherine, she hardly got into the explanation when she said, "Oh, I know all about it, Mama. Dorothy told me." She was so relieved that she hadn't thought to ask how Dorothy knew so much.

She decided that she'd ask Dessa to do it. Maybe Sammy would understand if Dessa told her.

Samuel was resting on the daybed in his room. He could hear Dessa moving about in the kitchen and wondered what she was preparing for his dinner—smelled like chicken and probably was. He remembered that Sammy had been chasing around in the chicken coop, and she and Jamie were yelling at that Plymouth Rock rooster. He was an ornery one, all right. He laughed to himself, closed his eyes and reflected on the last few years.

Since Dessa had been his cook and cleaning woman, his life had become more peaceful. He didn't even want to accompany his cousin Lonnie to Hot Springs like they had done since Belle passed away. Didn't seem to need to leave home, and, if the truth were known, he enjoyed living in the little house. There were too many memories of Belle in the big house. Things had worked out just fine, and tearing down the store removed a lot of the stress he'd been under. Never could find anyone to run it properly. That all helped, but mostly he enjoyed Sammy's carrying on. He just wished that Catherine could enjoy her as much as he and Dessa did. He soon eased into a deep sleep.

Dessa opened his door just enough to make sure that he was asleep, then went out the kitchen door to call Sammy. She was trying to get the new kittens to drink milk out of a saucer. Their mama had disappeared, and Samuel figured that a bobcat had taken her.

"Sammy, come heah a minute. Ah needs to talk to ya."

"Be there in a second. Look, Dessa, the little tiger one thinks I'm his mama. Look at him suckle my finger. Isn't he cute! I named him Hopalong and the black and white one Tom for Tom Mix. Jamie gets to name the other two."

"Heah, let's you and me sit out heah underneath the rubba trees. Give us some shade an' some privacy, too."

"Why you being so serious, Dessa? Is something wrong with Grandpa Samuel?"

"No, he fine. Youah mama want dat Ah have a little talk wid ya. Now, don't go an' git anxious on me. Ya ain't done anyt'in' bad. It's jes dat she t'ink Ah can explain bettah, dat's all."

Sammy had a puzzled look on her face but didn't offer a comment for once.

"She t'ink it time dat ya know 'bout how it is 'tween a man an' a woman. Ya knows, how dey make babies an'..."

"Oh, I already know about that. Junie Mae told me. She's already on the rag, 'cause she let me see it. Now she said that when a girl goes on the rag, that means she's able to have a baby. Is that so, Dessa?"

"Dat is raght. She havin' huh period an' every month she have it again..."

"She said that you can't make a baby unless the man plows your field and plants his seed. But she didn't really give me any idea how he does that except, she said, one night when her mama thought she was asleep, but she wasn't, Spike was doing his best to plant his seed in DeeCee. But it must have hurt something awful, 'cause DeeCee was moaning and carrying on. But that Spike wasn't about to give up and just kept on trying to plant that seed. She guessed that something must have been wrong with his planter, 'cause he couldn't get that seed in, so he finally just gave up and rolled over so tired that he let out a big sigh. Then her mama did the same thing, like she was exhausted or something. Guess it didn't work, 'cause DeeCee isn't going to have a baby best I can tell. Or maybe it just wasn't planting season."

Dessa couldn't help but smile. Ah best not tell Miz Carroll all dis. Best Ah jes tell her dat Ah had dat talk. Dis chile ain't ready foah no moah information 'bout dis baby business, an' Ah ain't ready ta be givin' huh any moah, eithah.

CHAPTER FIFTEEN

The new Canal Point School was ready by the opening of the school year in '35. The ten-room structure was reputed to be storm proof and was the pride of the area people. Sammy was so excited about the school that when the bus let her out, she made a dash for the big house to share her day with her mama and Dessa. Dessa was amused by her appearance, but Catherine just shook her head in dismay. Sammy's long pigtails were swinging out behind her, her shoes were tied together dangling from around her neck, and both her pants' knees were covered with dirt.

She hurriedly began the account of her day, but not before she grabbed a piece of corn bread out of the warm oven. Her teacher was new, Mrs. DuBose, and there were three new girls in her class and two new boys. She liked Betty Ann the best, 'cause she liked to play jacks and was real good with a yoyo and promised to teach Sammy how to roller skate. Not only that, but she never intended to miss a single Saturday afternoon movie matinee, not in her entire lifetime—just like Sammy.

Jamie was almost as exuberant as Sammy. He had made a new friend, and his name was Bobby Baker, who used to live in Ocala and whose daddy trained horses when they lived there. His daddy was the new production manager at the cannery Herb Gold had built. He hated fishing as much as Jamie, but sure liked to foot race, and most of all he liked to ride bikes. He had promised Jamie that he'd ride up to see him sometime, if his parents would let him.

"How do you like your teacher, son?" Catherine asked.

"She's real nice. Her name is Miss Folsom, and she used to live up in Aucilla, and she doesn't have a husband. She said that she was a maiden lady, whatever that is."

"That means that she's not married, dummy!" Sammy answered, her mouth full of corn bread.

"That's enough, Sammy. First, you don't talk with your mouth full, and secondly, you don't need to talk that way to your brother."

"I'm sorry, Jamie. It's just that sometimes you are so dumb."

"I am not dumb! You're the one who's dumb, 'cause Mary Catherine said so!"

Dessa interfered. "You two quit botherin' youah mama. Soon's Ah'm t'rough wid dese clothes, Ah'm gonta go pick some beans fo' youah Grandpa's dinnah tomorrow, an' ya can hep me wit de snappin'."

"Oh, I want to ride my bike down to see Betty Ann. Can I, Mama? Can I?" Sammy shouted.

"After you deliver the cream to Mrs. Harrington." Catherine was amused. Normally all Dessa had to do was suggest something and Sammy was eager to do it. Maybe Sammy is being weaned. I hope so. Dessa has too much of a hold on her. I don't care what Patrick thinks.

"And I want to go play with Bobby, Mama, can I?"

"After you've done your homework and only if Sammy will go with you. Is that all right, Sammy? Where does Bobby live, honey?"

"He lives in the townsite in that yellow house next to the Methodist church. He said I could come play today, and he'll ask his folks if he can come here tomorrow."

"Sammy, you'll have to be home in time to practice that Etude piece you messed up yesterday. You've got to learn to concentrate more like Mary Catherine does. She's already three years ahead of you and will play at the next school assembly." Catherine glanced at Dessa, who was folding the ironed sheets. "I believe our children are growing up on us, Dessa. What do you think?"

"Sho 'pears so, Miz Carroll. I t'ink it nice fo' dem ta have new friends. Ah sho do. Now maybe Dessa git some work done. An' Sammy, youah granddaddy want ya ta play dat new piece fo' him when ya git it perfect. He lak dat one de bes'"

I'm too hard on Dessa, Catherine thought. I guess I don't appreciate her. I need to mend my ways, as mama would have said. She's been so down because that son of hers won't even answer her letters. I wonder that she even bothers to write him. Alpha said that she wrote both of them every month, and only twice has that woman taken time out to acknowledge her letters. Alpha told Daddy Samuel that she sends a dollar bill in every letter to that ungrateful girl. No, I'm too hard on Dessa. She has a hard row to hoe.

⸙

The Pahokee Blue Devils, formerly Pahokee High Gladesmen, were having their final football game of the season Thanksgiving weekend—it had become traditional. The newly named football field, Lair Field, named for Dr. W.H. Lair, a prominent pioneer, was gayly decorated with blue and white crepe paper streamers and balloons. Their opponent was Okeechobee, and the Hunter boys, along with their wives, were in attendance.

"Would you just look at those Hunters," April Mosely whispered to Ruby Whidden. "I can tell you right now that Lenore didn't buy that suit at Joe Kahn's. Bet it's 100% wool, too. Nosiree! She wouldn't be caught dead buying anything out in the Glades."

187

"April Mosely, that's not true! I saw her just last week buying her little boy some toys at Denton's Hardware Store, and Mildred Horne said that she and Eben are already signed up for the New Year's Dance the Legion is sponsoring at the Pavilion. You going? Paul Ricky and his Rhythm Boys are playing, and Mildred said they've already sold over a hundred tickets."

"Might and might not. Haven't made up my mind yet, but if I do go, you can bet that I'll buy my gown right here in good old Pahokee. Told Nola Dragon the other morning that I'm partial to blue, and she said that she was going to Miami to buy for Christmas and would keep that in mind. Now that's service. You wouldn't get that personalized service in West Palm Beach, I can tell you. Nosiree, I'll do my spending right here in my home town. Not like some people I know. You been in Nola's new shop?"

"No, haven't had a chance." Ruby wished she could say something but knew that April would probably never speak to her again. She was her friend and should feel comfortable telling her that she let that Buck Colson walk all over her. Been keeping company with her for over a year and just about never took her anywhere. And I just bet he hasn't even asked her to the dance. No wonder she's gotten so bitter. Seems to wear a scowl all the time. She used to be a lot of fun, but no more. Only place he takes her is to the movies, and every time I'm in the diner he's in there eating. Bet he never pays for a single meal.

<hr>

"Why are you so amused, Hon?" Lenore rolled over and asked. "What have you done now? I know it's for Rahn's birthday, so don't try to hide it. Come on now, you bad boy, what have you bought him now?" she murmured close to his ear. "If you don't tell me, I'm going to tickle you. Yes I am, Eben!" She flung the silk sheet off them and started working her fingers around his neck going lower and lower while he tried to remain perfectly still. When she got to his biceps and slowly worked her long fingers around his arm, he gave in.

"I give up! You vixen! You know how to torture a man, don't you?" He grabbed a laughing Lenore to him, and they soon forgot their playfulness.

"I could easily devour you, woman!"

"I'll not stop you, my love. Not now, not ever!"

Eben was in their dressing room and tossed Lenore's dressing gown to her when they heard James outside in the hall. He knew better than to disturb them. When she joined him in the large dressing room off the bath he watched her in the mirrored wall. I've never seen anyone else with her grace of movement. She's like a ballet dancer. How do you suppose that this creature could have come from Johnny and Nora? It baffles the mind. In another time in history she would've been a princess or a queen. No one with her beauty and grace could have escaped a connoisseur's eyes.

"Why are you smiling?" she whispered. Her arms were quickly around him as she pulled him to her. He loosened her gown and said, "I want to look at you from every angle. I want to hire an artist to paint you. NO! I mean it. I want a painting of you just like this."

"Eben, no. I'd be too embarrassed."

"I'd be in the room with you and you'd be draped discretely. Please, my Lenore. I want it."

"But someone might see it. I'd die if they did. I don't mind if you see it, because I know it would please you, but someone else might and..."

<hr/>

Rahn's first birthday was celebrated in style. Lenore and Eben decided to have some of the area children and their mothers over for an afternoon tea, and then they would celebrate that evening along with other friends. Rahn had just begun to walk but was still hesitant and could say bye bye and mama and daddy like most one-year-olds. Dressed in a sailor suit with his brown ringlets and happy smile, he was the photographer's perfect subject.

Lenore and Eben were on the back patio when Alpha brought Rahn to them. General was on Alpha's heels but showed no jealousy toward Rahn. Eben had said that it was because General had not taken to him like he did to Patrick. "He'll always be Patrick's dog," he had said. Lenore rose to take Rahn, but Eben intervened.

"Come to your daddy, Rahn. James and I have a surprise for you." He looked at Lenore, who began laughing along with Alpha. "All right, Alpha, what has he done now?"

"Ah'm not 'lowed ta say, Missus." But she continued to laugh.

James came around the garage leading the pony. It was black and white, and on its back was a small leather saddle with silver medallions.

"Eben Hunter!" Lenore exclaimed. She wanted to cry, she was so happy. I wish Mum and Da could be here for this. It's not fair. I try so hard to not think of them, but I can't stop. They need to be with their grandson.

After the afternoon guests left, Lenore went up to their room to rest. She could hear Eben and James playing with Rahn, who was being held on the pony by Eben while General barked excitedly. Lenore pulled the afghan over her and began to reflect on the past few years. I wonder what my life would have been like had I not met Eben. Probably gone to the teachers college in Savannah after working at the bank for a few years. That's the only thing I miss. I really wish I had become a teacher, but then I wouldn't have Eben and Rahn. I'm so selfish that I wish I had both. She was soon asleep.

Eben had gone to hunt quail and turkey with the boys and had suggested to Lenore that it would be fun to have a big dinner after Rahn's party. They could follow it with a theater party at the Prince Theatre, where "Barbary Coast" was playing. Alpha had prepared a rice dish made with coconut milk, popular in the Bahamas, along with a huge Glades vegetable tray with various cheeses and breads. Lenore had decorated the table herself, using the tropical foliage and palm fronds for the center piece, and their informal white bone china was sparkling on the dark green linen cloth with white napkins. She had placed a red hibiscus on every plate. She had become an accomplished hostess and seemed to have blossomed since Rahn's birth. Eben was very proud of her.

The main topic of conversation was the soon-to-be-opened golf course. The official date was December first, and Eben was to be one of the dignitaries chosen to cut the ribbon. "That'll mean a new outfit for my bride, huh, boys?"

All the women present said in unison, "For us, too." Lenore had already purchased a new dress at Kahn's Department Store. She had heard rumors that she and Eben didn't support the local economy and wanted to change people's opinions of them, especially now that Eben had decided to run for city councilman. Joe Kahn had promised that the turquoise silk print dress was one of a kind, and she hoped that he was right, and it was only $3.98, about a quarter of what she'd have paid in West Palm Beach. It wouldn't have upset her if another woman wore a similar dress, but Eben would have been incensed. He was so proud. It bothered her at times.

"Patrick, would you please make sure Jamie's hair is combed?" Catherine called from their bedroom. "And, Sammy, you'll have to let me re-braid your hair, too. This is one time that you're not going to embarrass me by your appearance. You know that we're all invited to Eben's for a get together after they turn on the Christmas lights." To herself she said, I can't believe that it's already December first. Where has the year gone?

"Mama, Bobby said that he'd meet me in front of Fletcher's Drug Store." Jamie called.

"No he won't, young man. You three will be singing at different times at the city hall, and I'm not about to fight that crowd all the way to Fletcher's. Sammy, did you hear me? Where is that child! Patrick, would..."

"I'm coming," Sammy shouted. Don't want to go to that blasted old party. I want to go to the skating rink with Betty Ann and Nina Ruth. Don't know why I have to go to a dumb ol' grown-up party. But she knew better than to make a fuss, 'cause Eben was her daddy's boss and had got her out of a lot of trouble with her daddy when he got Chief Cross after that Hawkins. She guessed that she owed Eben Hunter a favor, and it was indeed a favor for her to give up an evening of roller skating. Heck, she could even skate backwards now. She was almost as good as Betty Ann.

"See, I braided it myself. Betty Ann taught me how. See, you pull the hair around to the front and it's easy that way."

"It might be easier but it's looser, too. Here, let me tighten them a little. Why don't you let me put the braids across the top like Myrtle Smith wears hers? It's so cute like that..."

"No, Mama. That looks tacky!"

Patrick was in the doorway smiling as he watched them. Well, I believe that our Sammy is taking an interest in her appearance, after all. I know it'll please Catherine.

"Is that Walter honking out front?"

"I'll look, honey, but you take your time. He's a half hour early."

It was Walter, all right, with Clara and Clarissa in his new Pontiac. Paid $615.00 for it when he could have had a Chevrolet for only $495.00. That Walter always had to have the most expensive car he could find in the Glades, Samuel had commented. Clara had really been put out with him and prayed that they'd have a good bean season. They would surely need it.

When Patrick got out to the driveway, Walter was rubbing a spot off the hood with his handkerchief. "Don't you get that handkerchief dirty, Walter," Clara shouted, her lips pursed in disgust.

"Patrick," she yelled out the window, "Is Catherine wearing her new blue silk dress she bought at Nola's?"

"How would I know? When I last saw her she was running around naked as a jay bird, Clara!"

Clara threw up her hands, and he and Walter and even Clarissa laughed. "Only fooling, Clara. She's wearing it."

"Did you hear President Roosevelt's speech on the radio, Walt?"

"No, I was too busy trying to listen to Clara read *"The Everglades News"* account of the big bash Lenore Hunter and her lady friends had, eating lunch at that fancy La Chaumiere restaurant in West Palm Beach. I sure hope Eben and the boys make a bundle this year. The way those two spend his greenbacks, you'd think that he was the President."

"We're here, Clara. We'll all go to Eben's after the chorus performance in front of the city hall. We're so lucky that the rain held off. Why, this morning I'd have sworn that they were going to have to cancel everything, but just look at the beautiful night we have. Here, Jamie, I'll declare your hair looks like your daddy didn't even take a brush to it."

"It's 'cause his curls are so tight, Mama," Sammy explained.

"He won't know if you kissed him or if you didn't. Come on Catherine, and lets get started. Dessa will kiss him a million times before she puts him down."

She sighed loudly and said, "You're right. He's a kissable child. Clara," she shouted over the noise of the motors of the two cars, "I am going to enter him in the beauty contest at the Prince Theatre. As much money as we spend with the Pahokee merchants, I think that they owe us a silver loving cup." She laughed when she squeezed Patrick's arm. "Don't you, honey?"

They climbed into the sedan, and the three children squeezed into the back seat. "Mary Catherine, who is going to lead the choruses when all three schools sing? Do you know?" Catherine asked turning around so she could check the three of them again.

"It won't be Miss Branning and..."

"How do you know? Miss Branning is a real good music teacher, isn't she, Jamie?" Sammy interrupted.

"I know because Miss Mitchell told us so, smartie! And she also said that the Pahokee colored school was going to perform first, then would sing with your glee club and then with my chorus. Then Sheldon Upthegrove is going to sing a solo at the end—think it'll be "Silent Night"—and then the Christmas lights will be turned on all over Pahokee. So there!"

Catherine entered the conversation. "I don't think it's fair that the Pahokee colored school will participate and that they completely ignored the Canal Point school. Not fair at all."

"Junie said that Slick was going to drive her and DeeCee down so's they could hear me, but I told her that she wouldn't be allowed to go to the new woman's club for refreshments. She said they didn't care one whit 'cause they were going to the church hall in colored town, where they were going to have a wiener roast and hay ride. That sounds like a lot more fun then some dumb old..."

"That's enough, Sammy. I told you that you were going to Eben's, and that's that."

"Well, I for one am looking forward to it. I've heard that it's a beautiful home, and I'm sure that Mrs. Hunter will be wearing an elegant gown." Mary Catherine said theatrically, waving her hands.

"Patrick, why do you think they didn't invite the Canal Point colored school?" Catherine insisted.

"Probably because they didn't have to. If the people in Canal Point expect this town to be counted and continue to grow, they're going to have to incorporate. Now you've heard me say that a thousand times. These people are so afraid they'll have to pay a little extra in taxes that they won't get off their rear ends to do anything. Pahokee and Belle Glade are the coming towns around this lake."

"Sammy, I don't want you to get anything to eat before your glee club goes on, do you hear? All I'd need is for you to spill something on that white blouse. Don't know why Miss Branning insisted on white blouses and shirts for you kids. Guess it's because she doesn't have children that she doesn't know what a mess white can become in a hurry."

"Mama, is Marsh going to hafta spend the night with Grandpa Samuel?" Sammy asked.

"No, honey. He's going to go on home with Dessa soon as we get back. Why do you want to know?"

"I don't like to be with him when he's sick. What if he dies when I'm there?"

"What a thing to say, Sammy!" Catherine exclaimed. "Daddy Samuel isn't feeling well, but he's not dying. Really!"

⚘

Patrick lifted the sleeping Jamie out of the back seat, and Sammy and Mary Catherine soon followed, both rubbing their eyes. "You be quiet as a mouse when you go in, Sammy," Catherine warned. "I don't want you disturbing Daddy Samuel."

"I will, Mama. We sure sounded good, didn't we? Even Mr. Hunter said we did." She closed the car door and hugged Catherine around her waist as they walked to the back door of the big house.

"It was beautiful, honey. The entire program was wonderful. Pahokee should be real proud of this night. And, oh my, when the mayor pulled the switch and all the Christmas lights lit up, I was so proud I felt like crying..."

"Why, Dessa, what're you doing still up? Gray isn't sick, is he?" She saw Patrick, his face glum, push past Dessa and hurriedly come down the steps toward her. "What's wrong, honey? Is something wrong with...?" She knew. He didn't even have to say it. "It's Daddy Samuel, isn't it? Is he gone?"

Patrick pulled her to him and said, "Yes, he is. Marsh went to look in on him about 9:00 o'clock and found him. He died peacefully in his sleep, and Marsh said he had a smile on his face. I think he must have seen his Belle. I truly do."

"You'll have to go get Clara, honey," is all she could think to say.

When Sammy looked up at Dessa, who was still standing on the steps, she asked, "Did you go see Grandpa Samuel, Dessa? You sure Marsh knows he's dead, or do you think he just thinks that he's dead?"

"Marsh know, Sammy. Marsh been 'round lots o' dead folks in his time. He know."

"Then I want to go see him. I haven't ever seen a dead person, not in my entire lifetime." She reached for Dessa's arm, but Dessa pulled back.

"Ya gotta wait foah ya Aunt Clara and ya mama ta go ta him, Sammy. Dey his close kin, an' it's fittin' dat dey do him de honor."

"Is that a law or something?"

"No, it not a law, it jes de respect foah de dead ta have da close kin wid dem when dey die, dat's all."

"Well, will you go with me as soon as they're finished? I'm not sure what I'm supposed to do, and I wouldn't want to do something wrong to Grandpa Samuel. He was my special friend, and I don't want..." With that the tears began, and she was in Dessa's arms sobbing into her apron front.

Four days later Samuel Graham was laid to rest beside his beloved Belle in the Port Mayaca cemetery. There were tears but also smiles and laughter when someone would remember the good times. The ladies from the area churches brought food to the big house, and over two hundred Glades friends passed through the serving lines that cool Saturday afternoon. Patrick commented that there wasn't a place left on the house-wide porch where there wasn't a body, and Dessa had set up long tables in the little house as well.

Sammy had extracted a sworn promise from Betty Ann that she would remember everything that was worth remembering about the Saturday movie matinee and tell her every speck of it. "I wouldn't be missing it but for Grandpa Samuel. Like Dessa said, I have to pay my respects. He was my special friend, you know. He loved me more than buttermilk, and that was his most favorite thing in the entire world besides me."

There was a crowd at the cafe for a Tuesday morning, and April was holding court, as the saying went. "You're not going to believe who's running for city councilman?" April Mosely announced loudly to everyone in the Lakeside Coffee Shoppe.

"Now this comes from a reliable source, so don't think I'm making it up. Dunbar Anderson, that's who. And his best friend, Jessup Spearman, was the one who told me, too."

It was March, 1936, and everyone in the Lakeside was flabbergasted when she announced the news. Bill Elam spoke up, "Why's he running? Is it 'cause Eben's running and Dunbar can't stand it? Is that why?"

Pop Salvatore explained, "Jessup said that Dunbar wants to show Eben up. He really believes that he can win. Said that Eben's tainted money will cause the people of Pahokee to tell him how they feel about scoundrels like him pulling the wool over the eyes of decent people."

"And I thought that Dunbar was over that foolishness," April said.

"Doc Spooner said that the doctor in West Palm Beach had done a world of good for Dunbar, but this just goes to prove he was wrong. Dunbar'll get the pants beat off him. Folks around here are jealous of Eben. That's for sure, but they do respect what all he's done for the Glades. Dunbar has gotta admit that," James Latham said.

"Jessup said that Dunbar had been getting letters from someone who had some dirt on Eben, and he's willing to sell it to him, and Dunbar's gonna send the man money in exchange for his testimony. That's what!"

"You mean that the man doesn't even live around here? How does Dunbar even know that the man is telling the truth? He could get himself in a lot of trouble accusing someone falsely. He surely could."

"Jessup said that the postmark is West Palm Beach."

"Dat's all right, Mistah Carroll. Ah can do it. She worse off dan me." Dessa responded referring to Aunt Hannah, who lived in the shack beside the bamboo stand at the edge of the first acre of the Graham property. She had been ailing for the past few days, and since both her daughters had moved to Miami to work, there was no one to tend to her.

"I'll do it, Dessa. Aunt Hannah was real good to Junie before that Spike took her and DeeCee off to New Jersey. Uncle Walter said that he was escaping the law, 'cause he knifed a man at Silver City. I just hope the law catches him so Junie and DeeCee can come home. I sure miss her. Isn't the same around here without her, huh, Dessa?" Sammy asked.

"No, Sammy, it shuah ain't. She a good girl an' a good friend to ya, too."

"After I visit Aunt Hannah, maybe I can ride my bike down town to see Betty Ann, huh, Mama?"

"That'll be fine, honey. First, you've got to help Dessa with the dishes, and Mary Catherine, I want you to do the clearing up. Dessa has been low lately."

Dessa sniffled, wiped her nose on the back of her hand, then got her handkerchief out of her apron pocket. Alpha and James had come up last Sunday, like always, and told her some disturbing news. Now, mind you, she wasn't sure that it was John who was writing those letters and causing trouble for Mister Eben, but she'd bet a million dollars that it was. He had threatened that he'd get even, and she believed him.

She had worried over it for a week, and when she told Marsh that she wanted him to drive her to West Palm Beach so she could confront Andrea about it, he had agreed. He knew that she had to find out the truth, and that was the only way that she could. Who else could be sending those poison letters? John probably sent them to Andrea and had her send them to Dunbar. It wouldn't have been difficult for John to find out that Dunbar had it in for Eben. Everyone in town knew it.

Patrick had given Marsh permission to use the truck, and he and Dessa left about seven o'clock in the morning after Marsh had milked Aunt Maude. They wanted to arrive in time to confront Andrea before she went to church; that is, if she went anymore. Her mother had been a church goer, Dessa knew, and now that she kept the girls while Andrea worked in Palm Beach six days a week, she probably had some say about the girls' up-bringing.

Marsh pulled into Fern Street, and they could see that the car John had bought before he was sent up was parked in the side yard. Marsh looked at it and said, "I bet dat it don't even run. Don't t'ink dat Andrea even drive, an' it'll jes sit deah and get rusty waitin' foah him to get out. I jes bet."

"Dey's deah," Dessa said. "De windows is open and de curtains is billowin' outta dem. Hetty ain't evah gonta leave her windows open wid huh goin' ta church."

Marsh eased himself down from the front seat while Dessa did the same. She straightened her blue-flowered best dress, then grabbed her hat off the front seat. She heard Hetty talking, then she thought she heard Andrea. About that time the front door burst open, and Addy came rushing out. She buried herself in Dessa's full bosom, sobbing as she did.

Dessa was taken aback. John's girls had never shown her any affection before. Then she looked up to see Hetty and Andrea rush out. What's goin' on? is all she could think. I hope that fool son of mine hasn't escaped.

"Mama Dessa," Andrea shouted, "Have you seen John? Do you know where he is? If you do, you'd better get outta here fast 'cause the law has been houndin' us for two days."

"No, Ah ain't seen John. When ya say he escape? Ah gotta know, Andrea. Ah gotta know dis minute!"

"The police come heah last night and told Mama that he wasn't in the line-up Thursday morning. They have the law after him and three others who escaped with him. I'm afraid he'll come here, then what'll we do?"

"You'll talk him inta turnin' hisself in, dat's what ya do. He gonta eithah git hisself killed or he gonta cause you trouble. Ya gotta do it foah his own good, Andrea. He did wrong an' he gotta pay fo' it. Ya gotta t'ink o' de girls."

Hetty had been quiet until then. She sighed, then lit into him.

"Dat's jes what Ah tol' her, Dessa. He nuthin' but trouble an' got hisself inta runnin' dose numbers jes lak he know what he doin'. He wan' always bad. Jes seem ta come on him gradual lak. But Ah gotta protect mah girls, an' Ah'm shuah ya unnerstands."

"Hetty, he gonta get in moah trouble if'n he goes ta de Glades. He got it in foah a man deah, an' it ain't raght. Dat man ain't evah done anyt'ing ta John. He mah friend, an John know it."

Andrea got a scared look on her face and quickly looked at her shuffling feet. Dessa knew right then that she knew more than she was letting on.

"Andrea, do ya t'ink dat he be headed foah de Glades? Is dat what ya t'inking?"

"Mama Dessa, that is just what I am thinking. He hates Mr. Hunter with all the hatred he can come up with. He told me the last time I went to see him that the first thing he was going to do when he got out was to get even with him for sending him up. That's just what he said." She began to gulp, then sob. Her shoulders were heaving so hard that Hetty let her have it again.

"Dat's 'nuff, honey. He ain't evah been good 'nuff foah ya, an' he shuah ain't good 'nuff foah de girls. What kinda man do what he do? Not even God in his almighty kingdom want John. Not even God!"

Dessa looked up at Marsh, grabbed his arm and headed for the truck. "We gotta git ta Mistah Eben 'foah John do. Come on Marsh. Ah knows he headed dat way. Ah'm goin' foah de police soon's we git deah. If John show up heah don't tell him dat we been heah. Now Ah means it!" she shouted. Marsh beat her to the truck and when Dessa slammed the door, he wheeled out of the side yard as if the devil himself were chasing them.

Marsh talked Dessa into going to Canal Point to tell Patrick what they had found out about John before going to Pahokee. "He know what ta do, honey. Mistah Patrick is a smaht man. He go ta de police and de police listen ta him. Den he can go wahn Mistah Eben. Dat's de t'ing ta do, honey," he said softly, patting her arm lying limp on her lap.

"Ah knows ya right. Ah knows it."

Patrick went to Thornton's house to tell him about the escape, and Thornton telephoned Eben. He'd already been contacted by the West Palm Beach deputy and told Thornton that there were already several deputies there and that he'd sent Lenore and Rahn to Emerson's.

Patrick shook his head and informed Thornton that John was, according to Marsh, a snake and as wily as they come. He might be trying to get to Eben through Lenore and Rahn, and he couldn't believe that the sheriff's department hadn't thought of that. "Here, let me talk to him!"

"Eben, this is Patrick. I think that perhaps you'd better let me pick up Lenore and Rahn and take them up to the house. Catherine can do for them, and I truly think John won't show his face around his mama. He knows how upset she is with him. They'd be better off up at our place."

Eben thought on it and said, "I believe you're right. I'll call Emerson and tell him that you're on your way. And Patrick, thanks. I'll be the first to admit that I'm concerned. Very concerned." His voice trailed off.

⁓

Every light in the Hunter yard was ablaze when Marsh and Dessa arrived. They went to the back entrance and knocked loudly. They didn't have to wait long, because James and Alpha were just inside the pantry when they heard the truck pull up.

"Now Dessa, don't ya git excited. De police done been heah ta warn Mistah Eben 'bout John escapin'. We 'spectin' him an' maybe dose othah prisoners, too. Dey's killahs an' 'bout de worst kinda folks dey is, de police tol Mistah Eben. He got police all 'round dis house, and Mistah Eben had de missus an' little Rahn go ta Mistah Emerson's house fo' safety."

"No dey ain't, Alpha. Dey is at Mistah Carroll's. He 'fraid dat John git dem if'n dey is at Mistah Emerson's. Mistah Carroll want dat Marsh an' me come heah ta be heah in case John show up. He t'inks dat Ah can talk him inta givin' hisself up ta de law. But he don't know John. He ain't listen ta me in yeahs. Not in yeahs." She sat down hard at the kitchen table. When the tears started rolling down her shiny black face, Marsh went to her. She looked up at him and said, "He was such a good little boy, wan't he, Alpha?

So good an' always smilin', wan't he, Alpha? What happen ta dat little good boy, Ah wonders." She put her head down on her crossed arms and sobbed.

Alpha looked at James and shook her head. She hadn't seen her friend cry like that since her husband's drowned body was brought to her. She was so young and John just a little tyke. Dat's de last time Ah evah see Dessa cry. Den an' now. Den an' now.

They could hear shuffling feet rush past the windows. Marsh checked the back door handle again, just like he had done a dozen times since they had got there. He turned toward Dessa and murmured, "I t'ink sometin's goin' on. Deah is commotion out deah."

About then they heard a shot coming from the back. Marsh saw Dessa heave, hardly catching her breath before the next one. Then the moaning started with her hand trying to stifle the sound. He motioned for Alpha to go to her but needn't have. She could see how distraught she was and was quickly beside her.

"Shhhh. Shhhh. It gonta be ovah in a little while. Heah, put youah head down heah so's Ah can stroke youah worried brow, Dessa. Gonta all be ovah in a little while, an' den youah Johnny be wid his daddy, an' he be holdin' him an' singin' lak he use ta when he a little tyke. 'Member how Johnny lak ta heah Innes sing de island songs. Mah, but his feet dance an' dance..."

The next volley of gunfire sounded across the black night. Dessa sat up straight and said, "He gone, Marsh. He gone. Mah Johnny gone ta be wid his papa. Innes take care o' him. He sho love his little boy...."

CHAPTER SIXTEEN

"Dunbar's keeping to himself," Jessup explained to the gathering after church services. "He's withdrawn from the race, as is fitting, and going about the days being the farmer he always was. At least since I've known him."

"He's ashamed of himself, Jessup, and you know it—as well he should be. He had no cause to make up all those stories about Eben, and him basing it all on hearsay, and from a criminal, too. Shame on him," Vivian Combs added.

"It'll be a long time before he can hold his head proud in this town, I'll tell you," Rodney Connell said.

"Don't think so," Jessup replied. "He's already making amends."

"And how's that?" asked Nellie Latham.

"He's working with the FFA boys at the school and even donated ten acres of his own land for them to farm. Not only that, he's starting a scholarship to be awarded to the top student of the FFA. And guess how much it is."

"How much?" they asked in unison.

"One thousand dollars, that's how much. And he's naming the scholarship after his little brother who was killed by a train in Kansas. Calling it the Gordon Anderson Scholarship. No, Dunbar is making a real effort to do right by all of us."

"Seems to me," Lester Hatton said, "that he's doing just what he was accusing Eben of doing. You know, trying to use money to buy our approval. Sure seems to me that's the case."

***

Patrick and Catherine were sitting on the front porch having a glass of iced tea before her afternoon nap. Patrick began reading from the *Palm Beach Post*, chuckling as he did. "Listen to this, honey. Some enterprising farmers, or fools, planted 400 acres of pineapples between Lake Worth and Lantana. They'd be better off if they put it in green beans. Did I tell you that Jones' packing house got $4.35 a hamper on Saturday?"

"Yes, you did, and you also said that by Thursday Elmer said that the price will be down to probably $2.50 or less. How are we going to send Mary Catherine to college on that kind of money? I'm really concerned about the children's education. I'm sure that she'll get some kind of scholarship, but the Woman's Club only gives $200.00 and the Rotary not even that much. Now, how far will that go at the Florida State Women's College? Not far at all."

"I told you that I didn't want you worrying about that. We've got a little time yet. Two more years to go."

"That might be a lot of time to you, but it surely isn't to me."

He rose and went over to her, bent down and kissed the top of her head and said, "Go on and get your nap while Gray is sleeping. You're just worn out, that's all. And besides, we should have the other heirs paid off by then and can concentrate on the children. Will feel good to own this place outright, won't it?"

She rose, patted his back affectionately and said, "It'll be a big relief, all right. There is no way that we'd have been able to afford this place if Eben hadn't bought our land up at Chancey Bay. Oh, I know that he paid a fair price for it, but he could have got it for a lot less, and you know it. Other men would have taken advantage of you. He's a good man, and Lenore has been good for him. She is not high and mighty like some say. She's a sweet woman and dotes on little Rahn."

"He said that he'd be real glad when we get a phone. What do you think? Hickerson's put a phone in the grocery store last week, and most all the people in the town site have one. Would you like one?"

"You know I would, and I know that Mary Catherine would. She was moaning just last night about having to ride her bike down town every time she needed to ask Dorothy something. But I'm afraid we can't afford one yet. Let's think on it."

"I hadn't planned on saying anything to you just yet, but Walter has been thinking about leasing Stuckey's filling station. Now, don't look like that! He'll keep on farming with me and helping Hunters', but like you have said over and over you and Clara would like more security. That would give them a monthly income and..."

"I wish you hadn't told me, Patrick. I just wish you'd waited until I'd had my rest. Now, I won't be able to sleep a wink. Not a wink!"

"I'm sorry, honey. It was thoughtless of me. As long as you're awake you can stew on another idea. Stu Carpenter is thinking of running for sheriff, and he asked me if I'd be interested in becoming his deputy if he wins. What do you think about that?"

"Now, I know I'll not sleep a wink, Patrick Carroll! A deputy, and hafta use a gun and shoot people and hafta..."

"Now Catherine, it's not like that at all. It's not nearly as dangerous as dusting crops or..."

"I don't want you to fly an airplane either..."

"Then what in the heck do you want me to do? Farm for the rest of my life and worry about the children's education and...?"

"Patrick, you're yelling at me! What will Dessa think?"

"She'll think we're having a loud discussion, just like every married person I know has. That's what!"

"Now you've gone and done it, fellow! Now you've awakened Gray. So you go tend to him since you awakened him, and I'll just go to bed and stew about all the unpleasant things you just told me. And just what are you laughing at, Patrick Carroll? Just what?"

"I was just thinking how much our Sammy looks like you when you're mad, Mrs. Carroll. That's what! And I don't mind chasing that three-year-old one bit. As a matter of fact, it'll give me a lot of pleasure while I tell him about his daddy planning on becoming a law man."

She stopped then. "You are serious, aren't you?"

"Dead serious. But first we've got to get Stu elected."

"Now, I am worried..." she sighed loudly and closed the bedroom door forcefully.

<hr />

April Mosley and Buck Colson were married the summer of '36. They didn't want a fuss, according to April, so they ran away to Georgia. Most said that Buck was so cheap that a trip to Georgia saved him from paying for a honeymoon.

"What're we gonna do without April's pies, boys?" Cletas asked while whirling around on the counter stool trying to impress the new waitress of the Lakeside Coffee Shoppe. "She turned into the best pie baker in these parts."

"Now that we got a bakery, maybe that's why she finally gave in to old Buck. Maybe she thought that since we got Tillis' Hometown Bakery with those award-winning fruitcakes that we just don't need her."

"Hell, he ain't ever cleaned off a counter like Miss April, especially when she wears those low necked blouses. Whew! Does get a fellow's heat up, she does!"

"Now, Cracker, you'd best watch your talk. Buck might get jealous if he hears you talking like that."

"Hell! He never did before! Just kept sitting there stuffing his fat face fast as he could shovel it in. Frankly, I think April could've done a lot better than Buck Colson. A lot better."

"Not to change the subject, but Denton's Hardware Black Bass contest has just been claimed by none other then yours truly. Yessir..."

"Hey wait a minute, John T. It won't be over 'til September first. What'd you catch that's so special?" Ray, Jr. asked.

"Ten and three quarter pounds, that's what! Not more than two hours ago up at Port Mayaca, and just used a spinner, too. Took me near 'bout half hour to land it!"

"Why do you always hafta exaggerate, John T.?"

"Well, maybe not that long, but sure as hell felt like it. How much you want to bet that it's the winner? Any takers?"

No one answered, so he slammed his change down on the counter, and the new girl shyly took it. "Don't let him get to you, Betty Jean," Richard said. "He's an all-right guy but does like to brag. You'll get used to us regulars after a while. Took April a long time to learn to put up with us, and you'll soon find out that we're more bark than bite, huh, boys?"

The bell rang on the door as John T. left, and when Billy Rawles came in, the conversation turned back to fishing. "*The Everglades News* is gonna have a big article in it 'bout Echols' trip to Salerno. Hell, sea bass twelve to fifteen pounds each and blues and snook there for the grabbing. Millard Sapp caught a twenty-five pound jack and two snappers weighing in at eight pounds apiece. Now that's some kinda fishing!"

"When was this?"

"Just over the weekend."

"Damn! What're we sittin' here for, boys? Let's get a move on. I do believe we're gonna be in the money! Yessir! In the money!" "Hey, Billy, how much they paying for such as that?"

"I'm believing Martha will have a fit when I tell her how much money I can bring home from having such a good time! That's how much! And she can head for Pahokee Dry Goods and buy her that silk dress she's been eyeing for over a week. If this keeps up, boys, we're gonna have one helluva summer!"

***

The roaring of the thunder resounded across the Glades. Head clouds mushroomed in front of Marsh's windshield wipers. They were fighting a losing battle, he knew. Marsh had just let the last of the bean pickers out and was headed for home. Dessa gotna be glad to see dese cats Ah bought. Hope she make catfish stew wid rice lak she did in de islands. Bes not let on ta Sammy o' she be ovah fuh huh suppuh. Dat young lady sho love Dessa's catfish stew. Hummm!

The narrow road had no discernible sides, but he could make out the Australian pines that bordered it. They had been planted the length of the Palm Beach Canal. He loved those trees. They were so graceful! He loved to see them sway. Sometimes almost every limb had a red-winged blackbird perched on it. Soft, whistling sounds sent music across the open fields.

"Dey needs ta fix dis bumpy road," he said aloud. Ah needs ta talk ta Mistah Pat 'bout dose government quarters dey buildin'. Doubt dat Dessa would move, but maght be sometin' we need ta look inta. She been so down since John killed.

Bes make tracks, o' Aunt Maude t'ink Ah up an' die. Her udder gonta be 'bout ta bust. He laughed as he speeded up, ignoring the bumpy road. When the truck wrenched toward the field he quickly turned the steering wheel hard toward the canal. He felt the car leap—then it seemed to take to the air just like those red-winged black birds. He was surprised when the pine crushed his door. The murky canal water climbed up his limp body dissolving the muck from his black boots, then eased slowly up his pants legs. The light blue fabric became black. Slowly the truck's hood found the muddy bottom.

⌁

"Ain't lak Marsh ta do Aunt Maude lak dat, Mistah Carroll. He musta had trouble wid de truck," Dessa explained to Patrick. He was rushing around trying to get Gray dressed while Catherine was supervising the other three.

"Patrick, if we don't hurry we won't be there for the beginning. Patrick!"

"Dessa, I believe you're right about the truck. Now see! If we had a phone I could call the highway patrol to go look for him. I'm just surprised that no one has come up to tell me that he broke down on his way home, that's all."

"Patrick! Did you hear me?" Catherine called.

"Yes, Catherine, I and everyone including all the folks at Turnerville heard you."

"You don't hafta be ugly, mister. You know you have to carry out the flag to start it off. Don't know why you get yourself involved in anything as dumb as an old donkey baseball game, even if it is a fund raiser for Stu. I really don't!"

Patrick ignored her, and when he turned toward Dessa, he was surprised by her expression. "What's wrong, Dessa? Are you worried about Marsh?"

"It ain't a good feelin' Ah been carryin', Mistah Carroll. Now, ya go on wid youah fambly an' Ah go ovah ta de new folks from de islands who move inta DeeCee's quahtahs. Henry and Teena is good folks an dey will hep me go look fo' Marsh..."

204

"No, they won't! I'll drive the family over to Walt's, and they can go with him. He can carry that blasted flag just as well as I can. Don't you fret, you hear. We'll find Marsh." And with that said, he corralled the lot of them, and the only protest he got was from Sammy, who wanted to go with him and Dessa. He thought on it, but sensed that there was reason for concern. He too was worried. Sammy groaned that she wasn't going to sit with that cousin of hers, and Jamie said he didn't care if he had to sit on her lap as long as she kept her thumb in her mouth so he couldn't smell it.

———

Patrick and Dessa sped through the downtown section of Canal Point past the barber shop and drugstore. Patrick saw a truck headed for them flashing its headlights. It was Bill Erickson. When the two of them got out of their cars, Bill saw Dessa sitting in the back seat. He whispered something to Patrick.

Dessa knew, Patrick later told Catherine. She had known from the beginning, he thought. Those island Negroes seem to have special powers, just like Sammy always said. All she said was, "He was a good man, Mistah Carroll. A good man."

Marsh was buried at the Colored cemetery in Port Mayaca, and Patrick asked Dessa if she wanted to be beside him when she was taken. She replied, "No suh, Mistah Carroll. Ah wants ta be beside mah little boy, John." That's the only time Patrick saw her shed a tear.

———

Stu Carpenter was elected sheriff of Palm Beach County and, as he had promised, made Patrick a deputy sheriff. Walt and Clara leased the filling station in downtown Canal Point, and, as Catherine often said, "My life changed from that very moment." She no longer could count on Clara to drive her to the grocery or downtown for their afternoons or anywhere, for that matter. Clara was now a bonafide bookkeeper. She'd taken a corre-spondence course and had graduated with high honors. You would have thought that she had graduated from Harvard with a Ph.D., according to Patrick. The way that woman carried on about her new position irritated the entire town. If she doesn't mend her ways Walt won't have a single customer, they said.

They need not have worried. Walt was a natural born salesman and had every chair he could beg, borrow or steal lined up in front of the station. Must have had a dozen of 'em, and a story teller warming each seat, every one of them trying to out do each other in their tales about the olden days. When they got tired of that, they'd walk across the hard road that ran in front of the station and drown a few worms in the canal.

Clara had a going concession of peanuts, cokes, chewing gum and cigarettes for their pleasure and had begun making sandwiches for their lunch. Every little ragamuffin who lived in the tiny wooden houses across the canal visited Miss Clara for candy, gum and soft drinks. She dearly loved children, and they seemed to know it. Catherine had to admit that her sister was the happiest she'd ever been, but Catherine was not.

<hr />

The children's bus had just pulled out, and Catherine and Patrick were in the kitchen finishing their morning coffee. Patrick decided that he was going to bite the bullet and have that talk with Catherine that he had put off for too long.

"Honey, you're just going to have to make new friends and rely on them to take you to the PTA meetings and prayer meetings. You can't count on me, and you know it," Patrick reminded her.

"And just whose fault is it? That I want to know. Oh, I know what you're going to say even before you say it. If I'd learn to drive I'd not be in this mess! Go ahead and say it..."

"It's true, Catherine. I'd be glad to teach you. Don't look like that! I've offered dozens of times, and you know it!"

"And then you'd have to buy another car, and just how do you think we can afford it? How?"

"We can buy one on time just like lots of folks do. Besides, Stu said that by next year I'd get a car furnished by the county. Heck, the new Chevrolets are only $495.00, and the new Ford at B. Elliott's is only..."

"Do you think we're made of money, Patrick Carroll? Do you? Everything's gone sky high. Do you realize that the new silk dresses at Pahokee Dry Goods have climbed to $4.95, and just last year..."

"Cease! Catherine there is no need in getting all upset about this car business! I'll ask Henry to drive you wherever you need to go, and this conversation will cease! Now!"

He turned, his fists clenched, and when he arrived at Henry's and Teena's he had calmed down enough to knock gently on the heavy wooden door. No answer. Then he remembered that they had both been hired by Bo Knight and his wife to care for her aged mother, doing the cleaning, cooking and gardening. Miss Bertha was mighty independent and liked to live in her own place and have her own servants.

When Patrick turned to leave he saw Dessa in the side yard taking in her wash. He hailed her, and she walked toward him. She had heard them shouting at each other and knew that things weren't going well but wisely had not said anything to anyone. If Marsh had been there, she'd have shared her observations with him. But she had been thinking on it.

"Dessa, do you know anyone around here who isn't working full time who could take Miss Catherine into town and to various places? You must know that she feels like a cat in a cage," he laughed nervously when he said it.

"Mistah Carroll, Henry's boy Sonny drive real good. He went to de grocery fo' me jes last week. He real smaht lak his sisters, who is at de college up in Tallahassee. An' he plan on goin' when dey out."

"Didn't know he was old enough to drive. Thought he was only about fifteen or so."

"No suh, he goin' on eighteen. He jes slight fo' his age. He'd do a good job fo' Miz Catherine, an' it hep him out, too. He do real good weavin' dose cast nets, an' he savin' his money fo' college. He read real good, too, an' is a nice young man. Got real good mannahs an'...."

"Thank you, Dessa. I think that just might be the solution. Catherine is out of sorts since Clara works at the station all the time. That should do the trick! Thank you."

When he slammed the back door, Catherine was nowhere in sight. He called, "It's taken care of, Catherine. Catherine, where are you?"

Gray came tearing around the dining room table yelling. "Mama's in bed, Daddy. She's got the covers over her head and she's crying."

"Damn! Damn! She knows that I have to leave. I'm already late. Catherine!"

"James, wheah's General? Ah ain't seed him all mohnin' long an' he ain't touch a speck o' his food."

"Oh, he probably in da stall wid Peppah. Nevah seed a dog take ta a pony o' horse lak he did. Ah go look soon's Ah gits dese fishin' poles ready fo' Miz Eben."

They heard the hall door slide open and could hear Rahn running toward the kitchen. "We're ready, James! Mama's coming, and Daddy said that we could fish 'til noon. And Alpha, Mama wants you to fix us a lunch. We're going to have a picnic by the lake."

"Ah bets Ah knows what kinda sandwich ya wants, Mastah Rahn. Bet it's gonta be peanut buttah and jelly, huh?"

"Yes ma'am, that's just what I want, and I'll go pull some bananas for me and my mama."

"Ya bes make shuah dey is ripe. Heah, James will hep ya wid de stool in case ya needs ta get de ones up high."

Should have saved my breath, Alpha thought, as Rahn sped past her, and out the kitchen door he rushed with James trying to keep up with him. Nevah saw a youngun grow so fast and change from a little boy ta a young man 'most ovah night. Hmmm. He sho lak Mistah Eben, he is.

She heard Lenore coming through the hall, and when she got in the kitchen Alpha decided to tell her about General. "Missus, we ain't seed General all mohnin', an' James said he ain't touch his brea'fust. You want dat Ah goes to da stall ta see 'bout him soon's Ah gits yo lunch fix?"

"I'll go, Alpha. If he's not well I'd like for Eben to take a look at him before he goes to the city hall for that meeting." She turned back toward Alpha to see what kind of sandwiches she was fixing and smiled when she saw the peanut butter jar out.

"Mastah Rahn an' James gittin' ya some bananas fo' ya picnic..."

"Then I'll just have a half sandwich, please. Think I've been gaining a little weight lately," she said chuckling. Alpha wondered if she might be dropping a hint for her. Oh, Mistah Eben be so happy wid anothah little baby. Ah sho hopes Miz Eben be wid chile.

She had hardly gone outside before Rahn and James came in with a dozen little ladyfinger bananas. "Here, Alpha, I'm going to help mama check on General. James said that he wanted some bananas with cream for his lunch and I pulled some for you too, Alpha."

Eben called from the hallway. "Where'd everyone get off to? Lenore! Alpha, have you seen my bride?"

"She go check on General, Mistah Eben. We ain't seed him all de mohnin'."

They heard Lenore and Rahn coming up the back steps and when Eben saw Lenore's expression he asked, "What's wrong with General, Honey?"

"He's not doing very well, I'm afraid. He doesn't seem to have a fever, but doesn't act like himself."

"I'll check him. Alpha, just a cup of coffee for me. I'll get something at the cafe after the meeting. Rahn, you want to help me with General?"

Eben bent down and had Rahn on his shoulders before they had gotten to the bottom of the brick steps. Lenore continued. "He's not himself, and I hope Eben will call Dr. Youngblood in West Palm."

"He gittin' up theah in age, Missus," James said. "Mistah Pat said dat not long ago. Mus be 'bout thirteen yeahs old by now. He jes showin' his age."

"I certainly hope so. Eben would be devastated if anything happened to him. I know that he's been too busy to hunt him like Patrick used to, but he still thinks the world of that dog, and so does Rahn."

When they heard Eben whistling, then they knew that he was worried. Eben never whistled unless he had a lot on his mind. Alpha saw Lenore bite her lower lip. She worried too, she thought.

"You were right, honey, he doesn't seem to have a fever, but he certainly isn't himself. If he's not better by this afternoon, then I'll take him to town to see Dr. Youngblood. Should be finished with the meeting by noon and I'll have lunch at Rotary. Do need to go up to the packing house to check on those new belts that Thornton said were not functioning right, then..."

"I'll be back right after we have our picnic. Do you want me to drive him into town? Lucy might be able to go with me." Lenore said.

"No, you and Rahn have your day, and I'll tend to him when I get back. He might have eaten something that didn't agree with him, that's all."

❦

I know that I'm being unreasonable, Catherine thought as she finished preparing their big meal. I don't know why I even bother fixing a big meal anymore. Bet anything he'll call and say that he won't be home 'til late and for us to go ahead with our dinner. I just bet. He knows how frightened I am about driving. Why can't he understand? I'd simply die if I struck someone and perhaps hurt them or even killed them. You read about accidents all the time. I just can't bring myself to do it. Wonder what he wanted? Think Gray and I'll walk over to Dessa's soon's these greens are done. I'm sure she knows.

She lifted the pot lid and tasted the collards. Need more salt, she thought. Gray was playing in the sand pile in the back yard. He entertained himself easily, and it was a blessing for Catherine, for there were no little ones around for him to play with except that white trash at Turnerville. Patrick thought it would be all right for him to play with them as long as they were supervised, but Catherine didn't think so. She wished that Aunt Hannah's girls hadn't moved to Miami. They seemed to have a baby almost every other year and Aunt Hannah made sure that the children were clean and had good manners. And you never heard a one of them use bad language either.

"Gray, I'm going over to visit Dessa for a little while. It's almost time for dinner, so you stay right there. If you hear the phone, call me, you hear?"

"You want me to go sit beside it, Mama?"

"No, honey, who ever it is will wait for me to get there, I'm sure. They know that we have our chores and can't sit by that thing all day long."

"Yessum," he said and resumed playing making motor sounds as he scooted his toy trucks over the sand mounds.

Dessa was hanging out another load of wash when she saw Catherine approach. Wonder if he tol' her 'bout Sonny drivin' her 'round. Well, if he din't, den Ah will. She been so down since Miss Clara went to de station.

When Gray looked up he was surprised to see General. He hadn't heard Mister Hunter's truck or car drive up, so ran around to the front of the house in hopes that he'd brought Rahn to play with him. But there was no one there.

"Mama, Mama, General's here to play with me. Look, Mama," he yelled rounding the house on his way to Dessa's. General didn't follow him. He just lay down on the sand path beside the big house.

"Gray, what are you yelling about? Is the phone ringing?"

He stopped short, out of breath, then proceeded to tell her about General.

"I didn't hear them drive up, did you, Dessa?"

"There isn't any car or truck, Mama. I already looked," Gray interrupted.

"Well, there has to be. He couldn't have walked all the way from Pahokee. It has to be four miles from Eben's. At least!"

Dessa put down the willow basket of dry clothes and slowly walked past Catherine toward General. She knew something was wrong. "Miz Catherine, Ah believes dat General's sick."

Dessa got up from examining General and asked Gray to fetch some water for him. "An' Gray, get dat cloth off mah clothes line so's Ah can bathe his face. He sho had himself a long walk an' is real tired."

"Dessa, surely you don't think that he walked all that way, do you?"

"Missus, dat is jes what he did. Ah hates ta say it, but old General come home ta die. Din't want ta say anyt'ing in front o' Gray, but dat's jes what he do, all right."

"I should call Patrick. He needs to be here. Do you think that we should take him inside the house where it's cooler?"

"Yessum, Ah do. He gonta wait fo' his master 'fo' he go. Ya bes git hol' o' Mistah Carroll, lak ya said."

"What next! What's going to happen next, I want to know!" She mumbled to herself all the way to the phone while Gray and Dessa helped General stand up and Gray held the bowl of well water coaxing him to drink. Dessa dipped the rag in the water and bathed his head gently. Gray petted him, stroking his long fur. When he began to cry, Dessa grabbed hold of him and said softly, "Gray, he old an' it be his time. All animals an' folks hafta die."

"I know, but he went away because of me. Sammy said I was the cause of Daddy having to sell him to Mr. Hunter. She said it."

"Sometime Sammy say too much. Now, ya listen ta Dessa. Yo daddy sol' him ta Mistah Eben 'cause Mistah Eben want him so bad. An' General was too jealous o' ya when ya was jes a little baby, an' yo daddy 'fraid he gonta hahm ya. Now, dat's de trut'."

"But Sammy said..."

"Sammy done got huh facts wrong, Gray. General love yuah daddy too much, dat's all. Dat's why he walk all de way from Pahokee."

He sniffed, wiped his runny nose on the back of his hand and helped Dessa bathe General's face.

<hr />

Yes, I know that he is at the jail, Mildred, but I need to get hold of him. We have a family emergency, and I need to talk to him. Please, have him call me as soon as possible. Thank you."

When Catherine hung up she suddenly realized that Eben and Lenore would be searching for General. "Oh my! I hadn't even thought about them. They must be frantic."

"Alpha, this is Miss Catherine. I know that Eben and Lenore must be having a fit about General missing but..."

"Miz Catherine, Ah don't know what ya talkin' 'bout. Miz Eben and little Rahn an' James at de dike fishin', an Mistah Eben in town, an' fah as Ah knows, General in de stall wid Peppah..."

"No, Alpha. General is here in Canal Point. Right here! Dessa said that he must have walked all the way here 'cause he's sick and wanted to come home to die. She said it!"

"My, my...Dey oughta be back from de dike in a little bit. Ah tells dem soon's dey gits heah. Do ya wants fo' me ta try ta git hold o' Mistah Eben? He say he be at de Rotary fo' his dinnah."

"Oh, would you please? I'm waiting for Patrick to call me. He's all the way in West Palm at the jail. He'll be so upset if he doesn't get here in time."

Catherine pulled the dining room chair out and sat. She could hear Dessa and Gray coaxing General up the back steps. "Miz Catherine, would ya please git General a ol' blanket o' spread o' somethin' soft fo' him ta rest on. He so tired."

"I'll get one right away. Patrick wasn't at the court house, Mildred said, but she thought he was still at the jail. He should be calling any minute now."

When the phone rang Gray ran for it and was talking to Patrick even before Catherine could get to it. "No, Daddy. Mama's fine."

"Let me have it, Gray," Catherine said grabbing the receiver from him. "Patrick, we do indeed have an emergency. It appears that General walked all the way here from Eben's, and Dessa said that he is real sick and came home to die. Now, I'm just saying what she said, but he seems so low. I called Eben's and Alpha said they were all at the dike fishing and that Eben was at a Rotary meeting. She's trying to get hold of him now. What do you want me to do?"

"Just hold on, Honey! I'll leave right away and will have Stu call Dr. Youngblood. He might want us to bring him in here to examine him..."

"Patrick, I doubt that it will be necessary, Honey. He's real low, and Dessa thinks..."

"I'll be there in no time..."

"Don't you drive like a bat outa hell! Oh my, why'd I say such a thing! I don't want you to wreck the car and get yourself killed and..."

"Catherine! Get hold of yourself! I'll be there in a little while."

⁂

Alpha met the threesome at the bottom of the steps. They could tell by her expression that she was upset.

"Is it General, Alpha?" Lenore asked.

"Yessum, it is in a way. He be up at Mistah Pat's house."

"Who drove him up there? Did Patrick come for him?"

"Noam. He walk, Miz Pat say."

"What do you mean? He couldn't have walked all that distance!" She turned toward James. "Could he, James?"

"Animals do funny t'ings when dey is ready ta die, Missus. He not doin' good, an' he know it be his time, Ah'm believin'"

"I've got to call Eben. He's got to do something."

"He done left de Rotary. Ah done try, Missus. Maybe he at de packin' house."

"That's exactly where he is. He said that he was going after eating at the Rotary meeting. Rahn, you go upstairs and get washed up, and Alpha will get you ready for your nap. Go on, now. Be a good boy for Mama." She kissed his cheek and rushed into the living room. Frantically, she searched for the number. "I can never remember that darned number. Oh, here it is."

Oh, I hope he's there. If he is then he can be at Patrick's in no time.

The phone rang and rang. "Where are those people? Oh, I forgot! They close for noon and won't be back for another hour. Darn!"

"James," she called rushing into the kitchen. "I'm going to drive up to Canal Point to see if I can find Eben. If I can't, then I'll drive on to Patrick's. Tell Alpha, will you?"

"Miz Eben, maybe ya bettah call Miz Pat. She maght have some news fo' ya."

"Yes, that's the thing to do. Thank you, James. I'm glad someone has a calm head around here."

"Catherine! It's Lenore. We just got back and Alpha told us about General. I've been unable to find Eben but..."

"Oh, Lenore. He's hanging in there, and Patrick is on his way from town. He should be pulling up any minute now. Dessa seems to think that he came home to die. But I don't know. Patrick had Stu put in a call to Dr. Youngblood. What good that will do I don't know."

"Eben planned to take him into town this afternoon if he was no better. He thought that he was just off his feed. He had no fever and just seemed lethargic."

"We'll call you back as soon as Patrick gets here and decides what to do, all right?"

"In the meantime, I'll keep trying to track Eben down. He'll be sick about this."

"Of course he will. He loves him almost as much as Patrick does. We know that. That was the only way Pat could have given him up. He knew how much Eben wanted him. Oh, here's Patrick. I'll call you later."

Patrick tossed his hat onto the living room table and headed for the back porch. "How's he doing, Dessa?"

"He jes waitin' fo' ya, Mistah Carroll. He do fin' now, won't ya, ol' boy?"

Patrick kneeled down and Catherine started crying uncontrollably. Dessa sent Gray to her. Patrick hadn't even removed his gun. Just sat down beside General and talked to him like he had been doing for most of his thirteen years. Talking and stroking. Talking and stroking. Dessa said later that old General was wearing a smile when he gave his last breath and that Mistah Carroll was bawling as hard as Miz Catherine and Gray.

<hr/>

Howard Sharp of *The Everglades News* called Patrick a few days later and asked if he could run a story about General. He thought that his long journey home to die was newsworthy. Patrick thought that it was a fitting tribute to his friend and even furnished pictures to accompany the story. There was one of General sitting beside Patrick, who was holding a basket filled with quail taken up at Fisheating Creek, and another beside Patrick just before they boarded Arden's plane for their trip to Georgia. But the one that the family liked the most was of General taken up on the top of the dike with nothing but big clouds behind him and the sun shining on his coat. Looked like he was wearing a silver lining, Samuel had said when he had seen it. Patrick had it blown up and framed and gave one to Eben. General's picture sat on his night stand, and Catherine told Clara that he said goodnight to that picture every night without fail.

Eben approved of Patrick's burying General in the side yard beneath the cypress tree. It had been his favorite resting place. Sammy supervised the making of the headstone. Was just a bunch of medium sized rocks that she and her buddies found at the lake, but they were chosen carefully and were almost the very same size. She thought that he'd like the cross shape. "It's simple, but elegant," she told Dessa. She'd heard Irene Dunne say that in the Wednesday afternoon matinee and liked the sound of it. Tried to use the saying every chance she got. "Why, Betty Ann, that is simple but elegant, don't you think?" Jamie accused her of talking fancy like Mary Catherine, but he said it only once. She saw to that.

CHAPTER SEVENTEEN

Patrick almost threw the copy of the *EVERGLADES NEWS* down on the floor beside his chair. Catherine saw him and was quick to respond. "What's wrong, hon? What's that Hitler done now?"

"It's not Hitler this time. I've been predicting it as well you know. They're closing the Canal Point branch of the Pahokee Dry Goods because of lack of business. Mark my word! That will be the first of many to close. Mark my word! It's only 1938, and by 1940 there won't even be a town!"

"Well, you know how all the farmers are moaning. Been the driest three months in the history of the Glades, Howard wrote just last week. With no crops people won't have any money to spend." She bit off the end of the thread and shoved the mending back in the mending bag.

Walking over to Patrick, she bent down. "Is that all that's bothering you, Hon?"

"No, it's not all that's bothering me. Those Roosevelts are stirring up trouble between the Coloreds and the Whites. Now, I know that the Coloreds need help. I'll be the first to admit that, but I just don't like the way those Roosevelts go about it. The Coloreds don't need Washington to hand them stuff. They need for Washington to teach them and train them. They don't need any handouts. They need to learn to stand on their own two feet and..."

"Dessa ought to go to Washington to teach them, Daddy," Sammy interjected. "Hey, Mama, is there any of that punch left over from Mary Catherine's party? I want to take some out to Dessa's."

"There is a full pitcher in the refrigerator, but I don't want you to take it all. What's the big occasion? What on earth are you two planning now?"

Sammy had her head inside the refrigerator checking for anything that might be good to take along with the punch. "Oh, I forgot to tell you. That slowpoke Harry finally got up enough nerve to ask me to the scout jamboree. I've been working on him near 'bout a month. Dessa gave me some pointers."

"Just what kind of pointers could Dessa give you, I want to know? And I hope you don't want me to make you a new outfit on such short notice, young lady!"

"Talk to you later!" Juggling the almost full pitcher of punch she executed the long back steps, then across the grassy back yard down to the muck land past where the quarters used to stand to Aunt Hannah's old house, where Dessa now lived.

Catherine looked a little out of sorts, Patrick observed, so he came to Sammy's and Dessa's rescue.

"Don't get upset, honey. Sammy probably had Dessa cast one of her spells on poor unsuspecting Harry..."

"If she did, I just hope that Irene doesn't hold me responsible. Why can't that child behave like other children? Mary Catherine never had to have spells cast on her beaus in order to get a date. She accepted their invitations or she declined. But then Mary Catherine is a young lady and I'm afraid that Sammy is just...what do you call it...? Uncouth—that's the word. She's uncouth and Dessa is not helping her one little bit, either. And here she'll be fourteen this very month!"

Sammy arrived at the small wooden house, weathered with age, and managed the two steps onto the front porch without spilling much of the punch or knocking over the huge ferns in the cans beside the door. Dessa opened the door and commented that Sonny needed to repair the screened door. Sonny had moved in with her so he could continue driving Catherine to town. He was company for Dessa and also did her shopping. His folks had moved to Sandcut to the new government housing, since Saunders had torn down the quarters. None of the Coloreds wanted to move. They liked having their own garden and chickens, plus they were only a mile from town and could walk if necessary. The government quarters were nicer but not much larger than the old quarters, and there was only one store close enough for them to walk to. It just made no sense for them to have to move.

"Now when Harry pick you up fo' de jamboree, ya gotta not act anxious. Ya gotta let him open de doah fo' ya an', mind ya, ya gotta sit lak a lady."

"His sister is going to drive us, and he said he was going to bring me a corsage. That's dumb! Everyone will laugh at me. You don't wear a corsage to a jamboree."

"Maybe his mama want ta make one fo' ya. She supposed ta be real good wit flowahs..."

"Oh, she's real good, all right. Everyone in the Glades knows that. But, Dessa, I don't want to wear flowers to a jamboree. Heck, it's just a wiener roast and games and..."

"Now, Sammy, ya got him ta ast ya so ya gotta go along wit him a little. Won't hurt ya a bit. Not a bit. Besides, ya gonta be goin' ta de nint' grade next yeah an' gotta staht actin' lak a lady."

"Well, the first one who laughs at me will get a black eye, I can tell you."

"No dey won't! It's time ya act raght! Ya know, lak ya tells me dat dey act in de movies. If dey laugh, den ya jes ignoah dem. Act lak ya don't even see o' heah dem. Ya wanted ta go, an' ya is goin', an' ya gotta make a good impression on ya very fust date."

"I just wanted to go because Betty Ann is going, and Harry and Donny are best friends. It was her idea. Don't know what she sees in that Donny

Padgett, anyway. I'll admit that he's handsome as all get out, and he sure can sing good, but he's not worth a fig when it comes to sports."

"Din't know dat Betty Ann was good at spohts. Maybe she don't care 'bout spohts."

"You're right on that. Caused us to come in third in the three-legged race at the relay races. Miss Maxwell told us that we were mis-matched. Heck, I'm a head taller than she is. Should've listened to Miss Maxwell. But I got the blue for every other race but the egg race. I didn't care one bit. Dumbest race I ever heard of. Running as fast as you can while holding an egg in a spoon. Didn't mind losing that one, I can tell you."

"Best ya finish up de punch. But let's save some fo' Sonny. He be maghty hot an' tired when he come from Sandcut ta see his folks. He say he almost got 'nough money ta go ta college fo' one whole yeah. Ain't dat nice. Makin' all dat money makin' dose cast nets, an' yuah mama's money from drivin' her all ovah creation sho help him."

"Mama said that when he does go that she's going to take driving lessons, but I bet she won't. I heard her talking to Miss Beulah and Miss Loretta just last week about getting rides to town to grocery shop and for choir practice. I bet I'll be driving before she ever learns."

"Don't be so hahd on ya mama, Sammy. Some folks jes don't lak ta drive, an' Ah'm one of em. Marsh try ta teach me, an' Ah almost run raght inta dat canal. Ah nevah try again."

⁂

"He's here, Sammy," Jamie yelled. "Harry's here, Sammy!"

"Stop that yelling, son, or he'll hear you," Catherine cautioned.

"I'm ready and have been for it seems like hours," Sammy said while straightening her brown and white, striped seersucker short set. Her mother had suggested that she wear it because the skirt that matched could be unbuttoned and removed, and she could join in the games that they usually played after the wiener roast.

Jamie tried to cover his laughter when Harry came in the front door carrying a gardenia corsage. When Sammy saw it she remembered what Dessa had said. So she thanked him nicely and turned to glare at Jamie. Catherine broke the awkwardness when she gushed over how big the gardenia was. "Undoubtedly, your mother grows the biggest gardenias in these Glades, Harry. How nice of her to think of Sammy. Now, how did she know that they are her favorite flowers?"

Why'd she say that? She knows that nasturtiums and sweetpeas are my

217

favorites. But guess they'd not make a pretty corsage. To Harry she said, "It sure smells nice, Harry. Thank you."

"We'd better hurry, Sammy, 'cause Blanche has to get home to help Uncle Pete with the milking, but she'll pick us up when it's all over. See you later, Mrs. Carroll."

Catherine watched them as they drove off and hoped that Sammy would be able to keep her temper if anyone said anything about the corsage. *Maybe I'm too hard on her. It's just taking her longer to mature than it did Mary Catherine. They're just different, as Patrick has said a million times. I wonder if she'll share her evening with me like Mary Catherine always does. That would be nice.*

"Jamie, you and Gray come to the back porch, and I'll read you a story before you have to get your bath. I don't want you two to fill that tub to the rim like you usually do. Last night I had to mop the entire bathroom. I declare that it was a lot easier on me when we used the old bathhouse."

"I like the new bathroom, Mama. And it was Gray who filled it, and he splashed a lot more than I did."

Gray made a face at him and climbed up on Catherine's lap. She tousled his brown curls and asked, "Did you do that, honey? Did you make your mama hafta mop that floor?"

He reached up and kissed her cheek and hugged her around her neck. "I didn't mean to, Mama. It was Jamie who said I could. Didn't you Jamie? Didn't you?"

"But it was you who asked to, and you know it."

"If you two don't stop this bickering, I'm not going to read to you. What's it going to be? Are you going to sit down beside me and let me read, Jamie, or are you and Gray going to fuss?"

They quieted, as she knew they would, for they both enjoyed hearing her read. "Now, where was I? Do you remember? What was Black Beauty doing?"

"I remember, Mama, he was..."

"Phone, Mama, the phone..."

"For heaven's sake! Now who could that be at this time of night? You two sit right here. I'll only be a minute."

"Why, Clara! What on earth's the matter?" Catherine paused then said, "I'm so sorry to hear that. We both know how hard that's going to be on both of them. No, I was just reading to the boys before their bath time. I'll send a note to Lenore and express my sorrow. What makes you think that she's going to her home in Georgia? Who said? And do you always believe everything that busybody says to you? Since when?"

"Be right there, boys. Jamie, you go ahead and begin the reading. Page twenty-two, I think. You know how much they both wanted another baby, Clara. How old is Rahn now? He can't be. My, my, already three and a half.

How's Eben taking it? I can't believe that I'm the last person in the Glades to hear the news. When did she miscarry? Two days ago? Now, I know that I'm the last person to hear about it. Why didn't Beulah and Hulda say anything to me while we were at the grocery yesterday, I wonder.

"Hey, I hafta go. The boys are beginning to get restless. I'll talk to you tomorrow afternoon at the station. No, I promise that I'll stop by. Sammy has to practice her piano piece at the school after her last class, and Hulda said that she'd pick me up so I could help with the other performers. Well, it is for the Everglades Fair in Belle Glade, you know. And you know Sammy. She's real excited that her class was chosen to perform. She's got to have it perfect, and I for one want her to. I'll walk over as soon as I'm through. Dessa is staying with Gray and will tend Jamie when he gets off the bus. Bye, Clara. I hafta go."

"Now, where were we? How far did you get, Jamie? But I said for you to begin without me. I don't care what Gray said. I think that you read very well for your age. You shouldn't say things like that to your brother, Gray. How would you like for him to say that about your reading when you learn to read? Huh? You'll start next year and we'll just see how well you do, won't we, Jamie?"

"Dessa's coming, Mama. I see her coming with the milk. What happened to Sonny? I thought that he was supposed to milk Aunt Maude."

"And so he was. I hope she's not letting him take advantage of her. He's a nice young man, but he sometimes..."

"Dessa, we're on the back porch. What on earth are you doing carrying that heavy pail of milk? Where is Sonny, anyway?"

"His mama's ailing, an' Henry sent Ralph up ta git him. She not too bad, but he bein' de baby, Henry want him deah wit him. Ah unnerstan'."

"Here, let me help you with that. Why didn't you let me know? Why, Jamie and I could have helped you."

"Ah din't wanta bothah ya on Sammy's big naght. Moah important fo' ya ta be heah wit huh on huh fust date. Dis is a important naght fuh y'all."

"He brought her a corsage, Dessa. and it smelled to high heaven, didn't it, Mama?"

"Jamie, that's quite enough from you, young man. Yes, it did smell nice. A gardenia, Dessa, and Sammy thanked him real nice, like she said you suggested. I've been meaning to tell you that I appreciate all the help you've been to Sammy. Growing up can be a trial."

"Ah lak heppin' Sammy wit huh problems, Miz Catherine. She comin' along raght well, Ah t'ink."

"But why're you so upset with me, Betty Ann? He deserved to be kicked! It's a good thing for him that I didn't give him a black eye, too! He had no right to make Harry lose the race. He's supposed to be his best friend, isn't he?"

"Yes, he WAS his best friend, Sammy Carroll! Those two are always joshing like that, and neither one of them thinks a thing about it. Why'd you hafta get in the middle of it, anyway? You just hafta boss everyone around you, and, frankly, me and Donny are getting sick and tired of it! Is this how you're gonna act when we get in ninth grade next year? Is it?"

Sammy was gritting her teeth and just about to explode, when Mr. Cox, the scout master, came to Betty Ann's rescue.

"Hey, you two! I thought that you were best friends. What's all this shouting about?"

"I'm sorry, Mr. Cox, but that Sammy has to boss everyone. Just because Donny couldn't keep up with Harry in the relay race and dropped the baton you'd have thought that he did it purposely..."

"He did, Betty Ann, and you know it! You saw him grin when he did it, just like I did. He knew how much Harry wanted to beat those Ogle boys, and you know it!"

"That was no reason for you to march your high and mighty self over to him and kick him for the whole team to see, Miss!"

"Now, girls, let's not have this. I'm sure that it was just a misunderstanding."

"No, sir, Mr. Cox. He grinned big as you please and threw that race sure as I'm standing here. And furthermore, Betty Ann knows it."

Harry came to Sammy's rescue just in time. "Mr. Cox, Donny and I are best friends, or I should say that we used to be. Sammy's right. He's not much in sports and just doesn't like to see me win. It's one of his faults, and we've had words about it before..."

"Why didn't you bop him one, Harry? Why didn't you?" Sammy questioned.

"Yeah, Harry, why'd you let a old girl fight your fight for you, huh, why?" Frankie Ogle yelled.

"Don't you stick your nose in Harry's business, Frankie Ogle, or you'll be hearing from yours truly!" Sammy shouted warming to the approaching altercation.

Mr. Cox knew that it was time to intervene. "That will be enough from all of you. There are ways of settling things without resorting to fighting, Sammy. That is one of the things that we scouts try to instill in our members."

"Well, begging your pardon, sir, but it would appear to me that you have your work cut out for you when one of your own members deliberately throws a relay race. That's like going to war and helping the enemy win. I hope you teach your members to be fair. That's what I hope."

Mr. Cox shook his head and said, "I think Sammy has a point, boys. Now, let's all shake hands and show your lady friends how scouts are supposed to behave. We are supposed to work hard and play fair. Donny, do you think that you owe an apology to Harry? If you do, then I think now is the time to make that apology."

Betty Ann turned around abruptly and headed for the bonfire. When Sammy followed, she turned and glared at her. "I think that you've caused quite enough trouble, Sammy Carroll. You can just look for another best friend, 'cause I surely am not gonna be her." And that said, she sat on the big pine log beside the fire and looked off into space.

Sammy gulped and didn't say a word for it seemed like forever, but decided that she had to get it off her chest. "Well, Betty Ann, I don't want to be your best friend if you can't see the injustice in what just happened. You can keep that old Donny Padgett for all I care. I have fair play on my side, and that's a heck of a lot better than a...turncoat boyfriend! That's what! He threw that race!"

⸻

Catherine heard the car drive up and when she turned on the outside light, she saw Sammy and Harry holding hands as they walked up the walk. She turned back toward the living room and listened behind the front door to the porch. I probably shouldn't be doing this, but how else will I find out what's going on. Sammy probably won't share with me like Mary Catherine does.

"I'm real proud of you, Sammy. I don't care what Betty Ann and Donny said. You were right to stick up for what you consider an injustice. Now Donny does have a lot of fine qualities, even if he does behave like he did tonight."

Catherine couldn't make out what he said.

"Why do you hafta always take up for him, Harry? You know he did wrong! I mean really! Sometimes you just hafta put your foot down. He shouldn't behave like that. I know one thing. I bet he won't ever do a thing like that again. He's ashamed about how he behaved, and I bet this has taught him a lesson, and from now on no one else will put up with his shenanigans. I betcha!"

They got to the front door and Harry held it open for Sammy. "You're a good friend, Sammy. Maybe we could be best friends. Hey, what ya say?"

221

"I'd like that, Harry. And please thank your mama for the corsage. That was real sweet of her." Grief! I sounded just like Mary Catherine. I've gotta watch it.

Catherine put her hand over her mouth, sighed and thought, I think Sammy's coming along just fine, like Dessa said. They must have had a real good time.

"Oh, there you are, Sammy. Goodnight, Harry. Give Irene my best. And thank you for asking Sammy to your jamboree. I'm sure she had a nice time."

Before she could question her about her evening Sammy asked, "When do you expect Daddy home, Mama? I need to talk to him for a little while."

"What is it, dear? You can talk to me. I know that I'm not as smart as your daddy about a lot of things, but I do have some answers."

"Oh, I know that you're real smart about all kinds of things." She sighed deeply and continued slowly. "It's just that I think Daddy knows more about relay races and throwing races and stuff like that."

"What on earth are you talking about, Sammy? What's this about throwing a race? You did go to the scout jamboree, didn't you?"

"Yes, of course, but there was a...a...discussion about honesty and fairness and stuff like that. You know about scout behavior, like Mr. Cox said. I thought that Daddy would know more about that sort of thing. I'm tired. Think I'll go on to bed. Night." She sighed again and reached up and kissed Catherine's cheek.

"Night, honey. Did you have a good time? You didn't say."

Sammy turned around and tiredly said, "It was a very interesting evening. Harry's real nice. We've decided to become best friends. Night."

"Is that like going steady, honey?" No answer. Catherine sat down at the dining room table and reflected on the limited conversation. I don't know one bit more than I did before I asked her about her evening. Either she's a very deep child or she's avoiding my question. Oh, my, I don't think I'll ever understand that one. I really don't. She, too, sighed deeply.

Sammy didn't get to see Dessa the next afternoon because of the music practice after school. She and Catherine waited at her Uncle Walter's station for Patrick to finish work. It was almost dark when he did, and they were both tired, ready for supper, and not much in the mood for conversation. But Sammy did tell him a little of what had happened at the jamboree, not knowing that Patrick had already heard about it from Jimmy Cox. He let her explain, anyway.

"What's this all about, Sammy?" Catherine interrupted.

"Mama, there wasn't any commotion, really. It's just that I want to know what Daddy thinks I should have done. Betty Ann's not speaking to me, nor is Donny. Not that I care that much, but I want to know if what I did was wrong. That's all."

"I wasn't going to say anything to you, honey, but Jimmy Cox called me at the station this morning and told me what happened. Frankly, he was very impressed by your stance on fair play, Sammy. He did suggest that you could have handled it in another way..."

"What did you do, Sammy? Surely you didn't get into a knock down fight on your first date?"

"No, ma'am, I surely didn't! I just kicked Donny as hard as I could. That's all."

"Now, Kitten, Jimmy said that Sammy made a point and that he was proud of her. But as I said, he also said that there was another way that she could have handled it, and I agree."

"What should I have done? Should I have gone running to Mr. Cox and tattled? Is that what he thinks I should have done?"

"I don't think that he would have thought of it as tattling, honey. You saw that Donny dropped the baton purposely, and Jimmy should have been told. That's all."

By then Sammy's face was red and she was about to burst. "Daddy, everyone else there would have thought I was tattling, and you know it! And another thing. If Mr. Cox had been paying attention to the race, he'd have seen it, too, and I wouldn't have had to step in and do what needed doing. Seems to me that a referee oughta do his job... seems to me."

"Now, Sammy, don't start crying. It can't be that important to you."

"Not important? Just lost my best friend, that's all."

Catherine and Patrick looked at each other. She patted his hand reassuringly. When they pulled up in the driveway, Jamie was the first one to get to the car. Out of breath, he haltingly announced that Gray had thrown up all over Dessa and that she was out in the bathhouse taking a shower and that he was to be the big man and watch Gray so Dessa could get cleaned up.

"What next!" Catherine exclaimed. She looked at Patrick, and when he looked at her, they began to laugh. When Jamie asked what was so funny, Sammy joined her daddy and mama, who by then had got the giggles.

Patrick patted Jamie on the head and said that once in a while you just had to see humor in any situation, and he continued to laugh. Jamie just shook his head, wondering what could be funny about Gray throwing up all over Dessa. He thought that they'd be *upset*, but his mama was hugging Sammy and saying that everything would work out and that she was proud of her for defending Harry and...Grownups just can't be figured, he deduced. Normally she would have had a fit about Gray throwing up.

When Sammy related the story later to Dessa, they, too, laughed. "I don't know for the life of me what was so funny, Dessa. I guess that we were all so tired, and I was *upset* about the whole mess, and Jamie was *upset* with all of us, that we weren't the least bit *upset* that Gray had thrown up all over you."

Patrick's prediction about Canal Point's boom days being over proved to be accurate. Pahokee's growth had doubled in a decade to almost 5,000 people, and celery was the Glades new money crop. The new Prince Theater had opened as had the new skating rink. Robert Lampi was appointed the new band director at Pahokee High School, and Eleanor Roosevelt continued to make her surprise visits to the new government migrant camps. The year was 1940.

The war in Europe had escalated with Germany having invaded Austria without firing a shot and had attacked Poland. France had declared war on Germany and, according to Patrick and the other men hanging out on Main Street in Pahokee at their weekly Saturday night gatherings, Hitler was going to gobble up the entire continent before he was through. And that wasn't all. That Japanese Emperor Hirohito was not to be trusted any more than Hitler. What with Japan and Germany trying to own the world, they worried about what was going to become of the allies.

Gray was in the second grade at Canal Point Elementary, and Jamie was an active eight grader. Sammy was now in the tenth grade at Pahokee High School and not as concerned about world affairs as she was about her immediate problem of having to decide if she should try out for the cheerleading squad or take lessons and try to join the marching band. As usual, she consulted Dessa.

"What do ya lak ta do de most, Sammy? Do ya lak ta jump an' holler and cheah on yuah team lak de cheahleadahs do, o' do ya lak to march up and down and blow a horn an' weah de blue and white uniforms? Huh, what ya lak de best?"

"Oh, the cheerleaders wear uniforms, too, Dessa. They're real cute! They have a big blue "P" on a white sweater and blue swing skirts and tights. And I do like to do the cartwheels and make the pyramids and travel with the football players to the away games and..."

"Well, seems ta me dat ya already made up ya mind."

"No, I haven't because the band gets to go to the away games, too, and I'd sure like to do all those fancy drills. Miss Mock said that I could try out for majorette and lead the entire marching band."

"Well, why don't ya try out fo' cheahleadin', an' if'n ya don't make de squad den ya can try fo' de majorette an..."

"But the try-outs all happen soon's school starts, and there wouldn't be time to do them all. Besides, I'd hafta take music lessons once I decide what I want to play, and that'd take forever."

"What's Betty Ann goin' ta do?"

"Well, it's for sure she's not going to try for cheerleader or the band either. And Donny is already in the band. She just wants to take typing and shorthand and bookkeeping so she can be a secretary when she gets out of school. She doesn't want to go to college. I guess she'll be so busy practicing all that she won't have time to do anything else. She's real smart in those business courses."

"Ah t'inks Ah got de solution. Try foah de cheahleadah dis yeah, an' den next yeah take de lessons in de summer an' join de band foah de followin' yeah. Dat way ya can do both. Huh, what ya t'ink?"

Sammy jumped up off Dessa's bed and hugged her, exclaiming, "Dessa, don't you ever die. I mean it! What would I do without you? I love you. Hey, is there any more of that fish stew? I could smell it even before I got half way here. What do you put in it to make it so good? Mama's never tastes nearly as good as yours."

"Best not tell huh dat, Sammy. Well, fust Ah takes a nice slab o' white bacon dat Ah've cut down ta de rind, den Ah slices up a bunch o' onions wit de green stems o' de young ones. Den Ah fry dem 'til dey all brown up raght smaht. Ah puts in de flouah a little bit at a time and stir it round real good. Now, heah's mah secret. Ah adds some o' Aunt Maude's rich cream an' some chicken broth, an' when dat gits jes so, Ah add a big bowl o' mashed potatoes. Ah don't evah put in de fish til de las' minute. Only wants it ta cook til ya can flake it inta little pieces. Hmmmm! Mistah Eben sho 'nuff love dat when Ah show Alpha how ta fix it." She almost said when he was in the islands but caught herself in time. She was going to have to be more careful, she knew. It was just so easy to talk to Sammy.

Mary Catherine had been accepted to Florida State College for Women in Tallahassee as had her best friend, Dorothy Simms, and they both planned to enroll in the drama program after the first year. Everyone said that Mary Catherine was a natural actress, and they expected her to be on the silver screen along with Irene Dunne and Greta Garbo.

Mary Catherine's senior year at Pahokee High had indeed supported the town's opinion of her acting talents. Sammy hadn't particularly wanted to attend the senior play with Mary Catherine in the lead role, but her parents prevailed. Rather than cause a fuss she went. "But I'm gonna sit in the balcony in case she forgets her lines and embarrasses me," she declared.

When the curtain opened on *The Night of January Sixteenth*, Sammy didn't recognize Mary Catherine at first—she certainly didn't recognize her voice, she later told Dessa. "And when it was over, I bet I clapped harder than anyone there. She was better than Barbara Stanwick, Dessa. Oh, I wish you could have been there. That was one night I was proud of my sister.

"She played Karen Andre, who was on trial for murder, and the jury was selected right from the audience. You should have heard Daddy's response when he was selected. He brought down the house when he said, 'I'll be unable to serve, Your Honor, because I'm acquainted with this woman, Karen Andre,' and everyone laughed. He was so dramatic when he said it."

Sammy loved having the big room all to herself and was relieved when Mary Catherine hadn't gotten homesick and come running home like that Janie Tucker had. That would have messed everything up. Catherine had allowed Sammy to have a girlfriend over for an overnight almost every weekend.

Sammy had made the cheerleading squad, and after football season planned to try out for the basketball team. All her friends said that she'd have no trouble, because she was a head taller than most of them. Catherine was glad that she took after Patrick's family. She had thought that Mary Catherine would have grown more, but she seemed to stop in the tenth grade and was no taller than she.

That Jamie was the one who had shot up, Dessa said. Never saw a young man take off like he did the summer of '40. Catherine had to buy him a new set of clothes when he and Sammy were confirmed at St. Mary's. Sammy had one of her dramatic fits when Dessa decided that she would not attend the confirmation ceremony because she'd have to sit in the back of the church.

"No you won't, Dessa. You're part of our family, and you'll sit up there with Mama and Daddy and the rest of our kin."

When she mentioned it to Catherine, she found out that was not the case. "Now, I know how much Dessa means to you, honey, but it just wouldn't look right."

"And why not? And don't say because she's Colored or..."

"That's exactly what I mean. It's just not accepted down here."

"That's dumb! Just dumb! Why would anyone care if she sat with our family? Mama, I can't believe you're saying this. I can understand how other people think, but not you, and certainly not Daddy."

When Catherine mentioned their dilemma to Patrick, he assured her that he'd straighten Sammy out on what was and what was not accepted in the South.

"Would you want to embarrass Dessa, honey? She knows that her sitting up front with us is not done down here, even if you don't. She knows her place..."

"Daddy, Dessa's place is with us. You know she's my best friend, and it won't be right for her to not sit with my family," she said sniffling.

"All right, young lady, then I want you to ask Dessa what she wants to do. If she decides that it's acceptable for her to sit with our family, then I'll accept her decision, but I know that she'll want to do what is right for you and us. That I know."

"Aren't you taking a chance on it, Patrick?" Catherine asked. "What if she decides to sit with us?"

"I think I know what her answer to Sammy will be. I believe that she wants to do the right thing by us. We're her friends, too, even if Sammy doesn't know it."

Patrick was right. "Don't you want to see me confirmed, Dessa? Don't you?"

"Dat would be real nice, Sammy, but ta tell da trut', Ah'd rather be raght heah cookin' up a real big feast fo' you an' de fambly. Now don't look at me lak dat. Ah mean it. Why Ah'm gonta make dat ambrosia ya lak, an Ah'm gonta..."

"You're not just saying that are you? Because if you are, then..."

"No, chile, Ah'm tellin' de trut'. Ah love ta cook fo' ya. Ya knows dat, Sammy." She patted Sammy's back and Sammy hugged her.

"Well, in that case, it's all right. But I sure wish you could be there when I hafta answer the Bishop's questions. Jamie and I know our catechism. Boy howdy! We've got all those answers down pat, the sisters in Belle Glade said. I think we surprised them with our knowledge."

Ah would sho love ta heah you an' Jamie do ya stuff, chile. But ya daddy's raght 'bout me sittin' wit ya. Dese folks just wouldn't lak it. Maybe some day...

They had hoped that Miss Mae could come down from Georgia for the occasion, but Joe called and said that she had failed so much that they didn't think she should make the trip. Patrick and Catherine decided that they'd all take off for a two-week trip to visit his family in Augusta that next summer. It had been a long time since they'd seen any of them.

"Alpha, ya don't look too good," Dessa declared while folding the wash. "Hey, han' me dose blouses o' Sammy's so's Ah can press 'em while dey still a little damp."

"Ya wouldn't look too good eithah if'n ya could see how down Miz Lenore and Mistah Eben's been since dey los' dat little baby. You'd t'ink dey be ovah dat by now. Been neah 'bout two yeah now. Miz Lenore spen' lots o' time up in Georgia wit huh folks. Mistah Eben sho miss huh when she go. She say dat she won't git ta be goin' now dat Little Rahn staht school. 'Magine him bein' six yeah old come Thanksgivin'. 'Magine!"

"Time sho fly. Dat Gray doin' real good in his schoolin'. Wish ya could heah dat little boy read. He somet'in' else. Ah'm gonta git dese done, Alpha. Den we can have ouah tea. Call James in so he can join us. Did Mistah Eben git in his plantin? Mistah Carroll late dis yeah on account o' his bein' dat deputy. De Missus was sho put out wit him, what wid Mary Catherine away at dat big college an' it costin' dem so much money."

"James, come on in heah an' have some tea wid us." Alpha yelled out the back door to James, who was sitting in Eben's new Buick listening to the radio.

He came running up the long back steps out of breath. "Guess what Ah heard on Mistah Eben's radio? De president done ast de government for 15,000 navy airplanes an' seventeen battleships an' a bunch o' submarines. We be in fo' a heap o' trouble wit dose Japanese folks, Ah'm believin'. Mistah Eben say just de othah naght dat he maght be called ovah ta faght dem 'foah it through. He say dat very t'ing, din't he, Alpha?"

"He too old ta go off faghtin'. Now ya bot' know dat. He too old." Dessa commented.

"No he ain't. No he ain't. He ain't much pas' fohty, is he, James?"

"Dat ain't too old ta faght a wah, Ah'm t'inkin'. He say most all de boys would be called up if'n we goes ta wah. He say dat very t'ing."

CHAPTER EIGHTEEN

1941 began with a bang. There was a new Elks lodge built in Pahokee, and a migratory camp school and nursery opened in Belle Glade. New crops of beans were ready for harvesting, and celery processing plants were opening in all the Glades' towns. A bumper crop was predicted, and everyone was preparing for the Glades Fair to be held in Pahokee in February. One of the highlights at the fair was to be a Hollywood style wedding for the lucky couple chosen. All the merchants were donating gifts, and couples who had been putting off their weddings suddenly decided that now was the time to get married. There was a long line at Bolton's Drug Store for the registrants.

The new Glades Hospital and a Western Auto store opened in Pahokee and Belle Glade as well. Most of the area's young men were being drafted. Camp Blanding in Starke, Florida, was their destination. The local women were busily knitting items for the Palm Beach Red Cross: sweaters, scarves, mittens, socks and caps for shipping to our boys overseas.

The skies over the Everglades were filled with airplanes from the Florida bases. Bombing practice was an every-day occurrence in the lake. The airfields at Clewiston on the southeast side of Lake Okeechobee and Morrison Field in West Palm Beach were training pilots for the British Army.

When President Roosevelt declared the second registration of men twenty-one years old and the National Defense Savings Bonds went on sale, everyone was brought into the effort. The elementary school children helped collect aluminum from the housewives. It was reported that enough aluminum was collected in Florida alone to build more than twenty-five fighter planes. Palm Beach County was the second highest donor. The scouts collected old newspapers for the defense drive, and a number of the area men were sent to the Norfolk Naval Training Station for a sixteen-week, intensive, aviation machinist course.

The spring rains played havoc with the crops that were headed for the new State Farmers Market in Pahokee. It was especially hard on the area farmers because of their new importance in the war effort. There would be no sirens blown at noon in Pahokee as in the past, because the sirens were to be used only as an air raid alarm. A new signal had to be worked out for the fire alarm, and even the church bells had stopped ringing.

Graduation exercises at Pahokee High School, that included students from the towns of Belle Glade and South Bay as well as Canal Point, were held in May. There were sixty-eight seniors getting their diplomas. *Kitty Foyle* was playing at the Prince Theater with Ginger Rogers and Dennis

Morgan as was Bette Davis's newest release, *The Letter*. But the favorite movie for the youngsters was *Little Men* with Jack Oakie and Kay Francis, who was Clara's favorite actress.

Football season was over, so Sammy didn't have to stay after school for cheerleading practice. She was allowed, on occasion, to visit one of her Pahokee girlfriends on a weekend so she could attend a Saturday dance or other school function and not have to wait for a ride home from Patrick, who worked long hours on those nights. Clara and Catherine would pick her up in the early afternoon on Sunday. December seventh was such a day.

"I'll only be a minute, you two," Clara called as she went into Fletcher's Drug Store for her new *Redbook* magazine. She was gone only a short time, and when she came out, it was with a burst, and she was yelling, arms waving in the air.

"Good grief, Clara! What's wrong?" Catherine questioned.

She could hardly talk. She stammered, "Pearl Harbor has been attacked by the Japs, and we're at war. It just came over the radio." She opened the car door in a daze and started the engine.

"Where is Pearl Harbor?" Sammy asked.

She turned around to see if there was a car coming and said almost in a whisper, "They think it's in Hawaii, but they're not sure. Someone said Hawaii."

"Clara, stop the car. Julian is coming out. He'll know."

He went over to the car and asked, "Catherine, do you know where Patrick is? We've gotta have some kind of meeting. We've gotta get organized," he said in the same daze that Clara was in.

All Sammy could think to say was, "Is Daddy gonna hafta go, Mama? Will they call him up?"

"No, honey, your daddy will be needed here. Besides, he's too old."

"Don't count on anything, Catherine," Julian said. "This might be a long, hard-fought war. We're not prepared for it. We might need every woman, man and child before this is over."

"I'll do my share, Mr. Chandler," Sammy said. "I'd go tomorrow if they needed me. Mama, we've gotta get home so I can tell Dessa. You know that she doesn't listen to the radio often. Heck, she might not even know that we need to get prepared."

Clara said, "I'm gonna drive as fast as I can, Sammy. I just bet that Walter and Clarissa don't know about it, either."

When Clara pulled up in the Carrolls' driveway, the front door burst open with Jamie and Gray fighting to get to the car first so they could tell them about the news. Dessa was in the doorway wiping her eyes. It seems that Walter had been listening to the radio when the news was announced, and he had called to find out if Clara was there. Patrick had also called to tell them that he was on his way home.

The December 8th *Palm Beach Post* devoted the first page to the war. President Roosevelt had asked congress to declare a state of war between the United States and Japan, and he was to speak to the nation the next day.

The Carrolls and Halls were gathered in the living room with Dessa in the dining room. They all surrounded the radio waiting for the president's speech. Patrick had turned the radio's volume high and did not have to warn anyone about speaking. Sammy went to the dining room and pulled out a chair, getting as close to Dessa as she could. They were holding hands when the president began to speak.

He warned the country that as Germany and Japan conducted military and Naval operations in accordance with a joint plan, Germany and Italy would probably consider themselves also at war with the United States. "We are going to win the war, and we are going to win the peace that follows."

No one shouted or gave any kind of response. Just silence. Finally, Patrick rose and went to Catherine. She was in his arms, and everyone began to cry, the men allowing tears to form, and the rest, including Sammy, shed tears unashamedly.

"We've got our work cut out for us on this one, huh,` Walter?" Patrick said.

"You bet we have. And as we were just saying Saturday night, we aren't ready for this one."

December eleventh Germany and Italy declared war on the United States the same day congress passed and the President approved resolutions declaring a state of war with them.

Christmas of 1941 was not the usual festive time at the Carroll household. The family had gathered with only Dessa helping to prepare the big meal. There was the usual stuffed turkey and roasted haunch of venison, as only Walter could prepare it, but the laughter was sparse. Mary Catherine tried to infuse some funny stories about college life into the conversation, but everyone's mind was on the war. Even Gray's excitement about his gifts from Santa Claus hadn't lightened the atmosphere.

"Mama, after I have my pie can I go play with my new fire engine? I won't get dirty, promise."

"Give me a kiss, son, and go play as much as you like. You don't have to stay dressed. Put on your overalls. They're at the top of your closet. You want to eat your pie later?"

"Miz Carroll, Ah'll fix him a piece an' he can eat it in heah wit me. Come on, Gray. Come ta Dessa an' we'll git dose overalls down in a jiffy."

"Thanks, Dessa. Gray, what kind do you want? Mary Catherine will cut it for you. You want the coconut cream or do you want the mince?"

"What are you laughing about, Patrick Carroll? I fixed one without all that bourbon, or did you and Walter lace both of them? I just bet that you did!" Catherine said, admonishing them but laughing at the same time. "Dessa, you smell both of those mince pies to see if they did, please. Really, you two!"

Dessa put her head around the kitchen door and called into the dining room, "You caught 'em, Miz Carroll. Bot' dose pies is flyin' high." She was glad to hear laughter.

※

1942 brought rationing of tires and blackout practice every Sunday for half an hour between 10:15 and 10:45. Jamie and Gray, who weren't allowed to stay up that late ordinarily, were allowed to stay up to help put the black cloth over the windows, even though the lights were turned off. Patrick felt that they should learn the importance of every aspect of defense. Most of the time Gray would fall asleep.

Air raid wardens met at the Pahokee Elks Club, and the navy training planes were constantly flying over Lake Okeechobee. No toothpaste or shaving cream was to be sold in tubes unless the buyer brought in old tubes to replace the new ones. And to add to everyone's woes, there was an outbreak of mumps and measles among the children in the Canal Point school. Gray was one of the infected.

A sewing room was set up at the new Pahokee City Hall for the ladies of the area, and gas was being rationed. There were ceiling prices put on food and goods for the war effort with extra sugar allowed only for canning. It was predicted that by fall coffee, sugar, fuel oil and meat would be rationed. They were. Penny coinage was reduced to conserve copper, and identification tags and finger printing were required for the Citizens Defense Corps.

※

It was the year that Sammy was graduated from high school. She had won her school letter in basketball, softball and cheerleading. She was also an excellent student and involved in chorus, the Latin Club and every activity she had time for. She had dated from the time she was in the ninth grade but had not gone steady with any particular boy. She was very popular and loved school.

When she was voted by her class as the most athletic and the wittiest, she was excited. But when they also voted her the most conceited, she was incensed. "The most conceited! Just who do they think they are?" she questioned Dessa. "And guess what that J.E. said! He said that I was the only one who wouldn't be upset about being named the most conceited, that they really wanted to name Norma Miller that, but she would have cried and carried on. So that's why they gave it to me! Imagine that! Now I'll hafta go through life as being named by my class as the most conceited!"

❦

"Mama, make sure when you bring Dessa to the auditorium that she sits on the end of the row," Sammy reminded Catherine. "And, Mama, you fuss at her if she doesn't wear her new hat. I mean it! She is not gonna sit at the back with all the other Coloreds!"

Sammy was in a dither. She wanted her graduation to go perfectly, and Dessa had promised to be there with the Carrolls. Sammy had threatened to not go through with the ceremony if Dessa didn't attend. "And I mean it, Dessa. This is the most important day of my entire life, and you've gotta be there. Besides, I hope to win the Best All Around Student Award. That's what I've been working for. Heck, I'm glad Harry beat me out as salutatorian. I'd have a fit if I had to make a speech in front of all those people."

"Why, Sammy, ya been makin' speeches all ya life. Dat would've been a honah fo' ya parents."

"But I would have bawled my head off, Dessa. I love school and don't want to leave it. Really, I don't. I love Pahokee High School. It's been my home. And with the war and all our young men being killed and all those in the Japanese prison camps, I wouldn't have been able to make a speech about our future, and...Oh, Dessa, what if we don't win the war? It's scary!"

"Come ta ya Dessa, chile. Come heah dis minute. Ya gonta have a gran' life. Ah'll see ta it! Don't ya cry 'bout ya futuah. Don't ya."

Sammy's head was buried in Dessa's lap.

❦

Sammy and her best friend Lois Wilson were enrolled in college in Tallahassee for the fall term. They had spent the summer volunteering as airplane spotters, using the old fire towers, and rolling bandages with the other young people of the area. She also helped Catherine and Clara can food from the spring crop. Winning the Best All Around Student Award had made her proud, but the once carefree Sammy had become quite sober. Her friends were going off to war.

Mary Catherine, going into her senior year of college, had worked in West Palm Beach for the summer and stayed with her Uncle Wash and family. Being a cosmetic counter girl at Burdine's had been fun and profitable. She was saving her money for her hoped-for trip to New York during spring break. She and Dorothy were determined to make a big splash on Broadway. That is, if the war went well.

⁂

Thanksgiving vacation arrived, and the Canal Point and Pahokee students arrived at the Canal Point bus station from Tallahassee. Sammy and Mary Catherine walked the short distance to the filling station and stayed with Clara and Walter 'til Patrick could be summoned for their ride home.

"This is a pain!" Sammy uttered to Mary Catherine. "I know what you're going to say, that Mama probably wouldn't have the gas to pick us up even if she drove, but you'll have to admit sitting up in that bus all day long was a bore."

"I didn't think so. If you'd read more the time would have just sped by."

"And when did you read? Your mouth was going a mile a minute. What on earth do you and Dorothy find to talk about when you're with her almost every blessed minute at school?"

"For one thing, miss, she had got a letter from Vance, and we were speculating about where he is stationed. We know that it's somewhere in the Pacific from the few things the censors let slip by. He and Dotty have a code, so she does know a little."

"I bet she's worried sick. Mama sent a clipping out of the newspaper about Vann Bardin and John Padgett being held in a Japanese prison camp. The article said that their parents were allowed to send food packages, but that they couldn't weigh more than eleven pounds. I don't know how they stand it."

"You two want a coke?" Clara asked. "No telling when Patrick will get here. I can run you on home if you want, but Patrick can get gas, where

234

Walter and I have to scrimp. That should be funny, what with us owning our own gas station, but it isn't, I can tell you. We are rationed just like everyone else."

"We'll wait for Daddy, Aunt Clara. Mama would have a fit if we let you use your gas on us. Actually, we could walk home and just let Daddy bring our bags later. What do you think, Mary Catherine?"

"These are my good shoes. I'd rather just sit here and wait for Daddy. I'll take that coke, Aunt Clara. I can't believe it's this hot in November."

"Are those the Ogle boys sitting on the locks underneath that rubber tree fishing, Aunt Clara?" Sammy questioned.

"Looks like them to me." Clara answered. "By the way, I like your hair like that. Always was partial to page boys. You heard that John got himself killed on a PT boat about a month ago, didn't you?"

"Why didn't Mama write me about it? I'm going to ask Dessa to write more often. Mama seems to have too much on her mind. She should have written me."

"Didn't think that you were very fond of the Ogle boys, Sammy. Last thing I heard, you were feuding with them."

"Aunt Clara, grief! That was when I was just a little girl. We aren't good friends, but then we're not enemies, either. She should have written me about John. I would have written Mr. and Mrs. Ogle and told them how sorry I was to hear the news".

Sammy began to fidget. "I'm getting antsy just sitting here. I'm going to walk on home, but I think I'll walk over and tell the boys that I didn't know about poor John. See you at home."

Clara turned to Mary Catherine and whispered so Sammy couldn't hear, "I think that Sammy has truly changed since she went away to school. Seems to be more caring somehow. The old Sammy would've acted differently, don't you think, Mary Catherine?"

"Yes, I'll agree. But you know, Aunt Clara, the war has affected all of us. I think she's a little bit sweet on Lois Wilson's brother Woody. Now don't you say a word about this to anyone. He's at the training field at Carabelle and has been up to see Lois a number of times, and I know for a fact that Sammy has gone out with him, but she'd die if she thought I knew. Just die!"

"Why, for heavens sake? He's a nice looking boy and certainly a fine athlete, Walter says. Why would she care if anyone knew about it?"

"Sammy is a very private person and doesn't want anyone to know her business. Now I don't care one whit if people know that I'm in love with Bruce Murray. I love him terribly and want the world to know it. Oh, we're not going to marry until after the war is over and maybe not even then. He knows that I have my heart set on an acting career and has always encouraged me. He's very mature, you know."

"I always did like Mildred and Verne Murray. Nice people and I've heard nothing but good about Bruce, Mary Catherine. Seems like you girls are making plans for your future even if there is a war on."

"Here comes Daddy! We'll pick Sammy up on our way home. Thanks for the coke and see you tonight. I guess Mama will be fixing the stuffing like always and you and Uncle Walter will be over?"

"Walter, do you plan to go over to Patrick's tonight?" Clara asked.

He put his head out the station door and said, "If I can get all this paper work done I will. Darned government makes it just about impossible to get your real work done anymore. Just about."

<hr>

"But, Eben, he's only eight years old. He's too little to go duck hunting!" Lenore lamented.

Eben kissed her on the forehead, turned toward the kitchen and replied, "You know that I've been promising Rahn that we'd go duck hunting on his eighth birthday for two years at least. You know that. Emerson's boys will be along and also Pratt Pope's boys, Monroe and Roy..."

"But they're all older than Rahn. Why Junior is at least twelve and Reddick ten..."

"Lenore, I've heard enough! I don't want to be cross with you, but you've become just too protective of Rahn. Do you want him to be a sissy? Do you?"

"You know better than that! I want him to be a well rounded individual, and you know it!"

"Then, that's that! There'll be no more discussion." Alpha rushed away from the kitchen door and resumed her cooking while signaling James with her eyes. She began humming. "Why, Mistah Eben, what ya wantin' fo' yuah brea'fast? Ah got biscuits in de oven and can fix up some eggs in a jiffy."

"That would be wonderful, Alpha. But tomorrow morning I don't want you to fix breakfast for Rahn and me. I'm taking him duck hunting, and we're going to leave before daylight to get to the blind. He's real excited about it. Emerson's boys will join us as will Mr. Pope's sons. Should be a lot of fun for all of us. I can confess to you now that the past few years have not been our greatest. But then I imagine that you know that. It's time that we relaxed a little."

"Yessuh, Mistah Eben, we been aweah 'bout ya trouble. It ain't easy ta be a fahmah, an' what wit de wah..."

"We'll do just fine, James. The government is counting on us to supply the armed forces with vegetables. That's no small task, you know. We have to have the cooperation of the Almighty."

"Oh, Ah knows dat fo' shuah, Mistah Eben. It ain't no small task."

"James, han' Mistah Eben dis hot biscuit while Ah git his eggs fried up."

"Is that my Rahn I hear, Alpha? Is it, James?"

And with that, Rahn rushed in out of breath and grabbed James around his waist. "My. my, Mastah Rahn, ya gits tallah evah time Ah sees ya, don't he, Alpha?"

"Ain't no doubt 'bout it, James. He sho do dat."

Lenore came into the room with her soft smile aimed at Rahn. "Ask Alpha for your juice, honey. Did you tell them about your hunting trip with your daddy?"

"What dis all 'bout, Mastah Rahn? Ya goin' on a huntin' trip wit ya daddy?"

"You're all making sport of me, aren't they, Daddy? You know as well as I do that he's been promising this trip to me forever."

Eben laughed heartily. "It'll take more than all of you to pull the wool over Rahn's eyes, huh, son?"

"They're just having a good time teasing me. I don't mind. Heck, Alpha and James have been doing that for all my life." He grabbed a hot biscuit off the cookie sheet and proceeded to butter it. Alpha got the guava jelly out of the refrigerator and handed it to him.

"I'll take one of those, too, Alpha, if I may. No, I'll sit right down here and eat with my men," Lenore added.

⌐━⟐⟐⟐⌐

When Eben went to Rahn's door to awaken him the following morning, Thanksgiving Day, Rahn was already awake and dressed. He had put on the new camouflaged outfit and already had his knapsack filled with biscuits that James had fixed for him.

"I believe that you're anxious to get your first duck, son. Don't make a sound, or you'll awaken your mother."

"Ha! Your mother is already awake, you two. Surely you didn't think that you could escape the premises without getting a goodbye kiss from me, did you?" Lenore asked animatedly as she grabbed Eben to her.

"And who would want to, huh, Rahn?"

"I'll shoot enough for all of us to have for our Thanksgiving dinner, Mama. That's a promise."

She sighed deeply while looking at the two of them. "If you get just one I'll be happy for you. After all, this is your first hunting trip. You can't expect to kill many during your first effort."

"Your mother's right, son. Your first time out is just that. You'll learn as you go..."

"But Junior bagged six on his first time out! He told me!"

"Junior is inclined to exaggerate, Rahn. Just like his daddy," and Eben laughed. "Heck, I can remember when Emerson went with me on his very first..."

"Hey, you two better get started! I think I hear Emerson right now."

She ran down the circular staircase and could see someone at the front door, but before she could get to it, James was there.

*

Dessa had awakened early as was her habit. She awoke with a chuckle. She was remembering about Sammy's first kiss. She had told Dessa that all the kids went diking after the ball games. "What's diking?" Dessa questioned.

"You know. We drive up on the dike and smooch our dates." Sammy looked at Dessa questioningly. "You do know what smooching is, don't you?"

"Is dat like sparkin'?"

"I don't know, but it's when you hug and kiss."

"Yeah, dat's sparkin' all raght."

Dessa began to hum as she went about her morning chores. Ah bets Sammy sleepin' in dis mornin'. She near 'bout exhausted last night when she finally got home. Nevah saw huh so tired.

"Sonny," she called. "Best ya git up so's ya can go ta ya folks' house for Thanksgivin'. Come on now, dis ain't de day to loll in dat bed. Git yuah skinny bones outa dat bed. Ah wondahs how ya so skinny when ya says how much dey feed ya at yuah college."

Sonny rolled over and had his usual grin on. "They do cook good, Dessa, but can't hold a candle to you or Mama. I told Mama I'd be up early, and Mister Patrick said he'd drive me when I was ready. I guess deputy sheriffs work holidays, too."

"Mistah Carroll work all de time. Holidays don't mean nothin' ta robbahs and killahs, he say. Ah'm goin' on up ta de big house ta git dat tuhkey stuffed. Ya wants me ta tell him dat ya ready?"

"Yeah, that would be fine. I'll just grab a corn dodger to eat on the way. I know Mama will have a big breakfast fixed for me."

"Sammy still in de bed, Miz Catherine?"

"Yes, and so is Mary Catherine. I think I heard Jamie and Gray talking though. Hand me that thread, would you please, Dessa? I want to sew up this bird so he'll keep his stuffing in this year. Why did Patrick get such a big one I wonder? Just going to be us and Clara and hers. He could have gotten a smaller one. He won the turkey shoot at the Elks Club, you know."

"Yessum, Ah knows dat fo' shuah. Jamie almost split hisself in two runnin' ta tell me 'bout it."

"All right. That does it. Do you think I put enough lard on it? I certainly don't want it to be dry."

"Maybe puts a little moah on de breast. Dat seem ta git dry de most."

"Good, I hear Patrick coming. He said he wouldn't be long. I hope he remembered to give Sonny that little fruit cake I made him. He dearly loves fruit cake. I believe he's put on a little weight, don't you?"

"He got a long ways ta go, Miz Catherine. Ah fussed at him already dis day."

Patrick came into the kitchen with a scowl on his face. "No long faces this day, Patrick. Now, I mean it. This is to be our day of thankfulness, and that means all day. What's wrong, honey?"

"Oh, it's this letter from one of our soldiers stationed at Ft. McKinley in the Philippines, that's all."

"Let me see that paper, because if there is any bad news in it, I'm going to cut it out and not let you read it."

Dessa began laughing at the two of them as Patrick tried to keep the paper away from Catherine.

"Heah come Sammy. She hep ya, Miz Catherine."

"Help you do what, Mama?"

The phone rang. "That'll be Clara, Sammy. Would you answer it, please. Don't know anyone else who'd call us this early in the morning and on a holiday, too."

"Hello, this is Sammy. Yes, he's right here. Is this Alpha?"

"Daddy, I think it's Alpha, and she seems to be crying. I could hardly understand a thing she was saying. Something about Master Rahn and hunting or something..."

"Here, give it to me. Yes, Alpha. Now calm down and speak more slowly, please."

The phone was on the china cabinet in the dining room. Everyone had gathered around Patrick. When Catherine saw his face become ashen, her hand went to her mouth and so did Dessa's. When Sammy saw their expression she started tearing.

Patrick gulped, turned toward them and said, "It appears that little Rahn Hunter has been killed. Eben took him duck hunting for his birthday and somehow he was shot. Alpha said that the doctor is with Lenore but that Eben won't leave Rahn. I've gotta get to him."

"Of course you do, honey. Dear Lord! What's going to happen next?" They were all crying by then, and when a sleepy Mary Catherine came out of the bedroom and inquired about all the commotion, Sammy told her.

"Daddy, can I go with you? I might be of some help. And maybe Dessa oughta go, too. Alpha and James are her best friends, and they might need her." Sammy murmured.

"Normally, I would say no, Sammy, but I think that Dessa's being there would be of help. Alpha acted like she won't be of much assistance."

"Do you want me to go with you, Patrick?" Catherine asked.

"I don't think so, honey. You and Sammy stay here, but I would like for Dessa to go with me."

"Where are Eben and little Rahn? Did Alpha say?"

"He's in that hunting buggy holding Rahn's body, and neither Emerson nor Dr. Spooner can get him to come out. He's locked himself in, it would appear. Alpha said that Lenore fainted, and when the doctor got there he and Thornton got her up to her room and to bed. The doctor gave Lenore something, and she's resting."

"What a horrible thing to happen, and on his birthday, too. I believe he'd be eight today. I don't know how Eben and Lenore will be able to stand this. I truly don't." Catherine said, holding Patrick's hand tightly.

"If they need me, please call. I'll get Walter to drive me to Pahokee. Now I mean it, honey. Our dinner can wait. We won't feel like eating, anyway."

"Mistah Carroll, Ah'll be wit ya in a minute. Jus wanta git mah hat an' change dis apron."

"Here, Dessa, take this one. It's clean and pressed. I was going to wear it for today, but I'd rather you wear it. Now, don't you argue. Sammy, go with Dessa and help her get ready." Catherine could be very forceful when she had to.

⁂

"Eben, this is Patrick and I need to talk to you. There is no need to behave this way when your wife needs you. Open this door this minute! If you don't, then I'll open it for you. Now, I mean it! Lenore needs you!"

Patrick could see him. His head was buried in Rahn's chest, and his body was heaving.

"I said now, Eben! This minute! You're needed in the house!"

Emerson stood beside Patrick. His hand was shaking so that he could hardly hold onto the door handle. He felt it turn and Patrick pushed him out of the way and wrenched it open. Eben and Rahn almost fell out of the buggy, but Patrick caught them with Emerson's assistance. Doctor Spooner had arrived, and he and Emerson took Rahn from Eben and rushed him to the doctor's car. Patrick held Eben up, and James grabbed his other side. They walked him into the kitchen, where Alpha and Dessa were.

"Who's with Lenore?" Patrick asked.

"Ah call Miz Bleech ta come. She an' Miz Lenore become good friends since dey been workin' at de Red Cross, an' she a nuhse, too."

"Good thinking, Alpha. Dessa, get Mister Eben a glass and, James, I want you to get him some sweetenin' from the dining room. At least, I think that's where he keeps it."

"Yessuh, dat wheah he keep it."

"Bring the bottle and make it bourbon. Alpha, how about brewing up some strong tea." Patrick looked at Eben. His head was down on his crossed arms resting on the kitchen table. The front of his jacket was covered with Rahn's blood, and his boots were caked with dried mud and blood.

"When the doctor returns, Alpha, I want you and James to get Mister Eben up to his and Miss Lenore's room, get him undressed and cleaned up, and then call me. He has got to talk. He's in shock right now, but we've got to make him talk. He can't go on this way. The sooner the better."

⸻

"No, Eben, I said for you to drink this. Every bit of it. Since when did I have to pour good liquor down you? I was just remembering sitting in my own kitchen about ten or so years ago..."

"It was summer of '32..." Eben said. Dessa glanced at Patrick and he at her and they both shook their heads up and down, thinking that they had broken through to Eben.

"Was it that long ago? I can't believe it!"

But not another word did Patrick get out of Eben that day. He drank the hot toddy, allowed James to assist him upstairs, but when Patrick got upstairs, Eben had barricaded himself in Rahn's room with the rest of the bottle and had locked the door. Disgusted with himself, Patrick returned to the kitchen.

"All right, Emerson. What in the hell happened? How could anything like this happen?"

Emerson was a wreck. "I don't know! Honest, I don't know. We were all crouched behind the blind, and when the ducks started flying off the lake, we all began shooting. Rahn was between Eben and Roy Pope, and the next thing I heard was Eben screaming. He just kept screaming. When I got to him, there was Rahn down on the ground with half his head blown off."

"Do you know who fired the shot?"

"Well, I know that it wasn't Eben. He's too good a hunter to do anything that dumb. It could have been one of the other boys over my way, but I don't know. I asked Junior and he denied it. I don't know if we'll ever find out. It was an accident, that's all. Just an accident!" By then he was sobbing uncontrollably.

Patrick patted him on the back and said, "That's all for now, but when things settle down, I'll have to question all of you. I don't want to, but I have no choice. You understand, don't you, Emerson? It's my job."

Emerson shook his head yes and murmured that he understood.

<hr />

Patrick was driving Dessa back to the house. "I think Alpha and James can handle whatever needs handling now, Dessa."

"Dat whole house full o' people. Dat give Alpha somet'in' ta keep huh busy. Dat's what she need, ta keep busy."

"Yes, that's what she needs." Patrick remembered how Catherine had kept Dessa busy when her John was killed. Marsh and Catherine had a long talk, and Marsh suggested it. It didn't cure anything—only time could do that—but it did help.

<hr />

Lenore's mother Nora came down from Georgia to be with her. Christmas was going to be rough, she knew, and it was. Eben had not come out of his shell and behaved like a zombie, Patrick told Catherine. "He just won't accept it. Maybe he's still blaming himself. That's what Lenore said. Said he kept saying that he shouldn't have rushed him so. That he should have waited 'til he was older."

"What good would that have done, hon? Whoever fired that fatal shot would have done it in all the excitement, no matter..."

"I know that, and so do you, but Eben doesn't. I don't know what's going to happen to them. Lenore has threatened to go back to Georgia with Nora if he doesn't make an effort to talk to her and comfort her. He is so distant, Alpha says."

"And this is when they need to pull from each other. This is the time when he needs to show his love."

"I'll be willing to bet that she returns with Nora. He goes up to the cemetery every day. She had wanted Rahn buried in West Palm Beach in the Catholic cemetery, but he wouldn't hear of it."

"I wondered about that. Clara had said it, but I didn't believe her. Poor, poor man. I thought that the inscription on his beautiful tombstone was so touching. I wrote it to the girls and remember, Sammy wrote that she and Mary Catherine cried and cried when they read it."

Tread softly for an angel hand
Doth guard this silent dust,
And we can safely wait our boy,
Our darling in their trust

"I cry every time I think of it. Don't know where they got the poem. Someone said that they had books with inscriptions in them to choose from, but I've never heard of such a book, have you?" Catherine questioned.

"Maybe it's a saying from one of their families. We'll probably never know. Have to go, honey. Why don't you and Clara plan to visit Lenore soon? I'm sure she'd appreciate it." Patrick said as they walked to the front door.

"We've already talked about that, but Clara thinks that Walter can't get along without her for even an hour or two. She beats all, she does."

<hr/>

Spring of '43 arrived, and Lenore was still in Georgia. Alpha had told Dessa that when she left the end of January, she had told Eben that she wasn't coming back until he called her and asked her, that she couldn't stand his silence, and if he truly loved her, he'd make an effort to heal. "But ya knows Mistah Eben. He too stubbo'n fo' his own good, he is. Jes too stubbo'n. Walk up an' down evah blessed night. Up an' down, up an' down. It git ta James an' me ta heah him. Ah been waitin' fuh dat black spell ta come on him an' sho 'nuff it heah. He in de wust black spell Ah evah seed him in."

"Mistah Carroll say he drinking lots, too. He real worried 'bout him.'"

"Mistah Thornton ast him ta go stay wit him and his missus, dat he only be blue when he in dis house. But ya ain't see him go up deah, do ya? No ma'am, he jes stay up in dat room o' dead little Rahn an' bawl his head 'bout off, dat's what. Ah told him de other day wat mah ma used ta say, 'What de eye cain't see de heart don't grieve', but he jes turn away."

The Lakeside Coffee Shoppe had big news that summer. Seems that Eben Hunter up and joined the Seabees and was on his way up north for training.

"Hell, he's too old for the navy. How'd he pull that off?"

"Thornton said that he is a good friend of Judge Chillingworth's in West Palm Beach and the judge was called up when he was forty-four 'cause he was in the reserves. Eben had him pull some strings for him so he could serve."

"Serve my eye! He just wants to get himself killed so he can forget about little Rahn, that's what!" said April, who had resumed her work at the coffee shop after Buck went overseas.

"Betty Jean Wetherington said that Thornton and his missus were moving into Eben and Lenore's house. What in the world do those two want with such a big place now that their girls are married and gone?"

"Well, I for one am glad that someone's living in it. It's too pretty a house to be sitting there empty."

"I guess that means Lenore ain't ever coming back here. Cora Bleech said she has enrolled in a teachers college in Savannah. The minute she heard from Eben that he was enlisting, she took off, got herself an apartment and started school. Poor thing. Now wouldn't you think that he'd know how much she needs him? I never thought of Eben as cold, but guess you just don't know folks and how they'll act under fire. Hope he does better than that in the navy."

Lenore got her first letter from Eben written on Thanksgiving day. She had no idea where it was mailed from, but she kept it in her lingerie drawer made sweet with the rose petals of the sachet. Every night she'd take it out and reread it. What he couldn't say in person he could write, she had told Nora.

244

"No, Mum, I want you to read it," she said when she went to the farm for Christmas. It's personal, but it's so beautiful. Everyone who has loved Eben and Rahn needs to read this letter. Here."

Nora took it but said that she wanted to read it in the privacy of her room, that she didn't want to cry in front of Molly, Timothy's widow. He had been killed at the battle of Bataan. She and the baby had moved in with the Aherns.

The letter was dated Thanksgiving Day somewhere in the Pacific

My dearest Lenore,

Now don't you start crying when you see the date of this letter because you know, or should know, that was and will always be the most important day of our lives. The day our beautiful son was born. Our beautiful Rahn Ahern Hunter. "My, isn't that a proper name for a boy", Father Flynn had said. "But where's his saints name?" Remember? So we added Michael just to satisfy him.

I tried so hard to forget all that happened until one day, after I'd been over here for only a short time, a friend said that he gets through these seas of mud and filth remembering every thing he can, good and bad. He said that he was able to go about the business of staying alive, remembering. So I tried it. And before long I arrived at the day when Rahn was born.

I felt a peace come over me that stirred my soul. I didn't know that I even had one. And from that day to this I've been able to remember all the days that we had him with us. His beautiful smile and loving disposition. Alpha always said that child had the prettiest smile she had ever seen. Remember?

He will never be forgotten as long as I have him in my heart. I know that you've always had him in your heart, but I just wanted to withdraw from the world, but most of all from you, my precious one. I felt so responsible.

This morning my friend died in my arms. He had given me so much, just as Rahn did, and I'll never forget him, either. So now I have two very special people to remember.

I love you more than I can ever say and wanted to tell you that. If I am fortunate enough to return from this hell, I want to be with you wherever you want to live, and I promise you that I'll never desert you again. May our beautiful Father hold you until we can be together.

Your Eben

Lenore began writing almost every night. Eben's letters were less frequent. She continued her schooling and had written him that she would like to stay in Savannah, that she loved the city and had made friends there. His response had taken two months to arrive. He, too, loved Savannah. They began making plans for the future.

The months dragged by, but her studies and visits to Springfield to the farm kept her sane, she said. But, she was becoming concerned. She hadn't heard from Eben in three months. Her friend Cora Bleech clipped out an article from *The Everglades News* and sent it to her. It was about the 61st Seabees known as "Old Timers" and about how important they were to the landing forces in the Pacific. They were the first Naval Construction Battalion to land on the Philippines with the liberation forces and were under constant attack by the Jap warplanes. Strafing raids did not let up. Machine gun bullets were buzzing around them like angry hornets while they unloaded the ships, cut roads through seas of mud and battled Japanese paratroopers alone.

Cora asked if she thought that Eben was with the 61st. She knew he was. Her concern quickened. Finally, when she could stand it no longer, she called Thornton in Pahokee to ask if he or the boys had heard anything, that she was worried sick.

They had not and were as worried as she.

The very next day she got a call from a navy nurse in San Diego, who said that a very important person wanted to speak to her. Lenore held her breath. She had trouble understanding him, but when the nurse came back on the line, she said that his bandages kept him from saying what he wanted to say, but he had written a message. She laughed when she said it, so Lenore felt that he was all right.

"He wants me to tell you that he needs you. That's all he wrote."

"Tell him that I'll be there as fast as I can. I don't know how, but I'll be there. I need him too."

Lenore called Thornton, and he said he'd pull whatever strings he could for her to get to California. He did, and she was on a train in two days.

❦

"Patrick, was that Thornton? What did he say about Eben?" Catherine called from the kitchen.

"He said that he was battered and that he had taken a good amount of shrapnel in his left thigh. They still don't know if they'll be able to save his leg, but Lenore was with him and was trying to get him moved to an eastern hospital. Living conditions in San Diego are awful, and she is bunking in with three other wives whose husbands are wounded, too."

"Poor thing. I just hope that Mary Catherine's Bruce is all right. She called from New York while you were out and said she hadn't heard a word from him in over three months. When is it going to end? When?"

❦

"There'll be a celebration in Pahokee the likes of which we never saw before," Jessup, hesitating, told Dunbar. "An' I don't care one whit if you go or not!"

"You've been drinking, Jessup. You rightly know that I'll be there to welcome Eben Hunter back and all of our other servicemen as well. Yes, those without legs and those half blind, but I'll be there, because, Jessup, I'm proud of them. I know what you're gonna say even before you say it, but I figure that Eben has paid his dues to our Lord above, and no matter how he came by all that money, he did his duty to God and his country. Yes, Jessup, I'll be the first to acknowledge it. He, too, has gone through hell!"

"What ya talkin' 'bout Dunbar?"

"You wouldn't understand, Jessup." But when Dunbar said that, Jessup, as sotted as he was, saw something in his eyes he had never seen before. Dunbar seemed to be in another world.

No, my friend Jessup, you wouldn't understand, because when Dr. Spooner told us at Rotary about Eben's condition after Rahn was killed, I remembered holding my brother Gordon in the same way that he had held little Rahn. And I remembered how empty I felt. And I remembered feeling so guilty when Mama saw me carrying him up to her. That look will be with me always. No, my friend Jessup, you'll never understand, but Eben did and does. He, like I, can never bury that feeling and that look I'm sure he saw in Lenore's eyes, just like I saw in my mama's eyes, and will never be able to forget. I didn't have a war to fight to help me forget. No, Jessup, I moved to the Glades and poured myself into this black muck and made a life for myself. You'll never understand. You hafta have been there like Eben and I were. We were there...

❦

Dessa hurriedly opened the letter she had just received from Sammy. Wonder why she's writing this so close to her Christmas vacation? Must be something important.

Hi Dessa,

Guess what! I've met MISTER RIGHT! Just like you always said. I finally met him. His sister Ona lives down the hall from me and he came up from Dale Mabry field to see her. I saw him in the park across from the dorm and it was LOVE at first sight. I'm not teasing! Just like you always told me I'd feel. He said later that he felt the same way.

I just had to tell you. Simply couldn't wait 'til Christmas.

Gotta go. Paul—that's his name—should be out front waiting for you know who.

I love you,
Sammy

P.S. Don't say a word to Mama or Daddy. I want to surprise them. BYE.

Sitting down on her bed she smiled. My chile found huh man. My, my. We gonta have us a weddin' in dis household soon. Sammy don't have de patience dat Mary Catherine have. Not my Sammy. And Ah knows dat Ah'm not gonta be sittin' in de back o' any church. Not dis time, Sammy. Dis time we gonta win dis one. Ah'm gonta be up deah wit ya mama and ya daddy wheah Ah belongs. You an' me gonta win dis time, Sammy. *My Sammy...*

About the author:

Ann O'Connell Rust is a native Floridian, a "cracker." Her parents were pioneers in the Everglades in the early part of the century. She has had an on-going love affair with romantic, old Florida all of her adult life, and three of her and Allen's five children live in the state.

She is a popular speaker/lecturer and is a feature writer for the magazine, *"Florida Retirement Journal."*

She and Allen spend their time between their home in Ocala, Florida, and their ranch in Wyoming.

Amaro Books

Are you unable to find *"Dessa"*
in your book stores?

Mail to:
AMARO BOOKS
9765-C S.W. 92nd Court
Ocala, Florida 34481

Please send check or money order (no cash or C.O.D.s)

Enclosed is $ _____ for books indicated.

Book Title: _____

Number of books: _____

Name: _____

Address: _____

City: _____

State: _____

Zip: _____

Please enclose $14.95 per book plus $2.00 for postage and handling of first book and $1.00 for each additional book. For hardcov-
er please enclose $19.95 per book plus $2.00 postage of first book
and $1.00 for each additional book. Florida residents add 7% sales
tax. Please allow 2-4 weeks for delivery.